BLOOD BROTHERS

A Novel

RICK ACKER

Kregel
Publications

Blood Brothers
© 2008 by Rick Acker

Published by Kregel Publications, a division of Kregel, Inc., P.O. Box 2607, Grand Rapids, MI 49501.

A book club reading guide is available by e-mailing the author at rickacker@kregel.com.

Library of Congress Cataloging-in-Publication Data
Acker, Rick
    Blood brothers : a novel / by Rick Acker.
        p. cm.
    Sequel to: Dead man's rule.
    1. Pharmaceutical industry—Fiction   2. Sibling rivalry—Fiction   I. Title.
    PS3601.C545B58 2008
    813'.6—dc22
                                                    2008015330

ISBN 978-0-8254-2007-8

Printed in the United States of America
08 09 10 11 12 / 5 4 3 2 1

For my brother, Richard Acker,
who didn't live to read the ending of this book.
He succumbed to colon cancer on the morning
of his thirty-eighth birthday, May 20, 2007.

In his "Final Jottings," written a week before he died,
he said, "Do not fail to seize the love of God,
which is available to you in the all-embracing
sacrifice of Jesus Christ."

Acknowledgments

F<small>IRST AND FOREMOST</small>, credit goes to my beloved wife, Anette, who is my muse, editor, and collaborator. Without her, this book would not have been possible.

I am also deeply grateful to the busy professionals who generously contributed their expertise to ensure the accuracy of this book. Gene Barnett, Ph.D., took time away from his job as vice president of regulatory/clinical affairs at Nascent Pharmaceuticals to provide invaluable advice on FDA procedures and drug trials. I also greatly appreciate the input I received from Professor Mari Golub, Ph.D., of the University of California, regarding neurotoxicology and primate drug testing. Laurelea Williams and Arnold Schuler, crack auditors in the California Department of Justice, brought years of forensic accounting experience to the passages dealing with financial fraud. *Og til familien Kjeldaas: mange tusen takk for deres anbefalelser om alt norsk.*

If the devil is in the details, then editors and test readers are every author's exorcists. Thank you to all the people who helped me spot typos, mistakes, and plot holes. Janyre Tromp and Dave Lindstedt provided dozens of suggestions and corrections that substantially improved this book. Michael and Gail Pyle and fellow DAG Karen Bovarnick also provided detailed and thoughtful feedback.

Brother shall be brother's bane
Cousins break kinship's bond
Hard is the Earth; Whoredom reigns
An Axe-Age, a Sword-Age
The shield cut through
A Wind-Age, a Wolf-Age
Until the world ruins
No man to another mercy shall show
—The Elder Edda

Chapter One

A Gift from the Past

A CHILL APRIL RAIN FELL outside Chicago's Field Museum, drenching the wide black umbrellas that protected the designer gowns, suits, and hairstyles of the arriving guests. They came in couples or small groups, checked their coats and umbrellas, and found their way to the reception in the Founders' Room, a venerable chamber with the feel of old money. The room's reception area held a collection of fine artifacts never seen by the general public. A massive, ornately carved fireplace greeted guests with a roaring blaze. Two large crystal chandeliers cast a soft light from the high ceiling onto the guests mingling below.

The room was full, but not too full—the mark of a well-planned event. White-coated servers maneuvered deftly among the clusters of chatting guests, offering appetizers or glasses of champagne. The selection of baked appetizers reflected a bias for salmon—perhaps because the hostess had been craving it when she planned the menu. Fortunately, most of the guests seemed to like salmon.

Ben Corbin, who did not like salmon, stood by a table of cheese-based hors d'oeuvres and watched his wife work the crowd. Two hours ago, Noelle had been a no-nonsense accountant, but now she had fully morphed into the role of society hostess: bright smile, well-coifed brown hair, unostentatious—but not inexpensive—diamond jewelry, and an elegant blue sheath dress that complemented her athletic figure and matched her brilliant sapphire eyes. Her dress had been let out a little in the middle to make room for her expanding belly; she was four months pregnant with their first child and just starting to show.

Shortly after Ben and Noelle had told his mother the happy news, she had commented to Ben that pregnant women "glow." Ben had privately questioned whether *glow* was an appropriate synonym for "exhausted, moody, and nauseated," but now he saw what his mother had meant. Tonight, Noelle glowed. She radiated happy expectancy and never tired of answering the same questions about how far along she was, how she was feeling, whether they had settled on names yet, and so on.

Ben put down his plate and sauntered over to intercept his wife as she walked from one group of guests to another. "Having fun?" he asked as he fell in stride beside her.

"Yeah," she said distractedly as she quickly scanned the crowd for new arrivals she hadn't greeted yet. There were at least two dozen, and more on the way.

Ben followed her gaze. "Too much fun?"

"Yeah. I've got to say hi to Senator Fintzen and Justice Gaido. Could you go talk to those people over there?" She nodded in the direction of a group just leaving the name tag table. "That's Gunnar Bjornsen and his family."

"No problem."

Ben walked over to a group composed of two young men in their twenties, an attractive woman of about fifty, and an imposing sixtyish patriarch. The younger men were both blond and handsome; otherwise, they looked nothing alike. The older one had slightly unkempt long hair, earrings in both ears, a paunch, and a Bohemian air. His younger companion had short-cropped hair, a lean, muscular build, and a well-tailored Brooks Brothers suit. *He looks like he just stepped out of a Young Republicans leadership meeting*, thought Ben.

Both men were over six feet tall, but they were dwarfed by the man whom Ben guessed to be Gunnar; he stood at least six feet four and still had the arms of a weightlifter, despite his age.

The two young men talked to the woman, an elegant, aristocratic-looking lady whom Ben assumed was their mother. The older man loomed over the little group, saying nothing, but scanning the crowd with intense, pale gray eyes. His craggy face wore an undisguised look of displeasure, though it wasn't clear what had upset him.

"Hello," Ben said as he walked up smiling. "My name is Ben Corbin. Thank you for coming to the reception tonight." He glanced at their name tags. "Are you related to the Bjornsens of Bjornsen Pharmaceuticals?"

The storm clouds on the older man's face darkened further. "I *am* the Bjornsen of Bjornsen Pharmaceuticals." His basso profundo voice had a Scandinavian accent.

Oops. Ben's smile didn't waver. "Pleased to meet you, sir," he replied, extending his hand. "Thank you for your company's generosity in making this exhibition possible. I know the museum is very excited to be able to display artifacts from a royal Viking burial. I'm personally looking forward to spending an afternoon or two in the exhibition hall."

"So am I," said the big man as he shook Ben's hand with a firm grip. "Gunnar Bjornsen. This is my wife, Anne, and our sons, Markus and Tom." The sweep of his hand identified the Bohemian as Markus and the Republican as Tom. "My brother Karl runs Bjornsen Pharmaceuticals now," he continued with a trace of bitterness in his voice, "so I never saw the final selection of pieces for this exhibition."

"Oh." Momentarily at a loss for words, Ben wished he had paid more attention when Noelle had briefed him on the guest list last week. "I . . . well, I hope you like the choices he made. I've seen pictures of some of the items, and they look terrific."

Anne Bjornsen took pity on him and changed the subject. "Are you the same Ben Corbin who won that lawsuit against the terrorists?"

Five months ago, Ben had discovered that a routine breach of contract lawsuit was actually a battle over possession of a deadly biological weapon. "That's me. I had a lot of help, though—and I had no idea I was up against terrorists when I took the case."

"I read about that in the papers," commented Gunnar. "Very impressive. But I assume litigating against terrorists isn't a standard part of your practice—or is it?"

"If I did that full time, I would have a very short career. No, that's the first—and hopefully the last—time I take on a case like that. My real specialty is business disputes: breach of contract cases, shareholder fights, things like that."

Gunnar looked at him with interest. "Is that so? I'd like to—" he began, but Noelle's voice over the speaker system cut him off. "Thank you all for coming. As you know, we're here tonight to celebrate the tremendous generosity of Bjornsen Pharmaceuticals. They have made it possible for the Field Museum to be the first American museum to display artifacts from the Oseberg excavations and the Trondheim Riksmuseum. Let's welcome Karl Bjornsen, president of Bjornsen Pharmaceuticals, to the Field Museum."

"Please excuse me," said Gunnar. He turned abruptly on his heel and headed for the door. The other attendees applauded as a large man approached the front of the room, where Noelle and half a dozen museum worthies awaited him. He appeared to be a bit shorter than Gunnar, but burlier, and he had the same fading blond hair and fierce gray eyes. He walked with the confident, shoulder-swinging stride of a man who was used to having people make way for him.

While all eyes were on Karl Bjornsen, Ben also took the opportunity to slip out of the room. He had never been a great fan of the windy speechmaking that went on at receptions and award dinners. Worse, when executives from corporate donors spoke, they often seemed to feel that they had been invited to do an infomercial for their companies. Now that Noelle had sat down in one of the chairs on the dais, Ben figured he could quietly escape. He made for the entrance to the exhibit hall, which was framed by wooden pillars and a lintel carved with entwined geometric patterns, mimicking the entrance to a Viking hall.

✠ ✠ ✠

Back at the reception, Karl Bjornsen walked up to the podium and looked out over the crowd. He recognized a dozen CEOs and other senior executives, several reporters, and the head of a large mutual fund. There were lots of decision makers here tonight, and that was good. "Thank you, Noelle," he began, with a smile and a nod in her direction. "And thank you, Field Museum. Without the partnership of this great institution and the hard work of its staff, this exhibition would not have been possible."

Polite applause.

"I am very lucky to be part of this great effort to bring treasures of ancient Norway to this new land. When I was a child growing up in Oslo, I remember going to the museums with my parents to see beautiful artifacts that had lain buried and forgotten for a thousand years. It thrilled me then, and it thrills me even more now, to share the glories of my ancestors with the people of this great city where I have made my home and built my company.

"But I would like to take a few minutes to tell you about a Norse treasure that is not locked in museum cases—a treasure that we can hold in our hands and that can change each of our lives. Last year, a hiker in one of Norway's national parks got lost in the mountains. He wandered for days, growing hungrier and weaker. He would have died of starvation and exposure if he had not saved himself . . . by starting an avalanche."

A few chuckles rumbled through the crowd.

"How does an avalanche feed a hungry man? The rock and ice that thundered away down the mountainside that day uncovered a cave that had not seen the light of the sun for a millennium or more. And in that cave were some leaves and seeds from an extinct tree.

"The hiker took those leaves and seeds and ate some—but fortunately not all of them. After he ate, he had a new will to live, more energy, and he was suddenly able to think of a way to escape from his predicament. He managed to rip open one of his hiking boots and pull out the steel shank. He found a sufficiently hard stone and struck sparks off it into a pile of dry grass and pine needles. Once he had a fire going, he made himself a torch and limped along the timberline starting fires at regular intervals, which he knew would get the attention of the park rangers pretty quickly. They did, and he was rescued." Karl paused for a moment to let his audience appreciate the story. "Quite a tale, isn't it?

"But why didn't the hiker think of that sooner? And where did a man on the brink of death get the strength to tear apart a hiking boot?

"The hiker was unable to guide the rangers back to the cave he'd found, so unfortunately whatever secrets it still holds have been lost again. But he did have some of the leaves and seeds in his pockets. Norwegian scientists began studying them, and what they found was truly amazing: the leaves, and particularly the seeds, contained complex compounds that acted together to make it possible for neural impulses to move through chains of nerve cells more efficiently and at greater speed. Theoretically, that means that these chemicals should make the subject's brain operate faster and his reflexes quicker.

"Theoretically, that's how it should work, but what does it *really* do? We knew the hiker's story, of course, but that was only one individual and was hardly a controlled experiment. I wanted to find out more, so my company licensed the rights to perform experiments on extracts from these plants and make products from them. Let me show you what we found."

The lights dimmed and a motor whirred as a screen descended from the ceiling. The crowd watched in complete silence.

Karl picked up a remote control from the podium and clicked. The screen came to life, showing two lab rats negotiating identical mazes. A digital display at the top of each maze tracked the rats' performance.

"The rat on the right has been fed an extract from the seeds," Karl said. "The rat on the left has not."

As the video proceeded, the rat on the right finished well ahead of the other rat.

"On average, rats with the extract finished mazes twenty percent faster than those without it.

"But those are rats. What about something closer to a human being?" He pressed another button on the remote. The scene on the screen shifted to show two rhesus monkeys struggling to open clear containers with complicated lids that looked like blacksmith's puzzles. Inside each container was an apple slice. Again, a digital monitor timed each monkey. "The results were even more impressive than with the rats. The monkeys who took the extract completed the same intelligence-testing puzzles in roughly thirty percent less time, and they were able to do more difficult puzzles than the control group monkeys. In fact, they did puzzles more difficult than rhesus monkeys had previously been known to solve.

"And there may be another benefit to this extract." He clicked the remote again and a picture of a monkey cage appeared on the screen. The cage was empty and two of the bars had been noticeably bent. "This is a picture we took last week. We left the bowl of apples too close to the monkeys one night."

A laugh ran through the crowd.

"But as often happens in science, our mistake led to a fascinating discovery: those cages are actually designed to hold larger and stronger monkeys than the ones we were using. There's no way that our monkeys should have been able to bend those bars—but they did! There was nothing wrong with the metal; we tested that. So the only possibility left was that these rhesus monkeys did something that rhesus monkeys can't do.

"We're doing additional studies right now, but our best guess is that the extract increases muscle strength by increasing the speed and strength of the electrical impulses transmitted by the nerves to the muscle cells. That's only a guess, but it happens to fit the facts as we know them today."

He turned off the projector and the screen recessed into the ceiling. "Many companies say that their products will 'change the world,' and virtually all of them are wrong. But I ask you to imagine a time when a firefighter can take a pill that will give him increased strength and speed of mind and hand before he enters a burning building; when our men and women in uniform can make themselves stronger, faster, and smarter than their enemies during battle." He swept his hands over the audience. "A time when any of us can make ourselves a little smarter and faster whenever we need to face life's challenges."

He held up a single leaf. "This came from a tree grown from one of the seeds found in that ancient cave. It is a gift from our past. It is also our future, and it is a future bright with promise. We stand here tonight at a meeting of the ages. Past, present, and future have come together, each enriching the other. Thank you for coming tonight. I hope you enjoy the exhibition."

‡ ‡ ‡

Ben crossed the threshold of the exhibit hall and paused to let his eyes adjust. The interior had been made to look like the longhouse of a Viking king. There were no windows, and the only light came from the entrances and strategically spaced "smoke holes" in the roof. Dark timbers covered the walls and sloped upward to form a steeply peaked roof supported by richly carved beams bearing images of dragons and serpents that intertwined to form complex patterns that confused the eye. Artifacts protected by Plexiglas cases were arranged to make them appear to be a natural part of the long hall. A collection of eight golden arm rings, each in the form of an emerald-eyed serpent swallowing its tail, lay carelessly arranged in an iron-bound chest, as if some warlord had tossed them there after returning from a raid. Two swords with gold-inlaid hilts hung from pegs on the wall, their bright blades still bearing the notches of long-ago battles. In a dark corner near the end of the hall, an ancient chair of exquisitely carved black oak sat in a rough circle with several modern copies, in which visitors could sit and imagine a conversation with the lord of the hall. To complete the illusion, one of the chairs held the hulking figure of a Norse warlord bent in thought and shadow, brooding over plans for his next conquest.

Ben decided to give his feet a rest and headed for the little grouping of chairs. As he got closer, he noticed that the clothing on the Viking mannequin didn't look right, though the light was too dim to say exactly why. As Ben approached, the figure stirred and looked up. It was Gunnar. "Ah, Mr. Corbin. I see that I'm not the only escapee from the hot air blowing out there."

"The speeches do start to sound the same after a while. I figured the exhibit might be more interesting than the people talking about it."

"Well, what do you think?"

"Pretty impressive, especially when it's empty like this. They've really created the atmosphere of another place and time. When I walked in here, I almost felt like I'd arrived early for a Viking war council and that any minute the king and his generals would walk in."

Gunnar regarded him with an odd, piercing look for a moment. "It's interesting that you should put it like that. I—" There was a noise behind them and Gunnar looked past Ben's shoulder. Ben turned and saw Karl Bjornsen walking up to them. "Gunnar!" he said in a booming voice. "I'm so glad you could make it to our exhibition." He was smiling, but it was the hard, predatory smile of the victor greeting the vanquished.

"I wanted to make sure you didn't screw it up too badly after I left," Gunnar replied. He stood and looked around. "It looks good. I assume someone else took care of it."

Ben shifted his weight uncomfortably and looked away, but Karl continued to smile. "You're right. I was so busy cleaning up the mess you left at my company that I didn't have time to work on this myself."

Gunnar's face hardened. "*Ditt selskap, sier du?*"

"*Ja. Og min teknologi som du stjal,*" Karl growled in reply.

17

Gunnar tensed and clenched his fists. "*Din helv*—" He stopped himself as he noticed a group entering the exhibit hall from the reception. "Excuse me; do any of you speak Norwegian?"

"Yes, I do," replied a matronly woman with white hair and a tentlike dress.

"How unfortunate. Since that is the case, I will limit my remarks to wishing you all a good night," Gunnar continued with an icy smile. "Even you, little brother." Then he pushed past Karl and out of the hall.

‡ ‡ ‡

Two hours later, the festivities were winding down. The bar was closed, everyone who wanted to see the exhibit had been through the hall, and most of the crowd had left. The Corbins had spent the past half hour near the door, saying good-bye to guests. At last, even Karl Bjornsen and his wife had gathered their coats and were on their way out into the blustery night. As Ben watched their retreating backs, he leaned over to his wife and asked, "What's the deal with him and his brother? I thought they were going to start fighting when they ran into each other in the exhibit."

"I told you about that," replied Noelle. "They founded Bjornsen Pharmaceuticals together decades ago. Karl was the chairman and Gunnar was the president, but they set it up so that neither of them could make any major decision without the other's consent. That worked fine for a long time, but about a year ago they stopped agreeing. It turned into a feud over control of the company, and Karl won. He forced Gunnar out in a proxy fight about a month ago."

Ben vaguely recalled seeing articles about the brothers' battle, though he hadn't read them. "That was in the *Tribune* a while back, wasn't it?"

"And *Crain's*," replied Noelle. "A couple of the board members didn't want to invite Gunnar tonight, because they thought there might be a scene."

"There *was* a scene." Ben recounted the incident in the exhibit hall.

Noelle sighed. "I'm glad it wasn't worse. It sounds like Karl gave Gunnar the bump just as their company was developing a new product that could be huge. I've never heard of anything like it."

"What new product?"

She looked at him first with surprise, and then with suspicion. "You snuck out before Karl's presentation, didn't you?"

"I knew the speeches would go downhill as soon as you stopped talking," he replied.

She smiled affectionately. "Good answer, but you missed a really interesting talk." She summarized the story of the hiker's discovery and the results of Bjornsen Pharmaceuticals' test results.

"Wow," Ben said when she had finished. "I'm sorry I missed that. So he's invented brain steroids, huh? I wish we'd had those when I was in law school."

One of the servers walked up with a question, and Noelle turned her attention to the aftermath of the party. "The caterer says there's seven pounds of grilled salmon left," she informed Ben a few minutes later. "What do you say we bring it home?"

"Brutus will love it," he replied. Brutus was their ten-pound cockapoo—fifty percent cocker spaniel, fifty percent poodle, and one hundred percent terror. Noelle had picked the breed, and Ben had picked the name. Brutus was still a puppy and had a huge appetite, particularly for human food.

She made a point of looking appalled. "No way are you giving it to the dog!"

"It'll stink up the fridge if we have it in there for more than a day," Ben countered.

"Okay. We'll take half, and it will be gone in thirty-six hours."

Ben knew she was up to the challenge. "Deal."

‡ ‡ ‡

Gunnar's car would have been uncomfortably silent had it not been for Markus's intermittent snoring. Tom nudged his brother, who was quiet for a moment before starting up the chain saw again.

Markus was drunk, as he generally was by late evening. After a contemptuous remark from his father in the parking lot, Markus had put in his iPod earbuds, tuned out his family, and fallen asleep by the time the car reached the highway. About fifteen minutes later, Gunnar said "Markus!" in an irritated voice. No response. "*Markus!*" he boomed.

His son bolted awake and cringed. "What?"

"You were snoring. Stop it."

"Yes, *sir*," Markus replied in a slurred mixture of subservience and resentment. He turned up the volume on his music and closed his eyes again. But he didn't snore.

Gunnar drove fast. He always did when he was angry. Early in their marriage, Anne would urge him to slow down, but she soon learned that there was no reasoning with him when he was like this. All she could do was wait for the storm to pass and pray that he didn't hit anyone. So far, he hadn't.

"Are you still planning on taking the boat out on Thursday?" she asked, hoping to distract him from his wrath.

"Maybe," he said.

"Did the weather forecast change?"

"No."

She debated whether to dig deeper and decided it was worth the risk. "Then why *wouldn't* you go sailing?"

He was silent for so long that she began to think he wouldn't answer. "I think I'm going to see a lawyer."

She leaned over and whispered, "About the boys' inheritance—about Markus?"

"No," he replied. "About the other problem male in the family."

‡ ‡ ‡

The Corbins walked into their Wilmette home and were energetically greeted by ten pounds of fur, tongue, and bark. "Whoa! Down boy!" said Ben as he tried to protect the pants to his best suit. "I just had these dry cleaned."

After Brutus's affections subsided, Ben and Noelle trudged upstairs, worn out by the busy evening. Ben changed into a pair of sweats and got ready for bed. Then he lay down and let his mind idle as he waited for Noelle to finish her complicated ritual for removing her clothing, jewelry, and makeup after society evenings.

His thoughts wandered for a few minutes, but he soon found himself thinking about the exhibition. The intricately worked gold, the weathered runic inscriptions, and the sense that he had been walking among the ghosts of warrior kings all percolated in Ben's tired brain. He imagined mist-shrouded fjords and mountain forests growing over the burial mounds of ancient Viking lords.

Noelle walked in, interrupting her husband's Nordic reverie. "Hey, honey," he said, "what do you think about maybe taking a trip to Norway? We've never been there, and it'll be a lot harder to take trips after the baby comes."

"That's true." She thought for a moment. Every now and then they had vaguely discussed taking another overseas vacation, but they had mostly talked about Asia, not Scandinavia. "We've also never been to China."

"Yes, but just imagine how good the Norwegian salmon will be. Also, I'll bet the plumbing is a lot more modern in Norway." Two years ago, they had spent three weeks touring southern Italy and Greece. During their travels, Noelle had found exactly one bathroom that was remotely acceptable by her standards.

"Those are excellent points," she responded. "But do you think you can take any more time off from work?"

Ben hesitated before answering. Shortly after his victory against the terrorists, and partly because of his sudden celebrity, he had settled a large trade secrets case on very favorable terms. The contingent fee portion of his compensation had amounted to two million dollars, plus one hundred thousand per year for at least the next ten years. That, combined with some good investing, meant that he no longer had to work unless he wanted to—and he often didn't want to.

He had a couple of cases that occupied about fifteen hours per week, and some pro bono work that took around five hours more, but that was it. He spent most of his time reading, working in his woodshop, or watching old movies. Noelle was not a great fan of her husband's newly relaxed lifestyle, and had said so on more than one occasion. Her question was therefore a dangerous one and needed a careful answer. "I *think* so. Things are starting to pick up at the office, but I should be able to make the time for a vacation. Besides, this will probably be our last chance before the baby is old enough to travel."

She thought about that for a moment and then shook her head. "Maybe *you* can take the time, but I can't. There's just too much to do. I've got two new clients with quarterly reports coming due, and one of them has SEC filings to make. And that's on top of all the other stuff I've got to do." Ben knew that most of that "stuff" involved catered brunches in large homes, luncheon board meetings, and charity dinners. He was surprised she hadn't put on thirty pounds even before she got pregnant. "Oh, and it looks like we're going to get invited to the Adlers' son's bar mitzvah. The Bishops and Gossards are likely to be there."

"That's nice," Ben replied with a yawn. "We can send him a card and a sweater from Norway."

"You mean we could if we were going to be there instead of at his bar mitzvah."

"You'd give up three weeks in the Land of the Midnight Sun for three hours making small talk with the Bishops and Gossards? They're nice people, but they're not *that* nice."

She looked at him with raised eyebrows. "You were thinking of taking three weeks off?"

"Okay, two weeks."

She shook her head. "I just don't have time, bar mitzvah or no. And neither do you. Going to Norway would mean even more time out of the office—and you couldn't possibly spend less time there without retiring."

Ben rolled his eyes. "If I take up shuffleboard and start complaining about how young people drive, would you stop bugging me about that?"

"No, I'd bug you about being boring." She changed her tone and tried again. "Do you remember what you said when we were thinking about going out on our own?"

He shrugged. "I said a lot of stuff. The only one that sticks in my head was that I was going to miss the free catered lunches at B&R."

"The one that sticks in my head was that you wanted to do something more important than defend the rights of Fortune 500 companies. Remember that? We prayed about our decision, and you said you felt that God was calling you to use your gifts to make a real difference in the lives of real people. What happened? Now that we've got money, is God calling you to spend more time sitting in front of the TV or to make Shaker chairs in the basement?"

"Man, you're hard to please! A few months ago, you were complaining because I worked too much. Now you're complaining because I'm not working enough. Make up your mind."

"I'm not saying you have to spend all your time suing people, I'm just saying you should do *something*. Maybe you could do some work for the Field. I could introduce you to some very interesting and charming people."

"There are plenty of interesting and charming people in the world," Ben replied testily. "Not all of them have five-thousand-square-foot homes and live on the North Shore. In fact, I'll bet a lot of them live in Norway. Who knows, maybe we can even find some rich people there for you to talk to."

She stopped getting ready for bed and glared at him. "Do you really mean that? Do you really think I spend over a hundred hours every month working for free just so I can talk to rich people?"

Ben sighed inwardly. Why did these speak-the-truth-in-love conversations always seem to happen when he wanted to go to bed? "That was a cheap shot, and I'm sorry. No, I don't think that's the only reason you do it, but I do think it's one of the perks. I mean, if there was nothing to it, would I have hit a nerve like that?"

"Let's test that little theory," she returned sharply. "Why don't I try hitting a few of your nerves, and then you can tell me whether there's anything to *my* comments. Deal?"

Ben chuckled ruefully and sat up in bed. "How about I apologize again and you forgive me and then I give you a back rub to soothe that nerve I hit. Deal?"

"No deal. As long as we're sharing constructive criticism here, I want a real answer out of you on why you think it's okay to spend ten hours a day putzing around here at home and only four or five in the office. And half the time when you're there, I see you playing solitaire on your computer or surfing ESPN.com."

"I need to remember to keep my door shut." He yawned. "Look, we've had a long night and I'm beat. Can't we talk about this over coffee and muffins in the morning?"

"No, we can't. You've been ducking this one for months. I want to hear what you have to say for yourself."

He flopped back down onto his pillow. "Okay, fine. The answer is that I worked my butt off for eight years after law school because I had to. Now I don't have to anymore. I kind of like the change, but I'm not as motivated as I used to be. Maybe I should be, but I'm not. It's a lot harder to drag myself out of bed at six o'clock every morning when the only reason I've got to go into the office is that I feel called to do it. Satisfied?"

She smiled. "Of course. I just needed to hear you say it. And I think you needed to hear yourself say it. Now, did you say something about a back rub?"

✝ ✝ ✝

Captain Tor Kjeldaas put the *Agnes Larsen*'s engines in reverse and pulled her out of the slip she occupied at the crowded municipal pier in Yuragorsk, a small but booming port city tucked away in the far northwest corner of Russia. It was a starless, rainy night and the seas were choppy, but the captain welcomed the darkness and the foul weather.

The *Agnes Larsen* was a fishing boat, but there were no fish in her holds tonight. The Norwegian and Russian processing plants had dropped the price they would pay for cod, and the crew of the *Agnes Larsen* were feeling the pinch. So they decided to supplement their income by importing fifty cases of vodka with them when they returned to their home port of Torsknes, Norway. The Norwegian government held a monopoly on sales of hard liquor and charged exorbitant prices—usually three times or more the price in neighboring countries. The result, of course, was a brisk bootlegging business over Norway's long and sparsely populated borders and coastline.

Captain Kjeldaas steered his little ship cautiously, his leathery face a picture of concentration in the dim, green glow of the instrument panel. He continually made minor adjustments to the wheel and throttle, his gnarled hands moving with great precision and delicacy despite arthritis and dozens of scars from a half century of working these waters. His experienced blue eyes scanned the black waters for the subtlest change.

April was a dangerous time for sailors on the Arctic Ocean, even in calm waters and bright daylight. Warmed by the spring sun, icebergs calved off from the polar ice pack and coastal glaciers, drifting for weeks or even months until they finally melted. They ranged in size from huge floating islands, which could be easily spotted and avoided, to small chunks that were little more than ice cubes and bounced harmlessly off even the thinnest hulls. The truly deadly bergs lay between these two extremes—jagged masses of ice that barely disturbed the waves rolling over them, yet could smash fatal holes into any ship unlucky enough to meet them.

The *Agnes Larsen* puttered along at only a few knots to minimize the risk from ice. Her speed was further reduced because the running lights were set as dim as possible to avoid detection by the Kystvakt, the Norwegian coast guard. Captain Kjeldaas was a careful and experienced sailor, but neither care nor experience were complete protection against the hazards of the Arctic Ocean. As he looked out through the rain-streaked pilothouse window, he saw an odd pattern in the waves a hundred meters ahead. He frowned and turned his craft a few points to starboard to avoid whatever was causing the water to behave strangely. Then a trough in the waves exposed a pale white mass several times the length of his ship. Most of it lay to port, but a long spar of ice jutted straight toward the bow of the ship.

The captain swore and slammed the wheel as hard to starboard as he could, but the wind and current pulled the little craft to port and she barely altered course. The captain gunned the engine in a desperate effort to give the *Agnes Larsen* enough power to answer her helm. She began to turn, but it was too late. "Hold fast!" he shouted to his crew as he braced himself against the pilothouse walls.

A second later, the ship lurched, shuddered, and tilted sharply to starboard. Men shouted incoherently belowdecks and objects fell and crashed. A loud, deep groan issued from the ship's timbers, accented by the squeal of ice on wood. Then came the sound the captain feared the most: a sharp crack followed by screams of "Water! Water! The pump!"

All at once, the *Agnes Larsen* rolled back to port and then rode level. The noises of wood and ice ceased, but the men still shouted belowdecks. Captain Kjeldaas swore again and hurried down to see how bad the damage was. The *Agnes Larsen* was too small to carry a lifeboat, so if the ship went down, he and his crew would be adrift in the frigid sea. Hypothermia would kill them a few minutes after they went into the water.

Water sprayed in from a half-dozen leaks, but the hull planks had buckled in only one place—and that was above the waterline. The men had already started the pump and were breaking out the emergency patching kit. The first mate looked up at Captain Kjeldaas with a giddy, relieved grin. "She'll be dry in half an hour, captain!"

The captain surveyed the scene again and nodded curtly. "Good." He turned and went back to the pilothouse.

As dawn broke, signaled only by a lightening of the gray sky, the *Agnes Larsen* limped into Torsknes. Water continued to drip inside the hull and the pump ran intermittently. The growing light showed that much of her paint had been scraped away on the port side, which also bore several deep gouges. Captain Kjeldaas knew where his share of the vodka profits was going. In fact, he'd probably have to make another smuggling run next week just to cover the cost of repairs.

The ship cleared the sea wall and came into view of the dock. Captain and crew had expected to see a truck waiting at the dock to take their cargo. Instead, they saw a police car. Two Kystvakt launches floated just inside the sea wall, lest the *Agnes Larsen* try to run back out to sea.

Captain Kjeldaas set his mouth in a hard line and headed for the dock. He'd lose his cargo, of course, and probably get slapped with a stiff fine. That would likely be all, though. There were enough ex-fishermen in the police force and judiciary to ensure some leniency when an old sea captain got caught in the time-honored practice of rum-running. Still, the loss of his cargo, a fine, and the repair bill for his ship would come close to bankrupting him. He'd have to find a way to make a lot of money fast—faster than he could smuggling vodka, and a lot faster than he could catching cod.

‡ ‡ ‡

The evening was a great triumph, Karl decided. *A great triumph.* He walked over to the living room window of his palatial sixtieth floor condo and looked out on the glowing Chicago skyline, replaying pleasant memories from a few hours ago—the interest and applause during his remarks, the enthusiastic questions about his new product from stock analysts and captains of industry, and the jealous bile in his brother's face and voice. With luck, Bjornsen Pharmaceuticals' stock would be up strongly tomorrow as reports of his presentation circulated.

His satisfied smile faded as he recalled a detail he hadn't focused on at the time. Gunnar had been talking with a younger man who seemed vaguely familiar, but whom Karl couldn't immediately place. He also recalled having seen the man with the hostess at some point during the evening. Who was he? And what had he and Gunnar been talking about in the exhibit hall during the speeches? Karl turned as his wife walked into the room. "Gwen, who was that man at the reception with Noelle Corbin?"

"In his thirties, brown hair, athletic build, good-looking, but a little on the short side?" she responded.

"You have an excellent memory of him," Karl replied drily. "Yes, that's the one."

She laughed lightly. Before marrying Karl fifteen years ago, Gwen LaCharriere had been a runway model known for two things: her elegant, raven-haired good looks and her reputation as a flirt—though she had always thought of herself as merely friendly. One of the things that had drawn her to Karl was the fact that he was confident enough not to be bothered when she talked to other men. Still, it was fun to tease him. "That's her husband, Ben Corbin. He was in the papers a while back—something about Russian terrorists."

Now he remembered. He stood silent for a few seconds, weighing the significance of this new piece of information. "Chechens," he said. "The terrorists were Chechens. They bought their weapons from Russian smugglers. Ben Corbin was the lawyer who beat the Russians in court and then hunted down the Chechens, wasn't he?"

"That sounds right."

Karl began to understand his brother's interest in Mr. Corbin. He also began to wonder just how much Gunnar knew about

Bjornsen Pharmaceuticals' activities. This situation bore watching. Close watching. In fact, it bore more than that.

Karl considered what to do next. When he and Gunnar were boys, one of their favorite pastimes was to spar with long sticks. At first, Gunnar always won, because he was older and had a longer reach than Karl. But Karl eventually learned that if he could strike the first hard blow, he could put his brother on the defensive and control the fight.

Chapter Two

The First Hard Blow

SHORTLY BEFORE 10:00 AM, Ben arrived at the offices he and Noelle shared and found five phone message slips waiting for him. Two were from other lawyers in cases he was handling. Two were from a Field Museum board member who wanted Ben to run for alderman, an idea that Ben had no interest in, but Noelle did. And one message was from a "Gooner Boornson." Ben laughed and walked back out to the reception area. "Susan, do you think this might be 'Gunnar Bjornsen'?"

Susan Molfino, the Corbins' receptionist and all-purpose office administrator, looked at the slip critically. "Sure. Actually, it could be pretty much any funny name that sounds more or less like that, if the guy saying it has an accent and hangs up before I can ask him how to spell his name."

"Oh, is that what happened? Did this guy have a deep voice?"

"Yeah. He sounded like a German James Earl Jones."

"That's him," Ben replied.

Ben had been half expecting a call ever since the reception at the Field Museum three nights ago. In the exhibition hall, he had suspected that Gunnar had wanted to talk about something other than Viking art—and it was clear that the Bjornsen brothers were on the brink of open war. With a pretty good idea of what to expect, Ben walked back to his office and dialed the number on the slip. "Gunnar Bjornsen," said the rumbling voice at the other end of the line.

"Hello, Gunnar. This is Ben Corbin returning your call. What can I do for you?"

"I need a lawyer to defend me. My brother, Karl, sued me. He claims I stole trade secrets from the company."

That was a surprise. Ben had been expecting Gunnar to be the one doing the suing. "I think I could help you with that. Would you like to sit down to talk about the case sometime soon? I'm free for about an hour this afternoon at one o'clock."

"I'll see you at your office at one," replied Gunnar.

"Great. In the meantime, could you fax or PDF me a copy of the complaint?"

"I'll fax it to you now."

While he was waiting for the complaint to arrive, Ben called Noelle, who had been at a client's office since 8:30 going over draft financial statements. For the year and a half since she and Ben had struck out on their own professionally, her accounting practice had mostly consisted of doing telecom reconciliations for her former employer—about ten hours a week. But her practice had mushroomed since she started doing pro bono work for the Field Museum. Board members, donors, and other wealthy friends of the museum regularly hired her or referred work to her—so much work that she was considering hiring another accountant. After three rings, she picked up her cell phone. "Hi, Ben. What's up?"

"I've got some good news," he reported. "It looks like I might be landing a high profile trade secrets case today."

"That's great!" she replied. "I'm going to be busy until about 2:30. Can you tell me about it then?"

"Sure, just call me when you're ready and we'll meet at the Mud Hole."

‡ ‡ ‡

At exactly one o'clock, Ben's intercom beeped. "Mr. Bjornsen"—Susan pronounced the name slowly and correctly—"is here to see you."

"I'll be right out." Ben walked out into the lobby and ushered Gunnar into the conference room. It wasn't big, but it had comfortable leather chairs, a hand-carved round oak table, and a pleasant view of Grant Park and Lake Michigan. Ben and Noelle had designed the room to be a relaxing and informal place that put clients at ease and took the edge off of difficult negotiations with opposing counsel or auditors. Normally, the room felt cozy, but Gunnar's size and tension made it a little claustrophobic. "Sit down," encouraged Ben. "Can we get you something to drink?"

He sat down, moving with surprising grace for a man of his size. "No. Have you read the complaint?"

So he wanted to get right down to business. That was fine with Ben. "I have," he said, sitting down as well. He took out two copies of the pleading and handed one to Gunnar. "I'd like to go over some of the key allegations with you. First, were you the head of new drug development at Bjornsen Pharmaceuticals?"

"I was. I was also the president."

"Okay. Did you have access to all of the company's product development information?"

"I did," Gunnar answered without hesitation.

"Including the formulas for the 'Neurostim' product?"

"That was Karl's name for it, not mine," said Gunnar. "I never liked 'Neurostim,' and I think someone else is already using it. But I know what he's talking about, and yes, I did have access to the production processes for it. In fact, I developed most of them."

"Did the company take any steps to keep those processes secret?"

Gunnar nodded. "Absolutely. We had a secure lab, nondisclosure agreements signed by all our workers, a password-protected computer system, and a number of other security measures."

Ben crossed a potential defense off the list he had jotted down a few minutes before Gunnar arrived. "And did those measures work?"

"Yes. As far as I know, no sensitive information ever leaked out of the company."

Ben crossed off another potential defense. His list was getting short. "All right, did you take the Neurostim production processes with you when you left the company?"

Gunnar shrugged. "I didn't take any documents with me, but I didn't need to. Everything is right here." He tapped his temple.

"Unfortunately, that counts, for purposes of the Illinois Trade Secrets Act," responded Ben. "You were the head of new drug development, and you developed a new drug. As a general rule, that means it belongs to the company—even if you didn't take anything except memories of how to make it. Is there any argument that this drug is not economically valuable?"

Gunnar shook his head. "It's very valuable. It's probably worth billions of dollars."

"Billions? How many billions?"

"It's tough to tell this early in the development process, but," he started ticking points off on his thick fingers, "the potential market is huge, the drug is probably impossible to copy, and there won't be any competition until the patent expires. The Department of Defense orders alone should be enormous; they're very interested in the drug and have said they'll probably want five to ten million doses every year. So the upside is basically unlimited, assuming the trials go well and the drug gets FDA approval."

"And assuming they have the formula to make it," added Ben. "This litigation is going to be World War III." He looked down at his list of potential defenses, each of which he had crossed off over the course of their meeting. He paused to look over the complaint one more time to make sure he hadn't missed anything. He hadn't. He looked up at Gunnar. "Mr. Bjornsen, I have to tell you that these are not good facts. Based on what you've told me, there's a strong possibility that the company's lawyers will be able to convince a judge and jury that the information in your head is a trade secret."

"So?"

"So you can't use it or disclose it. Basically, that billion-dollar formula has to stay permanently locked in your head."

Much to Ben's surprise, Gunnar relaxed and smiled broadly. Then he broke into a deep laugh. After a minute or so, his mirth subsided and he said, "Thank you, Ben. That's the best news I've had in weeks."

"Uh, great. Why is that?"

"Because I don't want to disclose it."

"And you don't want to use it?"

"Not while my brother is running the company. When he's gone, I'll be perfectly happy to go back and help them develop products based on this compound. Until then, I'll keep my trade secrets secret."

"Okay," said Ben slowly. "And does the company know all this?"

Gunnar looked at Ben oddly. "Yes, of course. That's why they sued me."

"I . . . I didn't see anything about that in the complaint," replied Ben as he leafed through the pleading. "Could you explain what you mean?"

"I'm the only one who knows how to grow the plants that they need to make it; without me, there is no new wonder drug. Karl wants to force me to tell him how to do it."

"I'm surprised they didn't put any of that in the complaint," said Ben. "This is pretty obscure. The closest they come is in the prayer for relief, where they ask the court to order you to 'return all documents or materials containing or constituting trade secrets of Plaintiff Bjornsen Pharmaceuticals.' But you don't have anything like that, do you?"

Gunnar shook his head with a pleased grin. "Like I said, it's all in my head. I didn't write any of it down while I was there, either. If I had, Karl wouldn't have sued me."

"I see," said Ben thoughtfully. "And now that I think about it, I also see why his lawyers drafted the complaint the way they did. Bjornsen Pharmaceuticals' stock is up twenty-three percent since Karl announced this new product. It would probably drop by at least that much if word got out that they couldn't actually manufacture the drug."

"It certainly would be an embarrassing press release to write," agreed Gunnar.

"So let's write it for him," suggested Ben. "We can put together a draft press release, send it to him, and threaten to give it to Bloomberg and the *Journal* unless the company drops its lawsuit."

Gunnar pondered Ben's idea for a moment, but then slowly shook his head. "No, let's not. The press will probably find out quickly in any event, but I don't want to be the one who tells them. Issuing that press release could damage the company—and I don't want the company harmed more than necessary. What I want is to win this lawsuit and get back in charge."

"Winning this lawsuit won't get you back into control of the company," said Ben.

"No, but winning the countersuit you're going to file will."

‡ ‡ ‡

Sergei Spassky sat behind a cluttered desk in his North Loop office, his long legs resting on a battered side table. His boyish face wore an amused look as he pored over the criminal record of Dr. Timothy Lesner, a prominent local oncologist. One of the doctor's partners had begun to suspect that he did not have an entirely pristine past and had hired Sergei to investigate. The detective quickly discovered that Dr. Lesner's past was in fact perfectly clean: no record of professional discipline, no criminal convictions, no outstanding IRS liens—not even so much as a parking ticket. Indeed, Sergei couldn't see how things could have been otherwise, given that Timmy Lesner had died fifty-three years ago at the age of two. Frank

Waboda—who was using Timmy's name and long-dormant social security number—was a different story, however. A very different story.

Sergei had finished the criminal file and was about to start writing a report to his client when the phone rang. "Spassky Detective Agency, Sergei Spassky speaking."

"Hello, Mr. Spassky. My name is Karl Bjornsen. I'm interviewing private investigators for a job, and Aaron Wiederman gave me your name."

"That was nice of him," replied Sergei, making a mental note to thank Wiederman for the referral. "What's the job?"

"Right now, all I need is background research and possibly some surveillance on an attorney. His name is Ben Corbin."

‡ ‡ ‡

Chris and Brett Giacolone, the two brothers who owned and operated the Mud Hole, liked to refer to it as a coffee studio rather than a coffee shop. They were artists; not mere baristas. Their customers forgave this vanity, partly because the Giacolones were from the West Coast and therefore were expected to be a little eccentric, but mostly because their coffee was really, really good.

Ben arrived first and ordered for both himself and Noelle. She walked in just as their order came up. "Hi. I got you a decaf cinnamon latte."

"No fat?" she asked. She'd put on a little more weight than the baby books projected and had started watching her diet more closely.

"No fat. *And* light on the raw sugar."

"Good job," she said with an approving smile. "Let's find someplace to sit." She looked around the narrow, dimly lit studio for a free table.

"Actually, let's go for a walk," said Ben. "I'd rather not talk in a room full of people."

She looked at him curiously. "Okay, let's walk."

They sipped their coffee as they strolled through the Loop, the downtown office district that got its name from the loop of elevated rails that bordered it. The skyscrapers that edged its busy streets came from every decade from the 1890s to the 2000s, forming an open-air museum for architectural students. They also formed excellent wind tunnels, channeling and sharpening the lake breezes into blustery winds that whistled down Chicago's streets. Noelle shivered and snuggled in closer to her husband's side. "So, what's up?" she asked.

"Bjornsen Pharmaceuticals has sued Gunnar Bjornsen for trade secret theft, and Gunnar has asked me to represent him," Ben announced with a modest smile.

Noelle looked at him open-mouthed. "When you say Bjornsen Pharmaceuticals sued him, you really mean Karl Bjornsen, don't you?"

"I do indeed," replied Ben, his smile broadening. "This should be a high-profile trade secrets case, *plus* we may be able to swing a trip to Norway."

"But you said no, right?" Noelle's voice was urgent. "You told him you couldn't take the case."

Ben looked at her dumbfounded. "No, I told him I'd be happy to take the case. Why would I turn it down?"

"Because I'm on a committee with Karl's wife! Because I just finished working with Karl on that Viking art exhibit!" She hurled her empty coffee cup at the opening of a nearby trash can. "Because you should know better than to get into the middle of a fight between two such important people. This'll only cause trouble for us; you've *got* to get rid of this case. Can't you refer him to somebody else?"

"No, I can't," replied Ben. "What is it with you? You've been bugging me to take more important, high-profile cases. Now that I've taken one, you're bugging me to get rid of it."

"I didn't mean that you should take cases involving people I know!"

Ben spread his arms wide in helplessness. "Well, high-profile cases generally involve high-profile people, and you've gotten to know quite a few of those. Besides, there's not much I can do about it. Gunnar and I signed a retention agreement about an hour ago."

Noelle thought quickly. If Ben wasn't going to pull out of the case, she would need to do some damage control. Should she try to distance herself from the litigation by explaining the situation and telling people she had no control over what Ben was doing? No, people would interpret that as an announcement that she and her husband had disagreed about this and she had lost the argument. Also, Ben's lawsuits sometimes got ugly, and the more involved she was, the more likely she would be able to head off a nasty incident that could have repercussions for their lives. "If you're going to take the case, can I at least work with you on it?"

"So you can keep an eye on me, right?" replied Ben. "I thought you were overwhelmed by your accounting practice."

"I can make the time now that tax season is almost over."

He eyed her with a mixture of amusement and suspicion. "Oh, all right. I'll probably need accounting help on this case anyway."

"I thought it was a case about trade secrets."

"It is, but Gunnar wants me to countersue. He thinks there are fishy items in the company's financials. He'll send over documents tomorrow."

"What kind of fishy items?" Noelle asked apprehensively.

"Basically, he thinks Karl has been booking operating expenses as capital expenses."

"So he can amortize them and show higher profits."

"Exactly," said Ben. "It sounds like garden-variety accounting fraud."

"Which gets people put in garden-variety prisons," replied Noelle. This was one area of the law that Noelle, like many other accountants, had studied in some depth over the past few years.

"That's what Gunnar has in mind," acknowledged Ben. "Karl can't very well run the company from jail, so Gunnar will come back as president."

"I see," said Noelle unhappily. And she did, all too clearly.

‡ ‡ ‡

The phone rang on Karl Bjornsen's broad walnut desk. It was his private line. He looked at the number on the caller ID and frowned, but picked up the phone. "Hello, Karl Bjornsen."

"Hello, Karl. It's George from Cleverlad. The products you sent are selling extremely well, especially the sedatives. We'd like to order another shipment."

Ordinarily, product orders would be handled by the company's sales staff, but Cleverlad.ru was not an ordinary account. "Great, I'm glad to hear it. We can send you another shipment in three weeks," replied Karl.

"Actually, we'll need it in two weeks. We'll also need to increase the shipment size by fifty percent."

"Fifty percent? For all products?"

"Yes and yes. Like I said, your products are popular."

Karl made some mental calculations. "I can send you a shipment in two weeks, but it can't be any larger than the last one. We simply don't have sufficient availability of certain products you want, particularly the sedatives."

The line was silent for nearly half a minute. "We can accept that for now, but future shipments will need to be bigger." He placed a slight, but unmistakable, emphasis on the word *need*.

"Thanks for your order," Karl replied and hung up.

‡ ‡ ‡

George Kulish frowned and drummed his fingers spasmodically on his desk. His slender, pale hand looked like an albino spider having a convulsion. It bothered him that Karl Bjornsen had not been willing to increase the size of his order.

Business was growing fast, and George needed to find a way to make sure his suppliers kept pace, particularly established suppliers with quality products. Suppliers like Bjornsen Pharmaceuticals. There was a huge market for prescription drugs sold without prescriptions, and George intended to dominate as much of it as possible. The easiest way to do that was to buy his products from legitimate suppliers, who made consistently high quality drugs and sold them wholesale at a fraction of the prices charged by fly-by-night underground labs. Most legit companies wouldn't deal with people like George, of course, which was why it was vital to keep Bjornsen in line.

If Karl decided that doing business with Cleverlad.ru was no longer worth the risk, George would have a serious problem. Cleverlad paid a premium over Bjornsen Pharmaceuticals' list prices, but what if someday that ceased to be enough to ensure that the Bjornsen drug pipeline stayed open? He would need to find or create a sufficiently powerful nonmonetary motivator.

George pulled up the to-do list on his computer and added an item: "Bad Thing for Bjornsen."

‡ ‡ ‡

Ben got back to the office and found a message waiting for him from Sergei Spassky. The two of them had worked closely together on the Chechen bioterrorism case, and they were now good friends. Sergei was also very seriously dating Elena Kamenev, a college friend of Noelle's, and the Corbins had been speculating for some time on whether they would get married. They had seemed very serious for a while, but recently Elena had started complaining to Noelle that Sergei wasn't willing to commit.

Ben tossed his empty Mud Hole cup in the trash and was about to hit the speed-dial button for Sergei's number, but the phone rang as he was reaching for it. The caller ID screen showed Sergei's number.

Ben picked up the phone. "Hey, Sergei. What's up? I was just about to call you with a new job."

"Let me guess: it has something to do with a guy named Karl Bjornsen." Sergei's voice had the telltale hollow sound of a speaker-phone.

"Uh, yeah. How did you know that?"

"Lucky guess. Bjornsen called me about half an hour ago. He wanted to hire me to investigate you. I told him I had a conflict, of course."

The muscles of Ben's stomach tightened. "Why's he investigating me?"

"I was going to ask you the same thing."

Chapter Three

Sergei Spassky

SPRING IN CHICAGO COMES last along the lakeshore. Lake Michigan's wide, gray waters hold the winter cold like a cherished grudge, which they give up only reluctantly as summer approaches. The influence of the lake, which is large enough to be accurately called a freshwater sea, extends inland over much of Chicago. The trendy residential neighborhoods that cluster along the shoreline north of the Loop feel Michigan's moods particularly strongly, enjoying its cool breezes in summer, but enduring its damp chill and clinging fogs in spring.

Sergei stepped out of his apartment building and into a morning that seemed to have been borrowed from mid-March. The temperature was somewhere south of fifty degrees and a thin mist blurred the edges of the buildings. He crossed the alley and walked to his parking spot, slipping his hand into his jacket and resting it on the butt of his Beretta pistol as he inspected his new black Mustang, dubbed "the Black Russian" by his friends, looking for signs that someone had tampered with it. He didn't really expect to find any, but he would rather be safe than sorry. He had been sorry once, and he still had nightmares about it.

Satisfied that the car hadn't been tampered with, he got in and drove downtown to meet with Ben Corbin. He hummed happily as he drove, looking forward to the meeting. He enjoyed working with

Ben, and not just because they had become good friends. Ben was a truly gifted litigator, and Sergei enjoyed sitting on the bench at the back of a courtroom and watching his friend work, particularly if he was using evidence that Sergei had helped gather. Another nice thing about Ben was that he ran his cases clean and lean; unlike many other lawyers, he did not send Sergei out to turn over every stone when there were realistically only one or two that might have useful information under them. This Bjornsen deal was going to be fun.

‡ ‡ ‡

As Sergei was leaving his apartment in Chicago, Kim Young was returning to hers in Los Angeles. She had spent the night celebrating the news that she had landed her first-choice internship for the summer— doing drug development research for Bjornsen Pharmaceuticals. They weren't the biggest or best-known company, but they were actually willing to let her be in the lab, running experiments on rhesus monkeys. And these were experiments that really mattered; she would be participating in preclinical trials for a major new product that was nearly ready to begin the FDA approval process. Even her boyfriend, David, was a little jealous—and he was in his first year of med school. As he had told her last night, "You are so lucky! That sort of work is usually only for grad students or even MDs. I can't remember the last time I heard of a college student landing a job like this."

Kim brushed her teeth and flopped down on her bed, feeling happy, tired, and excited all at once. She flipped open her cell phone and clicked through the night's snapshots. She paused at a good one of her and David. He had his right arm around her and their heads were leaning together. Laughter and intelligence sparkled in his dark, almost eyes and he smiled the wide, happy smile that first caught her attention eight months ago. She looked more critically at her own image. A friend had recently commented that she looked more Japanese than Korean, and she wasn't quite sure what that meant or whether it was a compliment.

After spending several minutes examining other pictures of herself, she gave up and her thoughts turned back to the upcoming summer. She gave her Hello Kitty pillow an excited hug. Then she shoved it under her head and closed her eyes. Only one thing bothered her as sleep began to fog her mind—an image of a cute, big-eyed baby monkey that floated up to her out of some National Geographic program she had seen years ago. She didn't like the idea of sticking a syringe into one of those poor little animals and shooting it full of some dangerous drug. Then she remembered that the pictures of the labs she had seen during her interviews had shown adult animals that were significantly larger and less cute. Reassured, she slipped into a deep and satisfied sleep.

‡ ‡ ‡

Later that morning, Ben, Noelle, and Sergei sat around the table in the Corbins' conference room. "So you want my help to run down the facts behind Gunnar's theory, right?" asked Sergei when Ben finished describing the case.

"Right," replied Ben. "You did a lot of financial fraud work at the FBI, didn't you?"

"Yes, but that's part of the reason I *left* the FBI. Financial fraud cases aren't much fun. Lots of documents, and not a lot of excitement. I'm happy to do this one for you, though."

"Lucky for you, Noelle has volunteered to do most of the document review and number crunching," returned Ben.

"Volunteered? Really?" He looked at her in surprise. "Thanks, Noelle. I don't know how Ben talked you into this, but I'll appreciate the help."

Noelle smiled wanly. "Don't mention it."

"What we're really looking for from you," continued Ben, "is some help figuring out where the smoking-gun documents are likely to be and then getting them."

"Ideally, you'll want an insider," replied Sergei. "That's how the Bureau and the SEC get a lot of their cases; an honest accountant inside the company, or one of their auditors, figures out that something is wrong and gives them a call. The only other time this sort of thing gets caught is when the fraud gets so big that they can't hide it anymore. But without a whistle-blower or some sort of public trouble at the company, it's really hard to prove accounting fraud."

"Bjornsen Pharmaceuticals is a public company," said Noelle. "That means their financials have already been reviewed by outside auditors whose job it is to spot this sort of thing—and who have been especially thorough recently because they don't want to be the next Arthur Andersen. If Karl Bjornsen is cooking the books, he's cooked them well enough to fool the auditors. And that means that he's probably also cooked them well enough to fool us."

"Unless we can find an insider, or they go bankrupt or have a restatement of earnings or something," said Sergei, nodding. "We can't sit around and wait for the company to implode, so we'll have to go hunting for an insider. Gunnar may know somebody who's willing to talk."

"I'll give him a call," said Ben as he jotted down a note to remind himself. "Let's switch gears for a minute. Is there any way I can tell if someone is investigating me? After Karl called you, Sergei, I'm guessing he called other people who haven't had the courtesy to tell me."

"Probably a good guess," replied the detective. "If all they're doing is background research on you—credit report checks and stuff like that—you'll never know. And if they're good, you'll never know you're being investigated no matter what they do."

"Great," replied Ben. "I've never thought twice about having a detective investigate a witness or an opposing party, so I guess I can't really complain. But it's still a little unsettling to think of someone digging into my past and writing up a report on me."

"Think they'll find the Speedo modeling shots from your junior year?" asked Noelle.

Sergei arched his eyebrows. "Speedo modeling shots? Really?"

Ben turned red and grinned. "Hey, I was a kid. I needed the money."

‡ ‡ ‡

Two hours later and four blocks away, Special Agent Elena Kamenev sat at her desk, trying to concentrate and failing completely. Her desk was part of the problem; it was one of dozens crowding the large bullpen room in the FBI's cramped offices on the ninth floor of Chicago's Dirksen Federal Building. On most days, she could tune out the conversations and other background noise, but not today. The agent who sat across from her had a loud voice and a bad phone, which meant that everyone within ten yards of him got to share in his conversations. He had been on the phone a lot today.

She got up to stretch her legs and clear her mind. At five feet nine, she was tall enough to have a good view over the bullpen. She could see several other agents moving along the narrow corridors through the complicated pattern of desks, bulletin boards, and other office furniture that extended to the far wall of the room. It reminded her disconcertingly of a rat's-eye view of a scientist's maze.

She sat down again, pushed her shoulder-length blonde hair behind her ears, and tried to focus. Still no good. The main cause of her distraction had nothing to do with her job. Her real problem was about a mile and a half away, sitting in an office. After nearly three hours in which she accomplished nothing, she gave up and called him.

"Hello, Spassky Detective Agency."

"Hi, Sergei, it's me. I'm hungry; want to have lunch?"

"Sure, lunch sounds good. Where do you want to go?"

"How about Singha?"

"I'll see you there in half an hour."

Forty-five minutes later, Elena and Sergei sat across from each other at a utilitarian wooden table, waiting for their food. He was wearing the leather jacket she had given him for his birthday. It looked good on him. It made his tall, slender physique look wiry and athletic rather than skinny. It also added a touch of maturity to his boyish face—or it would have if he'd been willing to wear his thick brown hair in something other than a flattop, which he insisted was his trademark. Despite the hair, he was subtly good looking—the sort of man that a woman may not think is handsome in a picture, but finds attractive after talking to him for half an hour.

They weren't in a booth, but the tables were far enough apart that the two of them could have a private conversation, which was the main reason Elena had suggested this restaurant. "Every time we come here, you order peanut curry, rice, and beef kebabs," she observed. "Is that a tradition or a rut?"

"Neither," he replied. "It's a wise decision. I've found the best dish on the menu, and I don't come here often enough to get sick of it, so why should I order anything else?" Their waiter arrived with steaming bowls of food. "See?" Sergei continued, pointing to his lunch and taking a bite. "Edible heaven."

Elena took a bite of her chicken stir-fry, chewed slowly, and swallowed. "Sergei, are *we* a wise decision?" she asked in Russian.

He stopped eating and looked at her with a startled expression. "What do you mean?"

Heart pounding, she put down her chopsticks and asked the question that had been formulating in her mind for the past two months. "You have seemed distant recently; sort of pulling back from me. Like you're having second thoughts about us. Are you?"

He took a deep breath and let it out slowly. "I would not call it 'second thoughts,' but I have been . . . well, wondering about some things."

"Like what?"

"Like whether I can marry someone who doesn't share all of my values, no matter how much I love her and how terrific she is in every other way."

Elena sat in stunned silence as long seconds ticked by. There was a roaring in her ears and she couldn't think. "What are you talking about?" she said at last. "What values?"

"Religious values. You know how important my faith has become to me."

Actually, she didn't know, though maybe she should have. She knew that he had come very close to death at the hands of Chechen terrorists about six months ago, and it had affected him. He smiled and laughed less after that. He also became quieter and more thoughtful. Sometimes she found him staring at nothing and absently rubbing a jagged scar on his left arm.

She also knew that he had started going to church most Sundays and reading religious books. She went with him a couple of Sunday mornings and listened politely when he felt the need to talk about religion. The topic didn't particularly interest her though, and she tolerated it in much the same way that she tolerated his obsession with the Bears—and the way she suspected he tolerated her interest in women's winter sports.

His dark moods became less frequent as the attack receded into the past, and she had thought that his fascination with religion would also fade. Apparently, it not only hadn't faded, it was pulling him away from her. The initial shock of that discovery began to wear off and she realized he was still speaking.

". . . and how we would raise our kids. I mean, not only is the most important thing in my life not important to you, you don't even believe it's true. I love you, Elena. I really do love you. I want us to work, but I'm not sure we can. Not like this."

"Are you really saying that you would leave me just because . . . just because I don't have the same religious opinions as you?" she asked incredulously.

"This isn't just an opinion I have; this is something I *believe* from the depths of my soul. It's changing my life. It can change yours too."

"I don't *want* my life changed. Can't you love me the way I am?"

"I *do* love you," he insisted.

"But you won't marry me."

He looked at her with the I'm-trying-to-let-you-down-easy expression that most singles recognize instantly by the time they reach thirty. "I've been praying about this a lot and—"

Suddenly she couldn't bear to hear any more. "Stop! Just stop!" She felt sick to her stomach. "I can't believe this is happening." Her voice shook.

Sergei reached across the table and put his hand on her arm. "Elena, I don't want—"

She pulled her arm away from him and wiped her eyes. "I have to go," she said as she got to her feet and grabbed her coat. Half-blinded by tears, she turned and walked out of the restaurant as quickly as she could.

Sergei rose to follow her, but didn't. He stood awkwardly for a few seconds, watching her go. Then he slowly sat back down, avoiding the curious eyes of the other diners.

‡ ‡ ‡

That Saturday, like all Saturdays, the Gunnar Bjornsens gathered for a family dinner. Sometimes they ate in and sometimes they ate out. Regardless of where they ate, dinner always began by 6:30, as Gunnar believed in punctual meals. And dinner always ended by 8:00, as Markus and Tom did not want to spend their Saturday nights with their parents. They took turns coming up with scheduling conflicts that prevented the dinners from running too long.

Tonight the family had gathered at Gunnar and Anne's house, an imposing Victorian mansion with a neoclassical facade located in the tonier part of Hinsdale, an old town on the Burlington Northern rail line west of Chicago. Gunnar had bought it two decades ago as a peace offering to Anne, who resented the fact that he was almost never home.

The family sat around a polished mahogany table in the formal dining room. Gunnar was at the head of the table, of course, and Anne sat opposite him. The boys were seated across from each other, with Tom on Gunnar's right and Markus on his left. Tom had come straight from a meeting with a potential client and was dressed in a well-cut gray suit and tailored white shirt. Markus had come from nowhere in particular and was wearing jeans and an old sweater that had sprouted several stray strands of yarn.

Tom was talking about his job as assistant branch manager for a brokerage house, a topic that usually interested his father. "And so, with more and more research available online, we figured that flat fee accounts were really the way to go for our more sophisticated investors. So far, it's been a big success; revenues for last quarter were up ten percent, and I've been given the budget to add a new broker to my team." He paused for a moment for his father's reaction, but none came. "You know, Dad, you and Mom are pretty active investors and you do most of your own research. One of our flat fee products might be best for you."

"What was that?" asked Gunnar.

"I was saying that you might want to switch over to one of our flat fee accounts."

"Why would we do that?"

Tom was about to repeat his explanation when Anne cut in. "Why don't you send us the paperwork. We can look it over and set up a time to meet with you next week."

"Uh, no problem. You'll have it by Monday afternoon."

They ate in silence for several minutes, during which time Markus and Tom both surreptitiously checked their watches. It was 7:25. Anne broke the silence. "Markus, how is your production coming?"

Markus had been eyeing the wine bottle and wondering whether his father would comment if he had a third glass. "Fine, just fine. We're beginning rehearsals for *The Gamester*. It's an eighteenth century play written by Edward Moore. I'm going to be understudy to Tom Kennison, who's playing—"

Gunnar looked at his watch. "I'm sorry, but I've got some things I need to take care of this evening. Thanks for coming. Have a great week." He stood, shook hands with his bewildered sons, and strode from the room.

"Couldn't take even two minutes of theater talk, huh?" Markus muttered as he refilled his wine glass.

Gunnar disappeared into his den. "It's not the theater," replied Anne. "Dad has been preoccupied lately. He spends a lot of time on the phone and the computer."

"I would too if I'd been sued," said Tom. "I'd want to know everything about the legal issues and the judge and . . . well, and about anything else having to do with the lawsuit."

"But you wouldn't get up in the middle of dinner to go do research," observed Markus. "Especially if someone was talking."

"Dad has some rough edges," Tom conceded, "but I can understand why he's distracted. After all, he's being sued by Uncle Karl."

Anne smiled and turned the conversation back to more comfortable territory. "Markus, you never finished telling us about your new play."

‡ ‡ ‡

Half an hour later, Markus and Tom sat in Tom's Mercedes SL65, driving back into Chicago. Night gathered in front of them, and the last rays of the vanishing sun lit planes flying into and out of O'Hare like gleaming fireflies. Markus sprawled on the passenger seat, watching the sky absently as Tom drove and the two of them talked about the Cubs.

"Do you remember when the company almost went bankrupt when we were in high school?" Markus asked suddenly.

"Vaguely," replied Tom. "What I really remember was that Mom took me shopping for a new Lexus for my sixteenth birthday. Then, a week later, she told me in sort of an offhand way that I wouldn't be getting a car that year—but she wouldn't explain why. No one told me about what was going on. I just heard you guys talking about it, like a year later."

"*Nobody* heard about it when it happened," replied Markus. "Not even Mom. Dad didn't say anything; he was just really moody and distracted for about half a year and wouldn't let her spend any money. Then he was back to normal. And then, about a year after that, he started talking about the whole thing like everybody had known about it all along."

Tom looked at his older brother. "He didn't tell Mom?"

Markus shook his head. "He never tells her when something is seriously wrong. He never tells anyone. He just clams up and deals with it on his own."

They drove in silence for a while and Markus leaned against his window and started to breathe evenly.

"At least Dad has a good lawyer," said Tom.

Markus stirred. "What's that?"

"Dad's hired a good lawyer, so at least he's not dealing with the lawsuit all alone."

"Yeah, but he needs more than good lawyers," replied Markus.

"What do you mean?"

"The real problem isn't that Dad and Uncle Karl are fighting. The real problem is that both of them care more about that company than anything else in their lives. That's not healthy."

"So says your shrink?"

"Yeah, and so say I. You think it's not true?"

"I don't know," said Tom. "Dad put a lot of time and effort into the company. He should be proud of it, and it should be important to him."

"He's not just proud of it," replied Markus. "He's addicted to it."

‡ ‡ ‡

Night had fully fallen in Hinsdale. A cool breeze blew through an open window at the Bjornsen home, carrying in the sound of a few early crickets and the high squeak of bats hunting mosquitoes and moths. Anne sat in the family room, listening to the night sounds and reading. Gunnar finally emerged from his den. "Markus was talking to you."

Gunnar stopped suddenly and jerked his head around. "What? Oh, I didn't see you there."

"Your son was talking to you when you got up from the table."

"Was he? I didn't notice."

"*He* did. And so did I. It hurts him when you ignore him like that."

Gunnar sat down heavily. The armchair he chose was sturdily built, but it nonetheless creaked under his bulk. "If he wants me to notice him, he should do something worth noticing. He's my first-born, but he has spent the last twenty-five years rejecting everything I've ever given him. Except my money. He's not like his brother."

"Do brothers have to be alike?"

Gunnar smiled ruefully. "I suppose they don't." He paused and stared into the middle distance. "We used to go fishing every Saturday." He smiled again. "No matter how late we had been up on Friday night, we would get up early and be out on the water by six, when the fishing is best. We'd take bread and cheese wrapped in wax paper and a big canteen of lemonade. We would freeze the canteen the night before and drink the lemonade as it melted. Those were good days."

Anne gave her husband a quizzical look. "I don't remember you ever taking Markus fishing."

"Maybe I should have. No, I was talking about Karl and me. We were never all that much alike, but we were close." He paused. "We were close once."

‡ ‡ ‡

It was Monday morning at Bjornsen Pharmaceuticals, which meant Karl Bjornsen was in meetings. He had found that meetings tended to make him unproductive both before and after they occurred, so whenever possible he scheduled them one right after the other and put them all on Monday mornings, which was his least productive time of the week anyway. "There's a Mr. Geist here for you," announced Karl's receptionist.

"Thanks, Michele. Bring him in." Thirty seconds later, she appeared with a man of medium height, bland face, and carefully unremarkable clothes. He was somewhere between forty and sixty, but it was difficult to pinpoint. He rarely got a second look, if he was noticed at all. But Karl could see that he was extremely physically fit and had hard, perceptive eyes that missed nothing. "Hello, Alex. All right, Michele. Please close the door on your way out."

"Good afternoon, Mr. Bjornsen." They shook hands and Karl motioned Geist over to his guest table.

"That was quick," Karl said as they sat down. "So, what did you find? What can you tell me about Ben Corbin?"

Geist reached into his briefcase and produced a one-inch-thick Velo-bound report titled Full Background: Benjamin S. Corbin. It had tabs marked Executive Summary, Personal, Professional, Assets, Criminal/Regulatory, and Other. He handed it to Karl. "There aren't a lot of pressure points. Corbin has no civil or criminal convictions and no record of professional discipline. He and his wife collectively have investments with a total market value of roughly one and a half million dollars, which probably generate an annual income of around forty thousand. They also receive roughly one hundred thousand dollars a year from a large structured settlement, in which Corbin shares under a contingent fee agreement. They have no debt aside from credit card balances, which they pay off monthly."

"No debt at all?" interjected Karl. "That's unusual."

"It is," agreed Geist. "That settlement I mentioned also paid Corbin a two-million-dollar lump sum six months ago. He and his wife paid off their mortgage and all their other loans and invested the rest."

"That's also around the time he won that case involving the Chechens, right?"

Geist nodded.

"Were those flukes?" Karl continued. "What's his reputation as a lawyer?"

"Corbin practices law alone. He shares offices with his wife, and the two of them use a single secretary. He has a good reputation, but he has handled mostly nickel and dime cases. One partner at a large firm said that Corbin didn't have the resources to handle a major case."

"That's useful to know," replied Karl. He jotted down a note to pass this information along to his lawyers. "What about his personal background?"

"He's the third child of a Chicago banker and grew up moderately well off. He played football in high school and made good grades there and in college. He got mostly Bs and Cs in law school, but he got straight As in courses like trial advocacy and moot court.

"He met his wife, Noelle, in college, and they married after his second year in law school, while he was a 'summer associate' at the law firm of Beale & Ripley. They offered him a job when he came back from his honeymoon and he took it.

"After six years at Beale & Ripley, he went out on his own last year. Shortly after that, he took on a case involving biological weapons. It received extensive media coverage and led to the breakup of a large terrorist cell."

"I'm familiar with it," replied Karl, who had run a Google News search on Corbin. "Anything else I should know about Mr. Corbin?"

"If there is, our searches didn't uncover it."

"All right, what about his wife?"

"As you already know, she's an accountant, who shares offices with her husband. She may have chosen her profession because she comes from a financially troubled family. Her father went through bankruptcy twice, and the family moved frequently because of money problems. Her mother worked two jobs, and both Noelle and her brother went to work when they reached sixteen, probably to help support the family."

"How was she able to afford college?" Karl said.

"She was valedictorian of her high school class and received a partial scholarship. She also worked part-time all four years."

"I'm impressed. Say, Alex, how much would it cost to have you say 'no' if someone ever asked you to investigate me?"

Geist smiled. "I get that question a lot. I'll send you my standard fee chart."

‡ ‡ ‡

Half an hour later, Sergei's phone rang.

"Hello, Sergei," said a man's voice—familiar, but Sergei couldn't quite place it. "It's Alex Geist."

"Hello, Alex," Sergei replied in surprise. "What can I do for you?" He hadn't spoken to Alex the Ghost for several years. Geist was an international intelligence and counterintelligence specialist who had worked for the CIA and military intelligence for decades before retiring and entering the half-life of consultancy. He had advised several foreign governments and a number of multinational corporations, including two that Sergei had investigated while he was at the Bureau. The Ghost's advice must have been good, because the FBI had come up dry in both investigations, despite the strong suspicions of the investigating team. Sergei had dealt with Geist regularly at the time, and the two had shared a cordial respect despite Sergei's certainty that Geist's clients were crooks.

"Are you doing any work involving Bjornsen Pharmaceuticals?" Geist asked.

"You know I can't tell you that. Why do you ask?"

"And I can't tell you that. All I can say is that if you're working on something related to that company, I suggest you be careful."

Sergei sat in stunned silence for a moment. "Alex, are you threatening me?"

"Of course not. In fact, I don't think your investigation—if you're conducting one—will bring you into contact with anyone who will threaten you. However, you may meet people who don't bother to threaten."

Chapter Four

Split the Baby

"THIS IS BJORNSEN," Gunnar's voice announced from Ben's speakerphone.

Ben picked up the receiver. "Hello, Gunnar. It's Ben Corbin. I just got an interesting call from Karl's lawyers."

"What did they have to say?"

"They're offering you a deal. If you will tell them how to make the Neurostim product, they'll drop the lawsuit and pay you a two percent royalty on all gross sales. You would also have to drop your countersuit. If not, they start a full court press—reams of discovery requests, motions, and so on. Basically, anything they can think of to drive up your legal bills and pressure you to settle."

"I'm not interested," replied Gunnar without hesitation. "I want my company back. I'm not interested in anything less."

"That's what I figured," said Ben. "Do you want to make a counteroffer?"

Gunnar thought for a moment. "Tell them . . . tell them that if Karl resigns as president and agrees never to be active in Bjornsen Pharmaceuticals again, I'll make as much of the drug as the company needs. I'll also drop my countersuit. I'll even give *him* a two percent royalty on the drug to keep him comfortable in his retirement."

"That's actually more generous than I expected you to be."

A low chuckle rumbled across the phone line. "If I thought there was any chance he'd accept, I'd take a harder line."

"Since the negotiations are likely to be short, I'd like to wait a few days before delivering your response. There are some things I'll need to do first."

‡ ‡ ‡

The courtrooms at the Daley Center courthouse are strictly functional. They have none of the marble and polished brass of the federal courts, or the ornate dark-wood elegance of old county seat courthouses. They are windowless boxes decorated in various shades of easy-to-maintain brown and gray. Short, durable carpet covers the floors, and utilitarian wood benches stand in rows behind the bar, a metal railing that separates the spectator gallery from the rest of the courtroom. In front of the bar sit two benches for witnesses and support personnel, and in front of those are two plain, oak counsel tables, one for the plaintiff's attorneys and one for the defendant's. The jury box is along one of the side walls. The bench, at the far end of the courtroom, is a massive and complex wood structure that contains a raised desk for the judge, slightly lower work stations for the court reporter and the clerk, and the witness stand, which is on the side of the bench nearest the jury box. The bailiff sits off to one side, though the task of keeping order is usually less demanding in civil courtrooms than in their criminal counterparts.

Ben sat at the back of the gallery in one such courtroom, watching the emergency motion call of the Honorable Anthony J. Reilly, the judge who had been assigned *Bjornsen Pharmaceuticals, Inc. v. Bjornsen*. Judge Reilly was in the Chancery division, the section of the Cook County Superior Court that handled all requests for "equitable relief," including Bjornsen Pharmaceuticals' request for an injunction that would force Gunnar to turn over the Neurostim formula.

The judge had been on the bench for less than two years and had only been in Chancery for a few months. Ben had never had a case before him and wanted to get a sense for how he ran his courtroom before he had to appear in front of him.

At thirty-six, Judge Reilly was the youngest judge in the Daley Center courthouse. He was a tall, athletic man, who had played basketball in college—albeit at a Division III school. He had bright red hair and a fair complexion that flushed easily if he got annoyed or embarrassed, both of which happened while Ben watched. At one point, the judge, whose background was in criminal law, blushed noticeably when he stumbled over a point of civil procedure and had to be corrected by one of the lawyers. Ten minutes later, he turned crimson when a lawyer ignored his instruction to avoid repeating arguments that had already been made in writing in the briefs.

Judge Reilly's rulings were a mixed bag. There weren't many that were clearly wrong, but a lot of them were questionable. The judge seemed to always search for a middle ground between the parties, regardless of what the law required. That worried Ben. He was pretty sure that the blitz of motions that Karl's lawyers had promised would be mostly meritless, but Judge Reilly wasn't completely denying many motions, regardless of their merit. What if the judge decided to compromise by granting only some of the other side's unreasonable requests?

Ben slipped out of the courtroom near the end of the hearing and headed back to his office. He stopped in at a deli and picked up a grilled prosciutto and avocado sandwich to eat at his desk while he worked. He was going to be very busy over the next few days.

He went straight to Noelle's office and found her leafing through a fat Redweld folder of documents festooned with annotated Post-its. He admired her delicate, pretty profile for a moment before interrupting her. "Hi, honey. Those the documents from Gunnar?"

She nodded. "Mm-hmm."

"Anything interesting?"

She nodded again. "It's not what I was expecting, though. You said you thought there was WorldCom-type stuff going on at Bjornsen Pharmaceuticals. There isn't. Or at least if there is, these documents don't show it."

Ben settled himself into one of the office chairs and took out his sandwich. "So what is going on?"

Her eyes latched onto the sandwich. "Prosciutto and avocado?"

"Yep. From the Washington Street Deli. Want some?"

She hesitated. "I probably shouldn't."

"I'm sure it'll go straight to the baby."

"Or somewhere nearby. No, thanks." She pulled her eyes away from the sandwich and selected a document from the Redweld. "WorldCom got into trouble for trying to make their books look better than they were. They would create fake revenue and hide their expenses to boost the profits they reported. Enron used different tricks, but achieved the same basic result. That's what virtually all public companies do when they commit accounting fraud."

Ben swallowed a bite of his sandwich. "Except for Bjornsen Pharmaceuticals, right?"

"Right." She gestured to the document in her hand. "It looks like they've actually fudged their numbers to *reduce* profits by three or four million dollars each of the last two years."

Ben raised his eyebrows. "That's weird. Are you sure?"

"No. Like I said, it looks that way. But these documents are incomplete; it seems like Gunnar just saved copies of random financial statements and wire transfers that caught his attention. Also, some of the key documents are in Norwegian. Gunnar translated them for me, but he's not an accountant. What I've just told you is a guess, but it's an educated guess."

"So why would Karl be trying to keep profits *down*?" Ben asked before taking another bite of his sandwich.

"Good question. I've heard of executives doing that to drive down the company's stock price, but only when they're planning a buyout and want the company's market value as low as possible. But that wasn't Karl's strategy. He's been trying to push the stock price up to convince the shareholders that he would do a good job running the company without Gunnar. Besides, reducing or increasing their profits by this much wouldn't move their stock price at all. Three or four million per year isn't a lot of money to a company like Bjornsen Pharmaceuticals."

"But it certainly could be a lot of money to a person like Karl Bjornsen, don't you think?"

"Maybe," conceded Noelle, "though he and Gwen seem pretty well-off already. Are you thinking of—well, what are you thinking of doing?"

"Sounds like Karl has had his hand in the company till. That should go in Gunnar's cross-claim."

"Don't you think you should have Sergei look into it first?"

"Not a bad idea."

"How long do you think that will take?"

Ben grinned. "How long would you like it to take?"

"I've got a meeting of the special exhibits support committee next Monday, and Gwen will be there. It would be great if you didn't accuse her husband of embezzlement before then."

"I'll see what I can do."

‡ ‡ ‡

Kim was enjoying her summer job. She arrived at Bjornsen Pharmaceuticals every morning at eight and put on a lab coat embroidered with "Kim L. Young, Medical Intern" on the left breast pocket. For some reason, the lab coat did more to make her feel like a real researcher than the actual work she was doing. She went to the bathroom at every opportunity during her first few days so she would have an excuse to look in the mirror and see a scientist looking back at her. She had dyed her hair back to its original glossy black and pulled it into a serious-looking ponytail. That, combined with the crisp new lab coat, made her look nothing like the trendy sorority girl she had been just a few weeks ago. She could see the future Dr. Young in her reflection, and she liked it.

She spent most of her days in a long, wide room lined from ceiling to floor with animal cages. On one wall were large cages that held two or three monkeys each. The cages on the other side of the room were smaller and held only one monkey each. A lab table with various instruments and documents ran down the middle of the room. The control group monkeys were in the multi-animal cages, while the monkeys receiving the drug were in the single cages. Ideally, all of the monkeys would have had their own cages, but doubling up the control group animals saved money. Besides, the monkeys seemed to like it.

Each morning, Kim and one of the researchers visited the primate room to feed the animals, clean their cages, collect urine and feces samples, give them their morning dose of the drug, check whether any of them were showing adverse effects from the drug, and so on. From the hallway, Kim could hear the monkeys chattering to each other, but when she opened the door they would invariably turn up the volume, breaking into a chorus of hoots and screeches, and rattling their cages. This unnerved her at first, but soon she discovered that they were trying to get the attention of her companion, a friendly, talkative young woman appropriately named Dr. Kathy Chatterton. Dr. Chatterton was a pretty blonde in her early thirties. Like Kim, she had grown up in Southern California and had gone to a big SoCal university—graduating from USC, the crosstown rival of Kim's UCLA. The two women immediately liked each other, and Kim thought happily that she had found her mentor for the summer.

Dr. Chatterton carried mini marshmallows in her pockets, which she distributed as rewards to animals that behaved themselves while she checked their cages. She confided to Kim that Dr. Gene Kleinbaum—head of animal studies at Bjornsen Pharmaceuticals—would probably blow a gasket if he knew the monkeys were getting marshmallows every day. Kim promised to keep her secret.

The part of her work that Kim enjoyed most was when she and Dr. Chatterton took a few of their charges to the exercise room, a spare storage room that had been converted into a makeshift monkey gym, complete with balls, tree branches, and a slide and climbing bars donated by a scientist whose children had outgrown them. Visits to the exercise room were treats for both the monkeys and their keepers. The monkeys got to run free and play, and the keepers got to relax and talk while nominally watching the monkeys through a Plexiglas observation window.

When the daily exercise was done, Dr. Chatterton and Kim put some fruit or marshmallows in the cages to coax the monkeys back, and then closed the gates once the animals were inside. After a few weeks of this, Dr. Chatterton let Kim handle this job on her own. It was a simple and safe task, perfect for an intern.

☦ ☦ ☦

A messenger delivered the promised full-court press to Ben's office the following Wednesday, forty-three minutes after Ben had called Karl Bjornsen's lawyers to tell them that Gunnar wasn't interested in their proposal. The documents nearly filled an entire banker's box. Ben sighed and signed for it. Then he took it into the conference room, where he could spread out the papers and go through them without worrying about accidentally mixing in something from the other piles on his desk.

An hour later, Noelle walked by and noticed him in the conference room surrounded by court filings. "What's up?"

"I got a care package from Bert Siwell. He's teed up half a dozen motions for hearing on the emergency call tomorrow morning."

"What kind of motions?"

Ben put down the motion he had been reading and stretched. "Let's see. There's a motion for a temporary restraining order that would require Gunnar to immediately turn over the process for making Neurostim, a motion for a preliminary injunction, a motion for a permanent injunction, a motion for expedited discovery, one hundred and fifty-three pages of discovery requests he wants expedited, a motion to dismiss Gunnar's counterclaim, and—last but not least—a motion for sanctions against both Gunnar and me personally."

"Sanctions? What for?"

"For daring to bring a counterclaim that is . . . hold on a sec, I can't do it justice." He searched the table for the sanctions motion, found it, and flipped through it. "Here we go—'for bringing a counterclaim that is so ill-considered, so patently frivolous, so clearly lacking any basis in fact or law, and so laughably puerile'— I'm pretty sure Bert had his thesaurus out by that point—'that it demands sanctions.'"

Noelle stared at him, her mouth and eyes wide in angry disbelief. "Is he serious?"

Ben shrugged. "He's obnoxious. He's also pretty funny, usually on purpose, and he's good on his feet, so he gets away with a lot."

"What a piece of work. So how is this is an emergency?"

"It isn't. What he's really doing is punishing Gunnar and me for rejecting his settlement offer. I'll be working on responses all night." He grinned. "But then so will Bert—or at least the people working for him. I just sent them our box half an hour ago. I hope they didn't have plans for dinner. I also hope you won't be seeing Gwen Bjornsen again anytime soon."

‡ ‡ ‡

Ben's dinner that night was leftover Giordano's pizza from the office fridge, washed down with the flat remains of a two-liter bottle of Diet Coke. He was on his second slice when Gunnar called. "I just read through the court papers you faxed to me. Some of the things they say are completely outrageous! Aren't there ethical standards against this kind of garbage?"

"Sure. Some of them are cited in the sanctions motion against you and me for daring to countersue Karl. I'm not too worried about that motion, though. It's not likely to be granted, so the best thing to do is ignore it."

"So you don't recommend asking for sanctions against Karl and his lawyers? I don't like letting someone punch me without punching back. It sends the wrong signal."

"Not in court," Ben replied. "Judges generally hate sanctions motions. Except in really extreme cases, like destruction of evidence or lying under oath, judges view these types of motions as the written equivalent of a temper tantrum. Throwing our own tantrum in return isn't likely to do us any good. I know it's tempting to respond in kind to this sort of insulting trash, but it really isn't a good idea. We shouldn't let it distract us from the motions that really matter."

"Like the motion for a temporary restraining order."

"Yes. Exactly. That's the one that worries me the most. If they get the TRO they want, you'll have to tell them how to make this new drug, and their case against you will basically be over."

"I thought that's what it meant," said Gunnar. "Do you really think the judge would do that to me?"

"He could. This judge has a real instinct to split the baby in every case that comes before him."

"Split the baby?"

"Yes. It's a reference to the Old Testament story of King Solomon and two women who were arguing over a baby."

"I know the story."

"Okay. Well, lawyers use the phrase 'split the baby' to refer to judge-ordered compromises, especially when the compromise isn't particularly fair or smart. For example, Judge Reilly might think he was compromising by denying the sanctions motion and granting the TRO, but that wouldn't be a compromise—it would be a total victory for Karl."

"I see," Gunnar said slowly. "Yes, I see. So how will you keep this judge from splitting my baby?"

✠ ✠ ✠

Three monkeys played in the exercise room, two from the control group and one of the test subjects. All three were related and knew each other well. The oldest and largest of the three had been the leader of their troop at the ranch where they were raised. He was named Bruce, because he had been the boss of the group—a Bruce Springsteen reference that Kim was too young to understand without explanation. The younger two monkeys were cousins and Bruce's nephews. They weren't twins, but they were so similar that they had been named Tweedledee and Tweedledum. Tweedledee had been injected with the drug; Tweedledum (Bruce's cage mate) was in the control group.

Most of Bjornsen Pharmaceuticals' monkeys were related. The company bought members of the same family group whenever they could, to make comparisons between animals as exact as possible and thereby get the most precise possible data on the effect of the drug.

Kim looked forward to playtime today. She and David had spent an hour on the phone last night talking about medical school. He had just received his final grades from his first year, and they had not been good. She sipped her chai latte and explained the situation to Dr. Chatterton. "So he's really stressed," she concluded. "He's afraid he's going to flunk out next semester. What do you think? Does it get easier after your first year, or is he in real trouble?"

"The first year is always a big adjustment," replied Dr. Chatterton. "You're not in college anymore, that's for sure. I don't think I slept more than twenty hours a week during my first year. Does it get easier after that?" She shrugged. "I don't know. There are a lot of people who don't come back after the first year, but most of those who do graduate."

"I'll tell him that. Maybe it will calm him down some. He's a great guy and everything, but he can be kinda intense sometimes. So, do you have any more words of wisdom for him?"

"Yeah. If he flunks out of med school, there's always law school."

Kim laughed. "I want to cheer him up, not make him shoot himself."

"Then you may not want to mention the law school thing. Just tell him he'll get through it."

Half an hour later, Dr. Chatterton went back to her office to take care of some paperwork and Kim went into the exercise room to retrieve the monkeys. Bruce went back into his cage without much complaining, but Tweedledee and Tweedledum were still playing and needed a lot of coaxing. Technically, Kim should have checked the ID number tattooed on each animal's abdomen to make sure the right monkey went in the right cage, but the numbers were hard to read and the animals didn't like it. Besides, Kim was pretty sure she could tell them apart.

‡ ‡ ‡

Judge Reilly held his emergency motion call at 8:30 AM, so Ben and Gunnar arrived in his courtroom at 8:15 and sat on the hard wooden benches while the judge worked through the cases ahead of theirs. At 9:05, the clerk announced "Bjornsen Pharmaceuticals versus Bjornsen."

Bert Siwell and Ben approached the bench and made their appearances. Karl and Gunnar Bjornsen were both in the courtroom and moved to the front benches when the case was called, nodding curtly to each other as they sat down. "Good morning, counsel," said the judge. "Between the two of you, you've filed no less than *eleven* emergency motions. Let's start at the top of the stack. You've both moved for TROs. Mr. Siwell, you filed your motion first, so I'll let you argue first."

"Thank you, your honor." Bert Siwell was a large man in height, width, voice, and ego. Thirty years ago, he had played right tackle at Northwestern. He had been a good offensive lineman for the same reason he was a good litigator: he was quick and could overpower most opponents. Also, he knew how to play dirty without getting caught. "My client, Bjornsen Pharmaceuticals, is asking for something that is both simple and crucial: it wants its trade secrets back. That's all we want in this motion.

"Some people take Post-its or paperclips home from the office. Gunnar Bjornsen may have taken a multibillion-dollar secret. If he did, his former employer is entitled to get it back, and that's what we ask for in our injunction papers. In the meantime, though, we're entitled to know what he's got. We're not even asking for him to give anything back at this point. We just need him to disclose what information walked out the door with him. But he won't do it.

"Why won't he do it? That's a very good question. Maybe he just wants to keep my client in the dark so he can negotiate a better severance package than he deserves. Maybe. But maybe the real reason is that he plans to sell my client's secrets to a competitor. If that's his plan, we need to know right now exactly what secrets he took from my client. We ask for a TRO requiring him to make that disclosure immediately."

The judge looked at Ben. "Thank you, your honor," Ben said. "This is going to be easier than I thought. My client has no intention of disclosing any secrets to any third parties. We'll agree to a TRO to that effect. What—"

"So why won't he disclose what secrets he took?" asked Siwell.

Ben suppressed his irritation. It was rude for one lawyer to interrupt another lawyer's argument or speak directly to his opponent rather than to the judge. Ben glanced up at Judge Reilly, who showed no sign of intervening. Ben continued his argument. "Mr. Siwell's TRO motion doesn't just request a list of the information my client allegedly took; he wants the information itself. What Mr. Siwell is asking for is to have his entire case handed to him on a silver platter. The whole purpose of his lawsuit is to force my client to turn over information. A TRO is not intended to be a way to shortcut the litigation process; it is meant to prevent an imminent harm, a wrong that is about to be done and cannot be undone by a later order of the court. The only thing Mr. Siwell has pointed to fitting that description is the claimed risk that my client will tell his client's secrets to a competitor. Mr. Bjornsen won't do that. In fact, he's willing to agree to an order requiring him not to.

"That takes care of the plaintiff's TRO motion. Now—"

"No it doesn't," interjected Siwell. "You must not have heard me before—why won't your client disclose what secrets he took?"

Ben smiled thinly and kept his eyes on the judge. "That brings us to our TRO motion. Mr. Siwell thinks my client has a multibillion-dollar secret. Is that the sort of information that should be entrusted to an embezzler?"

Karl stirred in his seat and muttered something under his breath. Siwell was apoplectic. "Your honor, I object! This isn't argument, it's slander! Mr. Corbin can't—"

"Your honor, please!" said Ben, raising his voice over Siwell's.

Judge Reilly held up his hand. "Counsel, you can respond when Mr. Corbin is finished."

"Thank you, your honor," continued Ben. "We moved for a TRO because there is substantial evidence, summarized in Gunnar Bjornsen's affidavit, that there is some questionable accounting going on at Bjornsen Pharmaceuticals. Furthermore, it appears that the problem goes all the way to the top—senior management was either cooking the books or knew that they were being cooked. That has to stop immediately. We ask the court to order that auditors be appointed to review the company's books and monitor all financial transactions until the completion of the trial on our permanent injunction motion. Appointment of auditors is particularly crucial if your honor is considering granting the plaintiff's TRO motion; there's no telling how much damage current management will do to the company if they get their hands on what Mr. Siwell says is a multibillion-dollar new product. We respectfully request that the court enter the proposed order submitted with defendant's TRO motion."

"Thank you, Mr. Corbin," said the judge. "Mr. Siwell?"

Siwell picked up a copy of Ben's TRO motion, holding it by the corner as if it were a dead fish that had spent several days in the hot sun. "Your honor, this is pure, unadulterated bovine feces." A chuckle ran through the courtroom, and to Ben's dismay, the judge smiled. "All of the allegations Mr. Corbin just made are provably false. Karl Bjornsen, the president of Bjornsen Pharmaceuticals, has canceled a full schedule of appointments this morning so that he could be here to respond to my opponent's fantasies, if your honor thinks it necessary. He will testify that they are all categorically false. This is a squeaky clean company with squeaky clean books. The defendant knows that, by the way. He was president of Bjornsen Pharmaceuticals until six months ago, which brings up another point—he would have been in charge of the kitchen during any book cooking.

"Plus, putting a team of auditors in charge of the company's finances would be an enormous and unwarranted financial burden, and would interfere with the company's financial decision making."

"Anything further, Mr. Corbin?" asked the judge.

"Yes, your honor. The auditors would only interfere in the company's financial decision making if the company was deciding to defraud shareholders like my client. All the auditors would do is to monitor the company's finances and stop any wrongdoing. And there would be no financial burden, because—"

"Your honor, there's no fraud here—" Siwell interjected.

Ben ignored him and kept talking. "If no fraud is found, my client will bear the cost—"

Siwell also kept going, "And no wrongdoing, except by Mr. Corbin and his client, who—"

The judge held up his hands. "Counsel, counsel." Both lawyers fell silent. "I've heard enough. I'm going to deny both TRO motions. Okay, moving on to the next items on our agenda. You both want preliminary injunctions. How long will it take to put on your evidence?"

They spent the next fifteen minutes haggling over when the preliminary injunction hearing would commence, how many days each of them would have to put on evidence, what deadlines would apply to pre-hearing discovery, and so forth. Judge Reilly denied the sanctions motion without comment.

Karl Bjornsen left as soon as it became clear that he wouldn't have to testify, but Gunnar waited until the end of the hearing and walked back to Ben's office with him. As they stepped through the glass doors and out into the wide stone plaza in front of the Daley Center courthouse, Gunnar turned to Ben, a broad smile on his weathered face. "So, you kept the judge from splitting my baby by giving it a conjoined twin. Well done."

Ben laughed. "That was basically the idea. I would've liked to have saved the twin too, but I didn't really expect to. I'm just glad Judge Reilly made the right compromise."

"So am I. What happens now that the TROs have been denied?"

"A lot. We need to get ready for the preliminary injunction trial, which the judge scheduled to start in exactly one month. Between now and then, we'll have to get all our evidence, line up all our witnesses, take discovery from the company to find out what evidence they plan to put on and what their witnesses will say, and respond to their discovery."

"You're going to be busy," Gunnar observed.

"No kidding. This is when the fun really begins."

‡ ‡ ‡

The next morning, Kim stopped by Dr. Chatterton's office as usual. They would normally chat for a few minutes and then go do the morning cage check together. But this morning, Dr. Chatterton was busy fighting with her computer. Apparently, a virus or spyware or something had made it past the company's firewall and infected her computer. She wasn't willing to call IT and confess—at least not until she was sure she couldn't fix the problem on her own. She asked Kim if she was comfortable doing the cage check on her own.

Kim promptly said yes and gathered up the clipboard and treat bag. She knew the procedure by now and was confident she could handle it alone. Besides, it would show good confidence and was something Dr. Chatterton could mention in a reference letter.

As she walked toward the primate room door, Kim noticed that the monkeys were unusually noisy this morning. Their screams and shrieks echoed down the hallway and were clearly audible throughout the lab area. But Kim had not worked with monkeys long enough to realize that the *tone* of their cries was also unusual—the sounds of animals that were badly upset, even terrified.

Kim opened the door and was nearly deafened by the cacophony. It seemed that each of the animals was simultaneously screaming at the top of its lungs while rattling the bars to its cage. "Calm down, guys!" she called as she walked in. She shoved her hand into her pocket and pulled out the treat bag. "Look! I've got marshmallows for you!"

For the first time, none of them showed any interest in the sweets. She stopped several steps into the room, realizing that something wasn't right. She looked around and noticed that the monkeys seemed to be focused on something at the other end of the room. She didn't see anything, but the lighting wasn't great and her view was partially obscured by the long lab table that ran down the center of the room. *Should I go get Dr. Chatterton?* she wondered. And what would she tell Dr. Chatterton? That the monkeys were loud and they scared her? *And how would that look in a reference letter?*

She cautiously walked between the rows of frantic animals, her clipboard in one hand and the bag of marshmallows still clutched in the other. The noise and tension in the room were beginning to get to her. She could feel her heart hammering in her chest and the adrenaline levels rising in her blood.

Something was odd about one of the control group cages furthest from the door—Bruce's and Tweedledum's cage. There didn't seem to be any activity in it and there was something on the cage floor that she couldn't quite identify. It was dark, lumpy, and liquid—as if something had been put in a blender with motor oil and then dumped out. She tried to focus and think, but that was impossible with a room full of monkeys screaming at her. She edged closer and leaned over the table to get a better view of the cage.

The first thing she noticed was Tweedledum. He was sitting perfectly still at the back of the cage and watching her. Unlike the other monkeys, he wasn't screaming or making noise. His fur was splotched with something dark, but he wasn't grooming himself. He just sat there, staring at her with dark, impassive eyes.

The second thing she noticed was that Bruce was missing. She dropped her eyes from Tweedledum's unnerving gaze and looked more closely at the mess on the floor of the cage. All at once she realized what it was.

Down the hall, Dr. Chatterton's mind was still focused on her computer; too focused to immediately distinguish the sound of the higher-pitch screams coming from the direction of the primate room.

Chapter Five

A Problem With the Control Group

KARL BJORNSEN GLANCED UP as the head of new drug development walked into the conference room, the sixth and final division manager to join the meeting. "Hello, Frank," Karl said. "Grab some lunch and have a seat. Gene, could you get that first row of lights?"

Karl got up and walked to the podium as the lights at the front of the room dimmed. The chatter died down and six sets of eyes turned to watch him. The entire company had focused on the Neurostim investigational new drug, or IND, application for the past six months, and in a few days Karl would lead them into their first key meeting with regulators to discuss it.

A projector whirred to life and the words "Keys to a Successful Pre-IND Meeting" appeared on a screen behind him in gold type against a background image of Bjornsen Pharmaceuticals' headquarters. "I don't have to tell anyone here how important our meeting is with the FDA next week. You all know it. You all have been working very hard to get ready for it. Your departments are all working around the clock. If I come in at five-thirty in the morning, I'll find Tina and her staff working on clinical trial protocols. When I leave at seven-thirty at night, I'll find my car blocked by the truck of the pizza delivery guy who's bringing dinner to Gene's crew."

Everyone laughed except Gene Kleinbaum, the head of the animal testing unit. He frowned nervously and his bald head gleamed brightly in the light from the recessed bulb directly above him. "I talked to him about that, Karl. It won't happen again."

"I don't mind, as long as you guys order one of those triple meat pizzas next time." Karl smiled warmly. "All of us have been working nights and weekends for the past month to get ready for this meeting. We all want it to go well. We all believe in Neurostim, and we know what it means to our company and our customers.

"But believing in our product is not enough. We need to make the FDA believe in it. And we need to make them believe in our ability to bring it to market safely. To do that, we need to remember two things." He picked up a remote control and clicked. The words "Keep Your Eyes on the Prize" appeared on the screen. "What's our overriding goal when we sit down with the FDA?"

"Find out exactly what they want in our IND application?" ventured Dr. Frank Chow.

"Nope," replied Karl. "That's important, but that's not our number one priority. Anyone else?"

"We need to make sure they agree with our protocols," said Dr. Corrigan. "If they don't sign off on those, the rest of our IND application will be meaningless."

"Also important," said Karl, "but also not our main goal. Our purpose—our overriding aim—is to make them *want* to approve this drug. When they walk out of that meeting, we want them to be as excited about this project as we are. We're not going there to make an academic presentation or have an intellectual dialogue with the scientists sitting around the table. We're going there to sell the FDA on Neurostim, and on this company. If we do that, everything else will fall into place.

"The FDA, of course, has a different goal. They're bureaucrats with checklists. They want to make sure we've jumped through all their hoops and complied with each of their ten thousand and one regulations. We need to be ready to answer all of their questions, but we can't let them distract us from the task at hand." He pointed to the screen behind him. "We have to keep our eyes on the prize. Whatever questions they ask, make sure your answers build their confidence in Bjornsen Pharmaceuticals and their interest in Neurostim. If they're convinced that we're a top-notch company making a revolutionary new drug, they'll feel a lot more comfortable checking items off their lists."

He clicked the remote again and the word "Teamwork" appeared on the screen. "The second key to success is teamwork. We've come this far because we're a team. A good team—the best I've ever worked with. No one person in this room can claim the credit for creating Neurostim; but without each of you, it wouldn't have happened. We all succeed together because each of us knows that he or she can rely on all of the others. And I know that I can rely on each of you in our meeting with the FDA. I know that each of you will be ready and will be on message.

"One quick point on delivery," he said as "Short and Sweet" flashed onto the screen. "Our presentations should be clear and short—and prepared with our meeting goals in mind. Don't try to give the FDA every possible piece of information or cautionary footnote. Tell them what the product does and why they should approve human testing. If they have questions, they'll ask you. If they don't, we can catch an early flight home and crack open the champagne."

He reached down and turned off the PowerPoint projector. "There's only one more thing I want to say. Not only will this be the biggest meeting we've ever had with the FDA, it will also be the first one we've had without Gunnar. It's unfortunate that recent events mean that he won't be here to share in our success, but that's the path he has chosen. There's no question that he was a terrific scientist and made a substantial contribution to the Neurostim project. But there's also no question that a unified team is stronger than one that's divided." He gestured around the room. "Imagine this meeting if Gunnar had been here. He and I would still be fighting about whether to meet with the FDA at all, and the rest of you would be looking at your watches and wondering when we would shut up so you could get back to work." There were several chuckles and a couple of knowing nods. "He's my brother and I love him, but the truth is that we're better off without him in the company. So I don't want any of you worrying about how we'll do at the FDA without Gunnar sitting at the table. We'll be fine. In fact, we'll be more than fine; we'll be spectacular. And don't think for a minute that that's a throwaway motivational line. It's something I know to be true. I've seen you in action time and again, and I have great faith in each of you."

He picked up his notes and stepped away from the podium. "That's it. Any questions?"

After a couple of seconds, Dr. Kleinbaum said, "Well, I don't really have a question. Just a comment."

"What's that?"

"Thanks. I can't speak for anyone else here, but I needed to hear that." He started to clap, and one by one the others joined in.

‡ ‡ ‡

Dr. Kleinbaum arrived back from the meeting to find Dr. Chatterton waiting outside his office. She saw him coming and walked quickly to meet him. "Gene, I need to talk to you right away."

He was about to ask her what the problem was, but one look at her face told him that he'd better wait until they were behind closed doors. "Of course. Come into my office." He guided her in and motioned her toward a chair as he shut the door. "So, what's up, Kathy?"

"One of the monkeys killed another one. It—"

He stiffened and held up his hand. "Test group or control group?"

"Control group."

"Both of them?"

"Yes."

He relaxed. "Okay, go ahead."

"It was awful. One of the interns discovered it this morning. I found her throwing up in the hallway outside the primate room. I went in to see what had happened and—" She paused and took a deep breath. "I've never seen anything like it. One of the monkeys had literally torn a larger monkey to pieces."

He nodded sympathetically. "Being caged can do terrible things to animals, no matter how well we treat them. Sometimes they become psychotic. I'm sorry our intern had to see that. I hope neither of you blame yourselves. It's not your fault."

She leaned forward and looked him in the eye. "I don't think you understand, Gene. The smaller monkey *disassembled* the larger one. The floor of the cage was covered with blood and body parts. That's beyond psychotic. It's almost like the monkey was on PCP or something. Also, the victim and the murderer grew up together. The victim was like a big brother to the murderer. I have never, ever heard of anything like that happening. Have you?"

Dr. Kleinbaum swallowed. "We'll have the monkey put down, of course. And we'll transfer the intern to our clinical testing program. We'll be finishing the animal phase soon in any event."

"You'll do a necropsy, right?"

He forced a small smile. "From what you said, the cause of death was pretty apparent."

Dr. Chatterton didn't smile, and her brown eyes flashed angrily. "I meant the other monkey."

"Why bother? You said they were both part of the control group."

"But what if he got a dose of the drug somehow? The monkeys get mixed up sometimes, particularly the younger ones, and we haven't been able to check the tattoos yet. Besides, we'll need to do a necropsy for the FDA."

He nodded reassuringly. "Those are good points. I'll take care of it."

"You'll order the necropsy?"

He shrugged. "I'll do what I can. We're behind schedule on our necropsies and toxicity tests from the dog and rat testing, but I'll see what can be done."

For a moment she looked like she might protest further, but then she smiled and said, "Okay. Thanks, Gene."

✠ ✠ ✠

Anne Bjornsen arrived home from lunch and saw the message light on her answering machine blinking. She punched the replay button and heard Markus's familiar voice.

"Hi, Mom. I just got a call from the director, and it looks like I'm going to be on stage for opening night. Jim Kennison broke his leg last night, so I'm going to be playing Mr. Stukely for at least the next month."

She sat down on a stool by the phone in the kitchen and pushed the speed dial for his number. He answered on the third ring. "Hi, Mom."

"Congratulations!" she said. "I just got your message. That's great news! It's too bad about Jim, though."

"Yeah," agreed Markus. "I always tell him to break a leg before he goes on. Last night's rehearsal is the first time he actually did it. He seemed to be in pretty good spirits when I called him this morning, though."

Markus spoke with the careful, precise diction that his mother had learned meant he had been drinking and didn't want to disclose it by slurring his words. She worried that he might get into trouble if he showed up at a rehearsal drunk, but decided not to say anything. Her comments on his drinking rarely did anything except irritate him. Besides, this was not the time to criticize him. "That's good. This is the first time since college you've had a major role on opening night, isn't it?"

"It is. I'm really pumped. I'll be in the reviews, for better or worse. This could be a huge break for me."

"Well, as soon as I get off the phone with you, I'm going to call the theater and order tickets for your first performance. I don't know what Dad's schedule is, but I'll be there."

Markus chuckled drily. "You need to check his schedule to know whether he'll show up for a theater performance? Really?"

‡ ‡ ‡

At 4:59 PM on the second day after the emergency motion hearing—one minute before they would have violated Judge Reilly's scheduling order—Bjornsen Pharmaceuticals produced its financial documents. They not only produced the two boxes of useful documents that Ben had requested, but also three dozen boxes of irrelevant material that needed to be weeded through. "Docudumps" were a fairly common hardball tactic among big firm lawyers litigating against small firms or solo practitioners. As one of Ben's former colleagues at Beale & Ripley once noted, "If you have to give the other side a needle to stick you with, wrap it in a haystack whenever possible."

Ben promptly gave the documents to Noelle. Throughout the next day, she sat at her desk poring through stacks of financial statements and backup documents. Sergei was thirty feet away, in the conference room, doing the same thing. Noelle and Sergei had each taken half the boxes and promised Ben they would be ready to give him the highlights by the end of the day, when he got back from interviewing potential expert witnesses. He was taking the deposition of Bjornsen Pharmaceuticals' CFO tomorrow and he needed to know enough about the company's finances to ask the right questions and spot any holes in the answers.

When Noelle was halfway through the first box, Susan called on the intercom.

"Emily Marshall is on the phone for you."

"Okay, put her through." Emily was the chair of the special exhibits support committee at the Field Museum, and a member of Chicago's old money aristocracy. She was a fixture in the society pages and seemed to be on a first name basis with everyone of significance in the city. Noelle had worked closely with her on the Viking exhibit, and the two had become close acquaintances, if not quite friends. Though Noelle would never have said so (particularly in Ben's hearing), getting to know Emily had been one of the chief rewards of the hundreds of hours she had put into that project.

"Hello, Emily. What can I do for you?"

Emily laughed warmly. "What can you do? I'm not sure there's anything left! You've already done more than we expected when we invited you to join. That Viking exhibit and reception were just terrific. I'm still getting compliments about them."

"That's great. It was a lot of work, but also a lot of fun."

"I know it was. I got way too many e-mails and faxes from you after ten at night. I think it would be a good idea if you took a break from the committee. You need your rest with the baby coming, and I know you have lots of demands on your time."

"That's sweet of you, but I'm fine," replied Noelle. "I really don't have much on my plate for the Field right now. Plus I love working with everyone; it's no burden at all."

"But it will be a burden. There are some big projects in the works right now, and I just wouldn't feel right asking you to work on them," countered Emily. "I'm going to have to put my foot down, Noelle. You know you need some time off and we know it too. We'd like you to step down and let someone with a less hectic schedule fill in for you."

Noelle realized what was happening and felt sick to her stomach. "Emily, be honest with me. Does the lawsuit against Karl Bjornsen have anything to do with this?"

"Well, I know that must be taking a big bite out of your schedule," Emily acknowledged, "and it must be stressful to see Gwen Bjornsen at meetings."

And having me on the committee makes it less likely that Karl will make any more big donations. "I understand. I . . . I think it would be best if I resigned, effective immediately." She hung up the phone and started to cry.

‡ ‡ ‡

Tweedledee still gazed out from the back of Tweedledum's cage, ignoring his gruesome handiwork. A padded restraint slipped quickly over Tweedledee's head and pulled him to the side of the cage, where it held him fast. He didn't resist. A heavily gloved hand holding a syringe expertly injected him with enough morphine to kill an adult man. Tweedledee flinched as the needle went in, but he made no noise and didn't struggle. He was used to injections.

The hand withdrew and the restraint slipped off the monkey's neck. He sat quietly for several minutes. Then he closed his eyes and lay down. A few minutes later, his breathing became uneven. A few minutes after that, it stopped completely.

The hands, now wearing only latex gloves, returned and checked for a pulse and other signs of life. Finding none, they picked up Tweedledee's body and carried it to a garbage can bearing the words "CAUTION: BIOLOGICAL WASTE." The can was already nearly full of the bodies of dead rats and beagles, which had been sacrificed and necropsied as part of other drug tests. The hands dropped Tweedledee's remains on top of the other dead animals and wheeled the can to a loading dock, where a row of similarly marked trash containers awaited proper disposal.

Ordinarily, dead animals would wait undisturbed until the next morning, when a truck would pick them up and take them to a nearby disposal facility to be incinerated. But one last indignity awaited Tweedledee's corpse. During the night, another set of gloved hands opened the can containing his body and shone a flashlight inside. Once his body was identified, a scalpel appeared and expertly sliced open his belly. Plastic-coated fingers quickly found his liver, excised part of it with the knife, and dropped it in a plastic bag. Then the light winked out, the lid went back on the can, and Tweedledee's remains were left in peace to await their cremation.

‡ ‡ ‡

"How did the first day of the deposition go?" asked Noelle as she and Ben drove home from the office the next day.

The deposition of Bjornsen Pharmaceuticals' CFO had started that afternoon at two o'clock. Illinois Supreme Court Rule 206 limited depositions to three hours, but Bert Siwell had persuaded Judge Reilly to waive the rule in this case. Ben had objected, but in retrospect he was glad he could take as much time as he wanted to question witnesses. He rarely had more than two hours' worth of questions for a particular witness, but Siwell rarely had less than three hours' worth of objections, arguments, and delaying tactics. "Actually, we're done," replied Ben.

"Really? Sergei and I had over forty documents for you to ask him about. Were you able to get through all of them? Did he have any explanation for why it looks like there's extra money coming in through that Norwegian subsidiary?"

Ben shook his head. "Siwell must have given him a memory pill that kicked in about ten minutes into the deposition, because he started answering every question with some version of 'I don't recall.' After that, Siwell objected to every question on the grounds that it called for speculation. When I pushed, he instructed the witness not to answer."

"What a crock! Can he do that?"

"No. If the witness doesn't know the answer to a question, he has to say so. His lawyer can't just tell him not to answer. Siwell and I argued about that for about half an hour and I threatened to call the judge before he finally gave in. After that, I asked about ten minutes of questions to establish that the CFO has no idea where the extra money came from or how Bjornsen Pharmaceuticals' Norwegian subsidiary keeps its books—other than that he assumes they comply with Norwegian law."

"So who knows then?"

Ben shrugged. "Someone in Norway; the CFO claimed not to know who. And Siwell made it very clear that he's not going to let me depose anyone there until after the preliminary injunction hearing."

"So he's completely stonewalling you. Unbelievable."

"Oh, it's very believable. Unfortunately, there's not much I can do about it between now and the preliminary injunction hearing." Ben turned into their cul-de-sac and pushed the garage door opener. "So, how was your day?" he asked as they pulled in. "Did Gwen Bjornsen say anything to you at the committee meeting this afternoon?"

"Actually, I . . . well, I resigned from the committee yesterday."

Ben stared at her in shock and nearly crashed into the back of the garage. "Huh? Why?"

She sighed. "Because they asked me to."

"They asked you to? Why?"

"I got a very nice call from Emily Marshall telling me how she and the other board members thought I was overloaded and needed a break. They were all worried about me because I'm pregnant and working so hard, you see."

"A little overprotective, but I see her point," Ben interjected.

She glared at him. "That *wasn't* her real point. I told her I was fine, but she told me I didn't have any choice. Then she made it pretty clear that what's really going on is that they don't want me on the committee because you're representing Gunnar in this lawsuit."

"So? Why do they care?"

"Because Karl and Gwen donated two million dollars to the museum last year, and Bjornsen Pharmaceuticals donated another three to fund the Viking exhibit. That's why."

"Oh." He rolled his eyes. "At least now you can stop working so hard getting to know people who aren't worth knowing."

"You know, when I got off the phone with Emily, I really wanted to talk to you. But I didn't, because I was afraid you might say something like that. I've kept this bottled up inside for the past day and a half because I knew I couldn't talk to you."

"I'm sorry. I wasn't thinking."

"Seriously, sometimes you have a real gift for saying exactly the wrong thing at exactly the wrong moment!"

"I really am sorry." He opened his mouth as if to say something more, but then shut it.

She looked at him hard. "But . . . ?"

"No. No buts now. Let's go in and have dinner. I'll make that chicken Caesar salad you like so much."

He started to get out of the car, but she stopped him. "No you don't! Tell me what you were going to say."

"You sure you want to hear it?"

"Yes, I'm sure. I don't want to have some big 'but' hanging over me all night."

"Okay." He hesitated and ran his fingers through his thick brown hair. "I was going to say that if you're going to be donating a lot of time to an organization, maybe you should pick an orphanage or something. And not one run by rich, society types."

"What's wrong with them? They're not all like Emily Marshall. Just because someone has money and style doesn't make them evil. Look at the Gossards or the Bishops or the—"

Ben raised his hand. "I'm not saying that they're bad, just that they might be bad for you. You should be putting time into a charity because you want to help people, not because you want to meet people."

"That's not what I was doing!" Tears started to roll down her cheeks. She wiped them away furiously, leaving little mascara smears under her eyes. "You don't understand; you never have!"

"What don't I understand?"

"That this isn't about me. It isn't even about us." She put a hand on her belly. "It's about our baby and the babies we'll have after this one. I've been working so hard to make sure doors will be open for our children."

"We did just fine before we knew the Gossards and Bishops, and I'm sure our kids will too."

"'Fine' isn't good enough for my children. They're going to have the best we can give them! There won't be any doors that won't open for them. Not if I can help it. And that means having connections."

"In other words, they'll have everything you didn't, right?"

"Yes. Is that so terrible? You think opportunities magically appear for everyone, because they did for you. Well, that's not how this world works, Ben. We're not all lucky enough to have parents who can pay our way through college and law school. We didn't all get golf lessons when we were growing up so that we could impress clients and senior partners on the links."

Ben sighed. "Don't get me wrong—I'm not saying we shouldn't try to give our kids every possible advantage. I'm just saying that's not what should drive who we know and why. For one thing, we won't be setting a very good example for our kids, will we? They'll go to Sunday school and learn that they should love their neighbors. Then they'll watch us in action and learn that they should really only love the *right* neighbors."

Noelle rolled her eyes. "Thank you for that sermon, Reverend Corbin. I'll keep those words of wisdom in mind."

‡ ‡ ‡

Later that evening, Gunnar sat in the recliner in his den, reading through the deposition of Gene Kleinbaum. Gunnar had hired Dr. Kleinbaum ten years ago to head Bjornsen Pharmaceuticals' animal testing labs, and had considered him a friend and a good scientist. But based on Dr. Kleinbaum's testimony, his morals or his memory were more flexible than Gunnar would have expected. Ben Corbin had caught him "misremembering" often enough that Gunnar was confident the judge and jury wouldn't believe anything Dr. Kleinbaum said. Still, it pained Gunnar to see a former colleague and friend corrupting himself to curry favor with the company's new control group. He mentally added Dr. Kleinbaum to the list of executives who would have to go once Karl was out of power. It was depressing how many good men and women in the corporate control group had prostituted themselves for Karl's stock option offers and fat bonuses.

He was about to put the transcript down and go to bed, when his home office line rang. He looked over at the phone and saw that the number on the caller ID had the 572 prefix that all Bjornsen Pharmaceuticals numbers shared. He didn't recognize the last four digits, however. He picked up the phone. "Hello?"

"Hello, Mr. Bjornsen," said a vaguely familiar female voice, speaking in hushed tones. "This is Kathy Chatterton. I work in testing and development at Bjornsen Pharmaceuticals."

He sat up and searched for a pen and some paper so he could take notes. "Oh, yes. Hello, Kathy. What can I do for you?"

"I'm working on the Neur—XD-463 animal testing program," she said, speaking rapidly and quietly. "One of the monkeys killed and dismembered another monkey. We put down the first monkey, but Gene Kleinbaum wouldn't let me do a necropsy."

He stopped writing. "What? Why not? They're required by the FDA."

"He said it was because both animals were in the control group, but I thought the killer monkey might have been accidentally switched with one of the monkeys from the test group, one from the cohort receiving the highest dose. So after the monkey was dead, I went very discreetly out to the biowaste disposal area and checked the ID tattoo. It was a monkey from the high-dose group. I also took tissue samples from the liver."

"Where's the animal's body?" demanded Gunnar, his voice sharp and commanding.

"They . . . all the waste would be incinerated by now. I'm sorry. I . . . well, someone could have seen me taking the body. I did take a picture of the tattoo with my cell phone camera, though. It's blurry, but you can make out the numbers."

Gunnar smiled. "Good. What about the tissue samples? Have you had them tested yet?"

"Yes. I just got the results back a couple of hours ago. There were high levels of both XD-463 and its known metabolites in the monkey's body. I called Gene at home to tell him and he was just furious. He said I was going behind his back and trying to destroy the company. He also said I must have screwed up the test and told me to save the rest of the tissue for him so that he could test it personally. I—"

"I need that tissue!" Gunnar cut her off. "I also need your cell phone pictures, the test results, and the lab notes from the attack incident."

"I was really hoping you'd say that, Mr. Bjornsen," she replied, her voice trembling slightly. "I knew Mr. Bjornsen—the other Mr. Bjornsen—wouldn't . . . well, I didn't think he'd listen to me, and I didn't want to go to the FDA and have them shut down the whole R&D department; but this can't get swept under the rug—not when we're getting ready to start human testing."

"Oh, it won't be," replied Gunnar. "You can trust me on that. I'll meet you in the east parking lot in half an hour."

"No, wait," she said hesitantly. "The security guards will recognize you and they might not let you in. Also, it will be all over the company by morning that you were here." She paused and then went on more confidently. "Maybe I should come over to your house instead. I have your address from last year's company directory."

"Good thinking. When will you be here?"

"It'll take me a little while to get everything together. I should be at your front door in forty-five minutes."

"Excellent. I'll be waiting for you."

Gunnar hung up the phone and smiled. He had a pretty good idea who would be replacing Dr. Kleinbaum after the litigation was over.

He tried to go back to reading the deposition transcript as he waited for Dr. Chatterton to arrive. He couldn't focus, though, so he got up and walked out to the living room. He turned off the lights for a better view and took a seat in an armchair across from a wide bay window facing the street. He looked out expectantly across the dark lawn to the quiet, twisting street, watching for a pair of headlights to appear around the bend.

"Gunnar, why are you sitting down there in the dark?"

He jumped in his seat and turned to see his wife at the top of the stairs in her nightgown. Her brown hair hung loose on her shoulders, framing her fine-boned face and long neck. "Anne, I thought you were asleep. I'm waiting for someone to drop off a package."

"Who delivers packages at eleven o'clock at night?"

"Someone who doesn't want to be seen by Karl's cronies," replied Gunnar. "Her name is Kathy Chatterton. I think you met her at the company Christmas party a couple of years ago."

"Yes, I remember her. She seemed very nice," said Anne as she came down the stairs. "What's in the package she's bringing?"

"Karl's head on a platter," he said with a grin. He looked at his watch. "I wonder what's keeping her. She said she'd be here five minutes ago."

Anne chuckled and patted him on the shoulder. "Patience has never been your strong suit, dear. I'm going to make myself a cup of peppermint tea. Would you like some?"

"Yes, thanks."

She disappeared into the kitchen and reappeared five minutes later bearing two steaming mugs. She handed one to her husband, who accepted it wordlessly. "I'm heading to bed," she informed him. "Give Kathy my best."

"I will, if she ever shows up."

"I'm sure she's coming as fast as she can," Anne replied. "Good night." She kissed Gunnar and went back upstairs.

At eleven-thirty, Gunnar went back into his den and dialed the number that had appeared on his phone's caller ID screen. No one answered. He hung up without leaving a message. At midnight, he was pacing in the living room and muttering to himself, a half-full mug of cold peppermint tea still clutched in one massive fist. By one o'clock, he was toying with the idea of driving up to Bjornsen Pharmaceuticals to look for Dr. Chatterton. He ultimately decided against it, and he finally went to bed at one-thirty.

The next morning, he was in a foul mood. He wasn't sure what had happened the night before, but he was beginning to think that Dr. Chatterton's story had been too good to be true. Maybe she realized there was something wrong with the tissue tests after she got off the phone with him. Maybe the whole thing had been a childish prank by Karl's toadies. Whatever had happened, Gunnar had gotten his hopes up. He had even foolishly bragged to Anne that he was about to get Karl's head on a platter. That memory grated on him as he showered and shaved. He muttered angrily to himself as he dressed, and avoided Anne when he went downstairs.

After his usual breakfast of grapefruit, toast, and brown goat cheese, Gunnar retired to the den. After he left, Anne turned on the TV. The local news was on and Gunnar could hear a perky female voice discussing the Cubs' relief pitching and other local disasters. He frowned and got up to close the den door, but then he froze with his hand on the knob.

"Police are investigating a fatal accident on the Eisenhower Expressway late last night," the news anchor said with a slight note of solemnity in her otherwise cheerful voice. "Katherine Chatterton, a Chicago research scientist, was killed in a single car collision just west of Mannheim. Police are asking for witnesses to call the number at the bottom of the screen."

Chapter Six

Human Trials

THE PRE-IND MEETING TOOK PLACE in a grim, windowless conference room with a long, slightly dingy white Formica table with wood trim. The gray cloth chairs around the table looked as if they belonged in a high school teachers lounge. A not-quite-clean whiteboard covered one wall. In a nutshell, the room was very federal.

So too were the half-dozen men and women across the table from the Bjornsen Pharmaceuticals team. They were a motley assortment of bureaucrats in two-hundred-dollar suits and scientists wearing short-sleeved dress shirts and ugly ties. Karl had instructed his team to dress accordingly—nothing too expensive or polished; nothing they would normally wear to a client presentation.

Karl had designated himself—the team member with the least to say—to take notes for the company. The discussions would be largely technical and there was little of substance he could add. He was there principally to assess the FDA's mood and manage the discussion around any roadblocks.

To Karl's satisfaction, the FDA team seemed receptive. They paid close attention during the presentations, leaning forward and nodding appreciatively when Dr. Chow discussed the improved mental performance of the test animals and played the video Karl had shown at the Field Museum reception. The FDA staffers asked very few questions during the company's presentations on its rat and beagle studies. The only point where the talks didn't go particularly well came when the FDA's pharmacokinetics expert started questioning Dr. Kleinbaum about the primate testing. "Why didn't you do a final round of blood and urine tests on the monkeys?" he asked, interrupting Dr. Kleinbaum's PowerPoint presentation.

"We had already run full sets of tests on the rats and beagles, so we saw no reason to do a full set on the monkeys too."

"But you did, except for the final post-trial round. Why skip that one?"

"Because we felt we already had sufficient data from the post-trial tests on the other animals."

"If you already had enough information from those tests," the government expert persisted, "why run the monkey trials at all? You know we discourage primate testing where it's not necessary."

"Ah, well, we believed primate testing was necessary here because of the significance of this product and the fact that rhesus monkeys are a lot closer to humans than rats or beagles." Dr. Kleinbaum wiped his palms on his pants and was beginning to get visibly flustered.

"So if the testing was necessary, why not do a complete set? Without the final round, your results are incomplete."

"Like . . . like I said, we—"

"That's okay, Gene, you can stop covering for me," Karl interrupted. "The real reason for the primate trials was to test the efficacy of the drug and make that little video you folks saw. Investors and stock analysts tend to be more impressed by monkeys than they are by rats or dogs. But tests with monkeys also get the attention of animal rights activists, so I had them stop the trials as soon as we had what we needed for marketing. That was a PR decision, not a scientific decision." That wasn't true, but the FDA didn't need to know that. Moreover, Karl suspected that they would find his story more believable than Dr. Kleinbaum's, which they clearly weren't swallowing.

Several of the FDA personnel chuckled or nodded, but the pharmacokinetics expert wasn't quite ready to give up. "So the video was made at the end of the trials, but before the post-trial tests were scheduled to be done?"

"Well, no," conceded Karl. "To tell you the truth, I wasn't aware that the primate tests were still going on, until one night I found my car blocked by a pizza delivery truck that was bringing dinner to the animal research team." The pharmacokinetics expert smiled and several members of the FDA team smiled and exchanged knowing, look-at-the-clueless-CEO glances. "I went inside to find the deliveryman and discovered Gene and his crew hard at work with the monkeys. I asked Gene whether it was really necessary to keep running tests on these animals. He responded that he probably already had enough data and could stop the trial."

"Now I understand," said the government scientist. "Thank you for your candor, Mr. Bjornsen."

The rest of the meeting went smoothly, and Karl said nothing more of substance. The government scientists listened closely to Dr. Corrigan's discussion of the clinical protocols the company would use during human trials, but didn't challenge any of her proposals. Then came the part of the pre-IND meeting that Karl hated: the wrap-up. The salesman in Karl wanted to close the deal, to do something to get the people sitting on the other side of the table to commit to Neurostim, or at the very least say something positive about the drug. But he couldn't. This was very much a sales meeting from his perspective, but not from the FDA's. They were there to make sure the IND application process ran smoothly, not to short-circuit it. They would not do or say anything that might indicate they had prejudged the application—and Karl couldn't ask them to. All he could do was smile, shake hands, and say good-bye.

The Bjornsen Pharmaceuticals team gathered in an airport bar for a postmortem, where they all tried to guess the FDA's intentions from the few delphic comments its members had let slip. The consensus view was that the government would approve the IND and allow human trials of Neurostim, though a minority of the team (Dr. Chow and Dr. Corrigan) thought the FDA would require another round of primate trials with a full regimen of blood and urine testing. After they had all finished their drinks, they headed home to put the finishing touches on the IND application and wait to see what the FDA would do.

‡ ‡ ‡

Back at Bjornsen Pharmaceuticals, Kim Young was having a slow day, which was fine with her. She'd had more than enough excitement over the past week. First, there had been the awful incident with the monkeys. Then she had been reassigned to the Neurostim clinical team just in time for the final frenzy, as they prepped senior management for their meeting with the FDA. She worked fifteen-hour days proofreading background memos, scurrying after documents that an executive VP suddenly decided he needed to see, double-checking data for PowerPoint slides, etcetera. And while she was caught up in the middle of all that, she got a broadcast e-mail announcement that Dr. Kathy Chatterton had died in a car crash.

Yesterday afternoon, the management team had left for the airport, and the pressure level in the office dropped to virtually nothing. Kim and the other members of the prep team had gone out for a beer to celebrate, but they had all been too tired to stay out late. Even Kim, who was usually up for a night of bar-hopping, was in bed by ten.

Now, she had little to do in the office, so she decided to call David. They hadn't spoken for more than five minutes in over a week, and it would be good to hear his voice. He picked up on the first ring.

"Hi, Kimmy. How are you doing? It's been quite a week for you, hasn't it?"

"Yeah, but it's pretty quiet here today. Everybody's waiting to hear how the pre-IND meeting goes. I'm just sitting here at my desk, missing you."

"I miss you too. I wish you were here. The hospital here is less than a mile from the beach, and there's this cool little boardwalk right on the water," he said wistfully. "It would be fun to go hang out there with you after work."

She leaned back in her chair and closed her eyes. "That sounds so great right now, I can't even tell you. I wish I could get on a plane and be there tonight. I just want to get away from here."

"Really? How come?"

"I guess I'm still kind of in shock about Kathy dying. It's so weird to walk past her office and see the door shut and the lights off and know that I'm never going to talk to her again. There's going to be a memorial for her this weekend. I think I'm going to go."

"That's a good idea. It should give you some closure."

She opened her eyes and began to twist her hair around her finger, absently hunting for split ends among the black strands. "Maybe. I don't know. I need closure about more than Kathy."

"You mean the monkey thing? That sounded pretty gruesome, but they've moved you into the clinical program, haven't they?"

"Yeah, but it's not like the people in the clinical program haven't heard about it. I'm sure they all think of me as the screaming intern who threw up in the hallway."

"If it had been me, I would've needed to change my pants afterwards," replied David. "Seriously, I wouldn't worry about it. Just stay focused and make sure the rest of your summer there is strong—which I'm sure it will be."

"I'm actually thinking of quitting. It's not just the monkey thing and the Kathy thing and the missing you thing; it's all of them together. Plus, it's always humid here and there are tons of mosquitoes and I don't know anyone and—"

"Are you nuts?" David broke in with sudden vehemence. "You've got the perfect summer job, and you want to quit?"

"It's not seeming so perfect right now. I had a lot more fun waiting tables at Tim's Tiki Hut last summer. I made more money, too."

"What would you rather have on your med school application and résumé—Bjornsen Pharmaceuticals or Tim's Tiki Hut? And imagine what interviewers will think if they figure out that you bailed out of Bjornsen so you could wait tables in LA. I can't believe we're even having this conversation."

"Maybe you're right. I guess it would be best for me to stay here."

"I know I'm right. Getting into a top med school is incredibly competitive. If you really want to get into UCLA, you're going to need every advantage you can get."

"Yeah, I suppose not too many applicants get to talk about spending their summers working on a cutting-edge drug."

"You've got to look at the long term. Don't just think of what sounds like fun right now."

"Okay," Kim said wearily. "I knew you'd help put things in perspective. I'll have two weeks to have fun and spend time with you after I get back to LA. Right now, I need to get in the right mind-set so I can crank on this clinical trial if the FDA gives us the green light."

"There you go," he replied. "That's my Kimmy. Hey, speaking of that trial, do you think you could get me in?"

Kim hesitated. "Are you sure you want to? I mean, it's an experimental drug that does things to your brain."

"The FDA won't allow human trials unless they're sure it's safe," reasoned David. "Are you worried because of the monkey thing?"

"Yeah, a little bit," she admitted. "Dr. Kleinbaum said he'd looked into it and there's no way that it was related to Neurostim, but still. Besides, your brain is important to me. I don't want anything bad happening to it."

"Don't worry. If the FDA says it's safe, and Dr. Kleinbaum says it's safe, then it's safe, particularly in the extremely low doses they'll use for a Phase I clinical. C'mon, even a low dose of this thing could give me a boost in school next year. And I really need a boost."

His request made her uncomfortable, but she trusted his judgment. Besides, what he said about the FDA sounded right. "I'll see what I can do."

‡ ‡ ‡

Ben looked up when Sergei walked into his office. "Glad you could make it. Have a seat."

The tall Russian sat down in one of Ben's office chairs. "I was in the neighborhood when you called and had a few extra minutes. What's up?"

"I got a call from Gunnar this morning. He said that a Dr. Kathy Chatterton from Bjornsen Pharmaceuticals called him last night and told him that she had information proving that one of Karl's executives was hiding bad test results from the FDA. She said she would bring it over to his house, but she never arrived. She was killed in a traffic accident on the way."

Sergei whistled. "You mean a crash."

"What? Oh, yeah. Exactly. Gunnar suspects that it wasn't an accident at all."

"What do you think?"

"I'm not sure. I'd like to know what the police think. If they think it was an accident—particularly if they have witnesses who say so—I'll feel a lot better. Can you look into it?"

"Sure. I still have some friends in the state police from my time at the Bureau. I'll make a couple of calls."

"Thanks. Anything you can find out before the preliminary injunction hearing starts on Tuesday would be especially useful. Speaking of the Bureau, do you think we should talk to Elena about this? Murder is usually a state crime, of course, but I thought the fraud-on-the-FDA angle might interest the feds."

"It might."

Ben started to jot down a note to call Elena.

So, uh, are you planning to call her?" Sergei asked.

Ben stopped and looked up. "Yes. Is there some reason I shouldn't?"

"Not really, but you should know that I don't think we're . . . well, that we're not together anymore."

"Wow. Really? The last I heard, you guys were pretty serious. What happened? Or don't you want to talk about it?"

Sergei thought for a moment and then nodded. "You know, actually I would like to talk to you about it. Want to go get something to eat?"

Ben glanced at his watch. It was five-thirty. "Sure. Let me just tell Noelle that I'll be taking the L home."

Twenty minutes later, they were sitting at a table in the Sidebar Grille, eating sliders and buffalo wings. "So, what happened?" asked Ben.

"We'd been dating for a while—more than dating, really. We'd get together for dinner practically every night, and we'd spend the whole weekend together. We even went to Russia for three weeks to visit each other's families."

"I remember that," said Ben, nodding as he spoke. "You two seemed really happy together."

"We were." He paused and gazed absently at the street outside for a moment. "We really were. She liked doing the same stuff I like; we could talk about each other's jobs and really be interested. In fact, we could talk for hours about pretty much anything and never get bored. I'd never had that with a girl I'd dated. Every other time, eventually I'd get bored with her or she'd get bored with me and we'd wind up staring at our food during dinner and waiting for the evening to be over. I never once felt like that with Elena. Not once."

"Sounds like a great relationship," said Ben. "What made you guys break up?"

"After we got back from Russia, my mom and my aunts started asking when I was going to marry her. So I asked myself, 'Am I going to marry her?' And I realized that I couldn't."

"Why not?"

"She's not a Christian."

"Oh." Ben paused. "I knew you guys went to church together a couple of times, so I kind of figured she was, but no?"

Sergei shook his head and took a sip from his glass. "She's about as agnostic as you can get. Religion just doesn't matter to her one way or the other."

"And it does to you. Yeah, that's a problem. I don't know what I would have done if Noelle hadn't been a Christian. I would've known the right thing to do—or at least I hope I would have—but actually doing it would have been really tough. Remember that hiker who got his arm pinned under a boulder and had to cut it off or he'd die? That's what it would have been like, except harder. It takes a lot of guts to break off a serious relationship over your faith."

Sergei brightened a little. "Thanks, I was hoping you'd see things my way. I've been catching flak from everyone else I've told. You remember my Aunt Olga, who works at the Petrograd restaurant? I haven't been there for two weeks because every time I come in she sits down at my table and starts telling me what an idiot I am being to let Elena go."

"Didn't she marry a mob boss?"

"I pointed that out to her, and she said, 'And we were happily married for thirty-six years! See? You should listen to me about these things!'" He scowled and wagged his finger in perfect imitation of Olga as he spoke. "Of course, she was *mafiya* too."

"There you go," said Ben, gesturing with a buffalo wing. "They were both criminals, so it worked for them. What if he had been in the mob and she hadn't? What if his whole life was dictated by that 'thieves code' you told me about, but she thought it was all garbage? It's the most important thing in the world to him, but it's nothing to her—just a bunch of meaningless rules made up by some low-lifes a hundred years ago. Maybe they wouldn't have been so happy together then."

Sergei nodded vigorously. "Yeah, that's it exactly. My mom keeps telling me I should marry Elena anyway, because 'true love conquers all.' You know what? I'm afraid she's right, and I don't want my faith to be conquered. I don't think Elena would ever come right out and ask me to stop going to church or anything like that, but it bugs her in a lot of little ways—when I go home early on Saturday nights so I can get up for church, when every other Wednesday night is booked for small group meetings. Things like that. And it would probably bug her more after we're married; then the money I'd be putting into the offering plate each Sunday would be ours, not just mine.

"But more than that, she doesn't share the most important thing in my life. I can't talk to her about it. I can't even argue with her about it. I've tried bringing it up a couple of times, and she just sits there waiting for me to finish talking, and then she changes the subject when I run out of steam. I can't live like that for the rest of my life."

"No, you can't," agreed Ben. "It's too bad, though. You two were good together."

Sergei sighed and rubbed his eyes. "We were a lot better than good."

‡ ‡ ‡

Anne didn't sleep well after going to see *The Gamester* on opening night. As Markus had correctly guessed, Gunnar hadn't used his ticket, but that hadn't kept Anne from enjoying the play, a revival of an eighteenth-century tragedy about a man who destroys himself through his addiction to gambling. Markus had been superb as the main villain of the play; he had given a nuanced performance that conveyed deep emotion without overacting. He had also looked handsome and digni-fied in the period clothes, which gave him a gravitas that his usual ratty outfits did not. Or at least that's what Anne thought.

Markus had been less sanguine about his performance. When she talked to him after the play, he had agonized over getting his lines slightly wrong a few times and having been off in his timing. Anne hadn't noticed either alleged problem, but Markus was sure the critics in the audience had. While they were talking, Mel Goldsmith, who covered the theater for the *Chicago Reader*, had come up and congratulated Markus on his first appearance in a major role. Goldsmith then made a few polite, studiously noncommittal remarks and left. As soon as he walked away, Markus plunged into despair because he was sure that if Goldsmith had liked the play, he would have said so clearly. Because Goldsmith had been reserved in his comments, Markus reasoned, he must have hated the play—or worse, hated Markus's performance. Crushed, Markus headed for home a few minutes later, where Anne had no doubt a bottle or two waited to comfort him.

Anne watched for the morning *Tribune* with trepidation. When it came, she immediately pulled out the Tempo section and hunted for the theater reviews. She found the item on *The Gamester*. The *Trib*'s reviewer described the play as "a surprisingly satisfying revival of a three-century-old morality play." He commented that Markus's performance "showed his newness to the professional stage in occasional technical missteps, but his portrayal of Stukely was strong and sure overall. Bjornsen's performance held real power and revealed a thorough understanding of the character. This was his first time in a major role, but it won't be his last."

Anne read the review two more times and then called Markus. It was only 6:30 AM, but she felt no guilt about waking him. He picked up after the first ring. "Hi, Mom!" he said brightly.

"Good morning, Markus. You're up early."

"Or late, depending on how you look at it. I couldn't sleep last night. I finally gave up at four-thirty, fired up the espresso maker, and started hunting for reviews on the Internet."

"Have you seen the one in the *Tribune*?" asked Anne.

"I did. There are also reviews in the *Reader* and on a couple of theater Web sites. They all liked it, which hopefully will mean strong ticket sales. We should have a good run."

"Great! What did they say about you? I thought the *Tribune*'s review was right on the money, by the way. You were terrific."

"Thank you," said Markus. "The other reviewers were also pretty generous in their comments about my performance. I think they're going a little easy on me because I'm new, but I'm not complaining."

"I don't want to hear any false modesty from you this morning. You were really good, and I don't want you to deny it. We are very proud of you."

"Is that the royal 'we,' or has Dad really read any of the reviews?" he asked, a note of bitterness creeping into his voice. "I know he didn't see the play."

"He hasn't had the chance to yet, dear. I haven't given him the paper yet."

"Did he ask for it?" Markus sighed. "Don't bother answering. I know what you'll say."

"Your father loves you," replied Anne softly.

"Sure. Fine."

"It's true, Markus," she insisted. "I'm not saying it because I want it to be true, but because it really is."

"Mom, he can't even see me; how can he possibly love me?" The bitterness was now mixed with anger and hurt. He didn't wait for her to answer. "He doesn't see anything outside of his little corporate world, and I'm about as far outside that world as you can get. You know how he is; you know better than I do. The only time he notices me is when I force him to by being a problem somehow. If I haven't embarrassed him in front of a major stockholder or something, he barely acknowledges my existence.

"All he cares about is that company. I don't, and he's never forgiven me for that. No, it's worse: he's ignored me for it. He decided I was a failure and moved on to Tom. He couldn't fire me, of course, but he might as well have."

"You didn't take the path in life that he'd hoped you would," Anne acknowledged, "but he truly does love you."

Markus sighed again and his voice sounded weary. "Oh, he may love me in a sense because I'm his son, but that's not really love is it? It's duty; it's an accident of nature. He has to love *me* because he's my father, but he doesn't love anything *about* me."

"How about you?" Anne asked. "Do you love anything about him?"

"I—" He paused. "Touché."

‡ ‡ ‡

George Kulish hung up the phone and frowned. His Chicago contact had just called to confirm that the Chatterton business was finished, and that the local police did not appear to be handling it as a homicide. The contract had been handled efficiently, quickly, and at a reasonable cost. George made a mental note to use the same man if he ever had a similar business problem in Chicago in the future.

Still, a frown wrinkled the skin of his smooth, pale face, and he drummed his fingers on the mahogany table of his dacha's sunroom. He poured himself a tumbler of twenty-year-old single malt scotch that was only a few years younger than he was. He gulped it down quickly, grimaced, and poured himself another one. He brooded as he waited to feel the relaxing warmth of the alcohol reaching his blood. It was not the killing that bothered him; it was the personal failure that had led to the killing. The Chatterton contract shouldn't have been necessary in the first place. He'd had little choice once the woman found the data-capture program on her computer, but it was his own sloppiness that had allowed that to happen.

Bjornsen Pharmaceuticals' security software was a few years old, but well-designed. George needed to hack his way past it in order to find useful dirt that he could use as leverage if Karl Bjornsen got out of line, and he had quickly decided that the easiest way to do that was with the username and password of someone with full access to the system. A techie from the IT department would have been ideal, of course, but stealing the cyber-identities of those types of people was difficult—and they were much more likely to discover the theft. So George had sent a run-of-the-mill data-capture program to various members of the research and financial staffs, attaching them to e-mails purporting to be messages from the recipients' colleges regarding an upcoming reunion. Dr. Kathy Chatterton had taken the bait.

Although Dr. Chatterton was not technically savvy enough to prevent her computer from being infected, she was unfortunately savvy enough to run a good spyware detector, which had spotted George's program. Once it did, she not only removed the program from her machine, she started trying to find out where the stolen data was going. Through foolish overconfidence, George had placed only rudimentary protections on the outgoing data stream, so there had been a significant risk that she would have succeeded in following it back to him.

Now she was dead and the threat was gone, but he was still no closer to cracking Bjornsen Pharmaceuticals' security wall and finding the Bad Thing he needed. In retrospect, his efforts had been amateurish—hardly better than a phishing expedition. He expected more of himself.

And to make his mistake even more painful, the last phone intercepts he had picked up had been very tantalizing. *Something* bad was brewing at Bjornsen Pharmaceuticals, but what? If only Dr. Chatterton had called or e-mailed a friend to gossip, George might have picked up the Bad Thing he needed. Instead, she had decided to run straight to Karl Bjornsen's archenemy, leaving George with no choice. He needed Karl vulnerable, but undamaged—and Dr. Chatterton had been on her way to damage him.

Her life would have been short in any event, but that action had shortened it further. He sipped his scotch and began to unwind as he watched the Arctic breakers crashing on the rocky beach below the sunroom window. He promised himself that his next effort would be a lot better planned and executed.

Chapter Seven

Sandbags

A HEARING ON A PRELIMINARY INJUNCTION MOTION is an odd hybrid. Unlike a normal trial, it generally comes near the beginning of a lawsuit, not the end. Also, the order issued after the hearing is only temporary and dissolves after the permanent injunction hearing at the end of the case. But it's also unlike a normal motion hearing, such as the competing TRO motions Bert Siwell and Ben had argued at the outset of the case. When lawyers argue motions, that's usually all they do—argue. They don't put witnesses on the stand or introduce documents into evidence. A preliminary injunction hearing, on the other hand, consists largely of attorneys presenting testimonial and documentary evidence.

Because preliminary injunctions are heard early in a case, the parties generally aren't fully prepared and haven't finished their investigations. Therefore, it's easier to hit one's opponent with a "sandbag"—a surprise witness or document that knocks out an opponent in the same way a sandbag dropped from the theater rafters can take out a stage actor.

Bert Siwell was famous for his sandbagging skills. Ben worried intermittently about what surprises his opponent might have in store for him, but he tried not to obsess. He knew that the best thing he could do was to focus on what he would do to Siwell, and not spend too much time thinking about what Siwell would do to him.

The hearing began on a bright, clear afternoon in early June—though it was impossible to tell that from the blank-walled, fluorescent-lit courtroom where Ben stood. He gripped the podium in front of him and faced Judge Reilly across the courtroom's well—the empty space faced by the bench, counsel tables, and jury box. The box was empty because, due to a quirk in the history of the law, juries are never used in civil cases that don't involve a request for money. Because both Ben and Siwell were only asking for injunctions at this point, neither was entitled to a jury.

Noelle and Gunnar sat at the counsel table to Ben's left, and Siwell and Karl were at the table to his right. The benches behind Gunnar and Noelle were empty, except for a few boxes containing potential exhibits and various other documents Ben thought he might need over the course of the hearing. The benches on the other side of the courtroom, however, were packed with a small army of paralegals and associates from Siwell's firm, several computers, a projector, a projection screen, and dozens of boxes. Two men in rumpled suits sat in the back row of benches. Ben was tempted to ask Gunnar if he knew who they were, but talking, even in a whisper, while the judge is on the bench is frowned on, and Ben didn't want to start the hearing by being rude to the judge.

Judge Reilly nodded to Ben. "You may present your opening statement, Mr. Corbin."

Ben straightened his notes for the third time and cleared his throat. He stood very straight, taking advantage of every inch of his five-feet-ten frame. "Thank you, your honor. The court will have to decide two questions at the end of this hearing. The first is whether a proven embezzler should be allowed to continue to run a three-hundred-million-dollar company."

"Objection," said Siwell. "That's argument, in addition to being dead wrong."

Judge Reilly looked indecisively from Siwell to Ben. "Your honor," replied Ben, "I'm only saying what the facts will show at the end of the hearing. I'm entitled to do that in my opening state-ment." He pointed to the empty jury box. "Besides, we don't have a jury that might be misled by argument. Even if I were arguing, your honor can simply disregard it."

The judge nodded. "Objection overruled."

"Thank you, your honor. As I was saying, the evidence will estab-lish that Karl Bjornsen has been siphoning millions of dollars out of Bjornsen Pharmaceuticals for his own use, and then falsifying the company's accounting records to cover it up. We can document at least eight separate incidents over the past two years in which he stole more than seven-point-four million dollars from the com-pany. Seven-point-four million dollars. And that's just what we know about. We're in the middle of discovery right now and more wrong-doing may come to light.

"From the founding of Bjornsen Pharmaceuticals until last year, Karl Bjornsen was the chairman of the board. His brother, Gunnar," Ben turned and gestured to Gunnar, "was president and CEO. But then Karl decided he wanted complete control of the company and forced his own brother out. When *Crain's Chicago Business* asked him why he did it, he said that one of the reasons was that he was 'tired of always having someone telling me no.' Someone needs to tell him no, and we ask the court to do it, either by installing a team of auditors to monitor his dealings, or—pref-erably—by removing him from office and appointing a suitable replacement until the board of directors can choose his successor." Ben snuck a look at Karl and Siwell, but neither one reacted visibly to his words.

"The second question the court has to answer is whether there is any harm in waiting until the permanent injunction hearing to decide whether to force Gunnar to give the formula for a multibillion-dollar product to the company while it's still controlled by Karl. As your honor knows, Bjornsen Pharmaceuticals isn't entitled to a preliminary injunction unless it can prove, among other things, that it will be irreparably harmed if the injunction doesn't issue. The facts will show that there is no harm—let alone irreparable harm—in simply waiting until the permanent injunction hearing. Before Gunnar was pushed out, he helped the company manufacture enough of the drug to do all the testing they have scheduled over the next six months. They haven't even been given permission to start human trials yet, and they're years from being able to bring the drug to market. They have all of the drug they'll need between now and the permanent injunction hearing.

"There's no harm in waiting. Quite the contrary; the real risk is that the company will get control of the drug formula while Karl Bjornsen is still in charge and has no one to tell him no. If he can't be trusted with a few million dollars, should your honor trust him with a drug worth billions?"

Ben glanced at his notes to allow time for his last point to settle. Then nodded to his right and continued.

"I see Mr. Siwell muttering over there, and I expect that in a couple of minutes he'll get up here and tell you that everything I've said is 'scurrilous sewage' or something like that. But it doesn't matter what I say, and it doesn't matter what he says. What matters is what the witnesses say and what the documents show. Facts are hard things to argue away, even when you argue as well as Mr. Siwell, and the facts will show that the only irreparable harm that is likely to occur between now and the permanent injunction hearing will come from Karl Bjornsen's continued use of the company's bank account as his personal slush fund. Thank you, your honor."

‡ ‡ ‡

Sergei would have been in the courtroom to watch opening statements, but he had other business that morning. He pulled up outside the Illinois State Police District 2 headquarters, a long, low building that looked more like an elementary school than a police station. He parked the Black Russian, went inside, and greeted the receptionist. "Good morning. Could you tell Detective Munoz that Sergei Spassky is here for him?"

A few minutes later, a burly Hispanic man in his early forties appeared in the waiting room. "Sergei, it's good to see you again. Did you want to talk here or go out someplace?"

"Good to see you too, Dan. How about the Dunkin' Donuts I saw a couple of blocks up the road? I could use a cup of coffee, and I'd be happy to buy you a donut."

"I've sworn off donuts since I took a desk job," replied Munoz, "but coffee sounds good."

They made small talk as they walked to the Dunkin' Donuts, asking about each other's lives and careers. They had worked together on a couple of cases when Sergei was an FBI agent, and they had gotten to know each other well enough to be friendly, but not well enough to be truly friends.

They arrived at the donut shop, Sergei bought their coffee, and they found an isolated table where they could talk. "So what's on your mind?" Munoz asked after they sat down.

"Kathy Chatterton. The doctor I mentioned in my voice mail. What's the ISP's take on her death?"

"I took a look at the file before I came over. It looks pretty straightforward—single vehicle accident on the Eisenhower. Based on the crash scene, there's no reason to believe it was a homicide. No evidence of tampering with her vehicle, no foreign paint on the wreck to indicate that she was pushed off the road, nothing like that. We've interviewed your Mr. Bjornsen, but we haven't found any independent evidence of foul play."

"Have you interviewed anyone from Bjornsen Pharmaceuticals? I wonder if they've got alibis that hold water."

Munoz shook his head. "We haven't, and we're not likely to unless we open a homicide investigation, which I'm not inclined to do. There's just not enough here—no threats, no physical evidence, no witnesses to the death."

"She died on the Eisenhower and *no one* saw it?" said Sergei. "I know it was late at night, but doesn't that seem a little odd to you?"

Munoz shrugged. "Not really. I'm sure people saw it, but they didn't call the police. That happens a lot. It doesn't change the bottom line—we have no witnesses. All we have is a guy who says the woman *must* have been killed because she was on her way to give him something important. It's a close call, but without more we're not going to open an investigation. If my budget hadn't been cut, I might look into it further, but we just don't have the resources."

"I hear you," said Sergei, who had been half expecting that response. "By the way, did you find anything in the car that looked like lab reports or a tissue sample? And were you able to pull images from her cell phone camera?"

"No, but that doesn't mean much. The car was heavily damaged by fire. The interior was completely burned out and the phone was fried."

"That could destroy evidence of some types of vehicle tampering, couldn't it?" asked Sergei. "And if the exterior was scorched badly enough, paint from another vehicle could be charred off, couldn't it?"

"Maybe," conceded Munoz. He put down his coffee and looked Sergei in the eye. "Why are you pushing this? Is it just because your client is paying you to, or is there something you haven't told me yet?"

Sergei looked back at Munoz silently for a moment, debating how much to tell him. "Dan, do you know Alex Geist?"

"Not personally, but I've heard the name. High-priced PI-slash-security-consultant, right?"

Sergei nodded. "He's working for Bjornsen Pharmaceuticals. I'm pretty sure he's on the other side of the same lawsuit I'm working on."

"You think he killed her?"

"I doubt it, but when I first got involved in the case, I got a strange call from him. He told me to watch myself, and I asked if he was threatening me. He said he wasn't, but that I might run into people who don't bother to threaten. I wonder if Kathy Chatterton ran into them first."

Munoz finished his coffee and stared thoughtfully into the empty cup for a few seconds. "Maybe I can free up some time to dig into this a little further."

‡ ‡ ‡

Bert Siwell stepped up to the podium. He wore a carefully tailored navy blue suit that hid his ample stomach and emphasized his wide shoulders. He gave the judge a confident, relaxed smile. "Good morning, your honor. Desperate drivel is probably a more accurate description of Mr. Corbin's opening, but I can live with 'scurrilous sewage.' By the end of this hearing, it will be patently clear to everyone in the courtroom that Karl Bjornsen has engaged in no financial wrongdoing. Mr. Corbin's client has not been involved in Bjornsen Pharmaceuticals' finances for years, and frankly never understood them. In fact, he nearly drove the company into bankruptcy before Karl intervened and appointed a CFO.

"Gunnar Bjornsen is a scientist, not an accountant, but as a courtesy the new CFO continued to allow Gunnar full access to the company's financial records. Based on the discovery we've received so far, it looks like Gunnar has spent the last several years saving copies of documents from every transaction he didn't understand and taping them together into a paranoid tapestry of alleged fraud. The company's CFO will be here tomorrow to explain each transaction in as much or as little detail as your honor desires, but for now suffice it to say that no competent accountant looking at all the facts could possibly conclude that there was any fraud here.

"Turning to the injunction my client is requesting, it was interesting to hear what Mr. Corbin *didn't* say. He didn't say that the Neurostim formula isn't a trade secret. He didn't say it isn't Bjornsen Pharmaceuticals' property. He didn't even say that my client won't be entitled to have its property returned at the end of this case. All he said was that there's no harm in depriving Bjornsen Pharmaceuticals of its property until then.

"No harm? Bjornsen Pharmaceuticals' stock price is down ten percent since the markets discovered that Gunnar Bjornsen is withholding information on how to manufacture Neurostim. That's harm. Every time the financial press covers the company, they bring up this litigation. That's harm."

He pulled a news clipping out of his notebook. "Just last week, the company announced that its second quarter numbers were better than expected and that it was raising its earnings forecast for the remainder of the year. Here's what Bloomberg said: 'Despite legal clouds over the ownership of its new flagship product, Bjornsen Pharmaceuticals reported strong earnings for the second quarter. It also raised its forecast for the rest of the year by two cents per share.'"

He put down the clipping and pointed to the two men in the back bench. "There are two members of the press corps here today, doing research for more stories that will run in tomorrow's papers. That, your honor, is harm." He turned and looked back. "No offense, fellas."

"None taken," said the older of the two men with a smile.

"And the harm will continue every day until those news stories say that the Neurostim formula is back in the control of Bjornsen Pharmaceuticals. We ask the court to order Gunnar Bjornsen to turn it over immediately. Thank you, your honor."

"All right," said Judge Reilly. "Mr. Siwell, are you ready to call your first witness?"

"Yes, your honor. We call Gunnar Bjornsen."

Ben and Gunnar glanced at each other in surprise. This was an aggressive move and one that caught Ben off guard. Lawyers almost never start their cases by putting the opposing party on the stand. A litigator's first goal is usually to put on his client's side of the dispute—a project the opposing party generally won't want to help accomplish. Siwell had given no hint that he planned to lead off by calling Gunnar, and Ben had therefore scheduled Gunnar's final witness prep for that evening.

Gunnar walked up to the stand, where the bailiff swore him in. When he sat down in the witness chair, his knees jutted up and he looked like an adult sitting in a child's chair. He felt under the seat for a knob that would adjust the height, but he couldn't find one that would work.

"Good morning, Mr. Bjornsen," said Siwell.

"Good morning," replied Gunnar as he gave up fiddling with the chair.

"You founded Bjornsen Pharmaceuticals thirty years ago with your brother Karl, isn't that correct?"

"Thirty-two years ago."

"I stand corrected. I take it you remember it well?"

"I do."

"And the two of you spent three decades building up the company together, didn't you?"

"Yes."

"You and Karl turned it into a decent company, didn't you? Not Eli Lilly, but not bad, right?"

"Oh, I'd say we're better than Lilly. They're a good company, but we're more nimble and I think we've got a better scientific team."

"I think I hear some pride in your voice," observed Siwell.

"I am very proud of the company," replied Gunnar. "Or at least I was until shortly before I left."

"You want what's best for the company, don't you?"

"Of course."

"And you're proud of the company's product development team, right?"

"They are very fine scientists."

"In fact, you were the head of product development at Bjornsen Pharmaceuticals, right?"

"That's right."

"Were you directly involved in developing any of the company's drugs?"

"I was involved in developing all of them."

"Directly involved?"

"Directly involved."

"So you were directly involved in developing Neurostim?"

"I was, but I didn't call it that."

"You called it XD-463, right?"

"Right."

"XD-463 is a very valuable drug, wouldn't you agree?"

"Potentially, yes. A lot of drugs that look good in early trials are ultimately failures, however."

"But you saw no indication that XD-463 would be a failure, did you?"

"Not in the early trials I oversaw, no."

Ben started to relax. So far, Siwell was just rehashing familiar and relatively harmless territory from Gunnar's deposition. He had rattled Ben and was getting in the basic background facts he wanted, but he wasn't doing any real damage.

"It would be fair to say you invented XD-463, wouldn't it?" Siwell asked.

Gunnar shrugged modestly. "I developed the process for isolating the active compound from plant material and manufacturing it, if that's what you mean."

"Thank you, that's exactly what I mean. You had help from other scientists during your work, didn't you?"

"On certain aspects of the project, yes."

"But not on others?"

"Correct."

"Is it typical for a researcher working in a company the size of Bjornsen Pharmaceuticals to work on his own on significant aspects of a major new drug?"

Gunnar shrugged again. "I don't know what's typical at other companies. I like to work on my own on some projects, and as head of product development that was my prerogative."

"So there are certain steps involved in making the drug that you developed entirely on your own?"

"Yes."

"And you never shared your discoveries with other members of your team, right?"

"No, I shared the results."

"But you never explained to them how you achieved those results, did you?"

"Not always," acknowledged Gunnar.

"And to the best of your knowledge, the process for making XD-463 is not commonly known in the industry, right?"

Gunnar nodded. "To the best of my knowledge, it's not known to anyone in or out of the industry except me."

"So if you'd been hit by a bus and killed, the secret formula for how to make XD-463 would have died with you, correct?"

"I suppose so."

"And that would be bad for the company, wouldn't it?"

"It would have been worse for Karl to get his hands on it," Gunnar replied, lines of irritation forming around his mouth and eyes.

"So by the time you were developing this drug, it was clear to you that the directors were going to vote you out as president. Is that right?"

"No. It wasn't clear until they actually did it, but I knew Karl was lobbying hard for that result."

"You knew that a vote on your continued presidency was set for the next board meeting and that there was a significant chance that you would be voted out, right?"

"I did," admitted Gunnar.

"And that timing wasn't a coincidence. You intentionally kept key parts of the formula to yourself so that you could use your knowledge as a bargaining chip. You—"

"That's not true!" interrupted Gunnar, glaring at the attorney. "I—"

"Just a minute. I'm not finished with my question," said Siwell, raising his voice slightly. "You thought that if you alone had the formula, you could force Karl to come crawling to you to make a deal, didn't you?"

Ben stood up. "Objection, he's arguing with the witness."

"No, I'm quoting him," returned Siwell. He gestured to one of his paralegals, who removed the cap from the projector, which was already on and warmed up. An e-mail chain appeared on the projection screen. At the bottom was an e-mail from Dr. Tina Corrigan to Gunnar that said, "There's a rumor you're leaving. Is it true? I sure hope not." Above it was Gunnar's response: "Don't worry. Without me, Karl can't make XD-463. Sooner or later, he'll come crawling to me and we'll make a deal."

So there's the first sandbag, thought Ben. "Your honor, if Mr. Siwell intended to use this document, he should have produced it in discovery. He didn't, and he should therefore not be allowed to use it here. This is a trial, not a game of 'gotcha.'"

"What this is, as Mr. Corbin should know, is a preliminary injunction hearing," responded Siwell. "That means that discovery isn't finished and occasionally he or his client will get surprised. As it happens, however, neither of them should be—Mr. Bjornsen wrote this e-mail, of course, and Mr. Corbin got a copy of it yesterday, which was as soon as my office could copy the disk it was on and get it to him."

"That's simply not true, your honor," rejoined Ben. "I was in my office all day yesterday and didn't receive any documents from Mr. Siwell."

Siwell held up a piece of paper. "Here's the receipt from the messenger service, which shows that the package was delivered at 6:23 PM yesterday." He turned to Ben. "When did you go home last night, counsel?"

"About five minutes before that," which Ben suspected his opponent already knew. He wouldn't be at all surprised to learn that Siwell's messenger had been told to wait to deliver the package until after he saw Ben had left the building. That would be impossible to prove, however, and making the accusation without proof would look paranoid and unprofessional. There was nothing he could do except grit his teeth and take the punch.

"All right," said Judge Reilly, "with that background, I'll overrule the objection. Mr. Siwell, you may proceed."

"Thank you, your honor. Mr. Bjornsen, you sent this e-mail, didn't you?"

"I don't have a specific recollection of it," replied Gunnar, the indignation gone from his voice and replaced by wary evasiveness.

"But you don't deny sending it?"

"I don't recall one way or the other."

"All right. Do you recall making statements similar to those in this e-mail?"

"It's possible I said something like that," Gunnar conceded.

"In fact, you remember doing it, don't you?"

Gunnar opened and closed his mouth. He looked up at the screen for a long moment, as if hoping that the damning words might change if he watched them long enough. "Now that I see that e-mail, I do have a general memory of saying something like that," he said at last.

Siwell closed his notes. "No further questions, your honor."

"Your witness, Mr. Corbin," said the judge.

"Thank you, your honor," said Ben as he walked up to the podium to do whatever damage control he could. "Mr. Bjornsen, were you angry at your brother when he was trying to have you removed as president of Bjornsen Pharmaceuticals?"

"I was."

"Would you have liked to see your brother come crawling to you to make a deal?"

Gunnar smiled. "I confess occasionally day-dreaming about that possibility."

"Does any of that mean it would be a good idea for Karl Bjornsen to have control of XD-463?"

"No."

"Why not?"

"Objection, your honor," said Siwell. "That question calls for a narrative and rank speculation. Also, Mr. Corbin has laid no foundation whatsoever for the testimony his client is about to give."

Ben glanced at the clock. "I hadn't planned to put on my case-in-chief today, your honor, but I'm happy to do it if the court would like. Once I do, it will be clear that Mr. Bjornsen's testimony is neither speculation nor foundationless. But that will take a while and I see that it's four forty-five."

"Well, now I have another ground for my objection," said Siwell before Judge Reilly could respond. "Mr. Corbin is not entitled to put on his case-in-chief in the middle of mine."

"That's something that Mr. Siwell should have thought of before he opened the door on this subject by blindsiding my client with that e-mail," Ben shot back. "We're entitled to fully respond to—"

"This is ridiculous," interrupted Siwell. "I didn't—"

Judge Reilly flushed and held up his hand. "We're not doing this again, counsel. Mr. Corbin, I recognize that your client was surprised today, and you can respond fully in your case-in-chief, but that will have to wait until Mr. Siwell is done with his case. Court is now in recess until tomorrow morning at nine o'clock."

"Thank you, your honor," Ben and Siwell said in unison.

Chapter Eight

Small Victories

IT WAS 2:00 AM AND THE SUN HAD SUNK as low as it was going to go. It hung near the horizon, casting long shadows in the sleeping town of Torsknes and turning the choppy waters of the quiet harbor into a million flashes of deep gold. A handful of crab boats chugged in or out between two battered stone and concrete sea walls that protected the harbor from the full fury of the Arctic Sea during winter. Two long rows of boats, mostly rigged for crab or cod, floated in their berths along a massive concrete pier.

One of them was Tor Kjeldaas's *Agnes Larsen*. She had been patched and repainted after her encounter with sea ice two months ago. Captain Kjeldaas had done as much of the work as possible himself, but the repair bills still had been more than he could afford, particularly after paying the fine necessary to get his boat back.

The grizzled old man sat on his boat's deck in dirty denim overalls, watching and waiting as a heavily loaded blue pickup truck turned off of Havnegate, Torsknes's main street, and onto the pier. The truck slowly rumbled up to his boat and stopped. "You are late, Ola Magnus," he called out as the truck's engine coughed to a stop. "I should have been out to sea by now."

"What could I do?" replied the other man as he got out of the truck. He was younger and cleaner than the fisherman, but had the same weathered look. "The shipment was late coming in from Oslo. Here, I can help you load. That will make up some time."

The two men worked in silence for the next half hour, taking boxes from the back of the truck and stowing them in one of the boat's holds. When they were through, they spread an old tarp over the boxes and took several hundred pounds of cod from another hold and dumped it on top of the tarp. The sun was warm, but the refrigerated holds were dark and cold. Both men were shivering and blowing on their hands when they finished working. The truck driver yawned and stretched. "Time for bed."

"For you, maybe," Kjeldaas replied as he squinted into the rising sun. "Cast off that rope at the bow before you leave."

The captain primed the engine and gunned it to life. He eased the little ship out of its berth and guided it toward open water and the shipping lanes that carried traffic between Norway and Russia. During the Cold War, the Norwegian-Soviet maritime border had been vigilantly patrolled by wary destroyers, bristling with weapons and sensors, which made undetected travel through these Arctic waters impossible. Now, there were only a few lightly armed ships of the Kystvakt, keeping a leisurely eye on the bustling traffic between Russian and Norwegian ports. Their main purpose was to protect their national fisheries from poaching, so they tended to cruise the fishing grounds and mostly ignored coastal traffic.

They did, however, make exceptions for known smugglers. As the fishing boat rounded a small cape of lichen-and-moss-encrusted stone, a cutter flying the Norwegian flag hove into view. A moment later, the radio in the fishing boat's pilothouse crackled to life. "This is Kystvakt vessel *KV Farm* calling fishing vessel *Agnes Larsen*. Come in, *Agnes Larsen*."

"This is *Agnes Larsen*," replied Captain Kjeldaas. He looked out the streaked window and saw two sailors emerge from a forward hatch to man the gun on the *Farm*'s deck. He could also see that the cutter was swinging around to match course and speed with his boat.

"What is your cargo, *Agnes Larsen*?"

"Cod for the fish market at Yuragorsk."

"We see no crew on your decks."

"This is the captain. It was late, so I made port in Torsknes and dropped them off. I am taking our fish to market by myself."

The radio was silent for several minutes and Captain Kjeldaas began to hope the *Farm* would leave him alone. But then the radio squawked again. "*Agnes Larsen*, prepare to be boarded for inspection."

The fisherman sighed and watched as the cutter let down an inflatable rubber speedboat with three sailors in it. The launch crossed the short distance between the vessels, pulled alongside the fishing boat, and tied up at the base of a rusty ladder. This maneuver, which had remained substantively unchanged for centuries, was necessary because it is virtually impossible to bring two vessels of any size close enough together on the open sea for sailors to cross between them without one ship bumping into the other and damaging both.

The captain greeted the sailors at the top of the ladder. To his dismay, he saw a familiar face.

"Good morning, Captain Kjeldaas," said a dour-faced ensign. The man had been on the previous inspection that had uncovered a hold full of unauthorized vodka on its way to a black market distributor in Torsknes. "What are you carrying this time?"

"Cod. I already told you."

"We will see." The ensign took his men back to the holds and kicked open the hatches. He shone a large flashlight into both. One held only cold darkness and a puddle of foul water. In the other, the beam revealed a layer of gleaming cod. The familiar, thick smell of hundreds of fish floated up through the open hatch. He turned to the fisherman. "What will I find under those fish?"

"More fish."

"Mmm," the ensign grunted. He looked down into the hold again. "Today, I will trust you. But if you were going the other way, I would go in there and move the fish or make you do it. Liquor smuggling is a serious offense."

"If you want to inspect me again when I go back to Torsknes this afternoon, go ahead. You won't find any vodka." This was true. He had made his regular vodka run two days ago and would not be doing so again for another week.

The ensign made no reply. He and his men got back into their launch and motored back to the cutter. The fisherman returned to the pilothouse and watched them go with a carefully expressionless face. Once the men were aboard the *Farm* and the launch was stowed, the sailors manning the deck gun went back inside and the Kystvakt ship turned and headed back for the fishing grounds, leaving a broad white wake.

As the cutter receded into the distance, Captain Kjeldaas allowed himself a triumphant grin. He opened a drawer under the radio and pulled out a bottle of vodka and a chipped glass. He poured himself a drink and raised a victory toast to the cutter's rapidly receding stern. "*Skål!*"

‡ ‡ ‡

Fifteen hours later, and more than four thousand miles away, Karl Bjornsen sat in the chair on the witness stand in Judge Reilly's courtroom. He wore a well-tailored charcoal gray suit with a red silk tie and a cream shirt that set off his tan. He smiled and looked relaxed as he testified. Despite being nearly as tall as Gunnar, he managed to find a way to look comfortable in the awkwardly designed chair. In fact, he gave such a favorable visual impression from the stand that Ben suspected he had worked with an acting coach.

Siwell stood at the podium, conducting his direct examination of Karl. Both men were doing a good job, which was no surprise. Direct exam is usually carefully scripted and practiced. Ben was certain that Karl and his lawyers had rehearsed Karl's testimony several times—just as he had rehearsed with Gunnar and would do so again before Gunnar took the stand a second time.

Because Siwell had put in a fair amount of background testimony through Gunnar, Karl's testimony focused on the two main issues in the case: whether he was defrauding the company and whether Bjornsen Pharmaceuticals would suffer any irremediable harm if their injunction request was denied. Accompanied by a slick Power-Point presentation from Siwell's graphics consultant, Karl talked at length about the financial controls at his company, the quality of their outside auditors, how stupid it would be for him to commit fraud in light of his large stock holdings in the company, and so on. Ben objected from time to time, but there was little he could do to keep Karl's testimony from turning into a marketing presentation on his responsible and ethical management style.

Karl then turned to the grave danger to Bjornsen Pharmaceuticals' stock price if the company did not have the full and unquestioned ability to produce Neurostim. Despite good news on all other fronts, he claimed, Gunnar's actions were dragging the stock down. If Gunnar wasn't ordered to turn over the formula immediately, Karl warned, the stock price could drop still further, doing damage to thousands of stockholders.

Siwell sat down and Ben Corbin took his place at the podium. Ben took a few seconds to arrange his notes before looking up at Karl. "Good morning, Mr. Bjornsen. Your company has a Norwegian subsidiary, doesn't it?"

"Yes."

"Do the auditors you mentioned review the subsidiary's financial statements and work papers?"

"Not the originals, but we give them translations."

Ben turned and pulled a stack of documents from a box on the table to the left of the podium. He handed copies to Karl, the judge, and Siwell. "Mr. Bjornsen, I've just handed you what's been marked as Defendant's Exhibit A. Do you recognize this document?"

Karl flipped through it. "Yes, this is a set of accounting detail reports from Bjornsen Norge AS, the subsidiary you mentioned. It covers the first quarter of 2007."

"These are some of the work papers that provide the backup for the financial statements?"

"That's right. This document is also used as a report for executives, so it contains more information than is typical of other detail reports I've seen."

"But the bottom line numbers from this document become entries in the financial statements, correct?"

"Yes."

"And your auditors get English translations of documents such as these?"

"Yes."

"But they don't actually audit the detail reports, do they?"

"I think they only audit the financial statements, not backup materials like these. Our CFO will know more about that, though."

Ben turned and pulled out another document, which he handed around. "I've just handed you a copy of Defendant's Exhibit B. Do you recognize this document?"

Karl froze and his face turned gray beneath his tan. "Where did you get this?"

Ben suppressed a smile. Gunnar had brought this document to Ben's attention and partially translated it for him. Siwell apparently didn't have anyone on his litigation team who read Norwegian and therefore hadn't recognized the significance of the document or discussed it with Karl. "I believe it came from the file cabinet behind the desk in your office. By the look on your face, am I correct in guessing that you recognize it?"

Siwell jumped to his feet. "Your honor, I object. This document was apparently stolen from Bjornsen Pharmaceuticals. It should not be received into evidence, and counsel should be sanctioned for attempting to use it."

"Your honor," replied Ben, "this document was not stolen. While my client was still employed by Bjornsen Pharmaceuticals, he asked Karl Bjornsen's secretary for a copy of Bjornsen Norge's accounting detail reports for the first quarter of 2007. She went into his office and found this in the file cabinet behind his desk."

"And your client will so testify when he takes the stand again?" asked Judge Reilly.

Gunnar nodded and Ben said, "Yes, your honor."

"All right, with that representation, I'll overrule the objection. You may proceed."

"Thank you. Mr. Bjornsen, this is also a set of accounting detail reports for Bjornsen Norge for the first quarter of 2007, isn't it?"

"It, um, it appears to be. I can't say for sure."

"Well, let's compare it to Exhibit A. The first pages of both documents are the same, except that the first page of Exhibit B has the words *Kun Internt Bruk* in the upper right corner. Do you see that?"

"Yes."

"That means 'Internal Use Only,' doesn't it?"

"It can be translated that way," acknowledged Karl.

"Now look at page eighteen of both exhibits. That's a table showing the net profits from Bjornsen Norge's largest customer accounts, isn't it?"

"That's what it looks like."

Siwell stood up again. "I object to this whole line of questioning. These documents speak for themselves."

Ben opened his mouth to respond, but the judge beat him to it. "Yes, but they speak in Norwegian. These appear to be key documents and I want to hear the witness's interpretation of them."

"Thank you, your honor," said Ben. "Mr. Bjornsen, the third account listed on Exhibit B is Cleverlad.ru. Bjornsen Norge made a profit of 3,100,493 kroner on that account. Do you see that?"

Karl shifted in his seat and hunched forward. "I do."

"Three million kroner is worth about five hundred thousand dollars, isn't it?"

"That, uh, that sounds about right, though you'd have to check today's exchange rate."

"Now I'd like you to look at page eighteen in Exhibit A. That's the same list of accounts, isn't it?"

Karl shook his head. "No, there seem to be some differences."

"Cleverlad.ru is gone and the profit total at the bottom is lower by 3,100,493 kroner. Do you see any other differences?"

"I haven't checked your math, of course. I don't see any other differences offhand."

"Now let's turn to page forty-three of Exhibit A. The word *Kostnader* at the top means 'Costs,' right?"

"Yes."

"The last item on the page says '*Andre Kostnader.*' That means 'Other Costs,' correct?"

Karl forced a smile. "Your Norwegian is very good, Mr. Corbin."

"Thanks. So your answer is 'yes'?"

He shrugged as casually as he could. "Sure."

"And this shows that Bjornsen Norge had 'other costs' of 400,983 kroner, right?"

"That's what it says."

"And page forty-three of Exhibit B shows a much larger sum for *Andre Kostnader*. To be exact, it's 3,100,493 kroner larger. That's the precise amount of the missing Cleverlad.ru account from page eighteen, isn't it?"

Karl flipped back in the report. His hands shook as he held the document and he quickly put it down. "Yes, that's correct."

"Would you agree with me that it looks as if what's happening is that someone is trying to hide two things: the existence of the profits from the Cleverlad.ru account and what is happening to those profits?" Ben's heart raced as he asked the question. If Karl had a good answer for this question, then Ben's entire cross-examination would be an embarrassing dud.

"Objection, calls for expert testimony," said Siwell.

"Overruled," said the judge. "He's the CEO of the company."

Karl kept his eyes on the document in his lap. "No. Or, well, I don't know. I'm not sure what's going on here."

"But if someone were skimming the profits out of the Cleverlad account and wanted to keep the auditors from figuring that out, they could do it by hiding those transactions in the detail reports and then creating a fake set of reports for the auditors, right?"

Siwell stood up again. "Objection. The witness already said he doesn't know what this document shows. This is just harassment. Mr. Corbin should save these questions for the company's CFO."

"Your honor earlier commented that these were important documents and said that you wanted to hear the witness's interpretation of them," Ben responded. "I think your honor is entitled to an answer. I also think you'll get a more accurate one if counsel is prohibited from using objections to coach the witness."

"Objection overruled. Mr. Bjornsen, do you recall the question?"

"Yes, your honor. I don't know whether or not these two documents could reflect the scenario Mr. Corbin described. That really is a question for our CFO."

"No further questions," Ben said as he gathered up his notes and returned to his seat.

"I have a few questions, your honor," said Siwell.

"Go ahead," said the judge.

The attorney strode up to the podium. "Mr. Bjornsen, are you an accountant?"

"No."

"Are you an auditor?"

"No."

Siwell lifted up the two financial reports. "Did you prepare either Defendant's Exhibit A or Exhibit B?"

"No."

"Have you done anything to check the accuracy of either document?"

"No."

"No further questions."

Judge Reilly looked at Ben. "Any follow-up, Mr. Corbin?"

Ben shook his head. "I'm finished with him, your honor."

"All right," said the judge, "you're excused, Mr. Bjornsen. That's all for today. I'll see you all here at nine o'clock tomorrow morning."

‡ ‡ ‡

Russian longshoremen unloaded the *Agnes Larsen* under the watchful eyes of Captain Kjeldaas. The cod went to a seafood factory that stood less than a hundred yards from Yuragorsk's municipal pier. The boxes went into an unmarked white van.

The driver of the van handed the fisherman an envelope and turned and got into the van. Kjeldaas opened the envelope. "This misses one thousand dollars," he objected, speaking in English, which was the lingua franca in Arctic ports. "The price we agreed was seven thousand."

The other man leaned out of the van, his heavily tattooed arm resting on the window frame. "The time we agreed was six-thirty. It's eight."

"The cargo came late to my ship, and we never talked about late charges."

"You want to talk to George?" He opened the van door. "Get in."

The fisherman frowned and the leathery skin around his hard blue eyes creased into a thousand sharp wrinkles. "No, but we never talked about late charges."

The driver shut the door and drove off without replying.

‡ ‡ ‡

Yuragorsk's waterfront district is a warren of narrow, crowded streets. Warehouses, fish markets, and factories jam every block. Business owners often treat the pavement in front of their buildings as a loading dock or parking lot, making the streets nearly impassible in places.

The white van crept along, swerving around pallets of frozen cod and king crab, barrels of diesel fuel destined for fishing trawlers, randomly parked forklifts, and other obstacles. The driver applied the horn liberally, but without malice, and eventually arrived at a featureless corrugated steel and concrete building with a small sign over the door that read Cleverlad.ru. Only two things distinguished the building from the structures on either side. First, it did not reek of fish or spilled petroleum products. Second, a thick fiber-optic cable ran along one side of the building before leaping to a utility pole.

The driver turned his van into a narrow alley—really no more than a walkway—and drove to the back of the building. He backed up to the building's loading bay, where another man, wearing gray overalls, waited. The driver parked and tossed the keys to the man in the overalls, then went to report to the boss.

The ability to walk into George Kulish's office was a rare privilege. It required clearance to pass through three layers of cutting-edge electronic security. The driver knew of only two people, including himself, to whom George had granted the right to pass through these defenses and step into the private elevator that whisked him silently to the top floor.

George's office was a climate-controlled room that took up about a quarter of the top floor and had its own generator. Along one wall stood a floor-to-ceiling bank of servers, and a huge, U-shaped desk was crowded with a half-dozen large flat-panel monitors. Behind the desk, in an ergonomically designed rolling chair, sat George. He was a small, thin man of about twenty-five, with gelled black hair. He wore black jeans, flip-flops, and a T-shirt bearing the spiked Q logo of Quake computer games. George's eyes flicked back and forth between the monitors, and his fingers flew between the six well-used keyboards that lay in a semicircle around him.

The driver cleared his throat and George glanced up for an instant before returning to the monitors. "Hello, Pyotr. You brought the Bjornsen shipment?"

"Yes, it is being unloaded now."

"Good. See that it is relabeled and repackaged at once. We need to send out forty-six orders of Vicodin by DHL tomorrow morning." He glanced at another screen. "Make that forty-seven. We also need to ship a hundred and ten of those perc-a-pops."

"I will take care of it."

"Good boy, Pyotr. Oh, before you do that, get me a double cappuccino from that new place down the block. They're the only ones who make decent coffee around here."

Pyotr didn't like being "coffee boy" for anyone, particularly a skinny little Ukrainian kid whom he could kill with one punch. But he knew better than to do or say anything that might offend George. "No problem. Sugar?"

‡ ‡ ‡

"Welcome home," Gwen Bjornsen called from the kitchen. "Your timing is perfect! Michel is just putting the finishing touches on dinner."

"Terrific!" Karl called back as he hung up his coat. "What is it?"

"Come and see!" called a man's voice with the hint of a French accent. "I think you will like it."

Karl walked down the hallway, his steps alternately echoing on the black Italian marble and hushed by the Persian throw rugs. He turned into the dining room and was greeted by a pleasant mixture of savory smells. The mahogany table was lit by three candles and two places were set. Covered chafing dishes of various sizes sat on a small cart beside the table. Beside the cart stood Michel LeClair, the Bjornsens' favorite chef. He used to work at the Skyline Restaurant, but now found it more lucrative to cook private gourmet meals for the wealthier members of Chicago's aristocracy. "Let me guess," said Karl, drawing a deep breath through his nose. "I smell beef and onions—no, probably scallions, and—" He heard footsteps coming up behind him and sniffed again. "And Chanel Number Five."

He turned and saw Gwen carrying an open bottle of Stag's Leap cabernet and two glasses. She smiled luminously and her large green eyes sparkled in the candlelight. "Very good," she said and kissed him. "Welcome home."

"Walking through that door is always the best part of my day, particularly when I know Michel has been here." He turned to the chef. "Are you ready for us?"

"Of course, of course. Please sit down." Michel gestured to the table and Gwen and Karl sat while he unveiled their dinner. To start, he had prepared a Mediterranean salad with walnuts, olives, and crumbled goat cheese. The main course, as Karl had guessed, was beef with scallions—filet mignon in wine sauce, to be exact. And for dessert, Chef LeClair had prepared a brandied crème brulée based on a recipe known only to him. "Shall I serve you tonight?"

"Thank you, Michel," said Gwen. "That won't be necessary. Just let me know how long I can leave the steaks in the chafing dish."

"They will be fine for at least twenty minutes. After that, the texture may begin to degrade. Have a good evening. I'll see you on Sunday."

As he left, Gwen poured them each a glass of wine. "So, how was your big day in court?"

"It couldn't have gone better," replied Karl with a broad smile. "I think I was really able to get through to the judge. Bert Siwell had some great PowerPoint graphics that added a nice punch to what I was saying. I think the judge has a much better understanding of the case now."

"That's great! Did Noelle's husband cross-examine you?"

Karl swirled his wine and shrugged. "He did, but he didn't score any points. Gunnar had loaded him up with a string of questions about the company's financials, but they didn't lead anywhere. I actually felt a little sorry for him by the end."

"It's funny you should say that," replied Gwen. "I was just feeling sorry for Noelle this afternoon."

"Really? Why is that?"

"I just found out that Emily Marshall asked Noelle to leave that committee I'm on at the Field Museum. I hadn't said anything to Emily, of course, but it was awkward to see Noelle at meetings when her husband was saying such awful things about you in court. And it's nice to know that Emily and the other board members value us. We're lucky to have such good friends."

"We are," agreed Karl as he took a bite of his salad. "But it's too bad that she's being punished for her husband's sins."

Gwen took a sip of her wine. "Yes. Noelle is very sweet, but he's a real disadvantage to her. Unfortunately, she's pregnant, so it's hard for her to do anything about it. Poor girl. I really do feel sorry for her."

‡ ‡ ‡

Bert Siwell began the next day's proceedings by putting Bjornsen Pharmaceuticals' CFO, Tim Hawkins, on the stand. Hawkins was a CPA and a certified fraud examiner, who had, he testified, been brought in to clean up the company's books after Gunnar had nearly driven the company out of business through financial mismanagement. Hawkins testified for nearly half a day about the cleanliness of the company's finances, the high caliber of its auditors, and so forth. It was dull stuff and he was not a compelling witness. Despite Bert Siwell's one-liners and other attempts to keep things interesting, Ben could see Judge Reilly's eyes glazing over after fifteen minutes. Objecting would simply wake up the judge, so Ben kept his mouth shut and watched.

Siwell finally finished his direct questioning at ten minutes to noon. The judge glanced at the clock on the wall. "Do you want to wait until after lunch to do your cross, Mr. Corbin?" he inquired.

"No, your honor," Ben said as he walked up to the podium. "This will be quick. Mr. Hawkins, is it typical for companies to have two sets of books with different numbers, one set for 'Internal Use Only' and one to show to auditors?"

"As I told Mr. Siwell on direct, that may be typical in Norway," answered Hawkins in a dry, professional voice. "I'm not familiar with their accounting practices."

"But here in the U.S., it's a sign of fraud, isn't it?"

"It can be, but it can indicate other things as well."

"But in the majority of cases, it indicates fraud, right?"

"Not if the second set of books is for tax accounting purposes," the CFO countered, making a steeple of his long fingers as he spoke. "The IRS's rules can be different from GAAP."

"Are tax accounting books typically marked 'Internal Use Only'?"

"No," conceded the witness.

"Okay, so putting aside the tax accounting possibility, is keeping two sets of books usually a sign of fraud?"

"I suppose so."

"In fact, it indicates fraud in the vast majority of cases, doesn't it?"

"I suppose that's the case."

"No further questions."

‡ ‡ ‡

By 10:00 AM, the drugs had been repackaged, relabeled, and reloaded into Pyotr's van. He and his team had managed to make up the time lost by the Norwegians and then some. He was in a good mood as he drove down the claustrophobic little alley and hummed along with Ludacris's "Money Maker" as it blared out of the van's tinny speakers. Maybe George would let him keep some of the thousand dollars he had saved when the fisherman showed up late, he reflected. Probably not, but maybe.

By 10:15, he was on the highway heading from Yuragorsk to Murmansk, the largest city in the area. Barring a major delay, he would have no trouble making it to Murmansk in time to meet the DHL early shipment deadline. There was a DHL office in Yuragorsk too, but he preferred to ship from Murmansk, in case the police ever decided to try to track any of the packages back to their senders. As a further precaution, he paid a DHL clerk to mislabel the packages to show that they had been shipped from a Moscow suburb rather than Murmansk.

The police shouldn't be a problem, of course; Cleverlad.ru was a licensed pharmacy and could legally import and export drugs. However, those exports were illegal in many of the countries where their customers lived. George had said that Western cops had tried to hack into the company's Web site at least twice, and there were rumors that they were pressuring the *militsiya* to go after businesses like Cleverlad.ru. Also, there was the fact that some of their higher-value imports came through unorthodox channels—such as the holds of the *Agnes Larsen*—and therefore avoided customs delays and duties. So Pyotr drove to the DHL office in Murmansk rather than the one down the block. You could never be too careful where drugs and money were involved, even in Russia.

‡ ‡ ‡

Neither side scored many points during the remainder of the preliminary injunction hearing. Siwell brought up Gunnar's "crawling to me" e-mail whenever he could and kept hammering on the fact that no one disputed that the Neurostim formula belonged to Bjornsen Pharmaceuticals. Ben countered by asking every opposing witness whether they thought it was okay for the company's president to keep a secret set of financials in a cabinet behind his desk.

The judge didn't rule at the end of the preliminary injunction hearing. Instead, he took the matter "under submission" and told the parties to return at 8:30 the next morning to hear his ruling. So both sides boxed up their extra copies of exhibits, highlighted transcripts, Post-its, pens, accordion folders, and other detritus that litters the legal battlefield.

Ben, Noelle, and Gunnar, who had insisted on helping carry files back from court, trooped back to Ben and Noelle's offices. They stacked the boxes against one wall of the conference room and sat down to do a postmortem on the hearing. "The judge didn't rule right away," observed Gunnar as he eased onto one of the padded chairs. "Is that good or bad?"

Ben shrugged. "It's bad in that it means that none of us is likely to be able to focus on anything for the rest of the day. Beyond that, I doubt it means anything one way or the other. This is a big decision for him as well as us. Whatever he does will probably show up in the papers and may even affect his reelection chances. I would have been surprised if he'd ruled without taking some time to think it over first."

"What do you think he'll do?" asked Gunnar.

"Tough call," replied Ben. "I've been wondering about that for the past few days. On the one hand, your brother and his legal team don't have any real response to those financials you found. I think it's pretty clear to Judge Reilly that fraud was committed and that Karl either knew about it or intentionally didn't know about it. Either way, he shouldn't be running the company, at least not without a team of outside auditors keeping a very close eye on him.

"On the other hand, Bert Siwell did a good job of hammering home that the XD-463 formula belongs to Bjornsen Pharmaceuticals. He also managed to use that e-mail pretty effectively against you to make it look like you're withholding information as a power play, not because you're concerned about what would happen if Karl got hold of that information."

Gunnar stirred in his seat and the leather chair creaked loudly. "I . . . I suppose I can see how the judge might have gotten that impression," he admitted. "So, how do you think he'll rule?"

Ben grinned. "Sorry, I was taking a while getting to the point, wasn't I?"

"You're a lawyer," Noelle said. "We expect you to take the scenic route."

"Well, we're almost there now," continued Ben. "The gutsy thing to do would be to grant both injunctions—let the company have the formula, but remove Karl or install an auditor to make sure none of the profits disappear into some secret account. I don't know if Judge Reilly is the type to make that kind of ruling, though. He's new to the bench, and I don't know whether he's got the decisiveness to do something like that.

"All of that is a long-winded way of saying that I really don't know what he'll do. He could grant both injunctions, he could deny both, or he could come up with some compromise that he thinks is fair. The only thing I *don't* think he'll do is grant one side's injunction request completely and completely deny the other side's. That's not his style. There won't be a big win for you or Karl, only a small victory or a minor defeat."

"I thought so," said Gunnar. "All right, I think I'll go home and pace a lot. It will be good exercise."

‡ ‡ ‡

"Bjornsen Pharmaceuticals versus Bjornsen," the clerk announced at 8:35 the next morning. Ben and Siwell got up from the court benches and stood behind the podium, each a little to one side. A scattering of lawyers sat on the benches behind them, waiting for their cases to be called. Gunnar had come downtown to hear Judge Reilly announce his verdict and sat on the bench behind Ben. Karl wasn't in the courtroom, which surprised Ben a little. Apparently, he had more important things to do.

"Good morning, counsel," said the judge. He held several typewritten sheets in his hands. "I've prepared a written decision, which you can get from the clerk after this hearing is over. I've considered the evidence and argument presented by the parties, including the demeanor and credibility of the witnesses while they testified, and I've decided to deny both injunctions. My reasons are laid out in my opinion, but in essence my decision is based on two facts. One, both sides raise substantial claims, but there will not be substantial prejudice to either from waiting for a full trial to resolve them. Two, both sides seek dramatic remedies. Neither party is asking me to preserve the status quo; you're asking me to change it, and you're asking me to change it in substantial ways. That may be appropriate after a permanent injunction trial where all the evidence is fully developed and presented to a jury, but not now.

"I realize that this is an important matter to both of your clients, so I will give this case priority on my trial calendar. Mid-August works best for me, but check your calendars and talk to my clerk to set a trial date. I also want you to submit a stipulation regarding pretrial dates within seven days."

‡ ‡ ‡

Karl Bjornsen sat in his office, waiting for a phone call he didn't want to come. Today was the thirtieth day since Bjornsen Pharmaceuticals had submitted its IND application for Neurostim. If the FDA wanted to issue a "clinical hold"—effectively a denial of the application—they had to act by today. The standard FDA procedure for issuing a clinical hold was for the responsible division director and project manager to call the applicant to discuss the hold, and then follow up with a letter a few days later.

So when Karl had arrived at the office that morning, he'd told his secretary to screen his calls and take messages, unless the caller was from Bert Siwell's office or the FDA. Bert's call had come four hours ago, delivering the news—which Bert had predicted the day before—that Judge Reilly had denied both preliminary injunction requests and was setting the case for trial as soon as possible. Bert was confident that he would win that trial, so his news had been essentially good from Karl's perspective.

Now he waited for more good news—or, more accurately, nonnews. He tried to read sales reports, but he couldn't concentrate. At 2:30, he gave up and put the reports back into his in-box. He got up and walked over to the floor-to-ceiling windows that lined two sides of his office, which was situated on the top floor of the combined office building and production plant that formed the heart of Bjornsen Pharmaceuticals. The research labs, the warehouses, and other ancillary structures clustered below him in a closely built complex, like the stronghold of an ancient king. He and Gunnar could have allowed more space between their buildings, but they had planned to keep growing and didn't want to have to scatter their facilities around the Chicago area like other companies. One of their favorite pastimes had been to sit in this office and debate where each new building would go and what it would look like. Karl looked down and pictured where the Neurostim wing of the factory would rise from the parking lot below him. "Now I can dream alone," he murmured.

But Karl's dreams were interrupted with ever-increasing frequency by glances at his watch. By 3:45, he could no longer even concentrate on his pleasant visions of the future. All he could do was stare at the clock on his credenza and wait for the minutes to tick by.

Finally, 4:00 came. The business day was done at the FDA's East Coast headquarters, and he knew there was no longer any risk that they might call. He waited five more minutes to be sure his clock wasn't fast. Then he strode across his office, opened his door, and smiled broadly at his secretary. "Michele, call the kitchen and tell them to pop the corks, cut the cake, and get the big conference room set for a party. We're starting human trials tomorrow!"

Chapter Nine

Discovery

"So, what do we do now?" asked Gunnar. It was the morning after the preliminary injunction hearing ended and he, Ben, and Noelle had assembled around the table in Ben and Noelle's conference room. A plate of breakfast pastries sat in the middle of the table and Gunnar and Ben had each taken one. Noelle contented herself with caffeine-free tea, though Ben had noticed her eyeing a lemon–poppy seed muffin.

"I've been giving that some thought," replied Ben. "We need to get ready for the permanent injunction trial, of course. August fifteenth is only about a month and a half away, and we've got plenty to do between now and then. But before we dive into trial prep, we need to decide what we want that trial to be about. If it's about whether you should give the formula for XD-463 to the company, we'll probably lose. If it's about whether Karl can be trusted with a multibillion-dollar asset, we have a shot at winning. We need to find a way to convince the jury that Karl is not fit to run the company."

"I thought you did a good job of that at the hearing," said Gunnar. "If a jury had seen that, I don't think they would have let him run a gas station by the time he left the witness stand."

"But that was only because I caught him by surprise," said Ben. "Karl actually did pretty well during most of his testimony, but once

143

those reports knocked him off balance, he fell apart. That won't work twice, though."

"So you need a new surprise for him," said Gunnar. "I still have a lot of friends at the company. I'll call them to see what kind of useful documents they can find. Is there anything in particular you're looking for?"

"Actually, don't do that," replied Ben. "Remember, you're not an officer or employee of the company anymore; you're an adverse litigant. You could get in a lot of trouble by trying to get confidential documents from the company without going through their lawyer."

"But if we have to go through their lawyer, how can we have the element of surprise?" asked Gunnar.

"We may not be able to," conceded Ben. "Surprise witnesses and evidence are more common in movies than in real courtrooms."

"If Gunnar were still an officer of the company, would that make a difference?" asked Noelle.

"Uh . . . probably," replied Ben. "But he isn't. Or is he?"

"Not Bjornsen Pharmaceuticals, but maybe the Norwegian sub, Bjornsen Norge. One of the boxes I looked through had the board resolution removing him as president of Bjornsen Pharmaceuticals, but it didn't say anything about Bjornsen Norge. The preamble said it was a joint board meeting of the two companies, so I assume that if they had voted him out of Norge's presidency, they would have done it then."

Gunnar's eyes lit up and he leaned forward in his seat. "That preamble is part of the form we use for all our minutes and resolutions. I don't think anyone has read it in years, except you.

"Bjornsen Norge has its own separate corporate structure. When it was set up, all the officers and directors were the same as for Bjornsen Pharmaceuticals. I doubt that its formal organization has ever been updated—there's never been any reason to. All of the stock is owned by the parent company, and all the decisions are made there; the Norwegian operation is basically just a sales office and warehouse. I wouldn't be at all surprised if nobody thought to remove me as president when Karl staged his coup."

"Let's confirm that as quickly and quietly as possible," said Ben. "If the company's president gives us permission to go through the corporate records, Karl and Bert will have a tough time arguing that we've done anything illegal or unethical. I'll bet we could find some very interesting nuggets if we poked around in Norge's files, especially if Karl and Bert don't have a chance to sanitize them first."

"Any change to the officers or directors of a Norwegian company should be a matter of public record," said Gunnar. "I can help you check the relevant databases."

"And I'll track down those documents I saw," said Noelle.

"That sounds good," said Ben. "I'm glad you read their corporate records more closely than they did. I'll do a little legal research to make sure we're playing by the rules." He paused. "You know, if this all pans out, we should probably make at least one trip to Norway to interview witnesses and review documents. That will be a significant expense."

"That won't be a problem," said Gunnar immediately. "As a matter of fact, I would have been concerned if you had said that you *weren't* going to Norway. I've worked in international business long enough to know how essential it is to actually be on-site. I'll help you set up witness interviews. I'm also friends with a senior accountant at Bjornsen Norge. He's semiretired now, but I think he still goes into the office regularly. He speaks good English and I'm sure he will be happy to help you."

The meeting ended a few minutes later, and Noelle and Ben walked Gunnar to the elevator. As they headed back to their offices, Noelle turned to Ben. "So you managed to swing the Norwegian trip you wanted when you took this case. Nice job."

"Hey, you heard Gunnar. It's 'essential' that we go. Besides, I couldn't have done it without you; I owe you for figuring out that Gunnar might still be president of the Norwegian sub. That could turn out to be a very valuable piece of information."

"Just let me eat as much salmon as I want while we're there and we'll be even."

Ben laughed. "Deal. And you can have that lemon–poppy seed muffin in the conference room. You earned it."

She smiled luminously, but shook her head. "No way. I'm saving myself now."

When Noelle got back to her office, she was surprised to find a message waiting for her from Anne Bjornsen. She put down her notes from the meeting and returned the call.

"Noelle, I just heard what happened with the Field Museum," Anne said a moment later. "I'm terribly sorry. Charitable boards can be very uncharitable."

Noelle felt as if a cold wind had just blown through. She had been so caught up in the litigation that she hadn't thought about Emily Marshall and her committee for days. It wasn't pleasant to be reminded of them. "It's not your fault."

"I still feel responsible. This all happened because you and Ben are helping my husband. Would you like me to talk to some people for you? I doubt that you'll want to be involved with that committee again, but the Field is a fine institution and there are other opportunities there. There are also a lot of other good organizations in town, and I have friends at most of them. Gunnar and I are very supportive of the Brookfield Zoo, for example."

"Thanks, but I'm pretty busy with Gunnar's case right now, and my baby is due in three months. This probably isn't the best time for me to get involved in something new. I really appreciate the offer, though."

"Well, I'm in the Loop today. Can I at least take you out to lunch?" asked Anne.

"Lunch would be great."

Two hours later, the two women sat at a table in the Walnut Room, the flagship restaurant in what many Chicagoans stubbornly continued to call Marshall Field's, despite the fact that it was now officially Macy's. Panels of richly stained walnut wood lined the restaurant's walls, and spotless white linen cloths covered each table, even at lunchtime. The Walnut Room was not the place to grab a quick lunch during a busy workday, but it was the perfect place to have a quiet conversation over a good meal.

Anne looked at home in the Walnut Room. She had the mature, slightly stately beauty of a wealthy woman who has aged gracefully. Her hair and nails looked as if she had just left a high-end salon. She wore a stylish white sweater twin set and pearl necklace that set off her light tan and flattered her trim figure. *I hope I look like that in twenty-five years*, Noelle thought.

"So you're due in September?" asked Anne.

"September 28," confirmed Noelle.

"How exciting! Is this your first?"

"It is," replied Noelle. "Ben and I are really looking forward to meeting him or her. We're already spending our weekends outfitting the nursery. Ben is building a chest of drawers in his workshop in the basement. Right now it's just a bunch of boards with markings on them, but it looks great in the pictures he showed me."

"I remember when Gunnar and I were young and looking forward to the birth of our first son. He built a crib—or at least he started to. I think there are still some old, half-finished pieces of wood in a corner in our attic."

Noelle laughed. "Now that Ben's busy again, I wouldn't be surprised if the same thing happens to us. I guess it's the thought that counts."

"You're in such a great time of your lives. Everything is new. Everything is in front of you. So many things are possible." Anne smiled. "I'm a little envious of you."

"And I'm a little envious of *you*," replied Noelle. "And not just because no one would dream of kicking you off a committee because of something your husband was doing."

"Oh, I wouldn't mind being thrown off a committee or two. It would be something of a blessing, really. These things can take on a life of their own, and getting off of them can be complicated."

"Really?" Noelle said with surprise. "I hadn't thought about it much, but I kind of figured you could quit whenever you wanted to. There are always plenty of people wanting to get on them."

"Which is actually one reason it's hard to leave them," replied Anne with a sigh. "Every invitation to join a board or committee I've ever received has been a compliment from a friend or, especially when I was younger, somebody doing me a favor. It's hard enough to say 'no' to the invitation, but it's even harder to quit after you join. You make friends and take on responsibilities. Unless you have an almost unarguable reason, you really can't pull out without causing hurt feelings or giving offense."

"I'll keep that in mind the next time I'm thinking about joining something," said Noelle. "It's easy to overcommit, isn't it?"

"It is. Or maybe a better way to put it is that it's easy to make commitments and sacrifices without realizing you're doing it. When I was your age, I tried to meet all the right people, worked at getting invited to all the right events, and volunteered for all the right causes. By the time I was forty, I had something scheduled four or five days a week, and if I didn't have an engagement for a particular evening, Gunnar would invite an important customer over for dinner."

"You didn't like socializing that much?"

"Oh no, I loved it. I felt that Gunnar and I had truly arrived, that we were part of the glamorous and successful crowd. That was a wonderful feeling, but I eventually discovered that I couldn't stop. There were board and committee events, of course, but there were also invitations to dinners and parties from our friends and Gunnar's business partners, and we had to throw parties and host dinners in return. And then one day it dawned on me that this was the life I had created for myself and I was powerless to change it." She paused and took a sip of her coffee. "Have you ever heard the phrase 'chasing after wind'? Well, sometimes you catch it—or it catches you. I suppose there's not much difference."

‡ ‡ ‡

Kim Young sat in a conference room at Bjornsen Pharmaceuticals with Dr. Tina Corrigan's team. Dr. Corrigan was a severe-looking woman of about sixty with sharp features, no makeup, and hair pulled back so tightly that Kim thought it must hurt. Her appearance intimidated Kim at first, but she soon found Dr. Corrigan to be warm and friendly. Her two lieutenants, Drs. Tim Black and Daruka Reddy, were also friendly—Dr. Reddy a little too much so at times. He was a tall Indian man in his late thirties with a habit of standing very close to attractive women when he talked to them.

Kim listened as Dr. Corrigan and two senior members of the clinical trials group picked participants for the Neurostim trial. Despite the relatively low compensation—only $1,000—offered in its ads, Bjornsen Pharmaceuticals had received more than three hundred applications for the thirty-five participant slots it had available for the Phase I trial. Dr. Corrigan had asked her newly acquired intern to put all the applications in a database for easier review by Drs. Black and Reddy, who winnowed the group down to one hundred. To Kim's dismay, David's application didn't make it into the pool of finalists.

The purpose of the meeting was for Dr. Corrigan and her team to pick the thirty-five study subjects from the hundred names on their list. "Okay, we've got seven slots left," announced Dr. Corrigan. "Who's left?"

"How about number eighty-four?" suggested Dr. Black, a gray-haired man of about forty-five with an incongruously boyish face.

"Another Caucasian in the age thirty-five to fifty cohort," responded Dr. Reddy. "We've got all we need of those. Besides, this guy is a cop, and we've got five of them already. What about seventy-two?"

"Good call," said Dr. Black. "Twenty-three-year-old Asian computer game tester. If we get any delta in reflexes and problem-solving, this guy will notice."

"All right, seventy-two is in," said Dr. Corrigan as she highlighted him on her list. "What do you think of fourteen and nineteen? One is an African-American firefighter in his thirties, the other is a white personal trainer."

"Both in," agreed Dr. Black. Dr. Reddy nodded.

"Four to go," commented Dr. Corrigan. "Suggestions?"

"Forty-six," said Dr. Reddy. "He's a twenty-one-year-old white varsity athlete at a Division I-A school. He'll also notice any performance change."

Dr. Corrigan paused and frowned. "We've got a lot of athletic types already. Also, have we checked on whether including him would violate any NCAA rules? Let's nix this one. Remember, we can afford to be picky for this study."

"We don't have a lot of other options," said Dr. Black. "Everyone else on the list is either a Caucasian between thirty-five and fifty or an athlete."

"How about a med school student?" asked Kim. "Twenty-three-year-old Asian. I checked and he meets all the subject qualification criteria."

The other three looked at her. "Um, sure, let's take a look at him," said Dr. Corrigan as she skimmed her list. "Which number is he?"

"He's not on the list," explained Kim. "While you were talking, I pulled up the full database and started flipping through the applications. I found this one and thought it might interest you. Should I print out copies?"

"Please," said Dr. Corrigan.

Five minutes later, Dr. Black said, "I like this guy."

"I don't know," said Dr. Reddy. "There's a reason he didn't make our one hundred name list: he doesn't fit our ideal subject model at all. He's not in a position that requires quick reflexes, strength, or instant problem solving."

"So what?" responded Dr. Black. "We've got that covered in twenty other people. This one needs to solve problems every day under high pressure in his classes. You were in med school; you remember. Plus, he's got some medical training, so he'll probably do a better job reporting the drug's effects than a cop or a jock."

"Okay, you've convinced me," said Dr. Corrigan. "Add David Lee to our participant pool. Nice job, Kim. Why don't you spend some time going through the database to see if you can find some other names that might be good fits?"

‡ ‡ ‡

The phone on Sergei's desk rang. He stopped cleaning up the piles of papers that had accumulated around his office while he'd helped Ben prepare for trial and picked up the receiver. "Sergei, it's Dan Munoz."

"Hello, Dan. What's up? Any news?"

"Sort of. I've done some more digging into Kathy Chatterton's death, but I still didn't find anything suspicious."

"Did you check her phone records and pull any e-mail accounts?" Sergei asked.

"I did. She was a very social young woman, so there was a lot to go through. None of it indicated that she had been threatened. I also talked to her mother and her boyfriend. She didn't report to either of them that she'd been threatened, and neither of them knew of anyone who would want to harm her."

"Okay, did you interview her boss, Dr. Kleinbaum? He's the closest thing I had to a suspect."

"I interviewed both him and his wife; she's his alibi for that night. They both say he was at home in bed when the crash occurred."

"Did you give them polygraphs?" Sergei pursued.

"No, and I'm not going to," replied Munoz, his voice rising a fraction. "They're not suspects or persons of interest. They're not even witnesses. And this isn't a homicide investigation. This is me doing some informal looking around because you asked me to and you've usually got good instincts."

"Sorry, Dan. I didn't mean to start interrogating you. I appreciate what you've been doing."

"Don't worry about it. But you know what, buddy? Not all hunches play out. Maybe Kathy Chatterton was so focused on delivering that stuff to Bjornsen that she drove too fast and didn't pay attention to the road. That kind of thing happens on the tollways and interstates. In fact, it happens a lot." He paused. "No offense, but maybe you were wrong on this one."

‡ ‡ ‡

It hit Ben the next morning as he and Noelle were driving into the office. "Mmmm!" he said as he took a sip of his caramel macchiato at a stoplight. He swallowed the hot coffee too fast and stifled a cough. "Nuts!"

Noelle turned to him. "You okay? What is it?"

"I don't think we're going to Norway after all."

"How come?"

"Bert Siwell. Maybe I can disappear for a few days, but if I'm suddenly gone for a week or two, he'll get suspicious. There's a good chance he'll figure out where I am. He'll know I'm not going on a real vacation six weeks before a trial, and he'll either guess where I am or use that PI he hired to track me down. Either way, he'll figure out where I am, and once he does, he won't have much trouble figuring out why I'm there."

"And then he'll probably figure out that Gunnar is still president of Bjornsen Norge."

Ben nodded. "Either that or he'll file an emergency motion to bar me from looking at Norge's documents or talking to its employees without him in the room. Then I'll have to explain everything to him and the judge. Either way, our chance to surprise Karl in front of the jury is gone and Gunnar is out as Norge's president. Oh well, a couple of days over there won't be enough, but it'll be better than nothing."

"I could go by myself," offered Noelle.

"That's okay. I wouldn't send my pregnant wife on a four-thousand-mile flight by herself to spend two weeks alone in a foreign conference room looking at documents."

"I know you wouldn't, but maybe your pregnant wife might volunteer to go anyway. Seriously, going to Norway won't be a big hardship. If I go, all I'll be doing is sitting on a plane and sitting in a conference room. And I cleared my schedule for this case. So if I stay here, all I'll be doing is sitting in this car or sitting in my office."

Ben snapped his fingers. "How about inviting Elena? She told you she could use a vacation, and I'd feel a lot better if you were with someone . . . especially someone that can handle an emergency." His eyes slid to his wife's expanding belly. "We could offer to pay for her ticket, and I could join you for a few days to check everything over."

"That really isn't necessary," said Noelle.

"It's not necessary," agreed Ben, "but I'd like to do it anyway. And it's not just for my own peace of mind. Traveling alone sucks; wouldn't you rather go with a friend?"

"Well, yeah. It's just that it seems kind of extravagant to pay a couple thousand dollars to send someone to Norway just to keep me company."

Ben smiled. "We can afford it, and sometimes I like to be extravagant with you. Now stop arguing or I'll have to send you both first class."

‡ ‡ ‡

Later that afternoon, Karl stood in the doorway to the greenhouse that projected from the north side of the lab building. The air was cool and humid, approximating an ancient summer high in Norway's mountains. A misty rain fell from sprinklers near the greenhouse ceiling, dampening Karl's hair and shoulders and the report he held in his hands. He ignored the chilly water and looked pensively at the rows of plants in front of him. "How did you do it, Gunnar?"

Myrica norvegicus is a large bush or a small tree, depending on one's point of view. Karl liked to call it a tree, because he felt that sounded more impressive. The tallest plant in the building was just over two meters tall and showed no signs of growing further, though Dr. Gustav Grundaum, the botanist Bjornsen Pharmaceuticals had retained as a consultant, cautioned that it was still too early to tell whether the plant had reached its full growth. Gunnar had once commented that he thought the trees would reach maturity quickly, but would have an extremely long lifespan in which they probably changed little. Karl later asked Dr. Grundaum about this; he agreed that such a life cycle would not be unusual for an Arctic plant, but said that it was impossible to tell how long they would live. After all, the oldest plant in the greenhouse was less than two years old.

Karl stepped up to one of the trees and regarded it thoughtfully. It had small, round dark green leaves and a scattering of tiny white flowers, though most of these had dropped off, leaving behind growing seedpods. He leaned forward and gently lifted one ripening pod for closer inspection. An extraordinarily valuable secret was locked inside there, one that had stumped him and everyone else at the company for the past year. The seeds would not grow. The lab staff had tried different types of soils, different moisture levels, different temperature levels, and every fertilizer they could find. One researcher had even tried playing Mozart for the seeds every day. Nothing worked.

In desperation, they'd hired Dr. Grundaum, the world's leading expert in Arctic plants. Twice a month, they flew him in from Canada, where he spent most of his time doing research. He would spend two or three days dispensing instructions and working on the trees. He had designed the greenhouse that now held them and had managed to keep all forty-two specimens alive and healthy. But he'd had no better luck at getting the seeds to sprout than anyone else had. He had tried heating them to simulate forest fires, freezing them to well below zero to mimic a Norwegian winter, soaking them in water, and dozens of other techniques. His current theory was that there was something wrong with their pollination technique. They had first used cotton swabs to move pollen from flower to flower and more recently had tried honeybees. Dr. Grundaum suspected that they needed to find the insect that had pollinated these plants millennia ago in Norway, and he had gone off to Scandinavia to research insects and talk to botanists there.

Yet Gunnar had somehow managed to get the seeds to grow. And he had done it without a million-dollar greenhouse or a world-class researcher for a consultant. Each of the forty-two trees in the greenhouse had started life in a pot on the windowsill in Gunnar's office. After Gunnar left the company, the lab staff had, of course, tried putting seeds in the same pots on the same windowsill using the same dirt, but without success.

When he forced Gunnar out, Karl had gambled that the company's researchers would be able to replicate his brother's work in creating Neurostim. When Gunnar stormed out of his office for the last time, he left behind a hodgepodge of handwritten notes, spreadsheets, and charts. Whether intentionally or not, he also left numerous gaps in his records, which made recreating his research extremely difficult.

Frank Chow and his research team from new drug development had worked hard and had managed to fill in most of the gaps. They now knew how to extract the active compounds from the leaves and seeds of the plants and turn them into useful medicine. In fact, they did better. In his hands, Karl held a now-damp report on the process developed by Dr. Chow's team; their products were purer and stronger than the extracts created by Gunnar, and they managed to squeeze twenty percent more doses from the same amount of plant material. But without more trees, they could only make enough Neurostim to supply the company's clinical trials, if they were lucky.

"So, how did you do it?" Karl repeated. He stared at the seedpod for several seconds, as if hoping it might answer him. Then he sighed and walked away.

Chapter Ten

Henrik Haugeland

ELENA HAD JUST FINISHED A MAJOR INVESTIGATION and was delighted to take some time off and fly to Norway with Noelle. Six days after Noelle's invitation, the two of them sat on a bench on Aker Brygge, a wharf in downtown Oslo that had been renovated into a boardwalk edged on one side by fashionable shops and restaurants. On the other side lay the deep blue waters of the Viken, the long fjord that led from Oslo's waterfront to the North Sea. A bright July sun rode high in a cloudless sky, despite the fact that it was nearly seven o'clock in the evening. Thousands of Norwegians and tourists were taking advantage of the long day and good weather—eating, drinking, boating, walking, fishing, shopping, or just sitting in the sun.

The two women had arrived that afternoon. Noelle was lethargic and didn't feel like doing much except lying in her hotel room and killing time until the evening, when they were scheduled to meet with Gunnar's accountant contact, a man named Henrik Haugeland. But Elena, who had traveled to Europe often enough to know that the best way to combat jet lag was to go do something vigorous, persuaded her friend to get out. They'd spent a couple of hours wandering around the Vigeland sculpture garden in Frognerparken and then headed to Aker Brygge for a seafood dinner at Lekter'n, an open-air restaurant on a converted barge that was permanently moored to the dock. The food had been good—the shrimp in particular were better than anything either of them had tasted in America. Now they relaxed at the small blue and white lighthouse where they had agreed to meet Haugeland. Ferries, tour boats, and pleasure craft maneuvered around each other in the dark azure waters of the busy harbor. The ancient Akershus castle looked down on them from a strategic seaside bluff on the other side of the water. Noelle still felt tired, but that wasn't a bad feeling to have while relaxing by the sea after a good meal.

A man of about seventy approached them. He matched the description Gunnar had given them: medium height and build, well-trimmed gray beard, very tan, bright blue eyes hiding behind old-fashioned round glasses, and an enormous nose. "Hello, I'm Henrik Haugeland," he said in accented but clear English. "Am I correct in guessing that you're Elena and Noelle?"

"You are," replied Noelle. "I'm Noelle."

"And I'm Elena," added her friend. "Pleased to meet you."

"Likewise," said Haugeland. "Gunnar told me only a little about why you are here. You are accountants who have come to audit Bjornsen Norge's books in secret for a lawsuit?"

"Sort of," answered Noelle. "I'm here as an accountant; Elena is mostly here as a tourist. I'd like to do some auditing work on the company's customer accounts, and you're right that it should be kept confidential and that it has to do with a lawsuit."

He stroked his beard. "Our office is not large, so you'll be noticed and will be the subject of much gossip and speculation. If you want to do your audit confidentially, you should visit after business hours or on the weekend."

Noelle nodded. "That's what I thought. That's fine; it will give me plenty of time to play tourist with Elena."

Haugeland smiled warmly. "No trip to Norway would be complete without a trip to a real Norwegian farm. Would you be interested in visiting mine for a good dinner after you're done looking at documents on Saturday?"

"I'd love to," said Noelle.
"Me too," added Elena.

‡ ‡ ‡

As it turned out, Noelle didn't get a chance to look at the documents until Saturday anyway. Bjornsen Norge's accounting team was at the office until late in the evening every day that week, calculating their second quarter numbers. It bothered Noelle to lose time, but at least the files were up-to-date and in good order by the time she finally did get to them.

On Saturday morning, Haugeland picked up Noelle and Elena at their hotel and drove them to Bjornsen Norge's facility. Sitting in the front seat with him was a boy who looked to be about twelve, whom Haugeland introduced as his son, Einar. "Some of the records you may want to see are in stacks of boxes," Haugeland explained. "I hurt my back on the farm last week, so Einar has volunteered to help you move boxes and find what you are looking for."

Bjornsen Norge was housed in a modern warehouse on an industrial section of Oslo's waterfront, with a half floor of offices facing the street. Haugeland guided them through a wide space filled with empty cubicles to a large room at the back. Three walls were taken up by file cabinets, while the fourth held a row of cubicles. Haugeland walked over to one of them and turned on the computer that sat on its neatly organized desk. He picked up a stack of computer printouts and handed them to Noelle. "Here are last quarter's customer account numbers. They are in Norwegian, of course, but I can translate anything that's not clear from the context. Einar works in our file room after school and can get you the backup for any accounts listed here."

"Great," said Noelle. "One that I know I'll want to see is Cleverlad.ru."

Haugeland smiled. "I thought you might."

"Really? Why's that?" asked Noelle.

"All of the orders for that customer come through our head-quarters in America, which is unusual. A European customer would usually be handled from here. Also, the file documentation is . . . unusual. You will understand when you see it." He turned to Einar. "*Einar, kan du hente papirene til Cleverlad kontoen?*"

The boy nodded and took off his Real Madrid windbreaker, revealing tattoos of a cat's face and a four of spades crudely drawn on his slender arms in bluish ink. He hung his jacket on a chair and walked out of the room. Elena got up quickly and followed him. "I'll go help him with the files," she explained as she left.

Five minutes later, Einar and Elena reappeared with two thin manila folders, which they gave to Noelle. She spent five minutes reading through them, occasionally asking Haugeland to translate something. Then she looked up and said, "Okay, where are the rest of the files for this account?"

"There are none," replied Haugeland with a smile.

"*None?*" Noelle stared at him. "All that's here are money order receipts and a few e-mails. Where are the purchase orders? Where are the shipping bills?"

Haugeland's smile broadened. "As I said, the file is unusual. The orders simply appear by e-mail or phone call from America. I have seen no formal purchase orders, and we never ship the products. A man simply arrives in a truck. He gives us a money order and we give him the products."

"Do you have any idea why this account is handled like that?" asked Noelle.

"I suspect that the amount of information in the customer file is kept to a minimum by intent. Whose intent I do not know, but the account is not included in the statements we send to headquarters. I have mentioned this several times, and each time I am told the omission is a mistake. But the mistake is never fixed."

‡ ‡ ‡

It was Saturday morning, and David Lee sat where he usually sat on weekends, doing what he usually did in his free time. He had been up for less than two hours and he still wore the boxers and T-shirt in which he had slept. His tousled head bent over the workbook on the kitchen table of his loft apartment. His right hand held a pencil with which he alternately scribbled on the sheets of work paper that littered the tabletop or blackened tiny ovals on an answer sheet that lay beside the workbook. A stopwatch stared at him, ticking remorselessly as he worked.

He finished the test and slapped the stop button on the stopwatch. Fifty-three minutes, a new personal best. He checked the answer sheet against a key in the back of the workbook. Twenty-eight out of thirty right, also a new best. He pumped his fist in the air. "Yes!"

He poured himself a fresh cup of coffee, picked up his cell phone, and hit Kim's number on the speed dial. "Hey, Kimmy, I took another one of those immunology practice tests, and guess what?"

"What?" asked Kim in a sleepy voice.

"I got twenty-eight out of thirty, and it only took me fifty-three minutes!"

"That's great," responded Kim with more energy. "You did pretty well on the last oncology test you took too, didn't you?"

"That's right. With any luck, I'll know both subjects cold by the time school starts. I'll be able to nail them and then spend extra time working on my other classes."

"That is so cool! I knew you could turn it around. In a couple of months you'll be back on top and laughing about last year."

He glanced over at his kitchen counter, where a card of little yellow pills lay, each in its own foil-backed plastic bubble. Over half of the bubbles were crushed and empty. "Uh, yeah. Any idea whether they'll roll over the Phase I volunteers into Phase II?"

"I don't think they've decided yet. But seriously, don't worry about it, David. You're doing better because you're smart, not because you're taking some drug. You'll do great, even after the study is over."

"I don't know, Kimmy. My scores have been going up ever since I started the trial, and I can really notice the difference now that I've reached the peak dosage. I hardly have to think about the problems; the right answers just jump off the page at me. It's the same when I read the textbooks too—I used to have to read the same thing three or four times to make sure I understood it. Now I can just zip through it once and it all makes sense. I also feel more alert and focused. It's sort of like the feeling you get from a good espresso, except you don't get all jumpy and distractible."

Kim laughed. "So it's even better than coffee? That's saying a lot coming from you. Be careful, I don't want you getting addicted."

"Hey, you know the only thing I'm addicted to is you."

"Aww, you're sweet."

"You too. I've got to get going. I volunteered to take an extra shift at the hospital lab today, and I need to get ready."

"See? That's the attitude that's going to get you ahead, with or without Neurostim."

"Thanks, babe. I'll call you tonight." He hung up the phone and looked again at the card of pills on his counter.

He walked into the bathroom to get ready for work, but his thoughts remained on the workbook and pills in the kitchen. Maybe he could stumble through his second year without more Neurostim, but that wasn't good enough. He didn't want to just *pass* his classes; he wanted to *nail* them. All through high school and college, he had been at or near the top of his class. Now there was a way for him to get back there.

"No way are they cutting me out of Phase II!" he declared to the empty apartment. "No *way!*"

He caught a glimpse of himself in the bathroom mirror and then took a good look. He seemed strong and self-confident, almost fierce. The diligent schoolboy look had vanished from his face and been replaced by something harder. He smiled and watched his reflection do the same. He liked this look.

‡ ‡ ‡

Noelle reviewed customer accounts until late afternoon, asking frequent questions of Henrik Haugeland and copying documents that looked interesting. The picture that emerged was essentially what they had suspected: the Cleverlad.ru account was clearly being handled so as to give it as low a profile as possible, but the files didn't reveal who had decided to handle it that way. Noelle also couldn't figure out why someone had decided to hide the account. None of the sales appeared to be illegal and there was no fraud or bribery taking place that she could see. She had half-expected to find that the drugs were being sold at suspiciously low prices, which might mean that the salesman who handled the account was taking part of the purchase price in the form of a kickback. But Cleverlad was actually paying *more* for the drugs than most other customers, which eliminated that theory.

By 5:00, Noelle was ready to call it a day. She had been getting up and taking a short walk every half hour like her obstetrician recommended, but she still felt very stiff and very pregnant. She stretched, pulled the scrunchy out of her thick brown hair and said, "Well, I'm done for today. I still need to look at the expense accounting files, but not tonight."

"I am busy tomorrow," said Haugeland, "but I can help you on Monday after hours."

"That would be great."

"And now that we are done here, I will call my wife so that she knows we are coming. She looks forward very much to having you for dinner."

Oslo holds more than one-tenth of Norway's population, and is by far the largest and most cosmopolitan city in the country. It is nonetheless small by American standards, and Elena and Noelle were pleasantly surprised by how quickly the modern buildings and shops of downtown gave way to close-set and immaculate tile-roofed homes, usually painted red, yellow, or white. Then the houses gave way to rolling fields of bright green pasture and golden grain. A gusting wind cast rippling shadows across the fields.

After they had driven for about half an hour, they turned onto a gravel track in the midst of a thick pine grove. They drove through the dappled twilight of the trees for several seconds. Then the green wall of needles parted and revealed a tidy, well-kept farm. "Here we are," announced Henrik, pointing to a rambling white farmhouse set in a south-facing nook between two round hills. A barn stood a little to the west, flanked by two smaller outbuildings.

They parked and went inside, where they were greeted by two women. They were about the right age for a mother and daughter, but looked nothing alike. The older woman was short and plump. She had a grandmotherly air and honey-blonde hair that was fading to white. The younger woman was tall, rail-thin, black-haired, and had broad, almost Asian, cheekbones. Henrik introduced the older woman as his wife, Sigrid, and the younger as their daughter, Katrine.

After introductions and a few minutes of small talk, they all sat down around a large, well-used dining room table. There were six of them, but the table could easily have held double that number. The Norwegians all recited a traditional Norwegian grace, which is sung rather than spoken, before passing around dishes of vegetables, potatoes, and meat cakes. "Like Swedish meatballs, except better," explained Henrik with a wink.

Neither Einar nor Katrine spoke much English, and they were clearly relieved to be excused when the meal moved to the coffee-and-conversation phase. "I don't mean to pry, but how did you come to adopt a Russian son?" asked Elena when there was a lull in the conversation.

Henrik looked at her in surprise. "I don't recall mentioning that he was Russian or adopted. How did you know?"

"I'm Russian and an FBI agent," she explained, "so I recognized the tattoos on his arms. When we were out getting documents, I tried talking to him in Russian. He told me that you and Sigrid came to his orphanage four years ago and adopted him."

"Unfortunately, there are many children in the orphanages with prison gang tattoos," said Henrik. "A lot of people won't give them a chance."

"Prison gang tattoos?" asked Noelle.

Sigrid nodded. "Einar lived in Russia until he was twelve, and spent most of that time on the street or in a child labor colony."

"In Russia, they send juvenile, um, offenders to labor colonies," Elena explained to Noelle. "They're really rough places; they make American reform schools, even the bad ones, look like summer camp. Kids in labor colonies pretty much have to join gangs if they want to survive." She turned to Sigrid. "So, he's sixteen now?"

"Yes, though he is small for his age," said Sigrid. "I think it is probably from bad nutrition. I do not think he ever ate enough before he came to Norway. He and his mother were homeless or living in single rooms for as long as he can remember. She died when he was eight and he had to feed himself after that."

"How awful!" exclaimed Noelle. "Didn't the police pick him up and take him to a shelter or something?"

The Haugelands shook their heads. "He hid from the police," said Henrik. "He survived by doing jobs for street criminals. He would be a lookout during drug deals, for example."

Elena sighed. "Pretty typical, as I'm guessing both of you know."

"Seriously?" asked Noelle.

The Haugelands nodded and Elena said, "There are a lot of kids like that in Russia these days. No one really knows exactly how many, but there are probably at least a million homeless children in the country. They lose parents to AIDS, drugs, alcohol, violence, or some combination of them. Or they're just abandoned because their parents can't take care of them anymore or don't want to. You see these kids in pretty much all the big cities; little ones begging and older ones selling themselves or standing around in groups. You can't get too close to them or they'll swarm you, asking for money and trying to steal your purse or wallet, especially if they think you're a rich foreigner. It just breaks my heart every time I go back, but there's not much I can do except give money to children's charities. It's great that you were actually willing to take in one of them and give him a chance at a new life. How is Einar adapting to life here?"

"It has been hard for him," conceded Sigrid. "Especially when he first came. He could not go to normal school, because he had no education and did not speak Norwegian. He stole from stores and from us because that was the only way he knew. He fought. He beat up one boy so badly that the boy went to the hospital. The boy was bigger than Einar and had . . . had . . ." She turned to her husband, "*mobbet ham?*"

"Bullied him," supplied Henrik.

"Yes, bullied him," continued Sigrid, "so the judge did not put Einar in jail. But the police arrested him four times for different crimes. That was a difficult time for him and for us, but he does much better now."

"He also had nightmares," added Henrik. "Sometimes he woke up screaming. Other times, we would find him standing in the hall in the dark, sweating and shaking."

"He was sleepwalking?" asked Elena.

"Yes," replied Henrik. "He would wake when we touched him or spoke to him. One of us would stay with him until he could sleep again. Sometimes it would take an hour or more."

"But it is two years since the last time," said Sigrid with a touch of pride. "He is now in a normal school and has good marks and friends. He also changed his name from Ivan to Einar to be more Norwegian." She paused and smiled at Henrik. "He studies to be an accountant like his father."

"He studies math and says he will become an accountant," corrected Henrik. "Time will tell whether he actually does. Not everyone has the charisma and magnetism to make a good accountant."

Elena laughed. Noelle turned and raised her eyebrows. "Why is that funny?"

"Oh, because he obviously has lots of charisma and magnetism," responded Elena. "He's a remarkable young man. I was picturing him as a future rock star, but that's pretty close to being an accountant."

The other three laughed. "You are right about Einar—he is remarkable," said Sigrid. "We are very proud of him."

"You should be," said Elena. "It's wonderful to hear about one of these street kids actually turning his life around. A lot of them wind up as unclaimed bodies in the morgue before they turn eighteen, and most of the rest are in prison. And I'm really impressed that you were willing to stick with him through the hard times. I've seen the flyers for some of these Russian adoption agencies. For some reason, none of them mention what kids like Einar must have been like when you adopted him. They all have these glowing descriptions of perfect little angels with no problems. I'll bet Einar was something of a surprise for you."

The Haugelands both smiled. "No, he is our eighth adopted child," Sigrid said. "We always picked older children who have trouble, because no one else will take them. We adopted Katrine when she was eleven. She was a prostitute and alcoholic. Now she helps us here and goes to university."

"One of our boys is a policeman," added Henrik, "and another is an automobile mechanic. One of our girls is a children's doctor, and the other stays at home with her three children."

"And the . . ." began Noelle. She paused with her mouth open for a heartbeat. "Do you have plans to adopt any more children?"

"Einar will be our last," answered Henrik. "In fact, the orphanage made a special exception to their rules so we could adopt him. They require younger parents, which we understand.

"To answer the question that you were too polite to ask, the other two children are no longer alive. The first boy we adopted died in a car crash. The car was stolen and the police were chasing him.

"Our second child, a girl, was a heroin addict. She was in a program here and she did well, but she left home after finishing secondary school and moved to Bergen on the west coast of Norway. She had no family or support group to help her there and she began taking drugs again. We knew nothing until one night the hospital called to say she was in a coma. By the time we got there, she was dead."

Elena stared at him. "So you adopted *eight* of these kids—six after the first two died." She shook her head in awe. "I can't even imagine what that must have been like. You two must be real saints. That is way beyond the call of duty."

"But it is well within the call of love," responded Henrik. "Love does call, you know. He calls us to do what we cannot do alone. He asks us to give without counting the cost, to walk through the furnace, to love the unlovable. He asks everything of us, and he has the right to expect it."

Elena was as silent and still as stone, but Noelle nodded. "Because he gave everything for us."

"Exactly," said Henrik with a smile. "We love because he first loved us. Sigrid and I could not have children, but we loved children very much and we knew we were called to be parents. There were long waits to adopt Norwegian children, so we went to a place where there was no wait, where if we did not adopt the children, no one would. We traveled to Russia and found that even there many people wanted to adopt the babies and small children with no problems. But the older children, especially the ones with disabilities or who have been in a labor colony, most of them are never adopted. They live at the orphanage for a few years and watch the babies and toddlers find parents while they are passed over. Then they are too old for the orphanage and they go back to the streets."

"Except the ones who come to live with someone like you," said Elena. "I can't even imagine the sacrifices you've made over the years."

"We made no sacrifices," said Sigrid. "We made choices. We chose to have children instead of more money or nicer vacations."

"Or enough sleep or clean cars," added Henrik. "Or knowing that I can always sit in the soft chair in front of the television and turn on what I want. I have to disagree with my darling wife—those were sacrifices, not just choices. I would make them again, of course, but I would have stronger rules about children eating and drinking in my car."

‡ ‡ ‡

Monday morning at 7:30, Karl Bjornsen walked into his office. His phone was ringing and a blinking light showed that it was his private line. He quickly walked over and picked it up. "Hello, Karl Bjornsen here."

"Hello. This is George at Cleverlad. I just saw an interesting article about your company. It says that you have developed a drug that makes people stronger and smarter. I think we could sell a lot of that. Please send me a sample."

Karl froze. "I'm sorry, George," he forced out, "but that, ah, that drug hasn't been approved by the FDA. We can't sell it until we have a green light from them."

"How long will that take?"

"I don't know. We're in the middle of clinical trials right now. They're going well, but they could take a long time. It will probably be at least three or four years before the drug is available for sale. I'm glad to hear that you're interested, though. We'll make sure to let you know as soon as the drug hits the market."

"That is a long time. Certainly you can make an exception for one of your best customers."

"I'm sorry, but I really can't. Selling unapproved drugs is a serious crime. The company would be shut down and I would go to jail."

The line was silent for several seconds. "You would also go to jail if the authorities knew you used the money from my company's purchases for bribes."

"I—I have no idea what you're talking about," Karl stammered.

"Yes, you do," replied George coolly. "For the last two years, the money my company paid to Bjornsen Norge was used to buy gifts and expensive vacations for some of your American directors and shareholders. Those same directors and shareholders then gave you complete control of the company. Through a convenient accounting error, both the money coming in from Cleverlad and the money going out in bribes got left off of your company's books."

"Someone has been telling you outrageous lies!" Karl said, consciously injecting indignation into his deep voice. "I can assure you that—"

George cut him off. "You waste your breath and my time. I have all the proof I need to put you in jail for a long time." He paused for an instant and continued in a more conciliatory tone. "You don't want that to happen—and neither do I. I want to keep doing business with you. I would never betray a business partner, so you want to keep doing business with me too, don't you?"

Karl's hand shook as he wiped the sweat off his forehead. "I . . . yes."

"Excellent! I will expect the sample by this time next week."

Chapter Eleven

History Lessons

BEN AND SERGEI WALKED THROUGH GARDERMOEN, Oslo's main airport. It felt good to stretch their legs, particularly for Sergei. Northwest Airlines' coach class seats had been designed for someone about eight inches shorter, which was bad enough. But he also had been seated next to two unaccompanied girls, roughly twelve and fourteen, who had alternately bickered and chattered throughout the entire eight-hour flight.

As they walked, Ben called Noelle on his cell phone to let her know they had landed and to finalize arrangements for the next day. They had scheduled an interview with Henrik Haugeland for the morning. Noelle thought he would make a good witness, but Ben wanted to see for himself. He also wanted to talk to Haugeland about some of the key documents Noelle had found over the past few days.

Sergei had come primarily to help Noelle with the document review, which was taking longer than she had anticipated. Trial was only four weeks away, and Ben needed both his wife and the documents soon. Also, Sergei could take notes when Ben interviewed Haugeland. Ben didn't want to take notes himself, because he might later need to put the notes into evidence. To do that, whoever took the notes would have to testify that the notes were accurate, and it would be awkward at best for Ben to put himself on the witness stand.

171

Ben finished his conversation as they reached the baggage carousel. "We're set for ten o'clock tomorrow morning at the hotel. They have a suite we can use for the interview."

"Good. Nice and convenient," replied Sergei.

"It's, uh, Elena's suite, so she'll probably be there."

"Okay."

"I just thought I'd let you know, in case, you know, you'd rather we made other arrangements or something."

"No." The tall Russian forced a smile. "I can take notes with her in the room."

"Okay, good."

They stood in silence for a few minutes, watching the scuffed metal conveyor belt and waiting for their luggage to emerge from the depths of the airport. "So, what are your plans for dinner tonight?" asked Sergei.

"There are a couple of seafood places on the water that got good reviews from Noelle," replied Ben. "I was thinking of trying one of them. Care to join me?"

"Sure, but what about Noelle? You haven't seen her for a week."

"Well, she usually has dinner with Elena, so we were thinking it might be best for you and me to have dinner together, and for the two of them to eat someplace else."

"Oh, come on. You're acting like we're in high school. Elena and I are both adults and we can act like it. We can have dinner with friends without making a scene. Seriously, I'd like to have dinner with both of you, and it wouldn't bother me at all if Elena is there too."

"Not at all?"

"It will be a little weird—I haven't seen her since we broke up, but I'll be seeing her tomorrow morning anyway. We might as well get the weirdness out of the way now; tomorrow we'll have work to do."

‡ ‡ ‡

On Tuesday morning, Berit Lundgren came to work at Bjornsen Norge. She wore her blonde hair back in a bun, and she was dressed in a charcoal gray suit that was slightly more conservative than is typical for a twenty-six-year-old. That was by design; she knew that her chances of getting ahead were better if she looked a little more serious than her peers. Also, it was useful camouflage.

She sat down at her desk in the accounting section and frowned. The seat was higher than it should have been; someone had adjusted it after she'd left the night before. Papers on her desk had been moved too—none more than a centimeter, but enough for her to notice. She went through each of her drawers quickly, but found nothing amiss. Maybe someone had borrowed her chair last night and temporarily put something on her desk. She leaned over to the woman in the cubicle next to hers. "Kjersti, was there a meeting or special project here last night?"

"Maybe. Einar said he was working late yesterday, though he was pretty mysterious about what he was doing. I also saw a couple of cars in the parking lot last night when I was driving past."

Berit stared incredulously. "They let Einar be here after hours? Unbelievable! I hope they had a security guard watching him like a hawk. You'd better check your desk to make sure there's nothing missing, and lock it when you leave tonight."

"Yeah, good idea." Kjersti rolled back to her desk. Berit stared at her computer screen, but didn't see it. *What was that little thug doing here last night?* Einar had never been caught stealing from the office, but she had heard about his legal problems elsewhere. She had also never liked the knowing way he looked at her when she came into the office a little high or when she developed a nosebleed. What business was it of his if she liked to party and had a wild side that no one at work knew about? As if he was any better. *What if he's been going through my desk looking for something he can use to blackmail me?*

She went through her desk again more carefully. She made a real effort to keep her personal and work lives separate, but she might have scribbled down a phone number or an address that she wouldn't want someone else to find. Twenty minutes later, she sat back relieved. Her desk was clean; if Einar had been digging for extortion leverage, he had come up empty.

Then she tensed again. *What if that's not all he knows about?* He had done prison time in Russia and might still have contacts in the Russian underworld. *What if he told someone where he works and they know about me?*

She hurried back to the file room and opened the cabinet drawer containing the Cleverlad.ru files. They stuck up slightly, as if they recently had been removed and put back. Her heart raced as she pulled out the boxes containing the expense accounting records for the past two years. They too looked as if they had been gone through.

Berit began to shake and sweat, but she resisted the temptation to go out to her car for a quick pick-me-up from the emergency stash she kept in her glove compartment. *I graduated at the top of my class from the Oslo Handelshøyskole,* she assured herself. *I can outsmart a street punk ten years younger than me.*

Thinking of her car reminded her of something Kjersti had said: She had seen a *couple* of cars in the parking lot. So Einar hadn't been here alone. Who had he been with?

Berit could feel herself calming down as her thoughts began to get some traction. *All right, first things first. I need to know who I'm up against. And how do I do that? Well, there is a good chance that they will be back. The documents they need are not all in one place, and they are not easy to find. Some were in that pile, but some were not. Yes, they will be back, and this time I will know they are coming. And I will be watching.*

‡ ‡ ‡

Karl called Gwen to let her know that he would be working late. She didn't ask what would be keeping him, and he didn't volunteer.

He read through the weekly ream of management memos, reviewed the résumés of the finalists for the research position left open by the death of Dr. Chatterton, and polished a presentation he would be giving to the directors on the quarterly financial numbers. He even cleaned out his e-mail in-box. He went out for Chinese food at 6:30, but was back at his desk by 7:30. He killed more time as the shadows in his office lengthened and the parking lot below his window emptied. He took out a chrome-plated hand exerciser that his secretary had given him for Christmas several years ago and squeezed it absentmindedly until it snapped in one of his powerful hands. The cleaning people came and went.

At 8:30, he decided it was time. He walked along the quiet hallway, past rows of empty offices, and stopped at the elevators. He stepped into an empty car, waved his key card in front of the sensor panel, and pushed the button for the second floor—where the research labs were.

He got off at the lab floor and walked to one of the conference rooms. His leather portfolio was sitting on a bookshelf in the back, right where he had intentionally left it to give himself a perfectly natural reason to come back down after hours. He retrieved it and left the room. Back in the hallway, he paused and glanced both ways. He was alone. Stepping across the hall to another door—one marked Authorized Personnel Only—he swept his key card across the security panel, pushed the door open, and walked inside. His eyes flicked over the shelves of numbered, pill-filled boxes until he spotted the one he was looking for: XD-463. To his relief, there was no quantity tally sheet on it. He grabbed five cards of pills, dropped them into his portfolio, and zipped it shut. Thirty seconds later, he was back at the elevator.

The elevator doors opened and Karl started to get on—and nearly walked into one of the night security guards. "Oh, I'm sorry, Mr. Bjornsen," said the flustered guard. "I should watch where I'm going."

"So should I," replied Karl. "How are you, Wayne?"

"Oh, I can't complain. Thanks for asking. Is there anything I can do for you tonight, Mr. Bjornsen?"

"Nope." He held up his portfolio. "I just remembered that I'd left a notepad in the conference room down here and came to get it." The elevator began to ping impatiently. Karl stepped aside to let the guard out and then stepped inside. "Have a good night, Wayne."

As the doors closed and the elevator surged upward, Karl leaned against the back of the car and let out a long breath. What if Wayne had come down a minute earlier and found him in the drug storage room putting pills in his portfolio? Well, he hadn't, but this was the last time Karl would take such a chance.

The sun had set by the time he got back to his office, filling it with dull reds and black shadows. He shut his door, unzipped the portfolio, and tossed the pills on his desk. There were seventy capsules—enough for a sample, but nothing more. And there was no way he could get enough to sell commercially, even to one customer, without terminating the research program and letting both the manufacturing and shipping departments in on what he was doing. That was impossible, of course, but so was refusing George's request. Karl had no idea how George had found out about the off-ledger gifts to a few key directors and shareholders, but he had. If that got out, Karl knew he would probably go to jail. Worse, Gunnar would march back into the company and assume complete control. Karl's jaw clenched. He would rather burn the company to the ground than let Gunnar have it.

So, what could he do? There were no good options, but which one was least bad? He stared at the pills for several minutes as the darkness deepened around him. Then he reached his decision, picked up the pills, and put them in an inner pocket of his briefcase.

‡ ‡ ‡

Tom and Markus sat in the bleachers at Wrigley Field. The evening air was warm and the wind was blowing out. Two innings ago,

Markus had caught a home run ball—unfortunately hit by the visiting Giants—which he had given to an eight- or nine-year-old boy with a glove and a Cubs hat in the row behind them. The Cubs were still ahead, though, and the Bjornsen brothers drank flat beer from plastic cups and were glad together.

"By the way, congratulations on the Financial Advisor of the Year award," Markus said. "Sorry I couldn't make it to the dinner on Thursday to celebrate. I didn't feel up to it."

"An acute case of Daditis?" asked Tom.

"Something like that," replied Markus. "Anyway, nice job."

"Thanks. Mom mentioned over dinner that you are going to be keeping your role in *The Gamester*, even though the guy you replaced is out of his cast and ready to go back on stage. That's a promotion, isn't it?"

Markus shrugged. "I guess so. We've had a very good run, and I'm sure they don't want to mess up our onstage chemistry."

"Well, Mom also mentioned that you've been asked to audition for leading roles in a bunch of other plays after *The Gamester* closes."

Markus smiled. "I don't know if I'd call three a lot, but—"

Tom gave his brother a friendly shove. "Listen to you! I practically have to force good news out of you. It's too bad you weren't there on Thursday; we could have made it a double celebration."

Markus's smile faded and he turned back to the game. "No, we couldn't have."

"All right, three of us could have."

"And Dad would have sat there and made comments that ruined the evening for everyone else."

"You just have to ignore him when he's like that," said Tom.

"Maybe you can. I can't."

"If it bothers you so much, why do you provoke him into criticizing you? For starters, why do you drink in front of him? I know you can go all evening without a drink; I've seen you do it. So why break his two-drink rule every time you see him? You should know he's going to say something."

Markus glared at his brother. "And *you* should know that if it's not my drinking, it's something else—the theater, my hair, my friends. If I'm going to have to sit there and listen to his crap anyway, I might as well be a little buzzed while I'm doing it."

"Hey, all I'm saying is that there are some little things you could do that would help take the edge off of family get-togethers, that's all. Make small talk about the drug business or Norway, laugh at Dad's jokes, don't react when he makes some crack about your lifestyle. Or if you're going to react, treat it like a joke and laugh. You're an actor; it shouldn't be that hard."

"Unlike you, I don't think having a civil dinner with my father should require me to act."

"Fine, it shouldn't. But guess what? It does. Pretend that he's some new producer that you have to make like you. I have to do that sort of thing all day long. You can do it once a week during family dinners."

"I'm sorry, Tom. I guess I'm not as good an actor as you. Or maybe being a glad-handing sycophant isn't an act."

Tom stared at his brother for several seconds. Then he said, "You know, I'm going to give you a pass on that one. I'm going to assume it was the beer talking."

Markus sighed. "It wasn't the beer. It was the jealousy. I've always been amazed by you. You've got a gift for making people like you, for fitting into any social situation. If you're stuck at a table with a bunch of golfers, you get them talking about all the courses they've played, and you seem genuinely fascinated by their stories. And if they have some bad jokes to tell, you'll laugh at every one.

"You're a chameleon. Whatever the situation calls for, that's what you are naturally, effortlessly. I can't do that, at least when I'm not on stage. I can't hide what I'm thinking and feeling. I can't make unlikable people think I like them. I can't pretend that the company is the be-all and end-all for me, or even that I think it's okay that it's the be-all and end-all for Dad. Sometimes I wish I could just blend in, go along and get along, but I can't." He paused and smiled wryly. "I guess I'm like Dad that way."

‡ ‡ ‡

Elena had just gotten back from her daily ten-kilometer run and was cooling off in her room when there was a knock at her door. She looked through the peephole to see who it was. Noelle. She opened the door. "Hi. Did Ben call?"

"He did. He and Sergei just got in. They'll be here in about half an hour."

"Great. How was their flight?"

"Pretty good. I think they're going to get unpacked here and then head out to dinner. I suggested that seafood place down at Aker Brygge."

"You're not going to have dinner with Ben?"

Noelle shook her head. "I'll see him when they get in, and then after they get back from dinner. Besides, we didn't want to leave Sergei on his own on his first evening in Oslo, and we thought it might be awkward for you and Sergei if we all went out together."

"Oh, I'm fine," replied Elena with practiced nonchalance, "but I think you're right about Sergei. The last time I saw him, we broke up in a restaurant and I walked out on him. That can't have been easy for him. I don't want to ruin his first evening here by having to see me again across a restaurant table."

"That might bring up some bad memories, huh?" said Noelle.

"It might. It's better that we see each other tomorrow morning. He'll be focused on work, which should make it easier for him."

"Yeah. So, what do you want to do for dinner? Want to try that French place in the Oslo City building?"

"Sure, that sounds good."

After Noelle left, Elena sat on the edge of her bed, cooling off after her run. Her mind kept replaying the lunch at Singha when she and Sergei broke up. She'd already gone over it in her head hundreds of times in the nearly three months since it happened, analyzing and weighing everything each of them had said, every gesture and expression. There was really no reason for her to think about it anymore, but it took an effort not to.

She sighed and forced herself to think about her visit to the Munch Museum that afternoon. Sergei was history, but he was recent history. In a few more months, she'd be dating someone else and Sergei would be a faint memory. In the meantime, all she could do was push him out of her thoughts whenever she found him there.

She was about to go take a shower when there was another knock on the door. She glanced through the peephole. It was Noelle again. "Hi. What's up?" Elena asked when she opened the door.

"Well, uh, Ben called me again. Sergei says he has no problem having dinner with us. He suggested that all four of us have dinner at Lekter'n."

"Ben suggested it?"

"Sergei suggested it," Noelle clarified.

"He did? Oh."

"I thought Sergei was just being polite, but Ben said he seemed to really mean it. I told Ben I'd talk to you and get back to him. So, what do you think?"

Elena shrugged. "If Sergei is okay with it, I certainly am. Did you guys set a time?"

"No. How about eight o'clock?"

"Perfect. I'll come over to your room at 7:45."

As soon as Noelle was gone, Elena took a quick shower and shaved her legs while mentally scheduling the remaining time before dinner. It was 5:40 when she got out of the shower. She could be at the Oslo City shopping center by 6:15. She would need to buy a new outfit. She had a suit that would be fine for tomorrow, but other than that she had mostly casual pants, tops, and shoes—the sorts of things that traveled well and were comfortable to wear while walking around museums and sculpture gardens, but were entirely inadequate for dinner with an ex-boyfriend.

She looked at herself critically in the mirror as she blow-dried her hair. She had spent a fair amount of time outdoors while in Norway and she had gotten a light tan, which was good. However, she was about a month overdue for a haircut, which was bad. She debated whether she should try to get an appointment with a stylist before dinner. She decided against it. The last thing she wanted was to have a stylist she'd never met before butcher her hair. Besides, Sergei liked her with long hair.

‡ ‡ ‡

Two busy hours later, Elena stood in front of the mirror again, making a last minute assessment. She had found a sweater, slacks, and scarf outfit that complemented her slender figure and long legs without being racy. The black fabric of the scarf also provided a nice contrast to her blonde hair, which hung a few inches below her shoulders. She wore it in a simple, straight style that was partially pulled back in an onyx-embossed hair clip. It had turned out pretty well, though she definitely would have to get it cut when she got back home.

She took a deep breath and walked next door to Noelle's room. She knocked and Ben opened the door. "Hey, Elena. It's good to see you."

"Hi, Ben!" she replied as she gave him a polite hug. She glanced over his shoulder and saw Sergei standing a few feet behind. "Hi, Sergei!" she said and hugged him too, making sure to use exactly the same tone and platonic embrace she had used with Ben.

"Hello, Elena," Sergei said. "I'm glad you could make it for dinner."

The four of them went down to the lobby and caught a cab to Lekter'n. It was not as crowded as it had been when Noelle and Elena ate there on their first night in Norway, so they were able to get a table right on the water. A brisk breeze blew across the harbor, ridden by seagulls that floated over the choppy sea a few feet from the edge of the restaurant. They hung virtually motionless in the air as they watched for herring in the waters below or scraps dropped by diners. Elena watched for a moment, marveling at their ability to seemingly levitate with only the occasional flick of a feather. She turned back to the rest of the group and caught Sergei watching her, though he instantly dropped his eyes to his menu.

After a few minutes of catching-up small talk, Ben said, "So tell me more about what you've found at Bjornsen Norge. Based on the little bit you gave me on the phone, it sounds like you've come across some interesting stuff in the past couple of days."

Noelle nodded. "I've been going through their expense account backup, and I've been coming across some questionable entries—trips to ski resorts for directors of the parent company, art purchases that seem to have been delivered to the homes of major shareholders, and things like that. The supporting documents aren't all in one place, of course. They're scattered through the files and they've been disguised as routine business expenses in a lot of cases, so finding them is a lot of work." She turned to Sergei. "By the way, thanks for coming over to help, Sergei. Henrik Haugeland has been working with me, but we really need someone else with experience reviewing financial documents and a good feel for when something isn't right in them."

"I only have a couple of days before I have to go back," he replied, "but in the meantime I'm happy to do what I can."

"I'd also love to help, of course," said Elena, "but unfortunately I've never handled any financial fraud cases."

"That really is unfortunate," commented Sergei with a smile. "You know, I think I still have enough pull at the Bureau that I might be able to do something about that. Do you want me to give your supervisor a call and see if he'll put you on a nice, big bank investigation with whole warehouses full of financial documents for you to look at? You'll be an expert in financial fraud by the time you're done."

Elena shook her head. "That's okay. I don't have your tolerance for danger and excitement; I'd burn out after a week."

Sergei raised his eyebrows in mock surprise. "You'll never know what you're missing."

"It takes a special kind of courage to do document review in a financial case," said Ben, patting Noelle's hand.

The waitress arrived with their food. After she left, Ben asked, "So, honey, what else have you found on your expeditions into the dark wilds of Bjornsen Norge's accounting files?"

"I'm pretty sure the money from that Cleverlad account has been going straight to the expense account to cover those questionable expenses. I'll need to track down more of the expenses to be sure the numbers add up, but it's looking that way so far."

Ben shook his head. "And let me guess: The directors and shareholders who went on ski trips and got art and so on all voted to kick out Gunnar."

"Yep."

"What a coincidence." He paused. "Why wouldn't Karl just bribe these guys out of his own pocket? Why do it through the company where he'd have to leave a paper trail?"

"He'd also leave a paper trail if he did it on his own nickel," Sergei said. "One of the first things the Bureau does in a fraud investigation is get the target's bank and credit card records. That's usually where the most obvious dirt is. This guy is not only keeping his records clean, he's keeping the records of his main company clean. We had to go all the way to Norway to figure out what he's been up to, and we only knew to make the trip because his brother happened to have a document in his files that pointed us here. If he was going to commit bribery, this wasn't a bad strategy."

"Plus it saved him about seven million dollars," added Noelle.

"That too," agreed Sergei.

"I'll need to put someone on the stand to testify about what you've found," said Ben. "Haugeland sounds like a natural choice. Is his English as good as advertised?"

"It is," replied Noelle. "He's fluent. He's got an accent, of course, but he's completely understandable."

"Good," Ben said. "Do you think he'd be willing to come to America to testify?"

Noelle took a bite of her grilled salmon and chewed thoughtfully for a moment. "I haven't asked him, but I think he would."

Ben looked at her in surprise. "Really? I hope you're right. It's one thing for him to give us quiet access to the company's records and explain some stuff to us off the record. Flying to America and testifying under oath that his boss has been committing fraud is something else, particularly since that boss is likely to be right there in the courtroom with him."

"That's true," said Elena, "but I'm sure that if Henrik thought that testifying was the right thing to do, he would do it, even if it meant personal sacrifice."

"That's quite an endorsement," responded Ben. "How do you know that?"

"Henrik Haugeland is a remarkable person," she replied. "I don't know if Noelle told you, but he and his wife adopted eight Russian street children because they thought it was the right thing to do. If he was willing to do that, I'm pretty sure he'd be willing to fly to Chicago and face Karl Bjornsen in a courtroom."

"I wish more people thought that was the right thing to do—and were willing to actually do it," Sergei said. "Adopting street kids, I mean. My cousin is a street cop in Moscow, and she has to deal with these kids all the time. A lot of them have virtually no education and have all sorts of problems—health issues, addiction issues, behavior issues. She says the worst part of her job is seeing some nine- or ten-year-old on a street corner and knowing that there's basically no hope for him or her. Their lives have already been destroyed. What inspired a couple of Norwegians to take in kids like that—*eight* of them, no less?"

"Love," replied Elena. "They have a lot of love for these children, and it's amazing how it turns their lives around."

Sergei leaned forward slightly and the late evening sun glowed in his dark brown eyes. "The kids' lives or the Haugelands'?"

"Both, really. They are an amazing couple. I think you'd enjoy meeting them and seeing them with the two children they still have at home."

"I'd like to," said Sergei. "By the way, I'd heard that they were Christian. Did that come up?"

"I think they said something about that." There was a brief pause in the conversation and Elena realized that all three of them were watching her. "You know, one of the things I like about religion—um, particularly Christianity, is that it encourages people to help those who are less fortunate, like those Russian street kids. That's a great teaching. I wish more people took it to heart."

"Mm-hmm," Noelle said, but no one else said anything.

"It's, um, really great to meet people who take their beliefs seriously," Elena continued awkwardly. "They remind me of my Aunt Darya—you met her, Sergei. She was one of the first real environmentalists in the old Soviet Union. She was always bugging the local officials to stop dumping untreated sewage and chemical plant waste into the river near her hometown. When they wouldn't listen to her, she personally marched up to the mayor while Gorbachev was visiting and dumped a bucket of river sludge on the floor right in front of them. She said, 'This is what you're doing to our beautiful river!' She went to jail for that, but the mayor was so embarrassed that he cleaned up the river before another national leader came to town. People like her and the Haugelands really make a difference. They make me want to find a cause I care about and make the world a better place."

Sergei leaned back in his chair, and for an instant Elena thought she saw something like regret in his eyes. Or was it disappointment? But he smiled and said, "I remember Aunt Darya. She is an impressive woman, and a powerful conversationalist."

Elena chuckled. "She likes to talk," she explained to Ben and Noelle. "Sergei spent three hours in her apartment last summer while my mother and I went to visit a sick relative." She turned back to Sergei. "She really liked you, by the way. You listen well."

The conversation moved off into anecdotes about colorful relatives and then onto other topics. The sun sank behind the shops of Aker Brygge as the four friends talked and laughed. The awkwardness and coldness that Elena had half-expected to exist between her and Sergei never appeared. In fact, quite the opposite; he was as funny and easy to talk to as ever. It felt as if they had never been apart. There was no overt romance between them, of course, but Elena wondered what would happen if they wound up alone together at some point over the next couple of days.

After a round of coffee drinks, they paid the check and headed back to the hotel. They chatted for a moment more in the lobby beside the elevators, and then Ben said, "Well, I think I'm going to head back to our room and do a little more work on my interview outline for Henrik Haugeland. Would you mind looking it over, sweetheart? You know him and I don't."

"Sure," replied Noelle. "Do I get a back rub while I'm reading?"

Ben grinned. "You drive a hard bargain." He pushed the up button on the elevator call panel. "Have a good night, guys," he said to Sergei and Elena as the doors opened. "We'll see you tomorrow morning."

Elena glanced at Sergei and he looked back at her. He stifled a yawn. "I think I'm going to turn in. I had a rough flight and I'm beat."

"Me too," said Elena. "I've had a busy day." They joined the Corbins in the elevator and they all rode up in silence.

‡ ‡ ‡

Ben was in a good mood the next afternoon. Haugeland would make a good witness. He knew Bjornsen Norge's accounting system extremely well and took the same view of what they had found in its files that Noelle had expressed at dinner. At least as important, he was an unbiased and articulate witness with no ax to grind. Bert Siwell would have a hard time undermining his credibility at trial.

Best of all, he was willing to come to Chicago to tell his story to a jury.

Ben had already sent a quick e-mail report to Gunnar, who would still have been fast asleep when the interview ended, and now he sat with Noelle at an outdoor cafe on Karl Johan, Oslo's main street and a popular tourist destination. Slottet, the main royal palace, stood at one end of the street and the Storting, or parliament building, stood at the other. A popular park ran along one side of Karl Johan, and dozens of shops, restaurants, and cafés lined the other. Ben and Noelle both ordered some strong, black Norwegian coffee and enjoyed watching the crowds stroll past.

Noelle had just started plotting what to do with Sergei and Elena, both of whom were safely away doing other things, but Ben's cell phone rang. He looked at the number on the screen and took the call. "Hello, Gunnar. Did you get my e-mail?"

"I just read it over breakfast," Gunnar's voice rumbled over the phone. "That's good news about Henrik. I'm glad that he's able to help, but your e-mail isn't the reason why I called. I received another e-mail this morning, this one from Finn Sorensen. Have I ever told you about him?"

"I don't think so. Who is he?"

"He's a botanist at the University of Oslo and an old friend of mine. He is the scientist who first studied the plant from which we make XD-463. He's also the one who first told me about it and helped my company buy some seeds from the Norwegian government.

"He wrote to tell me that a research team has found the cave that held the original seeds and leaves. He says it's not too far from Oslo and is worth a trip. An archaeological team from the University of Oslo is getting ready to study it right now. Since Dr. Sorensen knows them, he volunteered to cut through some red tape and arrange a guided tour for me. But since I won't be in Norway in the next week, I thought you might want to go, if you have time. You really shouldn't leave Norway without taking at least one hike in the mountains."

"It would be like visiting France without touring at least one winery, wouldn't it?" replied Ben. "Let me check with Noelle." He covered the mouthpiece on his phone and said, "They've found the mountain cave where the Neurostim plants came from, and Gunnar's offered to arrange a tour for us. What do you think?"

"I've done plenty of sightseeing already, but you go ahead. I need to spend a few hours number-crunching and organizing what I've found so far, so you'll be on your own for a while tomorrow anyway."

Ben nodded and uncovered the mouthpiece. "Sure, I'd love to. How's tomorrow?"

"I'll e-mail and ask. I'll also give him your cell phone number so that you can talk directly."

Over the remainder of the afternoon, it was decided that Ben, Sergei, and Elena would drive as far into the mountains as Elena's rental car could handle. Dr. Sorensen would meet them at a logging shack—the point where he said the roads got really bad—and take them the rest of the way. Elena, Ben, and Sergei went shopping for hiking boots and mosquito repellent, while Noelle stayed behind and congratulated herself for having the foresight to say no to Gunnar's offer.

‡ ‡ ‡

The next morning's drive into the mountains was scenic, but nerve-racking—especially for the driver. The modern highways around Oslo gave way to a winding, two-lane road that had a sheer drop on one side—protected by an entirely inadequate-looking guardrail—and a towering mountain on the other, its splintered stone face held in place by wire netting intended to prevent boulders from crashing down on motorists below. Elena drove as quickly as she felt she could, but she soon found herself leading a motorcade of frustrated Norwegian drivers.

They reached the logging shack where they had agreed to meet and found Dr. Sorensen waiting for them. He was a rangy man of middle height, who dressed and looked like a lumberjack on the verge of retirement. An old and battered Land Rover was parked behind the shack. He walked over as they parked and got out of the car. "Finn Sorensen," he said, greeting each of them with a firm, somewhat abrupt handshake.

They clambered into his Land Rover and set off up a rough logging road at a bone-jarring speed. As he drove, Dr. Sorensen kept up a running monologue, speaking at a near-shout to make himself heard over the sound of the engine and the constant rattle and thump of the stony, deeply rutted track. He gave them an animated lecture on the area's history from the last ice age to the present. "Down there," he said, pointing to a stream a hundred feet below the road, "we excavated mammoth bones and teeth last year. Maybe you heard of the famous finds on Wrangel Island? These fossils may be even more recent than those—from the time of the pyramids. We were much excited because of this and because where mammoths live, hunters may live also. This is how we found the cave that I take you to. We searched for caves and other places where mammoth hunters might camp. One of my students found this cave just last week."

"Are we close to it?" asked Elena, who was riding shotgun and had an uncomfortably clear view of the streambed below. If she had reached out her window and dropped a rock, it would have landed in the water far below.

"It is still about five kilometers," the scientist replied, "but soon we must walk. This road does not go very much closer."

A few minutes later, he stopped the car in the middle of the road—there was no place to pull over—and set the parking brake. They got out and followed him into a thick pine forest. There were no paths, no buildings, and no sign that any human being had ever set foot there before them. After the constant noise and vibration of the drive, the woods seemed preternaturally still. The wind whispered through the pine needles and they could hear the faint tinkle and babble of dozens of tiny streams and rills that raced downhill from the melting snow a thousand feet above them. The only other sounds were their footsteps and an occasional comment from Dr. Sorensen, who now led them single-file up a steep slope and thus could not lecture effectively.

After an hour and a half of vigorous hiking, they reached a sudden break in the trees, stepping out into a long, narrow clearing filled with broken stumps and downed trees. Shocks of brilliant green grass and clusters of wildflowers pushed up through gaps in the fallen timber. A sparkling brook flowed through a little gully in the middle of the grass and flowers before vanishing among the trees. It looked as if someone had driven a giant bulldozer through the area.

"What happened here?" asked Ben.

"Avalanche," said Dr. Sorensen, pointing to a wall of dirty ice at the far end of the clearing. "About one hundred meters of that glacier broke off and crashed through the trees to make this empty space." He started walking toward the glacier, picking his way among the logs and rocks. "Here it is!" he called. "Look on the stone below the ice."

A ridge of mossy rock about five feet high jutted out below the glacier. As they got closer, a large crack became visible. It was about three feet wide and four feet high. Dr. Sorensen pulled a small flashlight out of his pocket and ducked in. The other three followed, taking care not to bang their heads on the low entrance.

The blackness of the cave enveloped them, and the air inside was still and cold. After a few yards, they could see Dr. Sorensen's breath in the light of his flashlight and the light sweat on their foreheads turned chilly and a little uncomfortable. The vibrant scents of pine, sun, and water vanished and were replaced by a peculiar stale, lifeless smell—what Ben would later describe as "the smell of time."

They walked along in a half-crouch at first, but the cave expanded quickly and within twenty yards even Sergei, who was six feet two, could stand upright without fear. "You see there are no stalactites or stalagmites," said Dr. Sorensen, his voice sounding unnaturally loud in the underground silence. He shone the light around him to demonstrate his point. "Also, the walls are not smooth limestone, but rough granite with many sharp edges and points. This cave was not made by water like most caves. A great violence of nature ripped a hole in the mountains. Maybe that is a reason why they chose this cave."

"'They' chose it?" asked Sergei. "Who were 'they'?"

The scientist stopped and looked back over his shoulder. "I apologize. I told Gunnar, but I forgot to tell you. The berserkers. Have you heard about them?"

"No," replied Sergei. "What were they?"

"Odin's holy warriors. They had the strength of bears and the fury of a mountain storm. They—ah, we are almost at the end. I will show you some of them."

The cave expanded into an open area about thirty feet across and eighty feet long. The ceiling rose up higher than the flashlight beam could reach. Most of the floor was rough and uneven, but an area near the far end had been flattened. Wide, vertical black streaks on the rock walls behind the flat area showed where fires had once burned. In the middle of the smooth floor stood a low table of dark wood and several benches. "Come look on these and you shall see berserkers," said Dr. Sorensen as they picked their way across the granite floor. "But do not touch them. They are a thousand years old or more. The air and the dark preserved them, but they are very fragile."

They reached the smooth-floored area and Dr. Sorensen played his flashlight on the ancient objects. They were intricately carved in much the same way as the items displayed at the Field Museum, but the motifs were different; instead of the dragons, serpents, and abstract intertwining patterns Ben had seen in Chicago, here were savage images of battle or hunting, it was difficult to tell which. Groups of armored men carrying swords and spears fled before bears that gripped axes in their forepaws and stood on two legs among the dismembered corpses of their foes. Standing or floating over some of the scenes was the figure of a giant, one-eyed man with a bird on his shoulder. "Did the berserkers control these bear demons?" asked Elena.

"The berserkers *were* the bear demons," said Dr. Sorensen. "*Berserk* means 'bear shirt' in Old Norse. Some sagas say they went to battle wearing no armor, only wolf- or bearskin shirts. Others say they actually became bears. Before fighting, they went into the mountains to secret places. When they came down, they were in *berserkergang*, the berserker state of mind or being. In *berserkergang*, they were in a rage that made them very strong and very fast and they felt no pain in battle. Some stories even say their severed limbs would continue to attack their enemies until they were burned. Your English word *berserk* comes from these stories. Snorri Sturluson, for example, says—"

"What caused *berserkergang*?" asked Ben urgently. "Do you know?"

"The sagas say Odin—the figure with one eye and a raven on his shoulder—gave the berserkers their powers," replied Dr. Sorensen, "but, of course, that is not true. The main theory, which I teach my students, is that *berserkergang* was a mass hysteria, maybe increased by a drug."

"Do you know what drug?" asked Ben.

Dr. Sorensen smiled and held up a finger. "Ah, now you ask an excellent question, Ben. The berserkers vanished a thousand years ago, and the secrets of what they did in the mountains vanished with them. Now, here in this cave, I think we have the answer."

"They ate the plant that lost hiker found in here," said Ben.

Dr. Sorensen's smile broadened and he looked every bit the professor pleased with the answer of a clever pupil.

"Exactly."

Chapter Twelve

Problem Solving

At exactly 5:30 pm, a woman's smoky voice crooned "Ring, ring, ring" from the computer speakers on George Kulish's U-shaped desk. George glanced at the clock on the monitor and smiled. "Right on time."

He clicked on the videophone icon, and the screen was instantly filled with the fat face of Grigori Kurilev. Grigori was a gifted biochemist with nearly a dozen patents to his name. His employer paid him well, but not well enough to support the lavish lifestyle he enjoyed. So he moonlighted as a consultant to Cleverlad and a few other high-paying clients. "Good to see you, Grigori."

"And it is good to hear your voice," replied Grigori. "Someday you must turn on your Webcam so that I can see what the great George Kulish looks like. It is a little strange talking to a blank computer screen."

"I can turn on the camera, but of course then I will have to kill you."

Grigori laughed uncertainly. "Perhaps the blank screen is not so bad. You wish to know about the test results, yes?"

"Yes. How difficult is this drug to manufacture?"

Grigori waved a balloonlike hand dismissively. "Very simple. I can make it on my kitchen stove."

"Good. But would the ingredients be difficult to obtain?"

"Not at all. The active ingredients are caffeine and ginseng. You can buy them in any drug store."

"It is not . . . this drug does not contain a previously unknown plant extract?"

"No. I ran the chemistry twice. There is nothing there except caffeine, ginseng, and a couple of common binding agents. There are a dozen basically identical pills you can buy over the counter in any country. If you ground it up and put it in fizzy sugar water, it would be an average energy drink."

"I . . . I see. Thank you very much. Send me the report. Your fee will be wired to your Bahamian account today."

George clicked the End Teleconference button and the screen went blank. He stared at it for several minutes. So Karl Bjornsen had sent him fake pills. That act could not go unpunished. George's first inclination was to deal with Karl the same way he would deal with any cheating supplier—have him killed discreetly, but not so discreetly that his other business partners wouldn't hear about it and get the message. The problem, though, was that Bjornsen Pharmaceuticals was not just any cheating supplier—it was the exclusive source of Neurostim. One of the reasons for George's success was that he had learned to spot hot drugs early and lock up suppliers before his competitors knew what was going on. Neurostim was going to be huge, and if he played his cards right, he would be the only significant nonprescription source of it in the world. To do that, he would need Karl Bjornsen alive and cooperative.

George had hoped that the threat of revelations about his boardroom bribery would be enough to keep Karl in line, but apparently not. Karl was a smart man, smarter than George had given him credit for. His threat had been a bluff and Karl had called it. The collateral damage from following through on that threat was simply too high—George could not reveal Karl's misdeeds without putting a spotlight on Cleverlad's role, thereby cutting off his access to all Bjornsen drugs and giving the FBI and Interpol another avenue to track his company's activities. It was like being locked in a closet with

Karl and trying to threaten him with a hand grenade. He drummed his fingers on the arm of his chair. He would need to find another way to apply pressure.

The elevator chimed and he turned to see the doors open. Pyotr emerged, looking worried.

"What is it Pyotr?"

"We have a problem," the big Russian announced as he walked over with long, rapid strides. "There's someone at Bjornsen's Norwegian office going through their records about us."

"Who?" demanded George.

"Someone who is suing them, I think. I, uh, I don't have all the details. These people are coming in after the office is closed and looking at the records in secret."

"Interesting . . . interesting." George sat silently, deep in thought. Pyotr stood in front of him, shifting his weight uncomfortably from one foot to the other. A smile slowly formed on George's face. Then he laughed. "Pyotr, my boy, you said we had a problem. I think we have a solution."

‡ ‡ ‡

When Kim's call came, David Lee was sitting at an outdoor table at Sharkeez, sipping a margarita and going over old oncology exam questions. "Hey, Kimmy, how are you doing?"

"Well, um, I'd be doing better if I didn't have to give you bad news," she said.

He could picture her twisting her hair around her finger as she talked. She always did that when she was nervous and talking on the phone. He smiled at the mental image. "I didn't make it into Phase II, did I?"

"Nobody from Phase I did. They decided to use all new participants for Phase II. I hope you're not too disappointed."

He wasn't. He had been researching Phase II protocols since he and Kim had last talked, and he had concluded that there was a good chance Bjornsen would opt for a fresh batch of test subjects rather than include holdovers from Phase I. "It's a little bit of a letdown, but no big deal."

"Really?"

"Really. I've been thinking about what you said. You're right—all I really need to do is get back into my groove, and I can do that without Neurostim as a crutch. What will really help is getting through the oncology and immunology textbooks over the summer. I'm really developing a rhythm and I think it'll carry into next semester."

"That's great!" He could hear the relief in her voice. "I was actually a little worried about telling you about Phase II. The last time we talked about it, you seemed a little like, I don't know, like you might be stressed about going off Neurostim. I'm glad you're not."

He laughed. "I'm sitting at the beach right now, having a margarita, watching the sun set in the Pacific, and talking to the most beautiful girl in the world. How can I be stressed about anything? Seriously, don't worry about it; I'm fine. So, how are things at work? Any interesting stories?"

"Oh, yeah. Remember that guy I told you about? Dr. Reddy?"

"The one who wanted to know if you had a boyfriend?"

"Yeah, well guess what? It turns out he's married and has a family back in India."

"No way. Are you sure?"

"Uh-huh. Our team went out to lunch yesterday, and someone asked him, 'So, when are you planning to bring Keya and the kids over to the States?' He got all embarrassed and was like, 'Uh, I don't know. I'm not sure it will be possible.' Then one of the lab techs leaned over to me and said, 'Of course not. That would ruin his social life.'"

"Do you know if he just flirts with hot interns, or is it worse than that?" David asked, jotting down notes as he spoke.

"Oh, it's worse. I saw him dirty dancing with some girl at a nightclub last weekend. They left together in his Porsche."

"Wow, what a tool. It's a relief to know that my competition is such pond scum."

"For him to be competition, he'd have to be in your league. I knew right away that he wasn't, even if he does drive a better car."

"I thought you liked the Impala. I painted over the rust spots and everything."

She laughed. "Hey, I've got to go. I promised I'd call my mom tonight."

"No problem. Miss you."

"Miss you too. I can't wait until we're back together."

‡ ‡ ‡

Kim put down the phone and smiled. She had been worried about more than David's stress level and confidence. He had been acting a little weird since he started taking the Neurostim—nothing big enough or concrete enough to catch the attention of the research team, but things that someone who knew him as well as she did would notice.

For instance, last week he had told her a story about being tail-gated on the freeway by some guy in a Mercedes SUV who was drinking a cup of coffee while talking on his cell phone. David had slammed on his brakes and then hit the accelerator a split second later to avoid getting rear-ended. The other driver slammed on his brakes too, of course, spilling coffee all over himself and losing his cell phone out the window.

It was a funny story and Kim had laughed when David told it to her, but it was completely unlike him—or rather, completely unlike the David she had known at the beginning of the summer. The old David would have been irritated by the tailgater and probably would have said something to anyone who was in the car with him, but that would have been it. He would never have retaliated, particularly in such an aggressive and risky way. When she mentioned that to him, he had shrugged it off, saying that someone needed to teach the guy in the Mercedes a lesson, and that he was the right person to do it because Neurostim gave him fast enough reflexes to avoid an accident.

She hadn't argued with him, but she had secretly hoped that he would be off the drug soon and back to his old self. When Dr. Corrigan announced that there would be no overlap between the Phase I and II participants, Kim had been relieved, though she hadn't looked forward to telling David. But now that was over and he had taken it well. Problem solved.

She smiled again and picked up the phone to call her mother.

‡ ‡ ‡

Drs. Chow and Corrigan sat across the table from Karl Bjornsen in Bjornsen Pharmaceuticals' executive conference room. A projection screen stood at one end of the room and the lights had been dimmed. A small projector sat on the table, connected to Dr. Corrigan's laptop by a cable.

"Okay, here's the chart showing the different liver enzymes we monitored in each of our Phase I participants," she said as a slide appeared on the screen. It displayed a number of roughly flat lines bearing the abbreviations for various liver-related chemicals. "We won't have a complete picture of Neurostim's pharmacology and pharmacokinetics until at least the end of Phase II, but liver performance tests give us a good early read on the potential for problems, because most drugs are metabolized in the liver. You'll notice that the subjects' liver enzymes and functions are all normal, both at the outset of Phase I and at the end. The numbers float around a little, but they're all in the normal range. Two participants actually had their liver function improve, probably because we insisted that no one consume more than one ounce of alcohol per day during the trial."

"Blood pressure and cardiac function were both the same story," said Dr. Chow. "Could you show the next slide, Tina?" She hit a key on her computer and a new chart appeared on the screen showing various measures of cardiac health. "See?" continued Dr. Chow. "No change in blood pressure, resting heart rate, or any other heart function we measured. That's unusual, and positive, for a drug that has stimulant effects."

"So we've got a green light for Phase II?" asked Karl.

"The green light will have to come from the FDA," cautioned Dr. Chow, "but none of the data from Phase I gives me any reason to think they won't give it. The results have all been very positive. This looks like a safe drug, which is all they really care about, particularly at this stage."

"Good, good," said Karl. "Did Phase I give us any idea about how well it will work in humans? I know the protocol was set up to look at maximum tolerated dose, but did we learn anything about efficacy?"

"Most of the dosage levels we used in Phase I were pretty low," said Dr. Corrigan. "They resulted in blood levels of the drug and its metabolites that were near the bottom of the levels at which we began to see effects in animals. Still, we did ask participants to report any positive effects they noticed, and the anecdotal evidence was encouraging."

"It's nothing we can put in a press release," added Dr. Chow, "but it is quite positive. In fact, it excited me enough that I asked Tina to put together a highly unscientific chart to show you."

Dr. Corrigan clicked her mouse and a new slide appeared on the screen. It showed three lines: red, yellow, and blue. The y-axis of the chart was titled Dosage and the x-axis was titled Time. The red and yellow lines remained essentially unchanged across the chart, while the blue line rose sharply, particularly toward the right side of the slide. "The red line represents overall heart function," explained Dr. Corrigan. "The yellow line represents overall liver function. And the blue represents reports of positive effects from participants. We weren't actively monitoring drug efficacy during Phase I, but we had asked participants to report any effects they noticed."

"But the participants all knew what Neurostim is supposed to do, right?" observed Karl. "Just as a psychological phenomenon, wouldn't you expect them to start noticing and reporting positive effects as their dosage level went up, even if Neurostim didn't work at all?"

Drs. Chow and Corrigan both smiled.

"Yes, we would," said Dr. Chow. He nodded to Dr. Corrigan, who clicked her mouse again. A green line appeared on the chart. It rose from left to right, but at less than half the rate of the blue line. "The green line represents the reports of positive effects from members of the placebo group. As I said, the results are encouraging. Not scientifically reliable, but encouraging nonetheless."

"Yes," agreed Karl. "Yes, they certainly are. You two and your staffs have done some really first-rate work—which I'll let you get back to now. Thanks for stopping by to update me."

After the meeting, Karl walked back to his office, humming happily. Things were falling into place nicely. Now there was just one major loose end he needed to tie up before the trial started. After settling into his chair, he picked up the phone and dialed Alex Geist's number.

"Hello, Mr. Bjornsen," said Geist's monochromatic voice a few seconds later.

"Hello, Alex. I have a project for you. I'd like a report on Cleverlad .ru. They're an Internet pharmacy. I want the works—key employees, detailed finances, any legal or regulatory issues they may have, and so on. When can you have that for me?"

"What are your intentions regarding that company?"

Karl frowned. "Why do you ask? Are they a client of yours?"

"No, but based on press reports, they appear to be a client of yours."

"So what?" Karl said. Geist's hesitancy irritated him, as did being reminded of the fiasco in the courtroom. As Geist alluded, the business papers had reported Karl's awkward testimony about Cleverlad, which had created a PR headache for the company and had the potential to take some of the shine off of Karl's previously sterling reputation.

"Cleverlad is . . . of interest to us," said Geist. "My associates and I are not on friendly terms with them. In light of your relationship to them, I will need to know the use to which you intend to put the information you are requesting."

"Confidentially speaking, I'd rather not do business with them," replied Karl. "I'm hoping your report will help me cut our ties with Cleverlad."

"I see. Based on that representation, we are willing to provide you a dossier on both the company and its owner, Mr. George Kulish. I will also make you an offer: We will reduce our fees by fifty percent for this project if you will agree to share with us any information you independently obtain regarding Mr. Kulish or any entity related to him. We will keep any information you provide confidential and we will not resell it."

"What's your interest in Kulish?"

Geist didn't speak for several seconds. "I will share with you a piece of information that will not appear in the formal dossier, but which may prove important to you. Several years ago, we were retained to investigate an entity related to Mr. Kulish. One of our employees traveled to Russia as part of the investigation. He was killed in a plane crash. The Russian authorities determined that the cause of the crash was a flaw in the software that operated the plane's hydraulic system. We subsequently determined that the flaw had been deliberately introduced shortly before our employee boarded the plane. There have been other, similar incidents in which individuals unfriendly to Mr. Kulish have suffered unfortunate circumstances."

"I see," replied Karl. He wasn't surprised to learn that George Kulish was a murderer, but it was unsettling to hear that he had managed to kill one of Geist's people. "That's good to know. One other thing: I need you to get records of every phone call made between our Norwegian facility and George Kulish, Cleverlad, or any of its affiliates. I also need the same information for each of our Norwegian employees."

"Have they signed waivers authorizing release of this information?" asked Geist.

"Of course," replied Karl. "It's part of their standard employment packages. I'll send you copies."

"Excellent. We will have the entire report ready for you two business days after I receive the waivers."

"And if you find that any of our people have been talking to Cleverlad, let me know what else you can find out about them quickly," said Karl, crossing the penultimate item off his mental checklist.

"Of course."

"One final thing: I remember you saying that you used to have very good connections at a number of intelligence and law enforcement organizations, both on national and international levels. How current are those connections?"

‡ ‡ ‡

At 7:00 the next morning, David Lee sat down at his computer, turned it on, and put on his headset. As he waited for the computer to boot up, he glanced over his notes one last time. He opened his Internet phone program, activated the privacy feature to make the call effectively untraceable, and dialed Bjornsen Pharmaceuticals' main number. His heart raced as the phone rang. A woman's voice answered, "Good morning, Bjornsen Pharmaceuticals."

"Good morning. Could you tell Dr. Reddy that Keya is on the phone for him?"

A few seconds later, a male voice with an Indian accent said, "Hello, Keya."

"Hello, Dr. Reddy."

The line was silent for several seconds. "Who are you?"

"I'm your conscience."

"Is this some kind of joke? Who is this?"

"I know what you did last weekend, and I think I need to tell your wife."

The line was silent again, this time for nearly half a minute. David began to sweat and feared that he had overplayed his hand. He reached for his mouse and was about to cut the connection, but he heard a shaky breath in his ear and knew that all was well. "I don't know what you're talking about."

"Now you're lying too."

"What . . . what do you want from me?"

"You're working with a drug called Neurostim. Send one thousand ten-milligram doses to PO Box 4653 in Los Angeles, 90012."

"I can't do that. That much would be missed."

"No, it won't. Your company just issued a press release saying that they're starting a major, nationwide clinical testing program. They'll be using a lot of the drug and shipping it to participating labs around the country. It will be easy for a box to get lost in the mail."

"I will lose my job and get deported if I am caught," pleaded Dr. Reddy. "I might even go to jail. Can I just send you money? Maybe five thousand dollars?"

"No. Listen to your conscience. Send me the pills or Keya finds out what you've been doing. If I don't have them in one week, I'll call her. And if there are any problems when I pick up the pills, someone else will call her if I can't. Good-bye."

"Wait, I—" David clicked his mouse and Dr. Reddy's frantic voice vanished. He wiped the sweat off his palms and smiled. He was well on the way to locking in his supply of Neurostim through at least the end of next school year and maybe longer. Problem solved.

‡ ‡ ‡

Gunnar sat in the Corbins' office lobby, thinking pleasant thoughts. Ben had returned from Norway the day before and had called to suggest that they meet to discuss the agenda for the remaining three weeks before trial. Based on the e-mail reports Ben had sent from Norway, that shouldn't be too difficult. According to Ben, the meeting with Gunnar's old friend Henrik Haugeland had gone well, and Noelle Corbin's auditing project had borne the hoped-for fruit. They had a clear advantage over Karl now, so presumably the main pretrial task was to hold that advantage.

The door opened and Ben walked into the lobby, exuding measured confidence. "Good morning, Gunnar. Let's head back to the conference room."

"All right." They walked down the hallway to the little conference room that Gunnar knew well after more than a dozen visits. He sat down in his usual chair, took a sip of the coffee proffered by the receptionist, and listened to Ben.

"As I think you know, the trip to Norway paid off nicely. Henrik Haugeland should make a good witness, and the documents he helped us find will be useful. That's the good news. The bad news is that Karl's lawyers have been busy doing the same thing I have—filling sandbags and lining them up to drop on you at trial.

"We don't know what they've got, and they don't know what we've got. But that will all change in six days when we have to exchange witness and exhibit lists. Anything or anyone that's not on those lists can't be brought in at trial."

Gunnar nodded and chuckled. "So they have to put all their cards on the table, and so do we. I wish I could be there to see Karl's face when he finds out that Henrik is going to testify, and he sees all those bribery receipts on our exhibit list. He will go completely nuts."

"So will Bert Siwell," replied Ben. "One of the things we—or really I—have to do between now and then is get ready for Siwell's objections to our evidence. I did some research before we sent Noelle to Norway—enough to know we weren't violating any rules by talking to Henrik and going through Norge's documents—but there's a lot that I still need to do on that front.

"The second main agenda item is mostly on Sergei's plate. In fact, I think he's working on it right now. That item is doing background checks on all our key witnesses, particularly Mr. Haugeland."

"I can vouch for Henrik," Gunnar assured Ben, resting a massive hand on his lawyer's arm. "I've known him for over twenty years. If there were any skeletons in his closet, I'm sure I would know about them."

"I don't doubt it," replied Ben, "but I'm sure Siwell will have investigators digging into Henrik's past five minutes after we send over our witness list. We need to know what they'll find. There may be inaccurate information that we need to know about. I once had a client whose criminal record showed that he had been indicted and convicted in absentia in Canada for check forgery. It turned out that the real forger—who was never caught—had stolen my client's identity and used it to open bank accounts to launder the money. Fortunately, we found this out before trial and we were able to get his record cleared before he took the stand. If we hadn't discovered the problem until opposing counsel asked him about it in front of the jury, it would have been a disaster."

"I hadn't thought of that," said Gunnar. "That's a good point. All right, what else do we have to do before trial?"

"A million little things that will keep me busy, but that you don't need to worry about. The one thing I'd like you to do is give some thought to what you want to do if you win."

"What do you mean?"

Ben took a deep breath and looked his client in the eye. "Gunnar, you talked to Professor Sorensen about what he found in that cave, right?"

"Yes, he told me all about it. He said they found some magnificent artifacts. Once we win this lawsuit and I'm back in charge of the company, I'll have to see if we can arrange another exhibition at the Field Museum and include those."

"Did he also mention that he thinks the plant the hiker found in the cave was used by the berserkers?"

"Yes, he mentioned that. It's an interesting historical footnote. Once Karl finds out, I'll bet he comes up with some way to use it in a marketing campaign."

Ben stared at him for a moment with a look of surprise on his face. "Well, it's more than an interesting footnote, isn't it? It sounded like these berserkers turned into homicidal maniacs after eating the plant and doing whatever rituals they did. Is it a good idea for a company to sell a drug that might turn thousands of people into berserkers? And what about all the soldiers who will be taking the drug; what happens if someone goes berserk while they're flying a bomber or commanding a tank?"

Gunnar digested the news slowly. "That's . . . interesting, very interesting. Finn and I didn't discuss the berserkers in depth, and I confess that I don't know much about them beyond the fact that they were legendary warriors. But if the drug turns people into 'homicidal maniacs,' as you put it, I'm sure that will come out in the preclinical and clinical studies. The FDA will insist that they be designed to catch preliminary signs of behavioral problems long before the dosage levels are high enough for the subjects to become dangerous. That's what clinical trials are for, after all."

‡ ‡ ‡

Six hours later, Gunnar sat in an armchair in his den reading a dusty volume of *Aschehougs Konversasjons Leksikon*, a Norwegian encyclopedia he had bought thirty years ago, but rarely used. Its entry on berserkers was, like everything else he had found on the subject, short on useful data and long on speculation. It simply confirmed that the berserkers would work themselves into a rage during secret ceremonies, and that they were unstoppable in battle. The closest it got to hard facts on berserkers was the following: "In battle, they were enraged, biting their shields, howling like dogs; weapons could not touch them, they ate coals and walked through fire. Some have tried to explain their rage, '*berserkergang*,' as the

206

result of eating psychoactive mushrooms, but this is unknown from ancient sources."

That was hardly the level of certainty and detail he needed. Still, it was encouraging. XD-463 wasn't made from mushrooms, and it didn't appear to cause the kind of psychosis mentioned in *Aschehougs*. Both he and the company had invested a lot in XD-463. Much as he hated the idea of Karl running the company, he hated the idea of XD-463 failing even more. This drug was supposed to be their passage to greatness, to transforming Bjornsen Pharmaceuticals from a regional, middle-market player into a top five company. It would also transform both of the Bjornsen brothers from millionaires into billionaires, based on their large holdings of the company's stock.

His mind turned to the monkey incident Dr. Chatterton had told him about. He had remembered it during his conversation with Ben, but hadn't mentioned it, because he wanted to think about it more before saying anything. It did sound uncomfortably like the berserker behavior *Aschehougs* described—and it was unlike anything he had ever heard about monkeys. He shut the book and put it back in its place on the shelf. Then he began to pace back and forth across the den.

Should he take this to the FDA? If so, he would need something better than "if people taking the drug are provoked, they might howl and bite things." He needed to be able to point to hard evidence that XD-463 was dangerous and that human trials should be halted. Without that, he'd look like nothing more than a disgruntled former executive who was trying to embarrass his successor. He also risked humiliating and damaging his company over nothing.

Or should he do nothing more than pass his worries along to Karl? Gunnar doubted that his brother would intentionally sell a highly dangerous drug, even if billions of dollars were on the line. Instead, he would find a way to convince himself and his inner circle that the drug wasn't actually dangerous. Then he would sell it. He was fond of saying that "a good salesman always sells himself first," and he was a very good salesman.

Gunnar debated calling Finn Sorensen, but he glanced at the clock and realized it would be about 2:00 AM in Norway. He picked up his Rolodex and flipped through it idly. *Who do I know in the U.S. who might know about berserkers?* Then he realized the answer and smiled. "Markus," he said aloud.

When his sons were in college, Gunnar had required each of them to take at least one Scandinavian-oriented class, preferably one focused on international business. Tom had made the most of the opportunity, enrolling in an economics class during a month-long exchange program in Copenhagen. He had even managed to land a part-time job at the Copenhagen stock market. Markus, on the other hand, had sulkily chosen the least useful course he could think of—a poetry seminar deconstructing ancient Norwegian sagas. Maybe it hadn't been so useless after all.

He picked up the phone and dialed Markus's number. "Hi, Mom," Markus said a moment later.

"It's your father."

"Oh. Hello, Dad. What can I do for you?"

"Do you remember that college course you took on the Norse sagas?"

"Yes," said Markus slowly. "I actually took a couple of them. I have a minor in Scandinavian literature."

"Did you ever learn anything about berserkers?"

"Well, yeah. They're in a lot of the older sagas. Why do you ask?"

"Do you remember the drug I was developing when I left the company?"

"Not, uh, not really."

"The one that came from an ancient Norwegian plant found in a cave? The one that was potentially a huge breakthrough for the company?"

"That rings a bell, but I don't remember any of the details. Sorry."

Typical. Gunnar suppressed his irritation and said, "Well, a friend of mine in Norway found the cave, and he thinks the berserkers used it. He thinks they ate this plant to make themselves into super warriors. The company is testing a drug made from the plant, and I'd like to know more about berserkers so I can know how the drug is likely to affect people. I called you because I thought you might be able to help."

"I guess I should have listened more closely when you talked about work over dinner." Markus laughed nervously. "I saved some of my old textbooks. Should I, uh, go see if I can find something useful?"

"Please."

"Okay, hold on." The line was silent for several minutes. Then Gunnar heard the thump of books landing on a table and the rustling of pages. "All right, here we go. This is from Thorbjørn Hornklofi; it's part of a conversation between a raven and a valkyrie after a battle: The valkyrie says, 'Of the berserkers' lot would I ask thee, thou who batten'st on corpses: how fare the fighters who rush forth to battle, and stout-hearted stand 'gainst the foe?' Then the raven responds, 'Wolf-coats are they called, the warriors unfleeing, who bear bloody shields in battle; the darts redden where they dash into battle and shoulder to shoulder stand. 'Tis men tried and true only, who can targes shatter, whom the wise war-lord wants in battle.'"

"That sounds like a lot of what I found," replied Gunnar. "Is there anything more specific about them? Anything that indicates whether they were mentally unstable?"

"Let's see." Gunnar could hear more pages flipping. "Well, they went into some sort of frenzy during battle and no army could stand against them," Markus continued. "I'm not finding much about them during peacetime. There was a wise King Ivar who was a berserker, or he had been one anyway—he was a paraplegic by the time he became king." More flipping. "And some other kings kept berserkers in their courts, but it's not clear whether they were advisors or bodyguards, or maybe both. These are really old sagas and they're garbled in places. Plus, the berserkers were ancient history before any of these were written."

"Really? I hadn't realized that."

"Yeah. There's not much written record from Scandinavia before about 1200, and the berserkers were outlawed about two hundred years before that."

Gunnar chuckled drily. "I'd hate to have been the one who had to enforce that law."

"No kidding. I remember one of my professors saying he wondered how the government pulled that one off. Maybe that was around the time this plant went extinct; I'll bet the berserkers were a lot easier to deal with once they could no longer take their secret wonder drug."

"Good point," replied Gunnar. "I'll bet you're right about that. So, would these sagas have been written by the descendants of the people who outlawed the berserkers?"

"Probably. The sagas would have existed in oral form for a long time before that, though."

"But would you agree that whoever wrote the sagas—and whoever decided which ones to write down—probably was no friend of the berserkers?" persisted Gunnar.

"That's probably fair," agreed Markus. "Any berserkers left would have been outlaws. They also would have been followers of Odin, and Scandinavia had been Christianized by that point. Most of the saga writers show a bias in favor of Christianity and against the old Norse gods."

"So there are no firsthand accounts of berserkers from unbiased sources, right? All we have are stories written down centuries later by authors who probably didn't like berserkers?"

"That's pretty much right," agreed Markus. "Sorry I couldn't be more helpful."

"No, that's fine. This was actually very helpful. Thank you."

"You're welcome. And, uh, good luck with the drug and Uncle Karl and, you know, everything."

‡ ‡ ‡

Elena and Noelle were leaving in less than two days and there was a lot left to do. For Noelle, there were boxes of documents to copy, organize, and ship back to America. As soon as Henrik called to say that the office was empty, Elena drove Noelle over. Henrik and Einar were there waiting to help, so Elena decided to go take care of a few last minute things.

Her first stop was at the historic Nasjonaltheatret, where she picked up a ticket and English program notes for an abridged version of *Peer Gynt* that was playing there that evening. Then she hit the shopping district for one last visit.

This time she wasn't shopping for herself—she had to buy gifts for her parents and several other relatives whom she would be seeing during a weekend stop in Russia before flying back to the States. She had already decided that her parents would get sweaters. The other relatives were harder to shop for; the men would be happy with anything that said Norway on it, but the women would require more thought. They couldn't each get the same thing—that would mean that Elena didn't care enough to shop for them individually. However, their gifts had to look like they had cost almost exactly the same, otherwise Elena would appear to be favoring one relative over another. Also, whatever she bought had to be stylish enough to hold up her reputation as the glamorous member of the family who had been an international athlete and now lived in America.

She briefly considered getting something for Sergei, but decided against it. Their dinner together on his first night in Norway had gone as well as she could have hoped, and he had seemed like he was still interested in her, but nothing ever came of it. He never made any effort to be alone with her, and whenever they were together, he was friendly, but nothing more—though every now and then he would say something or look at her in a way that made her suspect that he was holding himself back.

Part of her wanted to give him a signal that she was interested, just to see how he'd react, if nothing else. But the other, wiser, part knew that it was better just to let him go. If he were still interested, he would take the initiative. If he wasn't, there was no point in pursuing him. So she didn't get him a gift.

She finished her shopping by 6:30, grabbed a quick dinner, and went to the theater. The play started at 7:30 and ran until 9:30. The play itself was a little disappointing. It was the story of an amoral Norwegian peasant named Peer Gynt, who traveled around the world having cartoonish adventures and behaving badly toward a series of women who nonetheless loved him. The rest of the audience seemed to be enjoying themselves, however, so Elena suspected that she might have enjoyed the play more if she spoke Norwegian. She did like the sets, however, and the dance scenes were fun to watch. Also, the musicians in the orchestra pit did a great job with Edvard Grieg's incidental music—most of which Elena had heard before and liked, but hadn't realized was part of the play.

She left the theater, walked back to the hotel parking garage, and got her car. The sun was nearing the southwestern horizon and was in her eyes as she drove toward Bjornsen Norge. She squinted at first, but as she got close to her destination a column of smoke obscured the sun and relieved the strain on her eyes. She assumed the plume came from one of the factories and power plants that dotted Oslo's industrial waterfront, but then an ambulance screamed past her and drove off toward the smoke at double the posted speed limit. A cold wave of fear washed over Elena and she floored the accelerator.

Her fear grew into panic as she turned the corner onto the street leading to Norge's parking lot and got her first view of her destination. Flames licked out of the windows of the office portion of the building and thick clouds of black smoke billowed skyward. In the middle of the parking lot stood the Haugelands' green Volvo station wagon. Beyond it, closer to the building, two fire trucks were surrounded by a crowd of firefighters pouring thousands of gallons of water onto the fire from high-pressure hoses. And a few yards from the fire trucks, the ambulance that had passed Elena had just pulled to a stop in front of two bloody forms lying on stretchers on the grass outside the building. Between the stretchers sat Henrik Haugeland,

212

a dazed and vacant look on his face. As Elena drove up, she caught a glimpse of Noelle's thick, auburn-brown hair tumbling over the side of one of the stretchers.

Chapter Thirteen

The Aftermath

Elena stood in the hospital lobby, staring at her cell phone. She had already dialed the number, but had trouble bringing herself to push the Send button. She took a deep breath to calm herself and pressed it. She brought the phone to her ear and listened. It rang twice and she almost hoped her call would go into voice mail, but it didn't. There was a click followed by a familiar voice. "Hello, Ben Corbin."

"Ben, it's Elena."

"What's up?"

"I'm at the hospital. I—"

"What happened?" asked Ben urgently. "Where's Noelle?"

"She's been shot in the leg and has smoke inhalation injuries, but the doctor says she'll be okay. She's in preterm labor, though. They're trying to stop it, but they don't know if they can."

"Shot? Smoke inhalation?" repeated Ben, his voice rising. "*What happened?*"

"I'm not really sure. I . . ." Elena closed her eyes and forced the words out. "I wasn't there."

"Where were you?"

"I was, well, I dropped off Noelle and then I went out shopping for my family," she confessed, fighting back tears. "Then I went—"

Ben cut her off. "Never mind. I'm going to get over there as fast as I can. Call me if there's any news." There was a click and the phone went dead.

Elena reflexively closed the cell phone and dropped it into her purse. She found an isolated seat near a window where the last light of the dying day cast a fading glow on the nearly empty interior of the Rikshospitalet lobby. She put her face in her hands and started to cry.

‡ ‡ ‡

"*Takk. Hvis jeg husker noe videre skal jeg ringe deg.*" Karl hung up the phone and gazed blankly at his computer monitor for several minutes, his mind whirling. The last thing he'd been expecting was a call from the Oslo police department. What the lieutenant had told him seemed surreal—Noelle Corbin apparently had made a secret visit to Bjornsen Norge with Gunnar's old conspirator, Henrik Haugeland. Someone had shot her and Haugeland's son and then set fire to the building. After the Cleverlad fiasco at the preliminary injunction trial, Karl had no difficulty guessing what Noelle and Henrik had been doing, but who had attacked them?

A loyal employee who discovered what they were up to? No, too extreme. Plus, that didn't explain the fire. A random criminal who broke into the building intending burglary, but was surprised to find someone there? That was possible; drug warehouses often had theft problems. Having found people—witnesses—in what he thought was an unoccupied building, the thief might have decided to kill them to avoid detection and then set fire to the building to destroy the evidence of his crimes. The police were leaning toward that theory, but Karl suspected that murder had been the intruder's main objective from the start.

Was Cleverlad responsible? Karl had expected that George would eventually discover that the "Neurostim" he had received was fake, but the magnitude of his retaliation—if that's what this was—surprised Karl.

Karl was half-inclined to let the matter lie, at least for the time being. Insurance would cover the fire damage and the Norwegian police probably would do a reasonably competent investigation, though he doubted they would catch the perpetrator.

Unfortunately, however, the perpetrator needed to be caught. Karl had no doubt whom Ben Corbin and Gunnar would suspect, and he could not afford to let them lay those suspicions out for a jury—or the Norwegian police. And how would that play out if the perpetrator was George or one of his henchmen? Karl frowned for a moment. Then his expression brightened as a new idea occurred to him. There was an opportunity here to make some real progress if the situation was handled right.

The phone rang again. This time, Gunnar's number appeared on the caller ID. Karl let it go to the answering machine, then played his brother's message. "Karl, it's Gunnar. I need to talk to you. Call me at home. It's not about the lawsuit."

Karl grinned humorlessly. Sure. Of course it wasn't about the lawsuit; it was about the fire and shootings. And of course it would never occur to Gunnar or his lawyer to try to tell the jury about those. And Gunnar would certainly never use the threat of that prospect to pressure his little brother ahead of the trial. Well, Gunnar and his threats could wait. Karl would call him back when events had unfolded a little further.

✠ ✠ ✠

Ben stood in the neonatal intensive care unit, looking down at his son. Eric Benjamin Corbin had been born while Ben was somewhere over the North Atlantic. He weighed barely four pounds and was pitifully thin and fragile-looking. Wires were attached to his tiny body in various places and ran through an opening in his incubator to a bank of monitors that displayed his pulse, respiration rate, body temperature, blood oxygenation, and several other vital statistics that Ben couldn't immediately identify. Ben reached out and touched the hard plastic of the incubator. It was blood-warm, since Eric's body could not maintain its temperature.

"He's beautiful, isn't he?" said Noelle from her wheelchair at Ben's side.

"He is," said Ben. "It's such a relief to see him lying there and breathing and to have you here beside me. I was scared to death after Elena called. I prayed the whole way over on the plane. The guy sitting next to me asked the flight attendant for a different seat. I think he figured I was a terrorist or something."

Noelle smiled up at her husband and took his hand. "Thanks— for praying for me and for getting over here so fast. I love you."

He smiled back and squeezed her hand. "I know. I love you too. Is there anything I can do for you now that I'm here?"

She leaned her head against his arm. "You're doing it now."

They watched Eric in silence. He opened his eyes and stretched and moved his arms and legs randomly for a few seconds. Then he closed his eyes and went back to sleep. "He's so tiny," said Ben. "He looks like he would break if I touched him."

"Dr. Bakke says he'll grow a lot over the next couple of weeks," replied Noelle. "She's pretty sure that he'll be fine, but for right now they want to be extra careful with him. He's been through a lot."

"So have you." Ben glanced at the armed police guards outside the nursery door. "I haven't heard much about what happened. Are you up for talking about it?"

She sighed and rubbed her eyes. "Sure. I've already talked about it twice with the police. Last night, I was marking documents for Einar—Henrik Haugeland's son—to copy. Henrik was in back looking at archived files. I heard Einar shouting and I went into the hallway to see what was going on. Einar was wrestling with some guy I'd never seen before and yelling at the top of his lungs. I ran back to look for a phone where I could call the police and try to get someone who spoke English fast. I heard some shots from the hallway and then a few seconds later the guy burst into the room where I was. He pointed his gun at me from about five feet away. Just as the gun went off, Einar came through the door and hit the guy's arm. The bullet hit me in the leg and I fell down. He and Einar started fighting for the gun again. Einar had already been shot; I could see blood on his clothes. Then the gun went off again and Einar was down too." Her composure started to crack and her voice shook. "I could see the hole in his back where the bullet had just come out. It was awful." She began to cry.

Ben bent down and put his arm around her. "That's okay, babe. Sergei's talking to the police right now. I'll get a report from him. I shouldn't have brought it up with you. Let's talk about something that makes you happy."

She sniffed and smiled through her tears. "Well, it would make me happy to hear you promise to change half of Eric's dirty diapers and get up with him on half the nights."

‡ ‡ ‡

Karl sat in a wrought iron chair on the balcony of his apartment, a glass of ice tea on a little table at his elbow. A light breeze ruffled the pages of the dossier in his hand, which had arrived an hour ago from Alex Geist's firm. The first section contained a detailed biography of George Kulish. He had been born in Kiev twenty-six years ago to an unremarkable family. His father was an engineer and his mother managed a local grocery store. George's teachers and parents soon realized he was exceptionally bright and did their best to give him a good education in the chaotic years around the collapse of the Soviet Union. They did a good enough job for George to receive a scholarship at MIT when he was sixteen.

George's years at MIT were troubled. He got straight As, but he routinely violated school rules. At first, the school tolerated his misbehavior on the theory that he was having difficulty adjusting to life away from home and living in an alien culture. But eventually they cracked down on him. He was expelled and deported in the middle of his junior year when the school caught him hacking into the registrar's computer system—a feat which the registrar's office had thought impossible—and changing other students' grades for money.

Back in Ukraine, George promptly landed a job with a computer security company. He worked there for two years and apparently did good work. He received large bonuses each year and was promoted twice. However, his employer ran into legal difficulties for helping some of its customers build security systems specifically designed to prevent government surveillance. The company shut down its Ukrainian unit as a result and George found himself unemployed.

Next, he began doing freelance consulting. His services were in high demand, particularly in the Ukrainian and Russian underworlds. He already had prodigious talents for both creating and hacking into computer security systems. He now branched out and began doing electronic money laundering and Web site design for several of the more sophisticated drug gangs and their front operations.

The turning point in George's career had come three years ago. A smuggling ring hired him to hack into the system of a financially troubled drug wholesaler in northern Russia and make its computers crash on the eve of a crucial shipment. The wholesaler would go bankrupt, and George's clients could buy it for a song at the bankruptcy auction. They could then use it as a front for their business, and it would probably even make some money on its own if competently run. All went as planned at first—George successfully wrecked the company's computer system and it missed the shipment deadline, losing a key customer in the process. It went bankrupt shortly thereafter.

But then George learned that the smugglers had decided not to pay his fee. Geist's report was unclear on how George made this discovery, but the results were soon obvious. Less than a week later, the head of the ring died when the electric fence at his dacha malfunctioned. The coroner ruled the death accidental and blamed a bug in the software that operated the fence. The police anonymously received copies of the other members' bank statements the same day and arrested them for tax evasion.

Meanwhile, the bankruptcy proceeded and George made it known that he intended to submit a bid for the wholesaler he had ruined. No one bid against him. He took possession of the company's assets and relaunched the business as Cleverlad.ru. He moved from Moscow to Yuragorsk and made it his base of operations. He quickly reached agreements with the local *militsiya*—law enforcement authorities—and within a few months, Cleverlad.ru and a cluster of affiliated entities were doing brisk business. George stayed away from traditional drugs like heroin and meth, which would have brought him into conflict with his former clients. Instead, he focused on selling prescription drugs without prescriptions.

American and European authorities soon discovered Cleverlad and tried unsuccessfully to get the Russians to shut it down. The *militsiya*, of course, had no interest in attacking George's company, and the national authorities had better things to do than go after a savvy and wealthy provincial exporter, whose main crime was violating foreign drug laws.

So the FBI and NSA tried taking matters into their own hands. Despite considerable effort, they were wholly unsuccessful. The investigation remained confidential and the dossier didn't say exactly what happened, but the only result of the American efforts was to knock Cleverlad offline for a grand total of six hours. The next day, one of the FBI agents on the case discovered that his bank account had been drained and his credit history wrecked. The investigation was closed two weeks later.

The rest of the dossier consisted of a long list of Web sites and companies known to be owned or controlled by George, a chronicle of murders and other major crimes in which George was implicated, and two relatively recent pictures of him. Karl held these up to the light and studied them. In one of them, George looked like a slightly geeky grad student. He was walking down the street, his thin shoulders slouched and nearly hidden by the folds of an over-sized hooded sweatshirt. His unruly black hair was pulled back in a ponytail, revealing a slightly receding hairline. Dark knockoff Way-farer sunglasses covered his eyes, and his hands obscured the lower part of his face as he lit a cigarette. In the second picture, he looked older and more dangerous: his hair was shorter and he wore a dark, well-tailored suit. His face was clearly visible in the second picture, and it wore a shrewd, calculating look that few grad students have developed.

Karl put down the report and sipped his ice tea thoughtfully. Getting to George Kulish would be difficult. He had built an impregnable electronic fortress around himself that the best minds in American and European law enforcement had been unable to crack. He was also adept at detecting and eliminating threats to himself and his businesses.

George was formidable indeed. Formidable, but not invincible.

‡ ‡ ‡

Ben and Sergei sat in the hospital cafeteria, each with a cup of steaming black coffee from a large stainless steel urn that stood at the end of the room. Sergei took a tentative sip and his eyebrows went up. "You know, the coffee here is actually really good."

"Not what you expect from hospital coffee, is it?" replied Ben, taking a sip from his cup. Two days' worth of stubble covered his face and his brown hair was uncharacteristically disheveled. "Noelle clued me in to it; otherwise I'd be out looking for a Starbucks right now."

"How's she doing?"

"Better than I expected. She's sleeping now, but she seemed to be herself while I was with her. The doctor said both Noelle and Eric should be fine. Both of them are past the most dangerous stage now."

"That's a real answer to prayer," replied Sergei. "So, how are you doing?"

"A lot better now that it looks like they're going to be okay," said Ben. "Man, was I scared coming over here on the plane. I kept picturing what it would be like to land and find out that the baby was dead or that Noelle had died during delivery because of the shock and blood loss of being shot. Thank God that didn't happen. I'm still mad, though, and the more I think about it, the angrier I get. Who shoots a pregnant woman?" he demanded. "What kind of animal does something like that?"

"Someone who needs to be behind bars for a long, long time," agreed Sergei. "The police have made catching him a high priority—not just because of what he's already done, but because of what he'll do next. If he would shoot a pregnant woman in cold blood, he doesn't have any limits. The people I talked to in the police department are very worried. Right now, they've got an arson, a drug theft, and two attempted murders to solve, but they think that list is going to get longer if they don't catch this guy quickly."

"Two attempted murders," repeated Ben. "Have you heard anything about Henrik Haugeland's son? Noelle said he got shot up pretty bad."

Sergei nodded. "The kid has two bullet wounds in the abdomen and one in the shoulder. He had lost a lot of blood by the time he got to the hospital. He's been in surgery twice since he got here."

"Any idea what his prognosis is?"

"No, but the senior detective said he'd seen a lot of bullet wounds and these looked bad."

Ben shook his head. "That's terrible. You know, if it wasn't for him, I probably wouldn't have a wife or a son right now. The guy who broke into Norge shot Einar first before he came after Noelle. Einar could have run away, but he followed the guy and kept him from getting a clean shot at Noelle. Then he basically took a bullet for her."

"Wow. He's a hero," said Sergei. "A real hero."

"He is," agreed Ben. "I hope I get the chance to thank him."

"If I hear anything more about him, I'll pass it along."

"I'll do the same," replied Ben. He took another sip of his coffee. "Do you know what happened after Einar got shot the second time? I've only heard the story up to there."

Sergei nodded. "The cops think the shooter used his last bullet on Einar. Then Henrik, who had been in the storage area in back, came in with an ax from one of those glass 'break in case of fire' boxes. The guy was out of ammo and ran. He'd already poured gasoline in strategic spots around the building, and he lit it on his way out."

"I didn't talk to Noelle about the fire. Do you know how she got out? Was it Henrik?"

"It was. He pulled her and Einar out of the building before the fire reached them. The fire department managed to save the warehouse, but the offices and file room were completely destroyed."

Ben rolled his eyes. "What a surprise."

"FYI, the cops say there are a dozen cases of drugs missing from the warehouse. Karl may be behind this and may have staged the theft as a diversion. If he did, it's working. Right now, the police are treating this as a warehouse burglary gone bad."

"Have you told them about Gunnar's case and Karl's fraud?"

"Some, but not much."

"What do you say we stop by and fill them in?" Ben asked with a hard-edged smile.

"Definitely, but not today. I'm going to check on Elena. According to the detective who interviewed her, she's taking this pretty hard."

‡ ‡ ‡

Sergei took a deep breath and knocked on Elena's door. A moment later, he heard the locks turning. The door opened and Elena looked at him with wide-eyed surprise. Her face was blotchy and what little makeup she usually wore was gone, but she wasn't crying at the moment. "I didn't know you were here. When did you get in?"

"I flew over with Ben. We got in around noon, and I've been at the police station and the hospital since then. I stopped by as soon as I could. I thought you might want someone to talk to."

"It's good to see you. I was at the hospital with Noelle until Ben came, but then I thought I'd let them be alone."

"Want to go for a walk?" he asked. "Nothing cheers me up like sitting in a hotel room by myself, but I know I'm a little strange that way."

She smiled. "A walk would be nice, but do you think it's safe? The shooter may come after me too."

"We'll stick to crowded places. Besides," he patted his side, "I'm carrying. It's not technically legal here, but I talked to the police and they made a couple of calls and they're okay with it."

Her smile widened slightly. "You're always ready to go out on the town, aren't you? I need a few minutes to get ready."

"That's fine. I'll wait for you in one of those chairs by the elevators."

Half an hour later, they were strolling down Kongensgate. A rainstorm had swept through earlier in the day, but the sun was out now and the city had a clean, fresh-washed look. Sergei tried making conversation on various topics, but he couldn't get Elena engaged. After his third attempt flopped, he said, "Okay, your choice. We can talk about last night or not. Just let me know what you'd like to do."

She bit her lip and walked in silence for several seconds. "I want to talk about it . . . or, well, I need to talk about it, I guess."

"'Need to'?"

"It was awful, absolutely awful. I haven't been able to sleep since it happened; I can't even turn off the lights." She took a deep breath and let it out. "I don't know how I'll be able to live with myself after this."

"What happened?"

"I dropped Noelle off in front of the building, and then I went downtown to do some last-minute shopping and see a play. When I got back, the ambulance was just pulling into the parking lot."

"You think you shouldn't have left, that you should have stayed with Noelle to protect her and Einar?" he asked.

"Basically, yeah."

He nodded. "I'd probably feel the same way in your shoes. You know what, though? This wasn't your fault. You had no reason to stay behind, no reason to know what was going to happen. And even if you had stayed, what would you have done? You'd have gotten shot and wound up in the hospital like Noelle and Einar—or in the morgue."

Elena looked down. "That's not completely true." She stopped and shrugged. "In fact, it's not true at all. I *did* know what was going to happen, or I should have, anyway. Two days ago, I saw a gray sedan parked across the street from the Bjornsen building. There was a man in it who seemed to be looking at a map. There was nothing suspicious about him. It was just one of those things you notice a dozen times a day."

"What the Kasman calls Bureauvision, right?" said Sergei. Mark Kasanin was a retired agent who trained new agents when Sergei and Elena were hired. One of the axioms he used to drill into his classes was to be aware of their surroundings. He gave every new class the same speech: "Everyone notices something unusual; you have to notice usual things. You have to be able to see the two or three totally normal details that put together are evidence of a crime. That's Bureauvision, and you'll need to develop it if you want to be successful here at the FBI."

Elena nodded. "Yeah. Anyway, I thought I saw him again yesterday. He drove past as I pulled into the parking lot to drop off Noelle. Then he drove by again going the other way as I was leaving." She paused and Sergei glanced over at her, but she kept her eyes resolutely on the sidewalk. "I should have made the connection, but I didn't. I was too focused on getting downtown to do my shopping."

"He matched the description that Noelle and Henrik gave the police, right?"

She nodded.

"Now I get it," said Sergei. They walked in silence for several seconds. "I won't tell you there's nothing to feel guilty about. You wouldn't believe me even if I said it."

"It would be a lie," she said, her voice cracking.

"Maybe. Everybody gets sloppy sometimes, and in our business sometimes people get hurt as a result. It's happened to me, and I paid for it by spending two days in a torture chamber. And I never would have made it out if you hadn't come in after me." He paused, but she didn't respond. "But I was the only one who got hurt; I got off easy compared to you."

"When I drove up and saw Noelle and Einar lying there covered in blood and not moving and the look on Henrik's face as he sat there next to his son—" Her voice trailed off into a sob. Sergei put his arm around her and guided her to a park bench. She put her face in her hands and cried uncontrollably. Passers-by glanced at them curiously, but kept their distance. After a few minutes, she took a deep breath and said, "It was the worst thing I've ever seen in my life. I'll never be able to forgive myself. Never."

"Of course not," Sergei said gently. "No one can forgive their own sins."

She nodded and sniffed. "I don't know if it will make things any better, but I'm going to talk to Noelle when she's stronger. I'm also going to talk to Henrik, but what about Einar? What if he dies?" Tears welled up in her eyes again. "What if he dies and I know it's my fault and I never get to tell him I'm sorry?"

"Then maybe we can have another one of those religion talks you used to enjoy so much. The Bible is big on forgiveness. But we can worry about that later. Einar is still alive, and we should focus on keeping him that way."

She looked up at him. "How?"

"Well, there's a church up the street that I visited when I was here last time. I plan to go there and pray for him when we're done talking. You're welcome to join me if you want. Or I can take you back to your hotel room."

She thought for a moment. "I'd like to come with you."

He nodded and suppressed the urge to smile. "Do you want to go now, or did you want to talk some more?"

"We can go now. It's just that, well, you know I don't necessarily believe in God, right?"

"Yeah, I know. That's fine. You can just sit next to me if you want; you don't have to pray."

"Actually, I'd kind of like to pray. I'm just wondering if it's, well, if it's okay."

"You mean, if there is a God, will he be offended if you pray to him without believing in him?"

"Yes."

He smiled and wiped the tears from her cheeks. "I haven't really thought about that one, but I'll bet that won't bother him. I'm pretty sure he'd rather have you pray with all your doubts than not pray at all." He stood and reached out his hand. "Come on, let's go."

‡ ‡ ‡

The bronze doors of the Oslo Domkirke stood open and a small sign in English and Norwegian announced that it was open to the public from 10:00 AM to 4:00 PM every day. The interior seemed cool and dim to Elena after the bright warmth of the late July day outside. There were no services or concerts that day, so the church was mostly empty and quiet. A handful of people sat or knelt in random pews, and a few tourists strolled around the edges of the sanctuary, reading plaques or talking in whispers and pointing at the richly carved altar or one of the windows. Elena and Sergei picked an empty pew and sat at the end by the central aisle.

Sergei bowed his head and closed his eyes, but Elena felt a little hesitant—almost shy—about joining him. She sat with her hands folded in her lap and let her eyes wander over the church.

The Domkirke was very different from the church she had attended with Sergei in America. Sergei's church had the look and feel of a well-designed convention center—good lighting, comfortable seats, a modern sound system, and large display screens on which songs or PowerPoint notes complementing the pastor's sermon could be shown. This church had none of that, but something about it made anyone who entered instinctively speak in a whisper.

The years lay thick in here, a deep layer of invisible dust that hushed the voice and stilled the spirit. The Domkirke's ancient holiness was almost palpable, hovering at the edge of her senses like a faint sound just below the threshold of hearing. Every day for centuries, men and women had come here to pray and praise, and their worship had left an indefinable residue, a scent of fire and incense that only the soul could catch.

The turmoil and pain gradually drained from Elena as she sat beside Sergei. The weight on her heart slipped off and she felt a deep peace filling her. It was like stepping out of a bitter winter storm and into a warm room with a crackling fire and a comfortable chair waiting. She felt a new and unexpected calm seeping into her soul. Then she suddenly remembered why they were there, and she bowed her head in prayer.

‡ ‡ ‡

At 8:15 the next morning, the phone rang in Judge Reilly's chambers, a half-decorated office down the hall from his courtroom. Boxes of books and memorabilia still sat along the walls and beneath the window that offered a panoramic view of the Chicago cityscape. So far, the only items to make it out of the boxes were some books, Judge Reilly's law school diploma, and a trophy naming him Midwest Conference Basketball Player of the Year for 1993. The judge sat behind his desk, wearing a slightly frayed dress shirt and tie. Bert Siwell was in a chair on the other side of the desk. The judge pushed the speakerphone button. "Mr. Corbin?"

"Yes, your honor." Ben's voice was distorted by the poor quality of the speaker. "Thank you for agreeing to hold this hearing telephonically and on short notice."

"That's not a problem," replied the judge. "I understand that there are circumstances beyond your control here. Mr. Siwell is sitting in my chambers. Are you both ready to proceed?"

"Yes, your honor," said both attorneys.

"Okay. Go ahead, Mr. Corbin."

"Your honor, due to the circumstances you just mentioned, defendant and counter-plaintiff Gunnar Bjornsen moves to continue the trial date for at least four weeks, preferably more. As set forth in our papers, my wife was brutally attacked in Norway, which caused my son to be born prematurely. Neither of them will be able to fly for at least a month. I would very much like to stay with them until they can return to Chicago. If I do that, however, I will be unable to represent my client at trial. Mr. Bjornsen and I therefore request that the Court continue the trial date for at least four weeks to allow me to be with my family during this time and still be able to spend at least a week preparing for trial when I return."

"Have you discussed this matter with opposing counsel?" asked the judge.

"I called him yesterday, your honor. He said that he couldn't agree to my request."

The judge looked at Bert Siwell in surprise. "Counsel?"

"Mr. Corbin may have misunderstood my comments, your honor," responded Siwell. "I couldn't agree to something as significant as a trial continuance without discussing it with my clients. That's all I intended to communicate to Mr. Corbin."

"If that's what he had said," replied Ben, "I would not have called your honor's clerk to arrange this hearing, and I would not have stayed up past midnight drafting emergency motion papers."

"I apologize if I was unclear," replied Siwell. "I would never attempt to practice gamesmanship with opposing counsel under these circumstances. But the bottom line is that I have talked to my clients, and they do not object to allowing Mr. Corbin however much time he needs to deal with this terrible situation. We have some concerns about why Mrs. Corbin was at Bjornsen Pharmaceuticals' Norwegian facility when she was attacked, but I'm sure those will be resolved in due course. What's important now is that Mr. Corbin and his family have the time they need."

"I was hoping that would be your response," said Judge Reilly.

"Incidentally, I noticed that his papers request four weeks," continued Siwell, "but we would understand if he required more."

"Mr. Corbin, your papers request *at least* four weeks. Is that what you would like me to order?"

"Four weeks would probably be enough, if nothing goes wrong either here or in Chicago, your honor, but I would prefer six."

The judge looked at Siwell. "Any objection to a six-week continuance, Mr. Siwell?"

"None, your honor."

"All right, the new trial date is October seventeen. Mr. Siwell, please draw up an order."

‡ ‡ ‡

Ben hung up the phone. He looked down at the notes scattered across his hotel room desk. Bert Siwell had been surprisingly accommodating just now and had completely reversed the position he'd taken just the day before. Why?

Maybe they really had misunderstood each other on the phone last night. Maybe, but Ben doubted it. Siwell had clearly known about the attack before Ben called and had asked several questions about what exactly Noelle was doing at Bjornsen Norge when she was shot. Ben had refused to answer and Siwell had refused to agree to a continuance—or at least that was the impression Ben had been left with when he got off the phone with his opponent.

Even if it was a misunderstanding, why would Siwell volunteer to give Ben *more* time than he had requested? There were some lawyers Ben knew who would bend over backward for a colleague going through a personal crisis, but Bert Siwell wasn't one of them. So why was he doing this?

Because Karl had told him to, Ben realized. After Ben called Siwell last night, Siwell must have called his client and been told to reverse himself. Karl Bjornsen wanted some extra time himself before the trial started. Ben swiveled around in his chair and looked out the window at the busy downtown street outside his hotel. *Karl is up to something, but what?*

‡ ‡ ‡

If Ben had been looking through binoculars, he might have seen Karl Bjornsen for a few seconds on the sidewalk about two blocks away. The big Norwegian was heading north, away from Ben, toward an upscale residential area of Oslo. After several blocks, he turned left and disappeared into a street lined with trendy, recently renovated apartment buildings.

Karl had arrived in Norway that morning on an overnight SAS flight. He had bought his ticket in person and had paid cash—which made the SAS security personnel uncomfortable, because it was much harder to track the purchase electronically. He also used cash to pay for all of his other travel expenses. To his secretary's consternation, he sent no e-mails mentioning this trip or even announcing that he would be out of the office. Instead, he left it to her to cover for him until he got back. He also did not activate his European cell phone. He had a satellite phone with him, but he did not plan to turn it on until he needed it.

He stopped in front of an apartment building, glanced at a scrap of paper in his hand, and went in. He found himself in a small, well-furnished lobby facing a locked inner door with an intercom box next to it. He sat down in a comfortably overstuffed armchair in a corner with a good view of the interior door, took out a copy of *Dagens Naeringsliv*, Norway's equivalent of the *Wall Street Journal*, and waited. If Alex Geist was right, Berit Lundgren would walk out that door in about fifteen minutes to go to a yoga class at a downtown gym.

Sure enough, a young woman matching Berit's description and the photo Geist had sent emerged fifteen minutes later. She was pretty, blonde, and looked healthy—hardly what Karl expected a cocaine addict to look like. She was dressed in workout clothes and was carrying a gym bag, iPod, and water bottle. Karl smiled and stood up. He folded the newspaper under his arm and walked over to intercept her, reaching the door in time to open it for her. "*Takk*," she said automatically. Then she glanced at him and froze in recognition. "Mr. Bjornsen?"

His smile broadened. "And you must be Berit Lundgren. Pleased to meet you."

"I . . . I recognized you from your picture. Were you waiting for me?"

"I was. I was in Oslo and thought I would stop by and talk to you informally. Do you have a few minutes?"

"I was on my way to the gym," she said, looking up at him uncertainly, "but, uh, of course I would be happy to talk to you."

"Good. I saw a park down the street. What do you say we go for a walk?"

"Sure."

They stepped out onto the sidewalk and turned toward the park. "How long have you been with the company, Berit? About three years?"

"Three and a half. Ever since I graduated."

"How do you like it?"

"I really enjoy it. Bjornsen Norge is a great place to work."

"And you've been a good employee. I've seen your performance evaluations."

"Thank you."

They left the sidewalk and entered the wide green spaces of the park. Yelling children and chatting mothers packed a playground about fifty meters away, but otherwise there were few people nearby—and none within earshot. "Sometimes even good employees make mistakes, Berit."

She looked at him nervously. "I—I—" she stammered.

"Sometimes they use cocaine," Karl continued. "Sometimes they do worse things, like give confidential information to outsiders. Sometimes they even get mixed up in arson and attempted murder."

She stopped and stared at him with round, terrified eyes. Her face was white beneath her tan. "That wasn't me! I—" She snapped her mouth shut.

"But you know who it was," said Karl, "or at least you can make an educated guess. You have been calling and e-mailing some people in Russia on a regular basis. Dangerous people. Maybe they were paying you for information, or maybe they were blackmailing you. It does not matter now. One day, you found a piece of information that would be especially valuable to them—you discovered that someone had been going through their files. And then you told them, right?"

She nodded and looked down. "I don't know how the Russians found out about me, but they said they would tell the company and the police about my . . . my bad habits if I didn't give them information and documents. But that's all I did. I swear it. I had no idea they would try to kill anybody."

Karl stopped and grabbed her arm—not violently, but with great strength. "What did you think would happen? What did you think your Russian friends would do when you told them someone was looking at those records?"

She looked up at him and started to shake. "I . . . I don't know. I just thought . . . I don't know what I thought. It was a terrible mistake and I'm very sorry." She paused and licked her lips nervously. "Have you told the police?"

"Not yet," replied Karl. He felt a surge of pity for her as she stood there frightened and quivering. "But they will have to know soon. In the meantime, you may be able to help clean up this mess."

"That would be great. I really appreciate this opportunity, Mr. Bjornsen. Just let me know what I can do to help."

"You can start by telling me everything you know—your contacts, exactly what information you gave them, and so on. And Berit—"

"Yes, Mr. Bjornsen?"

"Do not lie to me or hold anything back. If you do, I will find out and things will go badly for you. Very badly. Do you understand?"

"Yes, Mr. Bjornsen."

Chapter Fourteen

Witnesses

It had now been six days since the telephonic hearing, and Ben felt that he couldn't wait any longer to talk business with Henrik Haugeland. He hadn't heard any definitive news about Einar's condition, but he needed to start planning for trial. If he was going to have to try this case without Henrik's testimony, he needed to know now.

He knocked on the door to Einar's hospital room, and Henrik opened it. He looked tired and pale, but he smiled and his voice was lively. "Good afternoon, Mr. Corbin. How are Noelle and the baby?"

"They're doing well. Noelle will be on crutches for a few weeks, but she should make a full recovery. The doctor says she can be discharged in a day or two. Eric is doing well too, but he'll need to stay here for about three more weeks. How's Einar? We've been praying for him."

"Thank you," replied Henrik. "God has answered all our prayers. Einar will live and he has no brain damage. He does have damage to several bones and internal organs, so he will be in the hospital for several months and will have certain permanent problems. But he is in good spirits and we are all very happy with his progress."

"That's great. I'll let you get back to him, but when you have a few minutes, I'd like to talk to you about something else."

235

"We can talk now if you like. Einar just went to sleep and his mother and sister are with him."

"Okay, can I buy you a cup of coffee or something?" offered Ben.

"I have already drunk five cups today, but I would enjoy a short walk. I have sat in a chair for most of the day."

"A walk it is, then."

Five minutes later, they were strolling along a well-kept path that ran through a small glade of pine and birch trees behind the hospital. "What was it you wanted to discuss?" asked Henrik.

"Your testimony at the trial. I assume you'll want to stay in Norway until Einar is better, but if you have the time and inclination, I'd like to videotape your testimony so that we can play it for the jury. That's completely your decision, though. I'll fully understand if you'd rather focus on more important things, and I'm sure Gunnar will understand too."

"Would it be better for you if I came to America to testify?"

"I'm not asking you to do that," replied Ben. "I just—"

Henrik smiled and held up his hand. "I know you are not asking me to do it. I am asking if you would have a better chance of winning if I did."

"Well, yes."

"Then I will come."

"You really don't have to."

"I want to. You believe Karl Bjornsen was responsible for the attack on my son and your wife, yes?"

Ben pressed his lips together and looked Henrik in the eye. "Yes. I think he either ordered the attack himself or knows who did."

Henrik returned Ben's gaze, and there was a grimness in his face that Ben hadn't seen before. "So do I. I will do everything I can within the law to make sure he hurts no one else. Removing him from control of Bjornsen Pharmaceuticals will make him much less powerful, and hopefully much less dangerous. I will come to America to testify."

‡ ‡ ‡

Two days after Noelle left Rikshospitalet, she and Elena went for a walk in the Vigeland sculpture garden in Frognerparken, home to the granite and bronze "no waist nudes" that grace many postcards from Oslo. Noelle was still on crutches, so Elena had suggested that they visit someplace where they could sit down. But Noelle said she had done plenty of sitting over the past week and a half and would really like to get off her rear end, which she was convinced had grown significantly during her involuntary inactivity.

So Elena walked and Noelle hobbled along the wide, crushed-rock paths of Frognerparken. It was a very public place with crowds of tourists and a significant police presence, but a pair of armed undercover officers accompanied them nonetheless, strolling watchfully a few feet on either side of them.

They walked slowly and stopped frequently, both because of Noelle's condition and because it was a hot August day. Their conversation drifted fitfully among various banal topics—the statues they walked past, the weather, the relative merits of Norwegian and American ice cream, and so on. Noelle got the distinct impression that Elena wanted to talk about something, but was having trouble coming to the point, so Noelle did it for her. "So, by this time tomorrow, you'll be back in America," she said as they sat down on a well-shaded bench. "Looking forward to it?"

Elena stretched out her long legs and leaned back against the warm concrete of the bench. "Yes, I guess so. I don't want to leave you and Ben in the lurch, but things are piling up back at the Bureau and I can't keep asking people to cover for me."

"We'll be fine," replied Noelle. "But it will be a while before we see each other again. Was there anything you wanted to talk about?"

"I . . . well, yeah," Elena admitted. Her tan face grew serious and she sat forward. "I wanted to let you know how sorry I am about all this." Noelle opened her mouth to protest, but Elena hurried on. "No, wait. Just let me get this off my chest. I know you don't blame me, but I blame myself, okay? I blame myself for not spotting that guy in the parking lot. I blame myself for going shopping while you guys were busy making copies and stuff. I blame myself for not getting permission to bring a gun. I'm sorry and I wanted to tell you before I left. That's all."

Noelle realized that it would be useless to try to argue Elena out of her guilt. She patted her friend's arm reassuringly. "You're right. I don't blame you. Neither does Ben. And even if there is something we should blame you for, we forgive you. So don't worry about it—or try not to, anyway."

"Thanks, I appreciate that. I really do. Einar and Henrik said pretty much the same thing when I talked to them. Everyone's being so nice about this, so understanding." She sighed and smiled. "It almost makes it worse."

"Okay, then I take it back," replied Noelle with a wink. "I hate you and never want to see you again. Better?"

Elena laughed. "Much, thanks. Seriously, you've been a real friend about this. I won't be able to be here with you after tomorrow, but I, uh, I'll be praying for you."

‡ ‡ ‡

Being back in LA felt so good that even the rush hour traffic didn't bother Kim. She was heading west on Highway 10 and the traffic was completely gridlocked due to construction. She watched the sunset and sang along with the car stereo. Chicago had been a lot of fun, and working at Bjornsen Pharmaceuticals had been a great experience, but it was wonderful to be home. She had missed it more than she realized.

It also felt good to be driving to David's apartment. When she'd left for the summer, she had been a little worried about what would happen to their relationship. It was the first time they'd been apart for longer than two weeks, and she had heard stories about how the younger nurses went after med school students interning at the hospitals. But David had remained true. He had continued to seem a little odd even after he had gone off the Neurostim, but she hoped that was just a result of the strain of having been apart for so long.

He wasn't expecting her back until tomorrow, but she had finished up at Bjornsen a day early and had been able to change her tickets. She had told her parents, but decided to surprise David. She smiled at the thought of how he'd react when he opened his door and saw her standing there.

The traffic finally started moving, and half an hour later she was parked outside David's building. She reached into the back seat and grabbed David's gifts: a Chicago Cubs shirt and a large box of Fannie May Mint Meltaways. She spotted his battered Impala as she got out of her car and smiled. At this hour, he should be back from work, but it was good to see proof.

She went up to his apartment and pushed the doorbell. She could hear the chimes faintly inside, followed a few seconds later by David's voice calling, "Just a second."

A moment later, she heard approaching footsteps and David opened the door. Kim was surprised at how much of a difference a few months had made in his appearance. She could tell that he had been working out, which was a welcome change. The long, slightly messy hair she remembered had been trimmed and gelled into a professional-looking cut. The biggest change was in his face, though—there was a light in his eyes that was both exciting and a little disconcerting.

He stared at her for a second and she beamed back at him. Then he let out a happy whoop, yelled "Kim!" and swept her up in a passionate kiss. The candy and T-shirt she had been holding dropped to the floor and she wrapped her arms around his neck. She heard a couple of doors open and close as David's neighbors looked out to see what was causing the commotion.

He finally came up for air nearly a minute later. "Wow, you missed me!" said Kim as she picked up her packages. "I don't think you've ever kissed me like that before."

"Really? I should have," he replied. "It's great to see you. I wasn't expecting you until tomorrow."

"I know. I thought I'd surprise you." She bent down and picked up the mints and T-shirt and handed them to him. "Here are a couple of souvenirs from Chi-town."

"Thanks, these are terrific. Come on in. I've got a couple of good bottles of wine I picked up at a new little winery last weekend. What do you say we get a couple of glasses and open one?"

"Actually, I'm starved. How about going out for some dinner?"

"We could order some pizza," he countered.

"I've had pizza like four or five times a week all summer," she said, rolling her eyes. "Let's do something else. What about that little French place with the romantic candlelight?"

His face clouded and his eyes flashed. For a moment, she was afraid he would get mad, but then he smiled. "Sure, babe. Whatever you say; it's your first night back in town. Just give me a few minutes to get ready."

He turned and walked back into his apartment as she trailed behind. "Okay, I'll just wait in the living room," she said as he disappeared into the bedroom. As she started to sit down on the sofa, however, she realized that an hour and a half on the freeway had left her with an uncomfortably full bladder. She went into the bathroom, but saw an empty roll on the toilet paper holder. There weren't any other rolls visible, so she turned to the small cabinet under the sink.

When she opened the doors, she immediately forgot about her bladder. Crammed in among the bathroom supplies was a cardboard box full of pills. The pills weren't labeled, but Kim didn't need labels to recognize them. She gingerly picked up a capsule and emptied it onto her palm. The gray-green granules looked all too familiar. She sniffed them. As she suspected and feared, they had a woody, faintly bitter smell that she knew well from trips to the production floor at Bjornsen Pharmaceuticals.

She stood up slowly, threw the empty capsule in the toilet, flushed it, and washed her hands. Then she walked back out to the living room. She thought about just leaving, and took a step toward the door, but then she stopped. *No, I need to talk to him first.* She sat down stiffly on the sofa and waited for David to come out of the bedroom. At last, the door opened and he emerged wearing a white polo shirt and crisply creased khaki slacks—both new additions to his wardrobe since the beginning of the summer. "So, how do I look?" he asked with an expectant grin.

"You look great," she replied. "But, uh, David, I went into the bathroom while you were getting ready. There wasn't any toilet paper so I, well, I looked under the sink and—"

"What were you doing going through my stuff?" he demanded.

"I'm sorry. I had to go to the bathroom and I didn't think you'd mind."

David glared at her. "I mind you digging around in my cabinets!"

She dropped her eyes from his. "David, there was Neurostim in there, lots of it. It's totally illegal for you to have that."

"What I keep under the sink in my bathroom is my own business," he snapped. "I didn't get it from you, so why do you care? I didn't steal it or kill anybody, so leave me alone!"

"How did you get it?"

"That's none of your business."

"Yes, it is!" she shot back. "You got that from the company I worked for, and if anyone ever finds out—"

He strode over to the sofa and stared down at her. "No one is going to find out! Just drop it, okay? You're not back five minutes and you're already spying on me and trying to control my life!"

"David, this is serious!" she persisted. "I can't just—"

He grabbed both her arms, lifted her from the sofa, and shook her like a rag doll. "I said drop it!" he shouted.

He dropped her and she collapsed back onto the sofa. She gasped and stared at him dumbly for several seconds. "I'd better go," she said softly.

She started toward the door, but David got there ahead of her and put his hand on it. "I'm sorry, Kimmy. I don't know what came over me. I've been so stressed and under so much pressure because of med school and everything, and I just snapped. Can we just go out for dinner and pretend this never happened? We'll go wherever you want."

She looked up at him and saw the old David. The rage was gone from his eyes and voice, and he really did seem sorry. But how would he react if she said no? She forced herself to smile. "That's okay. You're sure you don't mind the French place?"

He smiled back. "Not at all. Maybe some romantic candlelight isn't such a bad idea."

† † †

At seven o'clock, Pyotr Korovin glanced at his watch as he waited in his van at the Yuragorsk dock. Then he looked again at slip nineteen, which should have held the *Agnes Larsen*. Instead it contained only oily black water and strands of a hardy brown-green seaweed that managed to survive in the polluted waters of the harbor. Captain Kjeldaas was late again, and it would cost him. Apparently, a one-thousand-dollar penalty wasn't enough to keep him on schedule, so this time it would be two thousand. He took the extra bills out of the envelope and slipped them into his pocket.

He wouldn't even try to keep any of the extra money this time. He was still trying to get back into George's good graces after partially botching the job in Oslo. The fire had gone as planned, but George had been furious to learn that Pyotr hadn't managed to kill *any* of the witnesses he'd found in the building.

Pyotr scanned the harbor and saw Kjeldaas's little ship chugging through a fleet of fishing boats on their way out to hunt cod and king crab. He got out of the truck and stood with his heavily tattooed arms folded across his chest as he watched the *Agnes Larsen* make its way to the dock. Kjeldaas was at the wheel and a man Pyotr didn't recognize was on deck, ready to toss the bow line. The stranger was a big man in late middle age with dark brown hair that was unnaturally free of gray. Pyotr assumed the man was a member of the crew, though he didn't have the weather-beaten look of a veteran fisherman or sailor.

Pyotr waited until Kjeldaas and the other man had finished loading the boxes into the truck. Then he handed the captain the envelope of cash. The Norwegian started to count it. "You were late again. You are lucky I pay anything, but I give you five thousand dollars."

"The agreed payment was seven thousand," protested Kjeldaas's companion.

"Who is this?" Pyotr asked the captain without looking at the other man.

"This is Dag," said Kjeldaas. "He is my new business partner."

"Instruct him how business works," said Pyotr. "When you are late, you lose money."

Dag's pale gray eyes flashed. "I will instruct you on how business works with me! You pay the agreed upon price, even if your shipment is an hour or two late. If we don't agree in advance on late penalties, there are no late penalties."

Pyotr smiled at the man's naïveté. "Maybe you would like to instruct this to my boss George?"

"Yes, I would like that," replied Dag. "Let's go see him."

Pyotr laughed. "Of course." He ostentatiously opened the door to the truck's cab. "Please get in. I drive you." Dag got in and shut the door. Pyotr walked around to the driver's side. Before he got in, he grinned at Captain Kjeldaas and said, "Maybe you need a new partner soon."

‡ ‡ ‡

It was 9:00 AM when George Kulish parked his black Porsche Cayman S in the Cleverlad.ru parking lot. He usually arrived by 8:00, but Pyotr had called at 7:30 to say that one of their smugglers had a complaint about the price he'd been paid for a late shipment and wanted to meet with George to talk about it. George enjoyed these "meetings" on a visceral level, but he knew he really didn't have time to attend them from start to finish. Besides, he usually wound up with blood and sweat on his clothes by the time they were over. So he decided to work from his apartment for an hour. He told Pyotr that he would be in by 9:00 and that the smuggler should be "adequately prepared" by then.

George walked up to the main door and waved a magnetic key-card over a sensor panel. The door clicked and he pulled it open. He walked into an empty hallway that had locked doors with their own security panels on either side. At the end of the hall was an elevator door. Instead of a magnetically keyed lock, the elevator had a state-of-the-art biometric lock that measured dozens of points on a person's face and allowed access only to individuals whom it recognized. At present, that was a very select group: George, Pyotr, and the warehouse foreman. The sensor was also backed up by a fingerprint reader, which was installed just to the right of the elevator door.

George pressed the elevator button, stepped to the side, and positioned himself in front of the biometric system's camera. He pressed his right forefinger against the glass of the print reader. The linoleum floor tiles in the hallway were dark gray and grimy, so George did not notice the fresh, black-red drip marks. Even if he had, he would not have been alarmed; but he would have made a mental note to remind Pyotr to clean up after his "guests."

After several seconds, the elevator door chimed and opened. George got in and rode up to his office, his mind absently running through the various things he'd need to take care of that morning after he finished with Pyotr's smuggler.

When George stepped out of the elevator and started walking toward his desk, he heard an oddly familiar male voice behind him. "Hello, George."

He whirled around and saw a man standing between him and the elevator. He must have been standing just to the side of the door when it opened.

The man was in his fifties and did not appear to be armed, but neither was George. Also, the man was much bigger than George and his arms were thicker than George's legs. George stared at him for several seconds. "Bjornsen?" he said at last. "Karl Bjornsen?"

The man smiled. "Very good." He gestured toward the desk. "Please, have a seat. And remember to keep your hands where I can see them."

"What are you doing here?" George demanded. "How did you get in?"

"We had a meeting scheduled for this morning, but maybe your friend at the dock forgot to tell you. We're both here though, so it doesn't matter. Please sit down; we have a lot of ground to cover."

George stared, open-mouthed, for several seconds and then laughed. "Yes, yes we do." He walked over to his desk and sat down. "In fact, I've been meaning to call you for several days. I understand there was a fire and shooting at your Norwegian facility."

"Yes, and we both know who's responsible."

"It's interesting you should say that. When the police watch the surveillance videos, they'll see a man enter and leave the building, and one camera will have captured a good picture of his face. They'll run him through their database and realize he's a German hit man who was recently released from prison. He'll deny any involvement, of course, but he won't have an alibi."

"How unfortunate for him," Karl said.

"Yes, very." George relaxed some as he talked, but he had been badly rattled by finding Karl here. No one had ever beaten a Kulish-designed system before, especially one he had designed for himself. He resisted the temptation to ask Karl how he had done it. "The police will want to know who hired him, but he won't be able to tell them. They will check his bank records, and I was thinking they would find a fifty-thousand-dollar wire transfer from you. But once I found out that you were in Europe and had taken a suitcase full of cash with you, I had a better idea. Here, watch."

He opened a window on his computer and a grainy black-and-white video appeared. It showed Karl standing on a deserted sidewalk handing a briefcase to another man. A newspaper rack behind them displayed a copy of *Die Welt*. "I didn't realize you had dyed your hair, so I may want to darken it a little in the video, but then I'm a perfectionist. There's also a different version of this video, showing the hit man talking to a well-known wholesaler of undocumented pharmaceuticals."

"A competitor of yours, no doubt."

"You're a perceptive man, Mr. Bjornsen." George shifted slightly in his chair and smiled. "Right now, there are only two copies of each video, one on this computer and another on videocassettes of the type used in a typical German security camera."

"And those cassettes are where?" asked Karl.

George's smile broadened. "I thought you might want to know. They're in a safe place, and they will stay there until either I'm convinced that you and I can find a way to do business together without you trying to cheat me, or I'm convinced that we can't. Once I make up my mind, one of those videos will find its way to the proper authorities."

Karl sighed and shook his head. "George, you should know by now that blackmail doesn't work with me—though, unfortunately, it seems to have worked on one of my employees. She gave you confidential documents. I need those back. I also need you to tell the truth about what happened at my company's Norwegian office." He reached into his pocket, pulled out a small video camera, and set it on the desk facing George. The red light was glowing. "I've taped our conversation thus far, but the sound quality probably isn't very good. Besides, you might argue that the voice wasn't yours. That will be harder to do with video."

George stared at Karl for several seconds. "Are you crazy? Turn that thing off and give it to me!"

"No."

George reached for the camera, but Karl batted his hand away. George's eyes turned to steel. "Give it to me, or you will not leave this building alive."

Karl set his mouth in a hard line. "Start talking, or you will not leave this *room* alive."

George looked into the unblinking eye of the camera for several seconds, thinking furiously. "I think there has been a serious misunderstanding. The person you really need to talk to about these things is Pyotr. He handles all interactions with our, ah, Norwegian affiliates. I will call him in here." To his surprise, Karl didn't object as he picked up the phone. There was no dial tone. He looked at the wall and saw that the phone wire had been ripped out of its jack.

"Pyotr and I have already had a conversation," Karl said calmly. "I want to talk to you. You're the one who can tell me everything I need to know—and I want to emphasize that you will need to be completely open and honest. No more lies, no more plots. Just the truth."

"All right. Okay. But before we do that, let me give you my entire file on your company. I do not believe I have confidential documents, but if I do, I want to return them, of course." As he spoke, he opened a large drawer in his desk and reached for the gun he kept there for emergencies.

"Of course," said Karl with a sardonic smile. George was no longer looking at him, however. He was staring into the drawer. His searching fingers had encountered not a gun, but something cold, round, and sticky. He looked down and found Pyotr's lifeless, blood-smeared face staring back at him. Rolling around the back of the drawer was a severed finger. He jerked his hand back and sucked in his breath. The bloody smell of new death filled his lungs and he threw up.

Karl waited until he was done before speaking. "As my Viking ancestors used to say, 'The severed head no longer plots.' I warned you once not to cross me. I will not warn you again. There were no files in that drawer; only this." George looked up and saw his gun in Karl's hand. "If you lie again, I will use it." He paused and put the gun into his waistband. "On second thought, I won't. The noise might attract attention." He held out his large, muscular hands. "If you lie, you will die the way your friend did. Now, are you ready to answer my questions?"

George sucked in a short, ragged breath and wiped his mouth with the back of his hand. He stared at Karl's hands. "Okay."

‡ ‡ ‡

Kim was in bed, but not asleep. For the two weeks between the end of her internship and the beginning of fall semester, she was staying with her parents in the room she had occupied since she was six. The Japanese *manga* posters she had loved during her teen years still adorned the walls. Yearbooks, journals, and the cheesy romance novels she used to read filled the bookshelf in the hutch on her desk. Even her old gym uniforms were still there, neatly folded in her sock drawer.

The posters had been a minor rebellion against her Korean immigrant parents, who disliked anything having to do with the Japanese, who had occupied their homeland for almost half the twentieth century. Kim didn't feel rebellious tonight, though. The rules and order she had grown up with seemed comforting now, not restrictive. They gave certainty. If only she were certain what to do now.

Tell Bjornsen Pharmaceuticals? She knew she probably should, but the personal cost would be huge. They would almost certainly call the police, who would arrest David. Their relationship would be ruined, of course, and his future would be destroyed. She couldn't bear the thought of that happening to the man she loved. Plus, the incident could damage her career as well—potential employers might not believe she was entirely innocent, and she had no proof that she was. Besides, what lab would want to hire a research scientist who dated guys that might steal the drugs she was researching?

Try to talk David out of using Neurostim? That's what she wanted to do, but she doubted it would work. She remembered too well the rage in his face when she had confronted him about the pills under his bathroom sink. That was not a scene she wanted to repeat. Maybe she could try calling him. She didn't really think it would do much good, but at least he couldn't be physically violent with her over the phone.

Tell her parents? She didn't know how they would react—they might do anything from barring her from seeing David to calling his parents to calling the police. She knew that they loved her and would do what they thought was in her best interests. She also wanted to turn the whole situation over to someone who would take care of it for her, or at least tell her what to do.

She had just made up her mind to tell her mother in the morning when her cell phone rang. She found her purse in the darkness and fished out the phone. David's number showed on the glowing screen. Her heart raced as she flipped open the phone. "Hi, David."

"Hi. Sorry for calling so late. Did I wake you?"

"No, I . . . I wasn't asleep."

"Good. I wanted to let you know that I'm really sorry about how I acted when you came over. I shouldn't have yelled at you like that or grabbed you. That was totally wrong, and I promise it will never happen again. Can you forgive me?"

"Of course I can, David. I just—I'm really worried about you. That wasn't like you at all; it was like you were a completely different person."

"I know. I've let myself get way too stressed about school. I feel all wound up and tense, and sometimes I can't sleep for days. I didn't realize how bad it had gotten until I snapped. I'm going to really try to relax and take a step back. I'll work hard and do my best, but I'll have to just let go and let the chips fall where they may." He paused. "I also wanted to let you know that I've been thinking about what you said about the box under my sink, and you're right."

"What was I right about?" she asked cautiously.

"Everything. It was Neurostim, and I shouldn't have it. I just finished flushing all the pills down the toilet, and I thought you should know."

Relief flooded Kim's heart. "Oh, David, that is such good news! Thank you, thank you, thank you!"

He laughed. "Hey, when you're right, you're right. Anyway, I thought you would want to know as soon as possible."

"You were right. I love you."

"I love you too." He yawned. "I think it's time that both of us get some sleep."

As the tension drained out of her body, Kim realized just how tired she was. She yawned too. "No kidding. Good night."

"G'night. I'll call you tomorrow."

Kim closed her phone and dropped it back into her purse. She snuggled down among her pillows and stuffed animals with a sleepy smile on her face, feeling as light and carefree as a feather on a summer breeze. A flicker of doubt hovered at the edges of her mind, but she pushed it away. David had lied to her before to protect his access to Neurostim, but just now he had seemed genuinely contrite. Besides, she would be seeing a lot more of him now that they were both in LA again. She could keep an eye on him for any odd behavior, and she would have plenty of opportunities to poke around his apartment.

It was a good thing he'd called her before she talked to her mom. That could have been a real disaster.

‡ ‡ ‡

Karl reboarded the *Agnes Larsen* with George Kulish in tow. Captain Kjeldaas stepped out of the pilothouse as they came aboard. He watched wordlessly as Karl took George downstairs and locked him into one of the holds. When Karl came back up, he asked, "Was that George?"

"It was," Karl confirmed.

The fisherman nodded impassively. "He is younger than I expected."

A siren wailed in the Yuragorsk streets and was almost immediately joined by another. "We should cast off," said Karl. He quickly untied the mooring ropes as Captain Kjeldaas primed the engine and coaxed it to life.

The fishing boat turned toward the harbor mouth and the open ocean beyond. Karl leaned against the boat's rusty winch and watched the slowly receding shoreline. The busy piers and waterfront streets were filled with honking vehicles and shouting men, but none appeared to be from the police and no one paid any attention to the *Agnes Larsen* as she chugged away. A couple of kilometers inland, a pall of gray and black smoke had begun to rise over the rooftops in the direction of the Cleverlad building. Karl smiled with satisfaction. "One good fire deserves another," he said to himself.

He opened a steel briefcase he had left onboard during his visit with George. Inside were his passport; thick wads of dollars, kroner, and rubles; and a bulky satellite phone. He took out the phone and dialed Alex Geist's cell phone. Geist answered immediately. "Hello, Mr. Bjornsen. Is your Russian business trip complete?"

"It is. I'm on my way back to Norway now. How did your meeting go?"

"As I expected, the American and Norwegian authorities will be grateful for any information you can provide regarding our mutual acquaintance." His voice was precise and even. "However, he and his affiliates will be very hard to extradite and are unlikely to be prosecuted in Russia. Therefore, any information you have will be of only limited use and value. Under these circumstances, the Americans will not grant you or your companies immunity. The Norwegians were less absolute, but still pessimistic. I am sorry."

"Don't be. Both you and Bert Siwell warned me of that likelihood. Do you think the authorities would change their minds if I could persuade our mutual acquaintance to give a videotaped confession and accompany me to Norway?"

The line was silent for several seconds. "I . . . Is this possible?"

Karl laughed. "Did I just flap the unflappable Alex Geist?"

Geist chuckled drily. "Answer my question first."

"It is very possible. My offer has a limited duration, however. I need an answer within the next hour, and I'll need the paperwork completely executed in two hours. I don't have the luxury of making this a negotiation. It's a take-it-or-leave-it offer, and they will have to act fast if they want to take it."

"I understand. I will call my contacts at DOJ and Kripos as soon as I get off the phone with you. I will also call Mr. Siwell and tell him that his writing talents are likely to be needed very soon."

"Excellent. I look forward to hearing from you."

The line went dead and Karl smiled and walked around to the pilothouse. He opened the door to the bridge, which wasn't much bigger than a large closet. Captain Kjeldaas glanced at him and gave a curt nod of acknowledgment. "How long until we reach Torsknes?" Karl asked.

"An hour, maybe an hour and a half."

"I may need to stay at sea for two hours or more. Will that be a problem?"

The fisherman shrugged. "We may get boarded by the Kystvakt, and they will check the holds. That is the only problem."

Karl nodded. "Do what you can to avoid them."

"I always do. Sometimes I win; sometimes they win."

"Well, if you win this time, I will double what I am paying to rent your boat today."

The fisherman wrinkled his leathery forehead and nodded appreciatively. "I will do what can be done."

Karl had no doubt that Captain Kjeldaas meant what he said. He was already getting $250,000 for the day's work—more than he was likely to net from a decade of smuggling runs.

Karl's satellite phone rang and he stepped back out onto the deck. He looked at his watch as he flipped open the phone. It had been only twenty minutes. "Hello, Alex."

"Hello, Mr. Bjornsen. We have a deal. Mr. Siwell is finalizing the papers now."

Chapter Fifteen

Openings

ANNE AND GUNNAR STROLLED ARM-IN-ARM down Hinsdale's oak and maple-lined streets in the night. No moon or stars shone, and the humid darkness was interrupted only by pools of yellow light cast by the wrought iron street lamps. The day had been unseasonably hot and humid for early October, though few fall days in the Midwest can fairly be described as "seasonable"—most are too hot or too cold, generally without advance warning.

The heat had eased some with nightfall, but the air remained heavy and warm, stirred occasionally by sudden, gusty breezes that held the promise of a thunderstorm during the night. "Is the trial starting next Monday?" asked Anne.

"Yes."

"How do you feel about it?"

"Fine."

They walked in silence for several seconds. "Are you thinking about it a lot?" she asked.

"What kind of a question is that?"

"The more you think about something, the less you talk about it."

Gunnar chuckled. "It has been on my mind," he conceded. "I've been fighting with Karl about the company for ten years. One way or the other, that fight is about to end. Except for the day I married you, I can't think of a more decisive time in my adult life. Either Karl will have the company all to himself, or I will—just in time to launch our first truly revolutionary drug. The other one will be standing on the outside, completely shut out."

"That will be hard on whoever is left out."

Gunnar shrugged. "It's his own fault."

"And if it's not him?"

"Oh, it will be. I'm feeling pretty good about this."

"But what if you're wrong?"

"Then I'm wrong," said Gunnar irritably. "That's a bridge we can cross when we reach it. There's no reason to ruin our evening by talking about it now."

They walked in silence for a few minutes. "Will Henrik Haugeland be staying with us while he's here?" Anne asked.

"Ben Corbin wants him to stay in a hotel until after he testifies. Otherwise, it could come out that he was our guest and that would make him look less impartial to the jury. After he's done testifying, I may invite him to stay with us. He and I will be very busy."

‡ ‡ ‡

Ben took Eric from Noelle, expertly positioned him, and started patting him gently on the back. After about a minute, Eric produced an enormous belch. "Nice work," said Noelle.

"I get a sense of accomplishment when he lets loose a big one like that," replied Ben as he put Eric into his bassinet. "I can actually feel him deflate."

Noelle smiled and patted the sofa next to her. Ben sat down and she put her head on his shoulder. "It's good to be home, isn't it?" she said.

"Oh, yeah. There's nothing like being back in our own house again. And I can't tell you how much I missed real pizza."

"I'll just be happy to sleep in my own bed with you beside me."

For the six weeks that Eric had been in neonatal, Noelle had slept on a narrow hospital bed in his room. Most nights Ben had been there too, but had been stuck sleeping in a vinyl reclining chair.

"That'll be nice," Ben agreed. "It'll also be nice not to have a nurse coming in every hour and turning on the light to do whatever it is they did with Eric."

"It was only a couple of times a night. The other times it was usually Eric wanting to be fed."

"Well, at least there will be fewer nightly interruptions," Ben replied. "To tell you the truth, though, I'm just glad he's okay and acting like a normal baby. And I'm glad you'll be okay as soon as that cast comes off your leg. I'm willing to go through lots of sleepless nights for that."

"Me too. We've been really blessed; this could have turned out a lot worse. It scares me that whoever attacked us is still out there. I'll be happy when they catch him and we can close the book on the whole thing."

"I don't know who pulled the trigger that night in Oslo," replied Ben, "but I still think Karl pulled the strings. I'd love to see him arrested, but first I'm going to take away his company and every penny he owns. Then the cops can have him."

"Speaking of cops, did you or Sergei ever get a clear answer on why no one is guarding us? I'd feel a lot safer if there was a squad car parked out front."

"So would I," agreed Ben. "My guess is that the police are watching every move Karl makes, so he's not likely to send someone after you again. It's tough to tell exactly what's going on, though—Sergei has been getting some pushback from his contacts in Norway. They say that their organized crime task force, Kripos, is handling the case now, so they can't talk about it. Sergei tried calling Kripos, but they say they have a confidentiality policy about ongoing investigations, so they won't tell him anything.

"Now that we're back in the U.S., we don't have to rely on the Norwegian police, of course. Sergei and Elena are going to try going through the FBI to see if they can get some answers, or at least get someone to keep an eye on you until Karl and his hit man are arrested."

‡ ‡ ‡

David sat at his kitchen table. Canned outlines on cardiology and advanced cytology, heavily highlighted textbooks, class notes, and practice exams formed a rough crescent around him.

His first round of exams started in just a few days, and his studying was not going well. He thought he would be okay on oncology and immunology, the two subjects he had studied over the summer, but the rest of his courses were giving him trouble. No matter how much he studied and memorized, it was so hard to keep everything straight, and some of the formulas he was supposed to be able to apply simply made no sense to him. Without help, he doubted he would do much better than a C average—better than last year, but still not enough to land a good internship.

He got up, stretched, and walked over to his hall closet, which held a small stack washer-dryer unit. He opened the door and paced up and down the hall for several minutes, pausing occasionally to look thoughtfully at the washer. Taped to the back of it were two large freezer storage bags that together contained 823 doses of Neurostim. Despite his promise to Kim, he had not flushed the pills, though he had cut his dosage to one-third of what he had been taking at the time of "the Incident."

The new dosage level seemed to be working—sort of. Since he had made the change, he hadn't experienced any more episodes of uncontrollable rage. Also, Kim had commented several times that he was "the old David again." He found himself getting irritable a little more easily than he had before, but he attributed that mainly to increased caffeine consumption with the beginning of the school year. On the other hand, he was still struggling in school, just not as much as last year. That wasn't good enough. Not for him.

He decided to go back to the old dosage level, but only until exams were over. Even if there were a direct link between Neurostim and the Incident—which he wasn't convinced of—he doubted there was much risk that he'd lose control again. He could handle high levels of the drug for a few days. Kim had told him that the human body processed Neurostim quickly, so if he caught himself getting agitated or losing his temper, he could just go off the drug for a day or two and his blood levels would drop back down.

He reached behind the washer, grabbed two doses of Neurostim and popped them in his mouth. He swallowed quickly and waited for the familiar sense of increased focus and alertness to hit him.

‡ ‡ ‡

Sergei found Ben in his conference room, getting ready for opening statements amidst piles of heavily highlighted transcripts, financial statements, notes, and empty Mud Hole coffee cups. Ben muttered and gestured as he ran through his points, occasionally jotting something on the outline in his hands. He looked up and saw his friend leaning in the doorway. "I didn't want to interrupt you in mid-argument," said the tall Russian.

"I've run through it five times and there's one point that bothers me each time: I want to tell the jury about the shootings and fire and leave them with the clear impression that Karl was involved. Bert Siwell will jump up and object, of course, so I need to make sure I have irrefutable evidence backing me up. Ideally, I'd like it if Karl had been indicted or arrested. I know none of your sources will tell you if they're getting ready to make an arrest, but what kind of vibe are you getting from them? Are they getting close to issuing an indictment or arrest warrant?"

"Tough to tell," Sergei replied. "I'm having trouble getting a clear read on what's going on. This is being handled by the IOCC—the International Organized Crime Center in D.C.—and they're playing it very close to the vest. I have a friend there, but the most he could do was imply that the Norwegians may have made one arrest already."

"Karl's hit man?"

"Could be. Whatever they're working on, it's bigger than the warehouse-robbery-gone-bad scenario the Norwegian police were talking about when we were there. Something like that wouldn't get an IOCC investigation, even if an American was a victim."

"Can you think of anything it could be other than that they're looking at Karl and Bjornsen Pharmaceuticals?"

Sergei shrugged. "Sure, but nothing that's very likely. If I were running this investigation, I'd look at the people Karl was bribing. I'd look at that company he got the money from—what was the name? Clever something? I'd look at local Oslo organized crime. I'd look at anyone who might have a motive to break into that warehouse or stop Noelle's work."

"But you'd look hardest at people who knew that Noelle was there in the first place, right?"

"Yes," Sergei agreed.

"And can you think of anyone more likely to know that than Karl and his minions?"

"Nope."

"Neither can I." Ben leaned back and folded his arms. "Is any of this confidential, or can I ask Karl about it on the stand?"

Sergei thought for a moment. "You can ask him about it as long as you don't mention the IOCC. My guess is that Karl will take the Fifth."

"Mine too," said Ben. "That's fine with me. I'll hammer him with that for the rest of the case. It's almost better than having him confess to a crime, because he's admitting that he's guilty of something, but leaving the crime up to the jury's collective imagination. And I'll be happy to help them imagine."

"Can you do that?" asked Sergei in surprise. "I thought lawyers couldn't comment when a witness took the Fifth. In fact, I didn't know you could force an opposing party to get on the stand and then ask him questions where you know the answers would incriminate him."

"Prosecutors can't do that to defendants in criminal cases," replied Ben with a broad grin, "but this is a civil case. I can make Karl get up there, I can ask him all the incriminating questions I want, and if he takes the Fifth, I can say whatever I want about it."

‡ ‡ ‡

On the first day of trial, the courtroom looked different than it had during the preliminary injunction hearing. The most obvious difference was the presence of a jury. Bjornsen Pharmaceuticals and Gunnar Bjornsen had both demanded money damages from each other, so both had a right to a jury, and both had exercised that right.

Jury selection had gone fairly smoothly, as both Ben and Bert Siwell had apparently developed similar profiles for their ideal juror: someone with a college degree or higher and experience in business or finance. Their jury pool, like most in Cook County courthouses, held few individuals meeting these criteria, so both attorneys were hesitant to use one of their strikes on a remotely acceptable juror. Thus, Siwell let an accountant onto the jury, even though she was more likely than other jurors to understand Karl's fraud and less likely to buy any rationalizations he might have developed since the preliminary injunction hearing. And Ben decided not to strike a retired sales executive who might identify with Karl.

Another difference from the preliminary injunction hearing was that Bert Siwell was opening first. Most lawyers prefer to give their opening statement second because that gives them the opportunity to respond to what their opponent has said and gives them the last word. Both lawyers had wanted to go second and had argued the issue to Judge Reilly the day before. He had heard them out, and because there were no clear rules on the issue, he had flipped a coin to decide who had to go first.

Siwell walked up to the podium and smiled at the judge and jury. "Good morning, your honor. Good morning, ladies and gentlemen. Thank you all for being here today. I personally *hate* seeing a jury summons in my mailbox, and I'm guessing that you do too." A few smiles and nods from the jurors. "I'd also guess that each of you has something you'd rather be doing right now than listening to me, and if you don't . . . well, if you don't, you need to get out more." Smiles from more jurors and a few chuckles. "So thank you. Without the sacrifice you're making, our system of justice could not function."

He gestured to a paralegal sitting beside a projector hooked up to a laptop. She nodded and tapped a few keystrokes. "Stealing is wrong," Siwell continued. As he spoke, the same words appeared in large letters on the screen facing the jury. "You'll be hearing a lot of complex scientific and financial evidence over the next few days, but what it will all boil down to is that Gunnar Bjornsen stole something from his brother's company and doesn't want to give it back. Now, the interesting thing is that I don't think you'll hear him seriously dispute that. I think you'll hear him sit in that chair," he pointed to the witness stand, "and tell you that he developed a drug formula while he was working for the company as their head of research, and now he won't give it to them. He'll also admit that his job was to develop drugs for the company and that any drug he developed—including this one—was the company's property.

"By the way, this isn't just any drug. There are hundreds of drugs developed every year that do everything from reducing earwax buildup to curing toenail fungus. But the drug Gunnar Bjornsen developed is special. Its name is Neurostim and it improves reflexes and makes the brain work faster. In tests with monkeys and rats, it actually made them noticeably smarter. Neurostim is worth billions of dollars to Bjornsen Pharmaceuticals and could save the lives of firefighters or police or our men and women in uniform—that is, it could if Gunnar Bjornsen turned over the formula for it and—"

"Objection," said Ben, rising to his feet. "That's argument."

"Sustained," said Judge Reilly. "Please stick to the facts, Mr. Siwell."

"I apologize, your honor," said Siwell.

Ben sat back down, carefully avoiding a look of irritation. Whether or not Neurostim would "save lives" was irrelevant to who should win this lawsuit, and it was improper and damaging for Bert Siwell to imply otherwise—though not improper and damaging enough for Ben to get a mistrial.

"It's a fact," Siwell continued, "that the formula for Neurostim is highly valuable. No one disputes that. It is a fact that every day that the company doesn't have that formula, it is losing money as a result. It is also a fact that Gunnar Bjornsen doesn't have a real explanation for why he shouldn't turn over the formula. When I ask him about that, I expect you'll hear him do what my five-year-old does when he's caught doing something wrong—try to change the subject. I'll say, 'Jack, did you put your brother's Matchbox cars in the garbage disposal?' and he'll turn around and say 'Well, he ate my bag of Cheetos.' That argument doesn't work at our house, and it shouldn't work in this courtroom.

"So when you hear Mr. Bjornsen and his lawyer going on and on about the company's accounting and finances, recognize what that is: it's an attempt to change the subject. I can assure you that all of those financial questions have answers, and unfortunately you're going to have to listen to them for hours. But as you're listening, ask yourselves, 'Does any of this make it right for Gunnar Bjornsen to steal the Neurostim formula?'

"In fact, ask yourselves that question while you're listening to *all* of the evidence in this case, because that's the question you're going to have to answer at the end of the trial. And once you've heard all the evidence, I think the answer will be as obvious to you as it is to me: it's time for Gunnar Bjornsen to hand over the formula for Neurostim and pay for the damage he has done by stealing it in the first place. Thank you."

Siwell gathered his notes and sat down, and Ben took his place. Siwell's paralegal shut off the projector, but Ben said, "No, no. Please leave that up." Startled, the paralegal looked at Siwell, who shrugged. She turned the projector back on and "Stealing Is Wrong" reappeared on the screen. Ben pointed to it. "You won't hear Mr. Siwell and me agree on much over the next few days," he said to the jury, "but we agree on that. Stealing is wrong, and that principle should guide your deliberations.

"You just heard that the drug Gunnar Bjornsen developed is a revolutionary drug worth billions of dollars. Who should own that drug? You just heard Mr. Siwell say that Bjornsen Pharmaceuticals should. Of course it should. No one disputes that. But contrary to what Mr. Siwell said, that's not the real question you'll have to answer in the jury room.

"The real question is, 'Who should control Bjornsen Pharmaceuticals?' The evidence will show that the current president is an embezzler, and worse. He stole millions of dollars from the company and used the money to fund a campaign of bribery to force Gunnar Bjornsen out as president of the company. And he may have done worse things to keep Gunnar from winning back control of the company. He is a man who will do whatever—"

Siwell stood and interrupted. "Objection, your honor. This is more argumentative than anything I said."

"Mr. Corbin, please stick to what you believe the evidence will prove," said the judge.

"Yes, your honor," said Ben. "You will hear some very troubling things about the president of Bjornsen Pharmaceuticals," Ben said to the jury. "You will have to judge for yourself what to make of them. By the way, Mr. Siwell didn't mention his name: it's Karl Bjornsen; he is Gunnar's brother.

"That right there tells you something. This is a man who forced his own brother out of the company they founded together, the company Gunnar devoted his life to for thirty years. And Karl did it by fighting dirty. As I mentioned earlier, he stole from the company and used the stolen money to bribe some of the company's directors to vote against Gunnar. Is that the kind of person who should be in charge of a major drug company, particularly a company that is developing a multibillion-dollar drug that affects the brain?

"Gunnar Bjornsen doesn't think so. That's why he refused to turn the drug formula over to the company while Karl is still in control. And that's why, after Karl had the company sue him, Gunnar countersued on behalf of the shareholders to take the company back from Karl." He paused for a moment and continued in a lower tone. "Gunnar loves his brother, but unfortunately he can't trust him. He can't afford to, not when the stakes are as high as they are in this case.

"Mr. Siwell gave you a question he wants you to remember while you're listening to the evidence in this case. I'll give you another: Do you trust Karl Bjornsen enough to give him control, not only of Bjornsen Pharmaceuticals, but also of this incredibly powerful and valuable drug? That is ultimately the question you will have to answer at the end of the case.

"And now I'm going to end the way I began—by agreeing with Mr. Siwell. Thank you all for being here today. You are being forced to give up a lot to sit here and listen to this trial, and both my client and I appreciate that."

‡ ‡ ‡

After watching the first day of trial, Sergei checked his watch and hurried out of the courtroom. Ordinarily, he would have gone back to Ben's office to help prepare for the next day's festivities, but this evening he had other plans. He quickly walked the two blocks to the Sidebar, where Elena was waiting for him. "Hi. Sorry to keep you waiting," he said as he walked up to her.

She smiled. "Actually, I just got here myself. Let's grab a table."

Five minutes later, they were seated in a leather booth next to a window with a view of the Chicago River. The brownish-gray water looked almost picturesque as it sparkled in the slanting evening sun. "So how did trial go today?" asked Elena.

"Pretty well, I think. They picked a jury and gave opening statements. Ben did a good job, but so did the other lawyer. They'll start putting on witnesses tomorrow. How was your day?"

"Good. I finally tracked down a witness I've been trying to find for three months, and he's willing to talk to us. Also, my computer died completely, so the office will finally have to buy me a new one, and I basically had the afternoon off."

Sergei laughed. "Sounds like a double win for you. What did you do?"

"I did what I could without my computer, which took about fifteen minutes. Then I spent the rest of the day reading that book Pastor Joe mentioned in his sermon."

"*The Practice of the Presence of God*, or something like that?"

"That's the one."

"That was quick. What did you think of it?"

"It was really interesting," she replied. "This monk, Brother Lawrence, wasn't all that smart or dynamic or anything, but people came to the monastery just to talk to him and see how he lived."

"Pastor Joe described him as being really spiritual, with people coming to sort of watch him. What exactly did he do?" asked Sergei.

"It wasn't really *what* he did but *how* he did it," she said. Her head bobbed slightly as she spoke, as it often did when she was excited. "He was just a regular monk who worked in the monastery kitchen, but he tried to 'practice God's presence' in everything he did, to let it flow through him continuously. He said that for him there was no difference between times of work and times of prayer, because he was always communicating with God and submitting himself to God's will, no matter what he was doing. Everyone around him was just amazed at how . . . how *real* God was in his life. You should read it."

Sergei smiled at her excitement. "I never thought I'd see you more interested in religion than I am."

"Neither did I. It's like . . . Have you ever been to the Grand Canyon?"

He shook his head.

"I went when I was in college," she continued. "It really takes your breath away, but you can't see it until you're almost on top of it. It's basically a big hole and the ground around it is pretty flat, so you don't see anything except a few buildings until you're close enough to the edge to look down into it. I remember hearing this old story about an Indian farmer who lived less than a mile from the canyon his whole life, but didn't know it was there. He knew the paths that led to his farm and to his neighbors' homes and to their village, but none of those paths took him close enough to the canyon for him to see it."

"Doesn't sound very realistic," observed Sergei.

"It's a parable; go with it," she said, giving him a playful kick. "Anyway, one day as he was walking home from his farm, a huge storm blew up and caught him in the open. The sky turned black and wind and hail pounded the farmer and nearly killed him. He saw some bushes off to the side of the path and ran to them. He hid under them until the storm had passed. Then he got up and looked around—and for the first time he saw the Grand Canyon."

"Mm-hmm," said Sergei.

"That's sort of like what happened to me in Norway," Elena continued. "Everything that happened there with Noelle and Einar pushed me out of my comfortable little world and to a place where I could see God. And once I saw him, I couldn't believe I'd never noticed him before. It was like . . . well, like living next to the Grand Canyon all my life and not knowing it was there. I've still got a lot of questions, but I want to know more. I *have* to know more."

Sergei nodded. "It sounds like you're about where I was last year."

"I really want to thank you for being willing to take so much time talking about this stuff over the past month," she said. "I know you tried to bring it up before, but I wasn't always interested."

He laughed. "Yeah, you weren't 'always interested' in the same way that ice isn't always warm."

She smiled sheepishly. "Maybe so. Anyway, I appreciate it."

He returned her smile and looked her in the eye. "Hey, I enjoyed it. I got to spend time with you, and that's one of my favorite hobbies, except maybe during the Winter Olympics."

She blushed slightly and looked out the window. "You've just never understood how thrilling a good biathlon can be."

He chuckled and opened his mouth to say something, but just then the waiter came with their meals. Once he left, Sergei cut off a bite of his steak, but stopped before he put it in his mouth. He looked at Elena, who was busy mixing her seafood Cobb salad. "You know, we've had a lot of good times together."

She nodded and stopped mixing her salad, but she didn't look up. "Yes, we did."

He put his fork down. "I was thinking that it would be good to get back together, but that won't work, will it? We're kind of past the dating stage, aren't we?"

She nodded again.

"But now that we've been getting together a lot as friends, it's . . . well, that's not enough for me. When we broke up, neither of us said anything about being just friends, and I think that was right. It's killing me to be just friends when we've been so much more. I don't know how you feel about this, but I was wondering if maybe we could start . . . not dating, but being more than friends again and maybe . . . well, maybe start thinking about where we might go long term." He took a deep breath and let it out. "What do you think?"

She looked up. Her eyes were dry, but her voice was unsteady. "Sergei, I can't let you do this to me again. I can't let myself start caring for you again, not like that."

He put his fork down. "Why not?"

She sighed. "Because I can't start loving you again and then have you pull the rug out from under me. Because I'm thirty-three and I can't waste my time on a relationship that's not really going anywhere."

"What do you mean I pulled the rug out from under you? You're the one who walked out on me, remember? We were having lunch at Singha and you stood up and literally walked out on me and left me there with everyone staring at me."

"Because you had just said you wouldn't marry me!" she said, her eyes flashing angrily.

"Well, I'm saying something different now."

"Are you? All I'm hearing is, 'Let's get back together and see what happens.'"

"Well, that's different, isn't it? I'm not saying I won't marry you anymore."

She shook her head. "I'm sorry, Sergei. That's not good enough." She smiled. "You'd better eat your steak. It's getting cold."

Chapter Sixteen

Damage

BEN SAT AT THE DEFENDANT'S COUNSEL TABLE, glancing back and forth between the jury and Gunnar, who was on the witness stand being cross-examined by Bert Siwell. Gunnar was doing as well as could be expected, but Siwell was good at cross. The jurors' body language was not encouraging—they were paying attention, which is rarely good when the other side is questioning a witness. They were also smiling at Siwell's one-liners, but not at Gunnar's deliberate, sometimes irritated responses. Gunnar's appearance didn't help: he was frowning occasionally and forgetting to look at the jury when he answered questions. He also was fidgeting with a pen and hunching forward in the witness chair, which made him look defensive and nervous. He *was* defensive and nervous, of course—virtually all witnesses are when they're being cross-examined—but juries nonetheless tend to react negatively when witnesses let it show. In Gunnar's case, his tension and posture made him look vaguely like a giant ape trapped inside the confines of the witness stand.

Siwell was scoring points on the topics Ben had expected, such as the "crawling to me" e-mail and the fact that Gunnar had developed the drug formula as part of his job duties at Bjornsen Pharmaceuticals and refused to turn it over to the company. That was about it, though. Siwell hadn't dropped any sandbags in this hearing—or at least he hadn't yet.

Then came the words Ben had been waiting for. Siwell turned to the judge and said, "I have no further questions for this witness, your honor."

"Any redirect?" Judge Reilly asked Ben.

"No, your honor."

"All right, you're excused, Mr. Bjornsen," the judge said with a nod to Gunnar. "Thank you." Gunnar nodded back and awkwardly maneuvered around the witness chair and out of the stand. "Are you ready to call your next witness, counsel?" the judge asked Ben.

"Yes, your honor. We call Henrik Haugeland."

Henrik looked and sounded like a stereotypical Northern European professor. He wore a black suit with a slightly old-fashioned cut and a conservative red and yellow striped tie. His gray beard and hair were neatly trimmed, and he wore steel-rimmed glasses with small round lenses. He listened gravely as the bailiff swore him in and repeated the witness oath in a clipped, lilting Nordic accent.

Ben walked up to the podium. "Good morning, Mr. Haugeland. Could you tell the jury your name and a little about yourself?"

Henrik turned to the jury. "My name Henrik Edvard Haugeland," he said. "As you can perhaps hear, I am a Norwegian. For twenty-seven years, I have been an accountant at Bjornsen Norge, which is a subsidiary of Bjornsen Pharmaceuticals. I tried to retire three years ago, but I was home too much, so after six months my wife asked me to go back to work at least part-time." Several members of the jury, mostly married women, smiled.

"Did you go back to Bjornsen Norge?" Ben asked.

Henrik nodded. "Yes. They had hired two more accountants to replace me, but neither one had very much experience in the pharmaceuticals industry, so the company brought me back for twenty hours per week."

"Do you know Gunnar and Karl Bjornsen?"

"Yes, I know them well. They both interviewed me when I applied for a job. The company was much smaller then."

"Who was the president of Bjornsen Norge when you first went to work there?"

"Gunnar Bjornsen."

"Is he still the president of Bjornsen Norge?"

"No, Karl Bjornsen, who is the chairman of the board, had Gunnar removed as president several weeks ago."

"While Gunnar was still president, did he ask you to search the company's accounting records for documents related to a Bjornsen Norge customer called Cleverlad or Cleverlad.ru?"

"Yes."

"And did you do that?"

"I did, with help from my son, Einar, and your wife, Noelle."

"These records, were they regularly kept in the course of the business of Bjornsen Norge?"

"Yes, these were the company's regular accounting files."

"Did Gunnar tell you why he wanted you to look at those records?"

"Yes."

"What did he say?"

"Objection, hearsay," said Siwell as he rose to his feet.

"Your honor, it's not hearsay, because I'm not trying to prove the truth of Mr. Bjornsen's statement to Mr. Haugeland," responded Ben.

The judge nodded. "You're just showing his state of mind when he was looking at the records, right?"

"Yes, your honor," Ben confirmed.

"All right. Objection overruled." Judge Reilly turned to the jury. "Ladies and gentlemen, the upshot of that little exchange of legalese is that whatever Mr. Bjornsen told Mr. Haugeland about why he wanted these records reviewed is not sworn testimony, so you shouldn't consider it evidence of the truth of what Mr. Bjornsen said. You should only consider it insofar as it helps explain why and how Mr. Haugeland carried out his review." He turned back to Ben. "You may proceed, counsel."

"Thank you, your honor. Do you remember the question, Mr. Haugeland?"

"Yes, I do. Gunnar told me that he believed that his brother, Karl, was embezzling the money that came in from sales to Cleverlad and was using false accounting entries to hide what he was doing."

"You said that you performed the search that Gunnar Bjornsen requested. What did you find?"

"Gunnar had been right about Karl," replied Henrik. "We found records showing that fifty million Norwegian kroner—a little over seven million U.S. dollars—had come in from a series of sales to Cleverlad over the previous four years. Those amounts showed on the Norwegian accounting records of Bjornsen Norge, but I found that a separate set of accounting statements had been prepared in America that did not include them."

"If seven million dollars of income was removed from the company's balance sheet, didn't that throw off all the other numbers?" asked Ben.

Siwell stood. "Objection, calls for expert testimony."

Ben started to respond, but the judge said, "This seems pretty basic to me. I'll let him answer. Overruled."

"The answer to your question is 'yes,'" said Henrik, "unless there was an offsetting entry someplace else. If such an entry were made, there would be two different numbers in the financials, but everything else would stay the same. That is what we found in Bjornsen Norge's financials."

"What was the offsetting entry?" asked Ben.

"It was actually a series of entries in the company's expense accounts," Henrik explained. "We discovered that a number of unauthorized expenses had been charged. They totaled almost exactly the amount of the Cleverlad sales. The remainder was just charged as 'office supplies' to make the numbers match."

"You said the Cleverlad money was used to cover 'unauthorized expenses.' Could you be a little more specific? What kinds of expenses are you talking about?"

"Art purchases, trips to ski resorts, cases of extremely expensive wine, that sort of thing. Expenditures of that type always require written authorization by senior level executives, but none of the files for these charges had the required approvals. In fact, many of them had little or no documentation at all, and what was there was often inaccurate. For example, one case of wine that cost over five thousand dollars was described as 'office supplies' in the supporting paperwork."

"I'd like to work in that office," commented Ben, drawing a chuckle from the jury. "Did you try to figure out who drank the wine, took the ski vacation, and so on?"

"We did."

"What did you find?"

"We could not trace all of the expenses, but for those that we could, we found that all of them went to shareholders and directors of Bjornsen Pharmaceuticals, which owns one hundred percent of the stock of Bjornsen Norge."

"Why would Bjornsen Norge pay for a ski vacation for a director of Bjornsen Pharmaceuticals?"

Siwell popped up again. "Objection, calls for speculation."

Judge Reilly looked at Ben uncertainly, so Ben volunteered, "This won't be speculation, your honor. I can ask some more foundational questions if the Court would like."

"Please do."

"Mr. Haugeland, are you aware that last year there was a vote of the board of directors of Bjornsen Pharmaceuticals regarding whether Gunnar Bjornsen would continue to be president of that company?"

"Yes. This was big news in the company."

"Excuse me, counsel," said the judge. "Mr. Haugeland, I thought you said that Gunnar Bjornsen was president until a few weeks ago. Did I mishear you?"

"It is more likely that I was unclear," replied Henrik diplomatically. "He stopped being president of Bjornsen Pharmaceuticals last year. He was president of Bjornsen Norge, which is a separate company, until recently."

Judge Reilly reddened slightly. "Thank you for that clarification; I think you did say that earlier. Please continue your questioning, Mr. Corbin. I apologize for the interruption."

"Not at all, your honor," replied Ben, who felt a little sorry for the judge, who was presiding over what was probably his first or second complex commercial case. "Mr. Haugeland, do you remember which directors of Bjornsen Pharmaceuticals voted to remove Gunnar Bjornsen as president?"

"I have not memorized their names, but I do have a copy of the resolution removing Gunnar and making Karl president in his place. The resolution lists all the directors who voted for it, all the ones who voted against it, and all the ones who did not vote."

"Do you also have a list of the shareholders who voted to elect the different directors?"

"I do."

"Did you compare those lists to the names of the individuals who got the wine, went skiing on the company's nickel, and so on?"

Henrik nodded. "We did. The directors who received these, ah, unauthorized gifts voted to remove Gunnar. The shareholders who received such gifts elected directors who in turn voted to remove Gunnar."

"All of them?"

"All of them."

"You said that you discovered all these things by looking at documents. Where are those documents?"

"They were destroyed in a fire."

"Was it an accidental fire?"

Henrik's face became grim and he shook his head slowly. "No."

"How do you know?"

"I was there when the fire started."

"Could you tell the jury what happened?"

274

"After we had finished reviewing the records, we had many documents to copy—documents that proved all the things we have been discussing today. I was at the company with Noelle and Einar after business hours and we were making these copies. I was in back where we keep boxes of old records. I heard my son yelling and a sound like firecrackers. There was an ax on the wall for fires, so I took it and ran out to the office. There was a man with a gun standing there. Noelle and Einar were lying on the floor. Noelle was shot in the leg. She was screaming and trying to crawl away. Einar was—" His voice broke and he looked down for several seconds. The courtroom was completely silent while he regained his composure. "Einar was bleeding from several places. He was not moving. I ran toward the man with my ax. He pointed the gun at me for an instant and ran away. Perhaps he had no more bullets. Once he was gone, I locked the door and called the police. Then I went to help Einar and Noelle.

"While I was helping them and waiting for the police and ambulance, I smelled smoke. I looked out the window in the door and I saw fire. I took Einar and Noelle out of the building. By the time I was done, most of the building was on fire. The fire department saved the warehouse, but the office and all of the records were completely destroyed."

Ben sneaked a quick glance at the jurors before asking his next question. As he hoped, they were all watching Henrik raptly. "Based on your review of those records and your knowledge of Bjornsen Norge, are you aware of anyone who would have a motive to shoot Einar and Noelle and start that fire?"

Ben expected Siwell to object again, but he stayed in his chair. "Karl Bjornsen and the individuals who benefited from the Cleverlad money," said Henrik. He looked directly at Karl, who was sitting in the front row of benches. "I cannot be certain, of course, but I strongly believe Karl was involved."

"Why is that?" asked Ben.

Siwell cleared his throat and both Ben and Judge Reilly looked at him expectantly, but still he said nothing. "Because Karl had a motive, for the reasons we already discussed," answered Henrik, speaking quickly as if he feared being interrupted. "Also, none of the shareholders or directors know what happens at Bjornsen Norge nearly as well as Karl. I think he discovered what we were doing, probably from a spy in Bjornsen Norge. Then he sent a criminal to stop us and destroy the evidence we found."

"No further questions, your honor," said Ben as he gathered his notes and returned to his seat.

"All right," said the judge. "Any cross, Mr. Siwell?"

"Just a few questions," replied Siwell as he rose and walked to the podium. "Good afternoon, Mr. Haugeland."

"Good afternoon," replied Henrik stiffly, but politely.

"Let me start with something I know is on the jurors' minds: how is your son, Einar?"

"He is out of the hospital now. He has pain in his back and side and one of his kidneys was destroyed. He tires easily and he limps, but with therapy he should lead a normal life."

"Good. I'm glad to hear it. And how is Noelle Corbin? She was pregnant at the time of the shooting, wasn't she?"

"Mr. Corbin will know better than I, but it is my understanding that both she and her baby will recover, though until her leg heals she will limp as well. Things could have been much worse."

"Yes, they could, and we're all relieved that they weren't. Now I'd like to turn to some matters that have more relevance to this lawsuit. I believe you testified that you have been an accountant at Bjornsen Norge for twenty-seven years. Is that correct?"

"Yes."

"How many other accountants does Bjornsen Norge employ?"

"That has changed over time. In the beginning, I was the only one. By the time I left, there were six of us."

"Would it be fair to describe you as the senior accountant there?"

"Yes."

"Would it also be fair to say that you know more about Bjornsen Norge's accounting records than anyone else?"

"Yes, that would also be fair."

"And yet this massive fraud occurred under your nose and you knew nothing about it until Gunnar Bjornsen asked you to review the company's records?"

"Well, the company has hundreds of customer accounts and thousands of expense accounts. I am not personally familiar with all of them. Furthermore, many entries are generated from transactions in America, such as when Bjornsen Pharmaceuticals signs a supply contract that covers both it and Bjornsen Norge. We cannot check the accuracy of those entries."

Siwell paused and raised his eyebrows. "That was a yes or no question. It sounds to me like you can't say 'no,' but you don't want to say 'yes.' Is that a fair statement?"

Henrik opened his mouth and then shut it. He smiled. "Yes, it is. I am perhaps defensive on this point. I trusted the people I work with, and clearly there is at least one person I should not have trusted. That lapse in judgment cost my company over seven million dollars and it nearly cost my son his life."

The corners of Ben's mouth twitched. *Nothing like asking one question too many, is there, Bert?* Siwell shuffled through his notes in search of a question that could resurrect what had looked like a promising cross-examination. After thirty seconds of silence, he looked up and asked, "Are you a certified accountant?"

"No. In Norway, very few accountants are certified. When I first entered the field, virtually none were."

"Did you ever bother taking the certifying exam?"

"No. I was able to get a job without it."

"No further questions."

"Do you have any redirect, Mr. Corbin?" asked the judge.

Ben half-rose in his seat. "No, your honor."

Judge Reilly nodded to Henrik. "You are excused, Mr. Haugeland."

Henrik nodded back to the judge. "Thank you, your honor." He stood and nodded to the jury. Each of the jurors nodded back to him.

‡ ‡ ‡

Kim walked into Hammerhead's Club and looked for David and his friends. It was two o'clock on a Thursday afternoon, but the bar was crowded. A number of UCLA students had headed straight for their favorite watering holes once they finished their morning exams. "Born to Be Bad" blared from a giant neon-lit jukebox against one wall, and crowds of students and the occasional disreputable professor stood in groups holding plastic cups of beer and shouting to each other.

David had just finished the second of two big tests and didn't have any classes until Friday afternoon, so he had asked Kim to come out and celebrate with him and some friends. After pushing her way through the crowd for five minutes, she managed to track him down. He was in a semicircular booth near one end of the bar with a group of six other young Asian men. He was near the middle of the booth, so when he saw her he hopped up onto the table, walked across it—nimbly avoiding his friends' beers in the process—and jumped down on the floor. He bounded across the floor and enveloped her in a passionate and beery embrace. "How's the love of my life?"

"Great. So, how did the exam go?"

"Awesome! Totally awesome! I knew every single question." He led her over to the table. "Hey, guys, this is my girlfriend, Kim Young. Kim, this is David C., Jason, Eric with a *c*, Colin, Erik with a *k*, and David Z. We got started about half an hour ago."

"Your David is drinking to celebrate," David C. informed Kim. "The rest of us are drowning our sorrows."

"A couple more beers and yours'll be embalmed," said Colin.

"Lighten up, guys," said David, putting his arm around Kim's shoulder. "It wasn't that hard. I'm sure we all did fine."

"Sorry, Dave," returned Colin, "not all of us remembered to take our genius pills this morning like you."

Kim felt David's body stiffen. "What do you mean?" he asked sharply.

Colin made some response, but Kim didn't hear it. She felt sick to her stomach and her head started spinning. She turned and ran blindly, her eyes filling with tears. She stumbled toward the exit as fast as she could, ignoring David's calls and the exclamations of the people she pushed past.

She collided with a wall of muscle and nearly fell down. A large arm steadied her and a vaguely familiar voice said, "Whoa! Hey, watch where you're goin'. . . Kim? Whatsa matter?"

She looked up and found herself staring into the wide blue eyes of Bedford Lavelle, a defensive tackle for the UCLA Bruins. Kim's sorority had volunteered to help tutor the football players when she was a sophomore, and she had helped Bedford with the basic calculus class he was taking. He was an enormous, slow-speaking man from Sallis, Mississippi. He had asked her out halfway through the semester and had been surprised when she turned him down; girls from her sorority apparently didn't do that to football players often. He wasn't bad looking and she would have said 'yes,' except that she had just started dating David. Also, Bedford had a reputation as a forceful drunk—not necessarily violent, but difficult to refuse.

Before Kim could say anything, David came running up. "What are you doing?" he asked as he reached for her arm. "Come on back. I'll buy you a drink and you'll feel better."

She shrank away from him, unconsciously moving further into the crook of Bedford's arm. "No, David! Stay away from me! You're taking it again!"

"That was just Colin talking out of his butt," he said, waving his hand dismissively. "He doesn't know what he's talking about."

"But I do! I know all about your 'genius pills.' I know! And I can tell you're taking them again!"

"Look, I just—" he began, taking a step toward her and reaching out for her again. Bedford's left arm curled around her protectively and his right reached out and pushed David squarely in the chest. "She said to stay away from her," he said firmly.

David stumbled backward and tripped over someone's foot. He fell, knocking over a small table. A pitcher of beer landed on his head and balanced there for an instant like a comical crown. Bedford laughed, as did several other bar patrons. "David!" Kim cried as she tried unsuccessfully to disentangle herself from Bedford's arm.

David sprang to his feet and lunged at Bedford, who reached out with his right arm to intercept him again. But David was too quick. He ducked under the football player's grasp and punched him in the side. Kim, who was now pressed against Bedford's other side, could feel the shock of the blow through his body. The big man grunted and pushed her away to free both his arms for combat.

The two men squared off in the empty circle that always forms when a bar fight starts, no matter how crowded the club is. It did not have the look of a fight that would last long: Bedford weighed roughly double David's 160 pounds. He also carried himself in a way that made it clear he had significantly more experience in these situations than David did. After a few seconds of feinting and circling, Bedford used a bull rush to crowd his smaller opponent into a corner by a pool table where he couldn't escape.

Kim pushed her way through the yelling spectators just in time to see Bedford hit David with a gut punch so powerful that it lifted him several inches off his feet. She screamed, but to her surprise David did not collapse. In fact, he hardly seemed to feel the blow. He punched Bedford twice in the face, his arms moving so fast that the larger man couldn't react.

Bedford staggered back and Kim yelled, "Run, David!" But David didn't run. He grabbed a cue from the pool table and swung it like a baseball bat. He hit Bedford on the left side of the head and the cue shattered. Bedford fell to the floor in a disorganized heap.

David jumped on top of the football player, grabbed his shaggy blond hair with both hands and began pounding his head against the uncarpeted concrete floor with all his might. Bedford did not resist.

Kim screamed again and ran forward, but someone held her back. She turned and saw a burly man wearing a blue Hammerhead's shirt emblazoned with the word *Security*. A second man with a similar shirt pointed a Taser at David and yelled, "Stop! Get off him!"

David ignored the order and smashed Bedford's head into the floor again. The bouncer pulled the Taser's trigger and two small needles attached to thin wires shot into David. He stiffened, let out a guttural shout, and collapsed on the floor next to Bedford.

The man with the Taser walked over to the two inert forms on the floor. He gave the two men a nudge with his toe, but neither moved. He swore, kneeled down between them and put a finger on each man's neck. The bar was now quiet, except for the jukebox. After a few seconds, he called out, "No pulse on either of 'em! Call 9-1-1, and someone help me with CPR!"

‡ ‡ ‡

Ben was in his office preparing Karl's cross-examination when the call came. Susan had gone home for the day, so the call rang directly through to Ben. "Hello, Corbin law offices, Ben Corbin speaking."

"Hello, Ben, this is Curt Grunwald at the U.S. Attorney's Office."

"Oh, good evening, Curt. What can I do for you?"

"We worked together pretty well on that Chechen case, and I'm hoping we can do it again. I understand that you're representing Karl Bjornsen's brother in a legal dispute they're having."

"That's right."

"And are you planning to put Karl on the stand tomorrow as a hostile witness?"

"I am," replied Ben slowly. He didn't like the fact that Grunwald was apparently on a first-name basis with Karl. "Why do you ask?"

"Karl is cooperating with us on a very sensitive investigation. We're concerned that confidential information may come out, either during your cross of him or Bert Siwell's direct, and that the press might publish some or all of it. That could be very damaging to our investigation."

"All right. What are you asking me to do?"

Grunwald hesitated for an instant. "Well, we'd like you to not ask him about that shooting and fire in Norway. Also—and I know this is a lot to ask—we'd like you to agree to a stipulation that can be read to your jury that says basically that the parties agree that Karl wasn't responsible for those crimes."

Ben sat in open-mouthed silence.

"Ben, you there?" asked Grunwald.

"I'm here. What . . . how do you know he isn't?"

"We and the Norwegians have investigated that incident pretty thoroughly, and we're convinced that Karl was not behind it."

"Well, I'm not convinced," Ben said sharply. "And with all due respect to you and your office, Curt, it will take more than your say-so to change my mind."

Grunwald chuckled. "I thought that might not satisfy you. I have authority to share some information with you under the same terms and conditions as last time. I'll fax a letter of agreement to you now. Sign it, fax it back, and we can talk."

"Fine." Ben hung up and went to check the fax machine. There was nothing on it yet. His mind whirled as he waited for the letter to come through. Whatever Karl had done to get the USAO to intervene on his behalf, it must have been pretty dramatic. Ben could not imagine what it was, but his mind's eye could now clearly see a huge sandbag hanging over his head.

The fax machine came to life and spat out Grunwald's letter. Ben looked it over quickly. It prevented him from using anything he learned from the federal government in *Bjornsen Pharmaceuticals, Inc. v. Bjornsen* or disclosing it to the press, but that was no surprise and was almost certainly nonnegotiable. He signed it, faxed it back, and picked up the phone.

Grunwald answered on the first ring. "Okay, here's the scoop, in general terms: There is a guy who Main Justice, the FBI,

Interpol, and a bunch of other agencies have had their eye on for the past three or four years. He's committed all sorts of felonies related to the Internet and electronic crime, particularly when it comes to selling drugs. But we couldn't do much because he was unextraditable.

"This guy was trying to blackmail Bjornsen Pharmaceuticals into selling him drugs illegally, so he staged the shooting and fire in Norway and threatened to make it look like Karl Bjornsen was responsible. I can't go into details, but Karl made it possible for us to arrest this guy. He also gave us evidence, which we have since confirmed through other sources, that he—meaning Karl—had nothing to do with what happened in Oslo. We—"

"Why am I only hearing this now?" Ben broke in. "You knew someone had tried to kill my wife and unborn son. You must have known that I was getting ready for trial against the guy who would look like the prime suspect to my client and me. And you wait until *now* to tell me this?"

"I'm sorry we kept you in the dark, but we had to. Here's the most confidential thing I'm going to tell you: This guy's customers and suppliers don't know he's been arrested. They think someone tried to kill him and that he went into hiding. He ran virtually all of his operations through e-mail and Internet Web sites, so we've been able to pretend to be him. We're gathering an incredible amount of intelligence right now. If we can keep this going for a few more weeks, we'll be able to take down dozens of major players. We'll be able to make a major dent in Internet drug crime.

"We hadn't said anything to you because we needed to keep this entire operation secret. If word leaked out prematurely, targets would vanish, start destroying records, and so on. We had to keep information about it strictly on a need-to-know basis. You might have *wanted* to know—and frankly I wanted to tell you—but you didn't *need* to know."

"Actually, I did," Ben said angrily. "You knew I was getting ready for this trial, right? Didn't it occur to you that it might come up that two people got shot while they were working on the case, and that a building full of damaging records got burned down?"

"We thought the case was about trade-secret theft and accounting fraud," replied Grunwald defensively. "We thought you might file a separate battery case against Karl, or seek evidence spoliation sanctions for the fire, but no, it didn't occur to us that in the middle of your trial you would suddenly put on a witness who would accuse Karl of arson and attempted murder."

"Well, it should have occurred to you!" Ben shot back.

"Well, it didn't. Look, I'm sorry, Ben. We were prepared to have this call as soon as you raised the issue, but you caught us by surprise. I finished reading the rough transcript of Henrik Haugeland's testimony ten minutes before I called you."

"You got the transcript from Bert Siwell, right?"

"Yeah. He called me this afternoon after your trial recessed for the day and told me what happened. He also said that he plans to have Karl testify about what happened, and tell his whole story, unless I can get you to agree to the stipulation I mentioned."

"Can . . . can he do that?" asked Ben.

"Ordinarily, no. Our agreement with him only allows him to disclose what he knows if he is required to do so during a legal proceeding. But because Bert represents the company, he could subpoena Karl and technically require him to testify."

Ben leaned back in his chair and closed his eyes. He could feel the sandbag crashing down on his head. "So he set us both up."

Grunwald paused. "Could be."

"Oh, he did," replied Ben. "Brilliant piece of work, too." He sighed. "Okay. Let me see if I have this right. My options are either to agree to a stipulation that will be read to the jury, saying that Karl wasn't responsible for the Oslo attack, or to have Bert put him on the stand to tell the whole story—in which case your ongoing sting operation probably becomes public."

"You got it."

"Not much of a choice is it?" He grimaced and shook his head. "I'll talk to Gunnar about it. I understand where you're coming from, but the ultimate decision is up to my client, of course."

"Of course. Thanks, Ben."

Chapter Seventeen

Closings

DAVID LEE'S PARENTS SAT BY THEMSELVES in the waiting room outside a surgery theater at the UCLA Medical Center. Kim Young had been there, but she was now in another room being interviewed—for a third time—by the police.

The waiting room had a collection of Bibles, Korans, Vedas, and other religious books in a plywood bookshelf, together with a random assortment of former best-sellers donated by charities, former patients, and their families. Cheung and Meiying Lee were not reading, however. Mr. Lee stared stoically out the window at the darkening parking lot outside, his back erect and his hands on his knees. Kim had offered to hang up the coat of his dark navy suit when he and Mrs. Lee arrived three hours ago, but he had declined and still wore it.

Mrs. Lee sat beside him, wearing a dress with a cheery floral print that contrasted jarringly with her pale, slack face. Her eyes were red and swollen, and she held a damp handkerchief in her hands. Her purse was still over her shoulder—a habit developed during her youth in one of Hong Kong's poorer areas, where putting a purse on a bench when one sat down was an invitation to quick-fingered thieves.

The waiting room door opened and a doctor in blue surgical scrubs entered. He looked tired and said nothing as he walked over and sat down in a chair facing the Lees. "I'm very sorry," he began. Mrs. Lee bent her head and pressed her handkerchief to her eyes. "We tried everything we could think of to save David, but we just weren't able to. You can see him now if you would like."

Mr. Lee nodded. "I want to see my son," he said quietly.

"All right, but I want to warn you that there is a large cranial incision. We cut away part of his skull in an emergency operation to relieve pressure on the brain and . . . the sight may be disturbing."

"Knowing he is dead is disturbing!" Mr. Lee said with sudden vigor. He stood up and Mrs. Lee stood with him. "Take me to him."

The doctor nodded and rose. He led them out of the waiting room and down a long, tiled hallway. The doctor stopped outside the door and said, "I'll let you be alone with him."

Mr. Lee turned to him. "Will there be an autopsy?"

"I'm afraid it will be necessary, given the circumstances of his death."

Mr. Lee nodded mechanically. "Good. I want to know what killed David." The Lees opened the door and walked in to see what had once been their son.

‡ ‡ ‡

It was a warm night and the Corbins sat on their deck eating Indian takeout. Ben had been in a deep funk ever since he got off the phone with Curt Grunwald, so Noelle had decided to cheer him up by getting food from Ben's favorite restaurant and opening a bottle of a Sauvignon Blanc he liked. He was still in a dark mood—alternately blaming himself for not having seen Siwell's trap, and wondering how he was going to salvage his case—but he appreciated what his wife had done and did his best to show it. He tried to push the case out of his mind and talk about their plans for the still-unfinished nursery and dream about what Eric might be when he grew up. Eric, meanwhile, lay in a bassinet beside the table, covered by a protective anti-insect net. He was sleeping soundly, which of course he did only when his parents were awake. A Beethoven piano concerto played softly from MP3 speakers on a chair next to the bassinet. Brutus was busy running around the yard, hunting June bugs.

The epiphany came to Ben as he chewed a bite of Tandoori chicken. "They have an agreement," he announced.

Noelle looked at him blankly. "What?"

"Karl has an agreement with the U.S. Attorney's Office. If he were just a witness and a good citizen who had helped arrest a criminal, he wouldn't need an agreement. People only make agreements when each side is getting something."

"So what do you think Karl is getting?"

"Immunity," he replied, taking a sip of his wine. "He must be getting immunity for something."

"The embezzlement, bribery, and so on, right?"

He nodded. "That's my guess. Whatever it was, he would have had to make a full confession to the USAO as part of the deal. They won't give immunity unless they know exactly what they're immunizing. And if it turns out that the facts are worse than the person getting immunity lets on, then the deal is off."

"So he would have had to be pretty open with them." Her eyes lit up. "Do you think you can get a copy of the immunity agreement?"

Ben pulled out his cell phone. "No, but I may be able to get something out of Curt Grunwald. I think I've still got his cell number from when we were working out a deal for Dr. Ivanovsky." He paused as he scrolled through the numbers in the phone's address book. "Yep, here it is." He pushed the Call button.

Grunwald answered on the third ring. "Hello."

"Hi, Curt. It's Ben Corbin. Sorry to bother you at home."

"That's fine. Do you have an answer from your client yet?"

"I'm still working on that. I've got a few follow-up questions for you."

"Fire away."

"Okay, you said that the government and Karl have an agreement. Does that agreement give Karl or Bjornsen Pharmaceuticals immunity for anything?"

Grunwald didn't answer immediately. "We normally don't disclose the details of witness agreements, particularly when they relate to an ongoing confidential investigation."

"But witnesses normally don't use loopholes in those agreements to force you to do favors for them in civil lawsuits, do they?" countered Ben.

"No, they don't," agreed Grunwald. "I'll tell you what; if your client is willing to agree to the stip you and I talked about, I'll tell you whether we gave Karl immunity for anything."

"And what he got immunity for?"

"All right, fine. I'll also tell you in broad strokes what the immunity covers—assuming any immunity grant exists."

"Deal. I'll talk to Gunnar and call you back."

Gunnar agreed readily, and fifteen minutes later Ben was on the phone with Curt Grunwald again.

"All right," Grunwald said, "I'm going to trust that you'll be reasonable when we negotiate the stip language with Bert Siwell. You're right in guessing that Karl is receiving immunity for his cooperation. So is Bjornsen Pharmaceuticals. Specifically, they're getting immunity for any crimes arising out of the sale of controlled substances to a certain dealer in illegal drugs, the failure to report income from those sales on their tax returns, embezzlement of the sale proceeds, and use of the sale proceeds for bribery."

Ben whistled. "That's quite a list. I hadn't thought of the tax evasion angle, and I didn't know about the drug dealing, but the rest of it is pretty much what I expected. It sounds like he'd need immunity from more people than just the feds. Are the state and the Norwegians part of the deal?"

"I can confirm that this is a multi-jurisdiction agreement."

"And can you confirm that the 'certain dealer' you mentioned is named Cleverlad?"

Grunwald was silent for a moment. "Why do you ask?"

"Because there were some odd accounting entries about them in Bjornsen Pharmaceuticals' books. I crossed Karl about them at the preliminary injunction hearing."

"I need to start monitoring your case more closely. I can't answer your question, but I'd appreciate it if you didn't tie the cooperation agreement too closely to Cleverlad."

"I . . . well, that may be hard. But I'll do what I can. By the way, do you plan to tell Bert Siwell about our conversation tonight?"

"Not unless he asks," replied Grunwald drily. "He seems to like surprises."

Ben laughed. "Yes, he does, though I'm not sure he's as keen on getting them as he is on giving them."

"I'll call you first thing tomorrow morning to hammer out the wording of the stip," Grunwald said.

"Sounds good. I'll be in my office at eight and I'll be heading to court at 9:15." He clicked off his phone and gave Noelle his first unforced smile of the evening. Then he lifted his glass and said, "To Curt Grunwald!"

‡ ‡ ‡

At 10:15, half an hour after the regular start time, the jurors filed into the jury box and sat down in their accustomed seats. Judge Reilly cleared his throat. "Good morning, ladies and gentlemen. I'm sorry that we kept you waiting today.

"This morning we have a little something to take care of before you hear from the next witness. Shortly before you came in, the lawyers informed me that they had reached an agreement on a statement that they thought should be read to you. I needed to talk to them about it for a few minutes to find out what they wanted read and why. I've decided that you should hear their agreed statement, which is technically called a stipulation."

The judge picked up a sheet of paper and read, "Plaintiff and counter-defendant Bjornsen Pharmaceuticals, counter-defendant Karl Bjornsen, and defendant and counter-plaintiff Gunnar Bjornsen stipulate to the following fact: Law enforcement authorities have concluded that Karl Bjornsen and Bjornsen Pharmaceuticals were not directly or indirectly responsible for the fire that occurred at Bjornsen Norge AS on July twenty-third of this year. They also were not responsible for the shooting of Noelle Corbin and Einar Haugeland that took place on that same day. You should disregard any evidence that may have implied the contrary." The jurors looked surprised, and Ben saw several of them scribbling in their notebooks.

The judge put down the stipulation and turned to Ben. "All right. Mr. Corbin, are you ready to call your next witness?"

Ben stood. "Yes, your honor. We call Karl Bjornsen."

The bailiff swore Karl in and he took the stand. As at the preliminary injunction hearing, he was well-dressed and exuded poise and confidence. "Good morning, Mr. Bjornsen," began Ben. "You are the president and CEO of Bjornsen Pharmaceuticals, correct?"

"Yes. I'm also chairman of the board of directors."

"Thank you. That was going to be my next question. You are the ultimate decision maker at Bjornsen Pharmaceuticals, right?"

"I answer to our directors, and ultimately to our shareholders, but certainly that's true on a day-to-day basis."

"Would it be fair to say that no major decision is made at the company without your input?"

"That would depend on exactly what you're calling a 'major decision,' but in principle that's accurate."

"Your honor, could we have a sidebar conference?" asked Ben.

Judge Reilly looked surprised, but he motioned Ben and Siwell up to the bench on the side opposite the jury. He leaned over and whispered, "Okay, what is it?"

"I'm about to start on a line of questioning that Mr. Siwell may object to," Ben replied, "so I thought I'd get an advance ruling rather than have my questions interrupted."

"All right, Counsel," said Judge Reilly. "What do you want to ask about?"

"Mr. Bjornsen has an immunity deal with the feds and other authorities. I want to ask him about what crimes are covered by that immunity grant."

"That is totally inappropriate!" exploded Siwell in a voice loud enough that several jurors reacted. "The whole purpose of the stipulation this morning was to prevent my client from having to talk about his cooperation with the U.S. Attorney's Office and other authorities."

"I don't plan to ask about his cooperation with the authorities," countered Ben. "I plan to ask about *their* cooperation with *him*. In order to get him to cooperate, they had to agree to give him immunity for crimes unrelated to what happened in Norway, but directly related to this lawsuit. That's a completely different subject and is not covered by our stipulation, your honor."

"This is incredibly irresponsible of Mr. Corbin!" Siwell said through gritted teeth. "If the defendants in the government's investigation found out about the terms of Mr. Bjornsen's cooperation agreement, they could use that to undermine the government's case at trial."

Ben suppressed a smile. His gambit had clearly rattled opposing counsel, enough so that Siwell was now making a rare tactical blunder.

The judge stared at Siwell for several seconds, and then said, "Counsel, unless the law has changed drastically since my days as a prosecutor, the defendants will find out about any witness cooperation agreements in any event. They have a constitutional right to know." He brushed his fingers across his lips and continued, "Okay, here's my ruling: Any objection to Mr. Corbin's proposed questioning based on the grounds described so far is overruled. Do you have any other objections you want to raise?"

"Not now," said Siwell, "though I may when I hear the actual questions."

"Fair enough," said the judge. "Go ahead, Mr. Corbin."

Ben returned to the podium. He now had the full attention of every juror, of course; nothing arouses a jury's curiosity like a sidebar conference. "Mr. Bjornsen, you have been cooperating with the government in its investigation of the shooting and fire in Norway, isn't that correct?"

"Yes."

"And in return for your cooperation, the government has given you and Bjornsen Pharmaceuticals immunity for certain crimes, correct?"

Karl blinked, and for just an instant he looked terrified. But he recovered almost immediately. "Not quite. Your question assumes that my company or I committed crimes. That isn't the case, to the best of my knowledge."

"Well, did you ask for the immunity grant, or was that something the government volunteered to give?"

"We asked for it."

"In fact, you asked for it from several different governmental entities, didn't you? You wanted immunity not just from the federal government, but from the Illinois and Norwegian governments too, right?"

"Yes."

"And you had specific items you wanted immunity for, correct?"

Karl nodded. "That's also true."

Ben looked down at his notes from his conversation with Curt Grunwald. "And those items were 'any crimes arising out of the sale of drugs to a certain dealer in illegal drugs, the failure to report income from those sales on your or Bjornsen Pharmaceuticals' tax returns, embezzlement of the sale proceeds, and use of the sale proceeds for bribery.' Is that true?"

"Essentially, yes."

"And yet your testimony is that you did all of that despite the fact that neither you nor Bjornsen Pharmaceuticals committed any of those crimes?"

"Yes, because there could very well be evidence of those crimes, even if they had not been committed."

Ben paused for a moment, uncertain what to do next. On the one hand, he did not want to ask a 'why' question on cross-examination, particularly when he had no idea what the answer would be. On the other hand, he couldn't leave a loose end that large hanging out there for Bert Siwell to start tugging on during his questioning. That could unravel all of Ben's hard work. "Would you agree with me that evidence of a crime often means that the crime has in fact been committed?"

"Yes, unless there is reason to believe that the evidence was planted. I had reason to believe that evidence of the crimes you mentioned had been planted in my company."

"But you couldn't prove it, could you?"

"No. We could prove—"

"I didn't ask whether there was something else you could prove," said Ben. "You couldn't prove that evidence had been planted at your company, correct?"

A flash of anger showed in Karl's eyes, but he concealed it quickly and smiled. "Now that you mention it, we could prove that some evidence had been planted. The problem was that, after the fire at our Norwegian facility, we could not prove that other troubling documents had been planted. We strongly suspected it, but we couldn't prove it. That's why we needed immunity."

Ben decided to play his last card. "Could you prove that documents had been planted in your own personal files?"

"Yes. In fact, you helped us do it. During an earlier hearing, you showed me two different financial statements for our Norwegian subsidiary, one that was marked Internal Use Only and one that wasn't. The numbers in the two statements did not match, which caused us to worry, of course."

Karl spoke smoothly and energetically, warming to his story. "Just as we started to investigate the mystery financial statements, I began to receive blackmail threats claiming that the company and I were engaging in bribery, embezzlement, and so on.

"We put two and two together, and started looking into our Norwegian operation. We discovered that a junior accountant there was working with an outsider on the extortion scheme. Among other things, she—the accountant—had for some time been sending fraudulent financial statements to my secretary, with notes saying 'For Mr. Bjornsen's files.' The presence of those documents in my files would, of course, implicate me and make me easier to blackmail."

"So you're saying that these extortionists were actually sending you the documents they would later use to blackmail you," remarked Ben. "Wouldn't you agree that that was a high risk—almost suicidal—gamble on their part?"

Karl shrugged and smiled. "Oh, I don't know. It worked, until you discovered one of those documents and surprised me with it the last time I sat in this chair. To tell you the truth, if you send something to a senior executive and tell him it's for his file, there's not a very great risk that he'll actually read it. If you send it to his secretary and tell her that it's for his file, there's virtually no risk at all.

"In retrospect, though, you're right. As I believe you know, the individuals responsible are in custody now and are charged with extortion and other crimes. Unfortunately, I can't go into detail because—as I believe you also know—this matter is the subject of an ongoing confidential law enforcement investigation."

Siwell stood up. "At this point, I'm going to object to any further questioning on these topics until Mr. Corbin has gotten approval from the U.S. Attorney's Office."

The judge looked at Ben. "Mr. Corbin, do you . . . how much further questioning do you have along this line?"

Ben thought for a moment. Karl was proving to be a much more nimble witness than he had been at the preliminary injunction hearing. He was lying, of course, but he was lying exceptionally well. Also, he was lying about a topic he knew better than Ben. Questioning him further was unlikely to be productive and could well prove dangerous. Maybe a talk with the USAO wasn't such a bad idea. "Your honor, I discussed these topics with the U.S. Attorney's

Office last night, but I'm willing to suspend this line of questioning for today so that they can review a rough transcript of today's proceedings and make a judgment regarding the propriety of my questions and Mr. Bjornsen's answers."

‡ ‡ ‡

Ben dropped the highlighted transcript on his desk and rubbed his eyes. "Are you sure about that, Curt?" he said into the Bluetooth headset clipped to his right ear. "He said a lot of stuff that sounded an awful lot like lies to me."

"He may be lying," Grunwald replied, "but he hasn't said anything that directly contradicts what's in our file. We've always operated under the assumption that he was guilty of the crimes he got immunity for, but he's been cagy about exactly what he admitted under oath or in writing."

"I thought witnesses had to make full confessions in order to get immunity."

"As a general rule, they do," Grunwald agreed. "And Karl insists that he has made a full confession. I can't give you the specifics, but he has always said, in effect, 'I didn't commit any of these crimes, but there may be documents showing that I did.' I think he's full of it, but most of the relevant evidence burned up. Besides, what he had to offer us made the deal worthwhile, even if he was lying. I know the whole corporate fraud angle is central to your case, but it's pretty tangential to ours."

"Okay, thanks anyway."

"Sorry I couldn't be more help."

Ben hung up the phone and walked down the hall to the conference room. Sergei was on his laptop, searching for useful information on the remaining witnesses listed by Bert Siwell on his witness disclosure. Noelle was at the table, sifting through stacks of financial documents produced by Bjornsen Pharmaceuticals, hoping to discover something that would disprove Karl's lies. Eric was in a corner, lying in his combination car seat and carrier and making random baby noises. "I just got off the phone with Curt Grunwald," announced Ben from the doorway.

Noelle and Sergei looked up at him. "What did he have to say?" asked Noelle.

"That he doesn't think Karl told the truth, but that he doesn't see any provable lies in his testimony."

"So he doesn't plan to go after him for perjury?" asked Noelle.

Ben shook his head. "That was always a long shot. Curt probably plans to use Karl as a witness during any prosecutions that come out of this investigation he's doing. It would be kind of awkward to do that if he was simultaneously prosecuting Karl for perjury. No, the most I was realistically hoping for was that he might give me some sort of hint if he saw something in the transcript that he knew was a lie."

Noelle raised her eyebrows. "Oh, I hadn't really thought about it from his perspective before. I guess he wouldn't want to destroy Karl's credibility, would he? I'm surprised you thought he would help you at all."

Ben shrugged. "Curt's a straight shooter and doesn't like it when people lie under oath. I also don't think he likes Bert and Karl much now that he's figured out they were using him to set an ambush for us. So I had hoped he might tell me if he knew Karl was lying, or at least react in a way that would make it pretty clear. But no such luck. How's your document hunt going?"

"Not so well. I've found a couple more examples of double sets of financials—one set listing the Cleverlad account and marked *Kun Internt Bruk*, and another set that doesn't have the marking or the account. But I haven't found anything that's inconsistent with Karl's new story. I even found a couple of notes from Bjornsen Norge saying 'Financial documents for Mr. Bjornsen's files' and things like that."

Ben's forehead wrinkled and he was silent for a moment. "Let me throw you a curveball. If all the documents we have are consistent with Karl's story, is it possible he's telling the truth?"

Noelle shook her head and Sergei said, "Are you serious?"

"I am," said Ben. "I was so convinced that Karl was behind the fire and shooting that I didn't see any of the signs that the law enforcement agencies thought he wasn't guilty—the lack of security for Noelle; the lack of information from Kripos, the FBI, and DOJ; the fact that Karl wasn't under arrest. I missed it all because it didn't fit my view of what happened. I should have seen Bert Siwell's trap a mile away, but I didn't. I don't want that to happen again. So let's at least think about the possibility that we may be wrong about this too."

Noelle shook her head again. "I think you're right to be careful, honey, but that's just not possible."

"Why not?" asked Ben.

"Because the documents Henrik and I saw looked and felt genuine. They weren't all in one place in the files; they didn't all look like they had ink from the same pen; they didn't all have the same handwriting. I've been involved in audits where there were forged documents, and it was pretty easy to tell they were forged. These didn't look forged."

"Do you think she should testify?" asked Sergei. "She's on our list."

"I'm sure she'd be great on direct," said Ben, "but the cross is pretty obvious. Imagine I'm Bert Siwell up there at the podium, wearing my sucking-up-to-the-jury smile. Ms. Corbin, is it possible for criminals to file forged documents in more than one location?"

"It is."

"Is it also possible for them to use more than one color of ink?"

"Yes."

"And is it possible for them to use more than one handwriting, particularly if there are two or more of them?"

"Yes."

"And in fact, wouldn't you expect reasonably intelligent criminals to take all of those steps if they could, particularly if one of them was a trained accountant?"

299

"I guess so."

"One last question, Ms. Corbin. Aren't you married to that pathetic lawyer over there, who's so desperate that he's putting his pretty little wife on the stand to try to save his case?"

Noelle smiled and got her mace out of her purse. "I'm sorry, Mr. Siwell, I couldn't hear that last question. Could you come a little closer and ask it again?"

Ben and Sergei laughed. "If I actually thought you might get to mace Bert, I would put you on the stand," said Ben. He looked at his watch. "We've got to get going. Sergei and I have to meet Gunnar and Henrik at the Italian Village in fifteen minutes."

"Eric and I will see you at home," said Noelle. "How late do you think you'll be?"

"Based on the last three, I'm guessing that we'll be done by nine or nine-thirty, so I should be home around ten."

"And then you'll have to do more work to get ready for tomorrow, right?" she asked.

He yawned. "Unfortunately, yeah. I don't know when I'll actually get to bed."

"You've been getting about four hours of sleep a night, even when Eric cooperates. How many more of these things is Gunnar going to schedule?"

"I think he's trying to put together one more meeting after tonight, but that will be it." He smiled. "I'll bet it makes you miss the old days when I used to sleep until eight and then watch ESPN or the History Channel until noon."

"Let me think about that for a second . . . no."

‡ ‡ ‡

At 8:30 the next morning, Dr. Daruka Reddy was pulling into the Bjornsen Pharmaceuticals parking lot when his BlackBerry buzzed at his hip. He eased into his parking place and pulled the device out of its holster. There was a red-flagged message from Dr. Corrigan to him and Dr. Black that read: "Neurostim Phase I participant just died. Meeting in my office to discuss at 8:45."

Dr. Reddy swore and hit the steering wheel with his fist. This was very bad news. If there was even the remotest chance that the death had any connection to the drug, the FDA was virtually certain to shut down their clinical trials indefinitely. He'd been on the Neurostim research and development team for almost two years, and it was his ticket to either a big promotion in the company or a cushy job someplace else. But if Neurostim turned into a black eye for the company, it could be a career killer.

He got out of his car and hurried up to Dr. Corrigan's office. He walked in at 8:40 and found Dr. Black already there. "Have a seat," said Dr. Corrigan. Sharp lines of concern showed on her forehead and at the corners of her mouth, accentuating her somewhat severe, no-nonsense demeanor. "When I got in this morning there was a voice mail and an e-mail waiting for me from UCLA Medical Center. They admitted a David Lee yesterday afternoon. He was the med student from Phase I. He arrived in the emergency room unresponsive and with no heartbeat. They declared him dead about two hours later."

"What happened to him?" asked Dr. Black.

"He got into a fight in a bar and one of the bouncers Tasered him. He collapsed, and by the time the police got there, he had no pulse and wasn't breathing. UCLA is doing an autopsy now and they promised to send us a copy of the results. They wanted the chemical profiles for Neurostim and its metabolites so they could look for them in his tissues."

"But there won't be any Neurostim in him," objected Dr. Reddy. "Phase I ended two months ago. His blood would have been clean two weeks after his last dose, three weeks maximum."

He leaned forward as he spoke and waved his finger authoritatively. "There are very likely other compounds in his body. He was in a bar, so there is likely alcohol. He is a medical student, so there is likely caffeine or other stimulants. Maybe there is cocaine or heroin or some other narcotic too. I saw a study a few months ago about the interaction of illegal drugs and Tasers. The authors examined all deaths in which a Taser was implicated and found that high doses of illegal drugs were the primary cause of most deaths.

"His body probably has all sorts of chemicals in it. What if some inexperienced lab tech finds a compound that looks similar to something from Neurostim and puts 'significant levels of Neurostim' in the report? The FDA will shut down our clinical testing program like this." He snapped his fingers. "We should not give them the Neurostim profiles. We should ask for tissue samples and run our own tests."

Dr. Corrigan pressed her lips together into a grim line as Dr. Reddy spoke, but said nothing.

Dr. Black cleared his throat. "Daruka has an interesting point," he ventured.

"Yes, he does," said Dr. Corrigan. "We can't really withhold the profiles, because there are a few pieces of information I haven't told you yet. UCLA knew he was part of Phase I, because our former intern, Kim Young, told them. He was her boyfriend and she was in the bar when he was Tasered. Kim also told the UCLA emergency room staff that she believed Mr. Lee had taken large doses of Neurostim recently."

All at once, the puzzle pieces fit together in Dr. Reddy's brain. The man who blackmailed him had known about his personal life and about Neurostim. Kim knew about both and probably gossiped with her boyfriend. In fact, he had a vague memory of her being the one who suggested Lee for Phase I. And the post office box to which he'd mailed the box of drugs had been in LA.

He stared at Dr. Corrigan with a fixed, stunned gaze. *Did she know?* His ears rang and he felt paralyzed. Sweat began forming on his forehead and hands.

"But how did he get it?" asked Dr. Black. He glanced at Dr. Reddy. "Hey, are you okay?"

"I . . . I'm fine," he stammered. "I just . . . this is a terrible development. Terrible."

"It is," agreed Dr. Corrigan, nodding her head gravely. "I'm as shocked as you are. We don't know where he got the drug, but the police are grilling Kim right now. She's a sweet girl, and I don't want to jump to any conclusions about her, but . . ."

Dr. Reddy took a deep breath and wiped his hands on his pants. "It's hard to believe she would put the entire company at risk just to steal some drugs for her boyfriend," he said, shaking his head sadly. "How terribly irresponsible."

"Do we tell Karl?" asked Dr. Black.

"I'd like your feedback on that before I make a decision," said Dr. Corrigan. "What do each of you think?"

"Well, he's got a lot on his mind with that trial," said Dr. Black. "Do we really need to say anything to him right now?"

"I don't think so," said Dr. Reddy. "Also, we don't know enough to say anything; better to wait until we hear from UCLA."

Dr. Corrigan nodded. "I'll tell him that one of our Phase I participants died and that an autopsy is being done. Anything more than that is unnecessary at this point. It would simply worry and distract him. There's nothing any of us can do until the autopsy results come back, in any event. I will ask for tissue samples so that we can perform our own parallel tests, though."

‡ ‡ ‡

Karl was not the last witness to testify, but he was the last one to affect the dynamics of the trial. For example, Bjornsen Pharmaceuticals' CFO testified, as he had at the preliminary injunction hearing, that two sets of financial books with different numbers generally indicated fraud. He also agreed with Ben that his company's subsidiary did indeed have two sets of financials with different numbers and that they very likely were the result of internal fraud. After Siwell took Ben's place at the podium, the CFO added that he had participated in the investigation of Bjornsen Norge's books and concluded that the fraud probably had been perpetrated by one or more individuals in the company's Oslo office. He hadn't reached any more specific conclusions because a fire had destroyed all of the backup documents, and various authorities had opened a criminal investigation—about which he could not, of course, testify. After that, both sides put on economic experts to explain why Gunnar's refusal to turn over the Neurostim formula had either cost Bjornsen Pharmaceuticals hundreds of millions of dollars (according to Siwell's expert) or nothing at all (according to Ben's). And so it went.

After the last witness testified and the lawyers had their final squabble about the admissibility of evidence, Judge Reilly informed the jurors that it was time for closing arguments. Ben stood up from his table and walked up to the podium with several sheets of scrawled notes. There were dark circles under his eyes and his face was pale and drawn. His voice, however, remained bright and lively. "Good afternoon, ladies and gentlemen. At the beginning of this trial, I asked you to keep a question in your minds as you listened to the evidence: Do you trust Karl Bjornsen? Do you trust him with a three-hundred-million-dollar company? Do you trust him with an incredibly powerful drug that affects the brain?

"I told you that the evidence would show that he is an embezzler, and it has. You heard witness after witness, *from Bjornsen Pharmaceuticals*, testify that there were two sets of books and that they showed fraud had been committed. By whom? The Bjornsen folks were a little vague on that.

"Could it have been Karl Bjornsen? He denied it, of course, but the rest of the witnesses put on by Mr. Siwell didn't. All they said was that someone in Norway was involved and that there was a fire that destroyed all the evidence. *But it didn't*. It didn't destroy those damning documents in Karl Bjornsen's own files. He has a convoluted story to explain how those got there, how they were planted by a brilliant, bold, and lucky criminal in Norway with a day job as a warehouse accountant. But there's a much simpler—and more believable—explanation: Those documents were in Karl Bjornsen's files because he put them there.

"And if those investigators from Bjornsen Pharmaceuticals really wanted to know what the destroyed documents showed, why didn't they ask Henrik Haugeland? He had been an accountant at Bjornsen Norge for nearly three decades. He knew what its books should and shouldn't show. Moreover, he knew *exactly* what those destroyed documents showed. They showed that someone had been embezzling money from Bjornsen Norge and using it to pay for extravagant vacations and gifts for the very people who put Karl Bjornsen in charge of Bjornsen Pharmaceuticals.

"Now unfortunately, just as Mr. Haugeland finished going through those documents—while he and his team were copying them, in fact—someone apparently got wind of what they were doing, broke into the building, shot everyone they could find, and burned all the records. Someone wanted very much to hide what those records showed, and it's only by the grace of God and the courage of Henrik Haugeland that they failed and that no one died. You may not have the documents in front of you, but you have Mr. Haugeland's testimony about them. He sat right there"—Ben pointed to the witness stand—"and answered the hardest questions Mr. Siwell could throw at him. When Judge Reilly gives you your instructions in a few minutes, he's going to tell you that you can take the credibility of the witnesses into account. I think you'll agree with me that no witness who testified during this trial was more credible than Henrik Haugeland." Two jurors nodded slightly and one smiled.

"A few words about the fire and shooting. We now know that Karl Bjornsen and Bjornsen Pharmaceuticals weren't responsible, even though circumstantial evidence pointed to them. Good. It's actually a relief to my client and me to know that they didn't commit those brutal attacks. But it really doesn't have anything to do with this lawsuit. Just because Karl Bjornsen didn't commit *those* crimes doesn't mean he didn't commit *any* crimes. I'm pretty sure he had nothing to do with the assassinations of John F. Kennedy or Martin Luther King Jr., but that doesn't mean he didn't embezzle money or commit bribery.

"In fact, the evidence showed that he did exactly that. He wanted control of Bjornsen Pharmaceuticals, and he was willing to break the law to get it. He was willing to use Bjornsen Norge as his personal slush fund. He was willing to bribe shareholders and directors. He was willing to falsify the company's financial documents to hide what he had done.

"Karl Bjornsen violated his trust as an officer and director of Bjornsen Pharmaceuticals. It is time for him to go. And on his way out the door, he should hand back the seven million dollars he stole. I ask you to enter a verdict requiring him to return that money. And on the section of the form titled Special Interrogatories, I ask you to answer *yes* to the question asking whether he committed serious misconduct, and *no* to the one asking whether he should be allowed to continue to hold leadership posts in Bjornsen Pharmaceuticals."

Ben paused and took a step away from the podium and toward the jury box. "Thank you," he said as he swept his eyes over the jury, looking each juror in the eye for an instant. "Thank you for your time and for your attention throughout this complex—and occasionally dull—trial. You have sat patiently while Mr. Siwell and I put on our evidence and made our arguments. Now it is our turn to sit nervously while you decide which of us is right." Smiles from a few jurors. "And I have every confidence that you will reach the right decision, a decision in favor of Gunnar Bjornsen."

Ben sat down and Siwell took his place as two paralegals quickly set up a projection screen opposite the jury. A projector and laptop already lay humming softly on their counsel table. Siwell laid a neatly organized binder on the podium and put a wireless computer mouse next to it. "Mr. Corbin may be nervous, but I'm not," he said as he opened the binder. "Why not? Because I saw and heard the same evidence you did and I know that there's only one verdict it can support—a verdict for Bjornsen Pharmaceuticals and Karl Bjornsen.

"I'm going to start by talking about the half of the case Mr. Corbin didn't mention, probably because he had nothing to say. This is a case about trade-secret theft." He clicked his mouse and the words "Gunnar Bjornsen Admits He Stole Trade Secrets" appeared on the screen under a video still of Gunnar, taken from his deposition testimony. Ben winced internally; Siwell had picked a good picture. Gunnar glared defensively at the camera, his face red and his mouth set in an angry line. "The evidence is undisputed. You heard Gunnar Bjornsen himself admit that he developed the formula for Neurostim while working for Bjornsen Pharmaceuticals. You heard him admit that the formula was both secret and valuable. And you heard him admit that he took it with him when he left. In short, you heard him admit every single element you'll need to find in order to find him liable for stealing Bjornsen Pharmaceuticals' trade secrets.

"The only question left for you to decide is the amount Gunnar Bjornsen should have to pay the company he robbed. He thinks he shouldn't have to pay anything. He claims that his actions didn't do any harm to his employer, but that's not what the evidence showed. I won't rehash all of the economic analysis you heard yesterday and this morning, but you heard that the drop in Bjornsen Pharmaceuticals' stock price combined with delays in its ability to bring Neurostim to market have cost the company over two hundred million dollars. Two hundred million dollars. That's how much Gunnar Bjornsen cost the company through his wrongdoing. But that's not how much the company is asking you to award." He clicked the mouse again and "$100 Million = Less Than Half the Cost of Gunnar Bjornsen's Theft" appeared on the screen. "In light of Mr. Bjornsen's long years of service and his many contributions, the company is only going to ask that he pay for less than half the damage he caused. I ask that you award Bjornsen Pharmaceuticals one hundred million dollars.

"Mr. Corbin thinks Bjornsen Pharmaceuticals should be deprived of its leader at this crucial juncture, just as it is developing a block-buster drug. The company's directors don't want that; they elected Karl Bjornsen just a few months ago, and they can elect someone new anytime they choose. The company's shareholders don't want it either; less than a year ago, they elected the directors who elected Karl Bjornsen. The only one who wants him out—other than the company's competitors—is Gunnar Bjornsen.

"I think we all know the real reason why Gunnar wants to see Karl forced out on the street. He had wanted Karl to come crawling to him and that didn't happen. He had wanted to be the alpha dog, the undisputed head of Bjornsen Pharmaceuticals, but that didn't happen either. In fact, the company's directors chose Karl to lead the company instead of Gunnar.

"So what did Gunnar do? He left the company and took the Neurostim formula with him. He held it hostage and tried to use it to blackmail the company into giving him Karl's job. That also didn't work—the company called his bluff and sued him to make him give back the formula.

"Gunnar knew he couldn't defend his actions, so he did what came naturally for him by this point: he launched another unjustified attack on his brother. He accused Karl of committing a number of very serious crimes, with virtually no evidence. Partway through this trial, he was forced to retract the most outrageous allegations—that Karl had arranged attempted murder and arson. And you heard what happened when Mr. Corbin questioned Karl about the rest of these imaginary crimes—his entire theory blew apart like a ripe tomato hitting a brick wall." A scattering of smiles and chuckles from the jury, but one well-dressed older woman rolled her eyes.

"To be fair to both Gunnar and his lawyer, crimes *were* committed and they did stumble across evidence of those crimes. But no matter how hard they try, they can't pin those crimes on Karl. Mr. Corbin thinks it's unbelievable that extortionists would try to plant incriminating documents in the files of an executive they wanted to blackmail. I don't know about you, but that makes perfect sense to me. And if you listened closely, you will have noticed that Mr. Corbin and Gunnar *never denied that someone was trying to blackmail Karl*. That's because they know it's true. So since we know that Karl was the target of a blackmail plot, is it really unbelievable that the blackmailers would have put some blackmail-worthy documents in his files?

"Mr. Corbin talked a lot about Henrik Haugeland. He said Mr. Haugeland was 'the most credible witness' you heard. That's flat-out false. If he had said Mr. Haugeland was an honest witness, I might have agreed with him, but Mr. Haugeland was *not* credible. 'Credible' doesn't just mean that a witness is telling the truth to the best of his ability; it means the witness is believable. Those aren't always the same thing, and they weren't here. Remember what Mr. Haugeland said, what his whole testimony led up to?" He clicked the wireless mouse again and a quote appeared on the screen: "'I strongly believe Karl was involved [in the shootings and arson at Bjornsen Norge]. . . . I think he discovered what we were doing, probably from a spy in Bjornsen Norge. Then he sent a criminal to stop us and destroy the evidence we found'—Henrik Haugeland."

Siwell paused to let the jury read the words on the screen. Then he pointed to them. "We know that isn't true. I'm willing to give Mr. Haugeland the benefit of the doubt and assume that he wasn't intentionally lying; that he really did 'strongly believe' those things. But it really doesn't matter. Either way, he was one hundred percent wrong—as even Gunnar and his lawyer now agree. That means Mr. Haugeland's testimony is, by definition, not credible. If he was so wrong on something so critical, can you really trust his other testimony? And even if you do, all he really said was that there were documents in Bjornsen Norge's files that were consistent with the blackmail plot Karl Bjornsen described—and remember that his testimony on this point was completely unchallenged by any witness or document. At least one of the blackmailers was an accountant at Bjornsen Norge, so is it really surprising that there would be documents in Bjornsen Norge's accounting files that would be helpful in the blackmail plot?"

He clicked the mouse again and Henrik's words vanished from the screen. They were replaced by an image of the verdict form the jury would receive. "So when you come back with your verdict, I ask you to answer *yes* to the special interrogatory asking whether Gunnar Bjornsen should return the Neurostim formula to Bjornsen Pharmaceuticals"—he highlighted and enlarged the interrogatory as he spoke—"and *no* to the interrogatory asking whether the company should be deprived of its duly elected president and chairman, Karl Bjornsen." He highlighted and enlarged that one too. "And I ask you to order Gunnar to pay for at least some of the hundreds of millions of dollars worth of damage he did to the company."

He clicked again and the screen went blank. "This is an important case. I know you know that. Billions of dollars are at stake. Karl Bjornsen's career and reputation are at stake. Thank you for taking time away from your businesses and families to be here. I know you had no choice, and that only makes your sacrifice greater. I ask you to take only a little more time, enough time to review the evidence carefully and fairly and make sure your verdict is the right one—a verdict for Bjornsen Pharmaceuticals and Karl Bjornsen." He paused and smiled. "And may your next jury service end after a morning of drinking coffee and reading the paper in the jury assembly room." Even Ben and Gunnar had to smile at that one.

‡ ‡ ‡

Karl sat in a chair on his balcony and watched the last remnants of the sunset fade from the western sky. A half-empty glass of petite sirah sat on a small table by his right elbow. He picked it up and looked at it thoughtfully. In the gathering darkness, the wine looked very much like blood. The consistency and smell were very different though. He swirled his glass gently for a few seconds, then drained it.

A hand touched his shoulder and he jumped, spilling several drops of wine on his white shirt. He snapped his head around and saw Gwen looking down at him. "Sorry, I didn't mean to startle you. Here, give me your shirt and I'll get it soaking. I'll make sure Maria takes care of it tomorrow morning."

"I didn't hear you come out," he said as he stood and unbuttoned his shirt. He handed it to her and she disappeared into the apartment.

She reappeared a minute later with the wine bottle, a second glass, and a fresh shirt. She stood for a moment in the rectangle of warm light cast by the dining room chandelier through the sliding glass balcony door. The diamonds at her neck and ears sparkled and she looked magnificent in her black silk cocktail dress. She embodied the image that aspiring luxury vineyards try to capture in their advertising. "You've been so tense recently," she commented as she filled their glasses. "Is it the trial, or something else?"

"A little of both," Karl replied as he slipped on the new shirt. "The jury deliberated for a little over an hour today without reaching a verdict. Bert thinks they'll go our way, but he isn't sure." He took a sip of his wine. "And Gunnar's up to something. I've heard from three different people that he's been meeting with directors and major shareholders over the past week or so. He has Ben Corbin and Henrik Haugeland and a detective put on a show about what a terrible guy I am. Then he makes a pitch for why they should vote me out and vote him in."

"That's outrageous! Can you stop him?"

"Bert says I probably can't. Gunnar is still a director and shareholder, so he probably has a right to talk to other shareholders and directors. Besides, it would send the wrong message. I don't want anyone to think that I'm afraid to have them hear what Gunnar has to say. Once we have the jury's verdict, I'll have my own meetings with the directors—if they're still necessary. In the meantime, though, it's putting me a little on edge."

"I can tell." Gwen stood and walked around behind him. She began to massage his thick shoulders. "Your muscles are all knotted up. Do you want me to set up an appointment for you with my masseur? He's really good."

"No."

She stopped kneading his shoulders and picked up her wine glass. "Speaking of Gunnar, I saw Anne and Markus the other day. They were having lunch at the University Club with Pat and Jacqui Gossard. Markus was the only one drinking. He had one of those little martini carafes and it was almost empty. Jacqui told me later that he actually drank *two* of those during lunch." She sighed sadly. "We both felt so sorry for Anne. It must be humiliating for her to have a son who behaves like that."

"I'm going to bed," Karl announced. He stood abruptly, knocking over the wine bottle. He grabbed the bottle and set it upright with a quick move of his hand, but not before a splash of red spread across the glass tabletop and began to drip onto the floor. He turned and walked through the door. "Good night."

"What has gotten into you?" Gwen demanded.

He stopped momentarily, but didn't turn to face her. "I'm under a lot of pressure. It will be over soon."

"I certainly hope so," she said icily to his retreating back. "I'd better get the old Karl back soon."

‡ ‡ ‡

Later that night, Anne Bjornsen woke to find herself in an empty bed. She looked at the clock; it was 11:35. She got up, pulled on her robe, and went to look for her husband. She found him in the den in his recliner. A brass floor lamp surrounded him in a pool of light, and a thick leather-bound book lay open on his lap. He looked up as she came in. "Trouble sleeping?" she asked as she stood blinking in the light.

He nodded. "I thought I'd come down and read something that would put me to sleep." He gestured to the book in his lap. "Markus got me thinking about the Norse sagas, so I pulled out my father's copy of the *Heimskringla*, the stories of the ancient Norwegian kings."

She smiled. "That would put me to sleep in ten minutes. How's it working for you?"

A low chuckle rumbled in his throat for a moment. "Not very well. I read the Saga of Olav Tryggvason and I'm more wide awake than ever."

"Is it a good story?"

"I suppose so. It's the tale of a king who liberates Norway from a Swedish *jarl* and builds it into a strong company."

"You mean 'country,'" interjected Anne.

He chuckled again. "I suppose I do. King Olav was a good ruler in many ways and accomplished a lot, but he could be . . . undiplomatic. He offended people. Eventually, his enemies gathered together against him and ambushed his fleet of longships at sea. There was an epic battle, and he lost. As the battle ended, he fell into the water and vanished. No one ever saw him again."

He stopped and dropped his eyes to the book in his lap. Anne stood in the doorway and waited for what was inside him to work its way out. After a long moment, he looked up again. "I was wondering what . . . after all of myself that I've invested in the company, what will happen if I lose?"

"What do you mean?"

"Well, if the company's gone, what's left of me?"

She smiled gently. "Will you have disappeared in defeat like King Olav?"

He closed the book and set it on an oak reading stand by the chair. "Yes."

She walked over and sat on the arm of the chair. "What will be left of you? Nothing, except the man I married almost thirty-five years ago."

‡ ‡ ‡

By 9:30 the next morning, Dr. Antonio Gomez had the preliminary autopsy reports ready. He picked up the report for Bedford Lavelle, clipped a circulation checklist to it, and tossed it into his out-box. That one had been easy—multiple skull fractures, torn cranial artery, and massive brain damage. There had been alcohol and trace amounts of steroids in his blood, but nothing that contributed to his death.

Dr. Gomez picked up the preliminary report for David Lee and frowned at it. This one was a problem. The cause of death listed was "heart failure due to unascertained causes," but that was simply medspeak for "I don't know."

Lee's body had several contusions, two broken ribs and a broken bone in his right hand, but no injuries that could explain his death. The emergency room staff thought they had detected intracranial swelling and an emergency craniotomy had been performed. But Dr. Gomez saw no noticeable swelling and ruled out both the alleged swelling and the craniotomy as potential causes of death.

There were two tiny holes in the left side of David Lee's chest where the Taser needles had hit him, but Dr. Gomez discounted these as a cause of death. He had seen the literature and knew that deaths allegedly due to Taser strikes invariably had other causes—generally lethal levels of illegal drugs already in the body.

Based on those studies and the behavior recorded in the police reports that accompanied Lee's remains and medical records, Dr. Gomez had therefore expected the toxicology reports to show very high levels of cocaine, PCP, or some other controlled substance. But they hadn't. Unsurprisingly for a med student several hours after a big exam, Lee had alcohol and caffeine in his system, but not in concentrations remotely near lethal levels. His adrenaline levels were also high—even for someone who was in the middle of a fight—but again not high enough to contribute to his death.

One possible culprit was the experimental drug Lee had taken. Both the drug and its metabolites were in his system, indicating that he had taken it recently. The levels in his blood and liver were above those reported by the drug company for Phase I participants, but well below the toxic levels established during their rat and beagle studies. Could the drug's interactions with caffeine or alcohol make it lethal? Maybe, but Dr. Gomez doubted it. The drug company had tested the drug's interactions with multiple common chemicals—including alcohol and caffeine—and hadn't found anything troubling. Besides, based on the drug's chemical structure, Dr. Gomez doubted that it would interact negatively with either one.

So what had killed David Lee?

Chapter Eighteen

Berserkergang

AT 2:15 THE NEXT DAY, Ben got the phone call he had been waiting for. "Mr. Corbin, it's Lisa Sinclair, Judge Reilly's clerk. The jury has a verdict."

"Great. We'll be there in fifteen minutes."

He hung up the phone, took a deep breath, and dialed Gunnar's cell phone number. He answered on the first ring. "Ben?"

"The jury is back. Can you be at the courthouse in ten minutes?"

"You know I can." The big Norwegian had spent the last two days wandering around the Loop because he wanted to be in the courtroom when the jury announced its verdict. "I'll see you there."

"I'll meet you in the lobby downstairs. North side." Ben dropped the phone into its cradle, grabbed his jacket, and hurried out the door. He speed-walked to the courthouse, cell phone to his ear the whole time as he briefed Noelle, who was at home with Eric, and Sergei, who was in New York on another job.

He found Gunnar in the courthouse lobby, and five minutes later the two of them walked through the doors of Judge Reilly's courtroom. The judge wasn't there, but the clerk and bailiff were in their seats. Karl and his team were already clustered around their counsel table, talking in hushed, tense tones. They looked up as Gunnar and Ben entered. The Bjornsen brothers exchanged curt nods as Ben walked up to the clerk's desk and informed her that everyone was there.

The clerk disappeared through a door behind the bench, and a few minutes later Judge Reilly appeared. Everyone in the courtroom stood and remained standing as the bailiff opened the door to the jury room and the jurors filed silently into the jury box and took their seats. They didn't make eye contact with anyone except the bailiff, and Ben thought they looked tired.

After the last juror took her seat, everyone else in the courtroom sat down. "Ladies and gentlemen of the jury, have you reached a verdict?" asked Judge Reilly.

A white-haired man—the retired sales executive whom Ben would have preferred to keep off the jury—stood up. "We have, your honor."

"All right, the parties will rise for the reading of the verdict."

The Bjornsens and their lead lawyers stood.

"What is your verdict?" asked the judge.

The jury foreman unfolded two sheets of paper, which Ben recognized as the verdict form. "On the claim of Bjornsen Pharmaceuticals against Gunnar Bjornsen for trade secret misappropriation, we find for Bjornsen Pharmaceuticals and against Gunnar Bjornsen. We answered *yes* to the interrogatory asking whether he should be ordered to return the Neurostim formula to Bjornsen Pharmaceuticals. We award Bjornsen Pharmaceuticals damages in the amount of one dollar." Karl shook Bert's hand discreetly, but Ben knew that was for the reporters in the back of the room—a show of victory on something that had been a foregone conclusion since the first day of trial. No matter what the rest of the verdict was, his press release would claim no worse than a mixed result. For his part, Ben was encouraged by the one dollar damages figure.

The foreman paused to turn the page of the form and the courtroom was perfectly silent except for the rustle of the paper. "On the claim of Gunnar Bjornsen, suing on behalf of Bjornsen Pharmaceuticals, against Karl Bjornsen for fraud, embezzlement, bribery, and mismanagement, we find for Karl Bjornsen and against Gunnar Bjornsen. The damages amount is therefore zero. We answered *no* to the interrogatories asking whether Karl Bjornsen committed serious financial misconduct and whether he should be barred from holding a leadership position in Bjornsen Pharmaceuticals."

Karl shook Siwell's hand again much more enthusiastically and smiled broadly at the jury. Ben glanced at Gunnar, who shrugged slightly, but otherwise remained impassive as murmurs rose from the gallery behind them. This wasn't the outcome either of them had wanted, of course, but it was one for which they were prepared.

Judge Reilly looked at Ben. "Mr. Corbin, would you like me to poll the jurors?"

"Thank you. I would, your honor."

"All right." The judge turned to the jury box. "Juror number one, do you personally agree with every aspect of the verdict that was just read?"

"Yes, your honor," said a petite blonde woman in the far right of the jury box.

"Thank you," replied the judge. "Juror number two, do you personally agree with every aspect of the verdict that was just read?"

A tall man sitting next to juror one nodded. "I do."

The only juror for whom Ben had any hope was juror nine, the accountant. Ben thought she had reacted particularly favorably to Henrik Haugeland's testimony, and if anyone on the jury had the financial sophistication to see through Karl's stories, it was her. When Judge Reilly reached her, she pursed her lips and paused before answering. "Well, I don't know, your honor," she said at last.

The courtroom became silent again and there was an uneasy stirring among other members of the jury. "If you do not agree with the verdict, then further deliberations are necessary."

Several jurors frowned, and it appeared to Ben that juror eight muttered something under his breath. "I . . . no, I agree with the verdict," said juror nine.

"Are you sure?" asked the judge. "If this is not your verdict, I want you to tell me now. You should reach your conclusions based solely on the evidence and the instructions I gave you and the other jurors, not the fact that you've been deliberating a long time and don't want to go back."

"This is my verdict, your honor," she said with a forced smile. "I'm sure."

"All right, if you're sure." He moved on to juror number ten, and Ben began to pack his briefcase. It was over.

‡ ‡ ‡

As soon as Dr. Gomez laid David Lee's pathology reports next to each other, the answer was obvious—or at least the question was. He raised his thick eyebrows and put down his coffee cup. "That's weird," he said to himself. He picked up the phone and dialed Neuropathology. "Hello, Neuropathology. Dr. Goldberg speaking," said a familiar male voice.

"Hi, Larry. It's Tony Gomez down in Autopsy. I've got a dead kid down here—UCLA med student, actually—with some unusual path reports I'd like you to take a look at if you have time."

"Sure. UCLA med student—what's the name?"

"David Lee."

"Didn't know him," Dr. Goldberg said with relief. "Still, that's too bad. What happened?"

"That's what I'm trying to figure out. He died after being Tasered during a bar fight with a football player more than twice his size."

"I heard about that. The football player died too, right?"

"Right," confirmed Dr. Gomez. "His autopsy report was pretty straightforward, but this guy has no obvious cause of death. The injuries from the fight didn't kill him, the Taser almost certainly didn't kill him, and the standard tox screen didn't show lethal doses of any drugs in his system."

"Heart abnormalities?" suggested Dr. Goldberg. "Burst aneurysm?"

"No, we looked for those too. Routine histopathology showed damage in the limbic nervous system, so we did some more in-depth chemical analyses and found a compound I hadn't seen before. Once I spotted it, I checked the results for the other tissue samples. It's there too, but in much lower levels."

"Ahh," said Dr. Goldberg as he realized the purpose of the call, "so you're thinking that this is something that built up in the nervous system and may have been the cause of death?"

"Yes, or contributed to it at least. One more thing—he was taking an experimental drug that affects the nervous system. The compound I spotted isn't part of the drug or one of the metabolites listed by the company that makes it, Bjornsen Pharmaceuticals, but there might be some connection."

"Interesting, interesting," mused Dr. Goldberg. "Yes, please send me the lab reports. I'd also like to see whatever you got from the drug company and anything else you think might be worth looking at."

"You'll have it this afternoon."

‡ ‡ ‡

Karl was driving back to the office for a victory celebration when the call came. "Karl, it's Bert. You're not going to believe what Corbin and Gunnar are doing now."

Karl sighed. "After fifty-five years of knowing Gunnar, I believe a lot more things than you'd expect. What is it this time?"

"Corbin just called to tell me that Gunnar is calling an emergency meeting of the board of directors for tomorrow night at seven o'clock to consider removing you as an officer of the company."

Karl laughed harshly. "Their timing is off by a couple of days, wouldn't you say? I thought they might pull this kind of stunt, but before the jury came back, not after."

"It's totally outrageous," agreed Siwell. "It would be laughable if it weren't for the inconvenience to you and the company. Do you want me to try to enjoin the meeting? I can have a team of lawyers work on the brief through the night and be ready to file when court opens in the morning."

"No," replied Karl. "I'm tired of screwing around with Gunnar. Let him have his meeting, and we'll put an end to this. I know all of the directors well enough to know that there's no way a majority of them will vote with Gunnar."

"Then why is he calling this meeting?"

"Spite." Karl spat out the word. Then he glanced at the speedometer and realized that his speed had crept from 75 to 90 as he talked. He eased his foot off the accelerator. "Either that or he expects us to try to stop the meeting. Then he'll argue that we're trying to hide something from the directors."

"Good point," agreed Siwell. "They want to hold the meeting at Bjornsen Pharmaceuticals. Do you want me to make them rent a hotel conference room somewhere instead?"

"Sure. Why make life easy for the other guy?"

"Words to live by," replied the lawyer.

‡ ‡ ‡

Dr. Goldberg was in Dr. Gomez's office two hours after he received David Lee's records. He was a small, precise man with quick, birdlike movements and a perfectly bald head. He placed a stack of papers on the corner of Dr. Gomez's cluttered desk. "This compound in the young man's brain is similar to several chemicals that have been tested in rat and nematode studies," he announced.

"What does that family of chemicals do?" asked Dr. Gomez, leaning back in his chair. "Anything that might have contributed to David Lee's death?"

Dr. Goldberg raised a finger. "Ah, you assume they all belong to the same family. They don't. One chemical affects the limbic nervous system, keeping it continually activated." He pulled out a copy of a journal article and pointed to a chemical diagram. "Look, see the molecular similarities there and there. Now, look at this." He flipped to another page and pointed to a series of bar charts.

Dr. Gomez leaned forward and pushed his thick black hair out of his eyes. "High adrenaline levels, just like Lee."

"Exactly," said Dr. Goldberg. He pulled out another article, this one marked with neatly annotated Post-it notes. "And here's the other study. This one is about multireceptor agonists in nematodes. I've tabbed the pertinent data."

Dr. Gomez took the journal from his colleague and skimmed through it quickly. Then he hunted for his notes from the Lee autopsy. He found them and compared them to the article as Dr. Goldberg watched with a smile of intellectual triumph. After a few minutes, Dr. Gomez uttered an expletive and looked up. "So this kid was in full fight-or-flight mode, *plus* he had something else amping up his nervous system?"

Dr. Goldberg sighed. "You sound like one of my students, Tony. I haven't studied this precise chemical, so I don't know how it interacts with the human nervous system. But it does share similarities with chemicals that have those effects on less-complex life forms."

"Wow!" Dr. Gomez pondered silently for a moment. "Wow. Well, someone better study this precise chemical. So where do you think it came from? A metabolite of that drug Lee was taking?"

Dr. Goldberg nodded. "That is the most probable source."

"The company didn't list it as a metabolite," observed Dr. Gomez, arching his eyebrows.

Dr. Goldberg shrugged. "I noticed that as well. Perhaps it was intentional, perhaps not. The chemical does not appear in high concentrations outside of the neural tissues, and it's not always easy to tell what by-products will result when the body metabolizes a drug. They may have missed it."

"Maybe. Well, I'm going to put it in my final report as a contributing factor, especially since I don't have anything else." He pulled out the draft report and started jotting notes on it.

"Will you notify the FDA?"

"Yeah, or I'll make sure the company does." Dr. Gomez stopped writing and looked up at his colleague. "The FDA will shut down their clinical studies, won't they?"

"Very likely, at least until the company performs significant additional preclinical testing."

Dr. Gomez whistled. "Some executive over there is going to go berserk when he hears about this."

‡ ‡ ‡

Kim walked up the steps at the West LA precinct station with her lawyer. She felt lightheaded, almost drunk. She remembered coming here as a wide-eyed fourth grader on a field trip. She had stayed very close to her mother, who had been a chaperone, because she worried that some of the people in the police station might be criminals who would attack her. Afterward, she had had occasional nightmares about being trapped in the police station without her mother or teacher to protect her. And now it was happening.

Her lawyer, a woman of about forty named Julie Neuhaus, had advised her to wear a conservative suit. Fortunately, the only suit she owned—the one she had last worn at her interview with Bjornsen Pharmaceuticals—was dark, navy blue wool, and its skirt ended below her knees. She wore her hair in the tight bun she used whenever she wanted to make an impression as a serious, responsible young woman.

Julie knew the station and guided Kim through the various layers of security. Soon they were sitting in a plain, windowless interview room. Across a scarred wooden table sat a large African-American man in his fifties wearing a herringbone blazer and a red tie. A small tape recorder sat on the table between them, resting on a phone book to prevent distortion from vibrations caused by, for example, putting a glass of water down on the table.

He took out a yellow legal pad with notes on it, turned on the tape recorder and said, "Good morning Miss Young, Miss Neuhaus.

324

Thank you for coming in today. My name is Frank McCormick, and I'm a detective with the Los Angeles Police Department. I'm going to ask you some questions, and I'd like you to speak clearly and give audible answers rather than nodding or shaking your head so that everything we say can be recorded.

"Miss Young, I see that you have an attorney with you. Is she representing you?"

"She is."

"And you are aware that you have the right to remain silent and that anything you say can and will be used against you in a court of law?"

This was now the third time Kim had been given the Miranda warnings. "I am."

"All right, you worked at Bjornsen Pharmaceuticals in Chicago over the summer, correct?"

"Yes."

The detective made a check on his pad. "When did you start and what was your last day there?"

"I started in the third week of June. I'm sorry, but I don't remember the exact date." She glanced at him quickly, half-wondering if he would challenge her. "My last day there was August fifteenth."

"What were your job responsibilities?"

"I was an intern. I did pretty much whatever I was told to do."

"That describes most jobs, doesn't it?" said the detective with an easy smile.

"Yes, I guess it does," replied Kim. "I spent most of my days doing different jobs in their new drug development program. Sometimes I helped the research team go through applications for our clinical trials. I also helped take data from animals and stuff like that."

"Did you ever go into the drug storage room located in the laboratory area of Bjornsen Pharmaceuticals?"

"I'm not sure. I went in there when I got a tour on my first day, but I don't know if I went in there after that." Realizing that she was fidgeting with her watch, Kim clasped her hands. "I might have, but I'm not sure."

"So if we found your fingerprints in there, that wouldn't surprise you?"

"I—I guess not."

"Did you ever go into the storage room alone?"

"I don't think so."

"Were you issued a keycard when you started working at Bjornsen Pharmaceuticals?"

"Yes."

"Did it give you access to the drug storage room?"

"Maybe."

Detective McCormick scribbled something on his pad.

"I think it gave me access to everything on the lab floor," Kim added.

The detective nodded. "You know what Neurostim looks like, right?"

"Yes. I saw it in solution form when researchers were injecting it into animals. I saw Neurostim pills in the storage room and on the production line where they were making it."

Julie put her hand on Kim's arm as the detective took notes. "He only asked you if you knew what it looked like," she cautioned.

"Oh, I'm sorry. Yes, I knew."

"That's all right," said Detective McCormick. "Did you have access to the production line?"

"I think everyone did," Kim replied.

"Including you, right?"

"Yes. You had to use a keycard to get into the building, but I don't think the production floor was specially secured. I do remember them having locked rooms where they kept some ingredients and products—narcotics and stuff like that. But the lines were in a big, open room."

"So, would it have been possible for you to walk into the production area and take some Neurostim as it came off the production line?"

"You're asking her hypothetically?" interjected the lawyer.

"Sure, hypothetically," agreed the detective. "Could you have done that?"

"Maybe, but there would have been people there and someone would have seen me and stopped me."

"Did you ever try?"

"You mean try to take Neurostim from the production floor?"

"Yes."

"No, I never did that."

He made another check mark on his pad. "And did you ever try to take any Neurostim from anywhere else, including the storage room in the laboratory area?"

"No."

Another item checked off. "Did you ever give Neurostim to David Lee, directly or indirectly?" he asked, reading the next question on his pad.

"No."

"Did you ever help him get it?"

"No."

He looked up. "I thought you helped him get into the Phase I clinical trial. Didn't he get Neurostim as part of that trial?"

"Oh, I'm sorry," said Kim quickly. "Yes, I didn't think you were talking about that. Other than that, I didn't help him get Neurostim. Never."

"Let's switch gears. You said that you found Neurostim under the sink in David Lee's apartment, right?"

"Yes, but he told me he got rid of it. I—" Julie raised her hand and Kim stopped short.

The detective glanced at the lawyer. "What were you going to say, Miss Young?"

"Just that I believed him. I thought he had gotten rid of it until I saw him in the bar."

"The day he died."

She looked down and nodded.

"I'm sorry, you'll have to speak up," he said.

"Yes. I believed him until then."

"All right. When you saw the Neurostim under his sink, did you touch it?"

Kim thought for a moment. "Yes, I did. I poured a capsule out on my hand and sniffed it to make sure it was Neurostim. Then I dumped it in the toilet."

"So you wouldn't be surprised if your fingerprints were on the Neurostim capsules we found in Mr. Lee's apartment?"

Kim felt a sudden urge to run out of the room. She could see the trap slowly closing around her, and she didn't know how to escape. "I . . . I don't remember if I touched any capsules except the one I threw away, so I guess the answer to your question is 'I don't know.' I was really upset."

"I understand," said the detective in a soothing, slightly paternal tone. "You were also upset when we talked to you on the day Mr. Lee died, weren't you?"

"Yes. I was very upset."

"Are you upset now?"

"No. Well, I'm a little nervous, but that's all."

Detective McCormick smiled sympathetically. "I'd be surprised if you weren't. When we talked to you last, we asked you if you knew how Mr. Lee might have gotten the Neurostim you saw under his sink. Do you remember that?"

"Yes."

"And do you remember saying that you didn't know, but that you were too upset to think clearly?"

"Yes."

"Since then, have you thought more about that—about how Mr. Lee could have gotten the Neurostim?"

"I have."

"Have you thought about it a lot?"

"Yes."

"And can you think of any way he might have gotten it?"

Kim's hands started to shake, so she put them under the table. "No."

‡ ‡ ‡

The Serena conference room at the Oak Brook Holiday Inn was full—overfull, in fact. Ben had made sure there would be enough seats for all nine Bjornsen Pharmaceuticals directors, Henrik, Bert Siwell, and himself. He had not counted on Karl inviting a couple of major shareholders or Siwell bringing a factotum of some sort. After several minutes of people standing around and grumbling, however, the hotel staff brought in more chairs and everyone was seated, though several non-directors had to sit against the wall rather than at the large, dark wood table. Gunnar had positioned himself at one end of the table, while Karl had seized the other. Each was flanked by his lawyer and an advisor. The directors were in the middle, like a battlefield to be fought over.

Gunnar stood to speak, but before he opened his mouth, Karl announced, "Before we get started, I wanted to let everyone know that there is an important issue we need to address as soon as Gunnar's business is done. We're about to start some critical emergency negotiations with the FDA that I'd like to discuss with you."

Ben was irritated, but he couldn't help admiring Karl's initiative-stealing tactic. Gunnar could either stick to his agenda and have a distracted board that was impatient to hear Karl's news, or he could give Karl center stage at the outset and then try to wrest it away from him later in the meeting. He opted for the latter. He sighed heavily and sat down. "All right, Karl. What are the negotiations about?"

Karl stood. "This afternoon, we learned that a participant in our Phase I clinical trial of Neurostim died and that the autopsy report will show Neurostim as a contributing factor. There's a real risk the FDA will shut down our clinical trials and send us back to square one as soon as we tell them, so I've requested an in-person meeting with senior staff in Maryland. I'm hoping we can persuade them that the lab that did the autopsy was wrong."

Several directors started talking at once while Gunnar watched stone-faced. Karl held up his hand and the room fell silent. "If we handle this right, I think we have a chance of nipping it in the bud. A good chance. The young man died during a bar fight, and our research team is convinced—"

"Stop!" Gunnar said loudly. Karl stopped in surprise and everyone in the room stared at Gunnar as he rose to his feet. "I called to warn you about this months ago, but you never returned my calls. Archae-ologists found the cave where the plant came from. It was used by the berserkers. The archaeologists think they ate the plant to make them go berserk before battles. You said this man was in a bar fight; how did it start? Did he act unusually aggressive?"

The directors stared at Gunnar in open-mouthed shock, but Karl recovered quickly. His strong face turned grim and he glared down the table at his brother. "You knew this for *months* and you did nothing but leave me a few voice-mail messages? Why didn't you pull me aside after court and say 'Karl, I need to talk to you?' Why didn't you send me a letter, or even an e-mail? Didn't you realize how reckless you were being?"

"*I* was being reckless with the drug?" Gunnar shot back. "Well, I hope I was the only one in this room. We're about to find out." He nodded to Ben, who got up and left the room. "During the trial, Ben Corbin and I both noticed how quick you were on the stand. Amazingly quick. Quicker than I've ever seen you in all the years I've known you."

"Thank you," Karl replied coldly, "but I'd appreciate it if you stopped changing the subject. We have a very serious situation with the FDA, and—" He paused for just an instant as Ben walked back in, accompanied by a woman carrying a medical bag—"and you just told me it's worse than I thought. Now if you'll all excuse me, I have to get back to the office. It looks like we're not as ready for our meeting with the FDA as I thought a few minutes ago."

He turned to go.

"Just a minute," called Gunnar. "I called this meeting and I haven't adjourned it yet. Sit down."

Karl remained standing. "Fine!" he snapped. "Take your vote so we can put an end to this farce."

"Before we vote, please let this young lady draw a sample of your blood," replied Gunnar calmly.

Karl looked incredulously at his brother. "What? Why?"

"To find out whether you're taking Neurostim. I think you are, and I think the directors are entitled to know one way or the other before they vote."

There was a murmur around the table, and the directors looked uncertainly between the two brothers. Karl's face reddened with anger and the veins on his bull neck stood out, but he managed to keep his voice calm. "Gunnar, I don't have time for your desperate games. The company doesn't have time. You're not even making sense. The blood work won't come back for days. You want us to sit here and wait until then to vote?"

"I just want to see you give a blood sample before we vote. If it comes back positive, we can have another vote." Gunnar unbuttoned his sleeve as he spoke and began to roll it up. "If it makes you feel better, I'll have a sample drawn too."

"This is outrageous!" said Karl loudly, his face darkening further. "I'm not going to stand for this . . . this completely unjustified invasion of my privacy!"

"Of course not," replied Gunnar coolly. "If you did, you would be out as president in two days."

"Enough!" shouted Karl, slamming his fist down on the table. The protective glass sheet covering the wood cracked from end to end. "This meeting is over!" He grabbed his jacket and stormed out, leaving stunned silence in his wake.

For several seconds, no one in the room moved. The only sound was Karl's footsteps fading down the corridor. Then everyone began to talk at once.

"Have you ever seen him act like that?" asked one director.

"When did we begin drug testing our executives?"

"Maybe we should start."

"Order!" called Gunnar in a booming voice. "Order! This meeting has not been adjourned!"

The chatter died down and the directors looked expectantly to Gunnar. "We still have a vote to take," he began.

"Hold on," interrupted Bert Siwell, standing as he spoke. "As the company's outside counsel, I can't permit this vote to go forward under these circumstances. I—"

"Don't you have a conflict?" asked Ben. "You're not just the company's lawyer; you're Karl Bjornsen's lawyer too. That's fine as long as his interests and the company's interests are completely aligned, but they aren't anymore, are they?"

Siwell froze for a moment. "Yes, they are, Ben. It's in Karl's interest to be president, and it's in the company's interest to keep Karl as president."

"The directors are about to have a vote to decide that," observed Ben.

"Let me give you a little lesson in corporate law, Ben. Decisions about what are and are not appropriate matters for the board to vote on are made by the company's attorney, not some random lawyer who happens to have wandered into a board meeting."

Ben leaned forward and put his elbows on the table. "Bert, if you try to interfere with this vote, I will call the Disciplinary Commission first thing tomorrow morning and you'll be explaining yourself to an ethics panel by the end of the month."

"Don't you threaten me!" shot back Siwell. But he sat down and said nothing more for the rest of the meeting.

The remaining directors voted six to two to remove Karl as chairman and president and replace him with Gunnar. Ben noted with satisfaction that the only two who voted against Gunnar were the ones Noelle had identified as bribe recipients.

Gunnar's first act as president was to fire Bert Siwell.

✢ ✢ ✢

Karl sat in his car in the hotel parking lot and brooded. He chewed over the evening's events again and again—or rather, they chewed over him. The injustice of what had happened gnawed at him. Gunnar couldn't beat him in a fair fight in court, so he sucker punched him during an "emergency" board meeting. And what was that "emergency"? That Gunnar wanted to ambush his brother, of course.

And he had played right along like an idiot. He had let Gunnar provoke him into a rage, and then that cheap hotel tabletop had broken at the slightest impact. That was a nice dramatic touch. *Gunnar probably planned it*, Karl thought, his anger building. *He's seen me talk often enough to know I sometimes hit the table or podium to make a point. He planted a piece of weakened glass in that conference room to make me look out of control.*

He had decided to sit in the car for a few minutes to cool off before driving home, but the longer he sat, the angrier he got. The rational part of his brain could plainly see what he should have done, how he could have managed the meeting so that he both avoided having a blood sample taken and won the vote. If he could have kept his temper, it would have been a simple matter to promise to have a blood test the next day if the board really wanted that. And then he could have handpicked the phlebotomist who did the test and taken steps to make sure the right results came back—or better yet, flown off to DC first thing in the morning and promised to reschedule the test. By the time he got back from the FDA negotiations, events would have moved on and the whole blood test issue would have been forgotten.

Knowing how he could have avoided Gunnar's trap only made him madder for having fallen into it. *"Din idiot!"* he muttered. *"Jeg kan ikke fordra—"*

He caught sight of Bert Siwell walking across the parking lot, followed by a minion, who hurried to keep up with him. Neither

333

one looked happy. Karl turned toward the hotel lobby door and saw three of the directors emerge. He couldn't make out their faces well enough in the fading light to read their expressions, and their body language told him nothing.

Gunnar, Henrik, and Ben Corbin walked out next. They stood for a moment in the well-lit area immediately outside the doors, talking and laughing. Then they shook hands and walked toward their cars.

Karl's jaw muscles bunched and his hands reflexively tightened into fists. He had known how the board would vote from the moment he walked out of the conference room, but seeing Gunnar and his team celebrate was still like a hard punch in the stomach. He felt an unreasoning urge to drive over and smash his car into that smug little group, but he resisted.

He watched as they started driving toward the parking lot exit. He found himself starting his car and following them at a careful distance. They split up as they reached the highway. Corbin headed north, and Henrik's rental car turned toward Gunnar's home in Hinsdale. But Gunnar didn't follow Henrik; he drove east, toward Chicago. *Toward the company*, Karl realized.

Karl's knuckles whitened on the steering wheel as his anger flamed into rage. So Gunnar couldn't wait to go visit his prize. He was going to show a copy of the board's resolution to the security guard and maybe get a congratulatory handshake. Then he was going to take the elevator up to the executive office suite and go into the president's office. He would sit in the president's chair and lean back with a smile on his face. He might even find a box and start dumping Karl's personal items into it—as Karl had done hours after he won the presidency.

The image was unbearable. Karl wouldn't allow it. He couldn't.

‡ ‡ ‡

Gunnar turned into the company's dark, empty parking lot. Karl pulled up to the edge of the driveway, but idled there, far enough away to be out of earshot. He watched as Gunnar parked in the president's space and got out of his car.

Gunnar stretched his legs and began to walk toward the building, but he stopped in surprise as Karl zipped in front of him and parked on the walkway to the building entrance.

"What do you think you're doing?" Gunnar demanded as Karl stepped out of his car.

Karl leaned over the top of his car and pointed a thick finger at his brother. "Leave!" he ordered.

Gunnar pulled a piece of paper from his pocket and held it out. "Here's a copy of the directors' resolution. You're not president or chairman anymore—I am. Now get out of my way and move that car before I have it towed!"

Karl did not move. "I don't care what you tricked the directors into doing. Stay away from my company."

Gunnar's eyes flashed and he walked toward the entrance. Karl stepped in front of him and Gunnar tried to push his way past. Karl's fist shot out, almost of its own volition, and struck Gunnar on the jaw.

Gunnar's head snapped to the side and he staggered back several steps. He regained his balance and stared at Karl with a mixture of shock and fury. A trickle of blood came from the corner of his mouth and he spat out a broken tooth. He walked back to his car, took off the jacket to his expensive, tailored suit and laid it carefully on the passenger seat. Then he came back, breathing heavily. "*Dette kunne vel bli din bane, lille bror!*"

Gunnar balled his massive hands into fists and threw a quick jab with his right. Karl ducked easily away from the blow—and straight into a left uppercut, falling victim to a bar-fighting trick Gunnar had picked up in his younger and less civilized days.

Karl felt almost no pain from the blow, but a red haze of rage filled his mind, and he was only dimly aware of what happened next. He fought with terrible strength and speed, intent not just on winning, but on destroying.

Less than a minute later, Karl landed three punches to his brother's head in quick succession. Gunnar stumbled backward, twisted his leg awkwardly, fell, and hit his head on the asphalt of the parking lot. He lay unmoving, stretched out on the blacktop.

Karl stood panting for several seconds. "Get up!" he shouted, but Gunnar did not respond. "I said get up!" He kicked Gunnar in the ribs. Gunnar twitched and moaned weakly before lying still again.

Karl's eyes moved back and forth between Gunnar's bloodied face and his exposed, vulnerable neck. A hard blow to the throat would certainly kill him. He got down on his knees beside his brother's head, his fists clenched and every muscle in his body tense. Sweat and blood dripped from his face and his eyes were empty and dark. Twice, he raised his hand for a killing blow, and twice he stopped. Then he lifted his fist a third time, and with an inarticulate roar smashed it down into the asphalt a fraction of an inch from his brother's head.

Karl rose to his feet and looked down on Gunnar's unconscious body. The sudden agony from the torn skin and broken bones in his damaged hand hovered unnoticed on the edge of his mind as he stared down into his brother's face. Then he turned and walked into Bjornsen Pharmaceuticals for the last time.

‡ ‡ ‡

Gunnar awoke to the sound of sirens. He opened his eyes and saw a confusing blur of moving lights. He blinked and squinted, and his vision cleared a bit, but he couldn't quite focus. He could discern, however, that a fire truck had stopped a few yards away, and could see men jumping off of it.

He tried to stand, but got no further than his hands and knees. His head pounded and spun, and sharp bolts of pain tore through his body. He heard running steps and a man's voice asked, "Are you okay?"

Gunnar lifted his head and looked up into the face of a young man in firefighting gear, who squatted down beside him, his face bathed in orange and yellow light. Gunnar was dimly aware of other figures running and shouting in the background. "I . . . I'm . . ." he began, but he had trouble finding words.

The firefighter turned and yelled over his shoulder, "EMT!" He turned back to Gunnar. "Don't try to get up. Just lie down and relax." He gently maneuvered Gunnar back to the ground. "Good, good. Now I need you to tell me if there's anyone left in the building."

"Building?" Gunnar replied groggily. He couldn't remember any particular building.

"That building right there." The firefighter pointed and Gunnar's eyes followed. He saw a massive building half-engulfed in flames. Sheets of fire spread up two of its sides and sent streams of sparks and coals into the night sky. Fire poured out of the lab windows where he had spent thousands of hours developing and testing new products. Long scorch marks already discolored what was left of the limestone cladding he and Karl had argued over when the building went up nearly twenty years ago.

"That's . . . it's the company," he said weakly. "Bjornsen Pharmaceuticals."

"I know," said the firefighter. "I need you to tell me if there are any people inside."

"It's burning!" Gunnar exclaimed in panic. "Stop it! Put it out!"

"We're doing everything we can, but right now I need you to focus," the firefighter said urgently. "Is anyone in there?"

Gunnar's head pounded and felt like it was full of cotton gauze, but he tried to concentrate. "Security guard . . . ground floor," he forced out. "Desk just inside . . . near some candy machines."

The firefighter turned and shouted, "Check for a security guard just inside on the ground floor!" He turned back to Gunnar. "Okay, is there anyone else?"

Gunnar looked back at the burning building, trying to remember. He noticed Karl's empty car parked on the path leading to the building entrance. That meant something, but he couldn't remember what. Something. "I don't know."

Two paramedics arrived and the firefighter jogged back to the truck. One man put a neck immobilization collar on Gunnar and carefully slid a flat "back board" under him while another checked his extremities for sensation, flashed a light in his pupils, and asked him who he was, where he was, what day it was, and so on. Gunnar could remember his name and recognized the burning building, but that was all.

As the paramedics worked on him, Gunnar helplessly watched the fire. More fire trucks arrived and their crews poured streams of water into the blaze, but still it grew. His shock and panic faded into despair and emptiness as the flames ate away more and more of his life's work. He tried to look away and slip back into the thick fog that enshrouded his mind, but his eyes kept coming back to Karl's car. Why was it there? Where was Karl? Finally, it dawned on him: Karl might be in the building. He grabbed the arm of the nearest paramedic. "The president's office . . . top floor."

The paramedic looked up doubtfully at the towering flames. "Is someone up there?"

"I think . . . I think my brother is."

Chapter Nineteen

After the World's Ruin

GUNNAR AWOKE IN THE HOSPITAL the next morning, remembering nothing that had happened after the end of the board meeting. A staff doctor told him it was the result of a concussion, one of a catalog of injuries that would keep him in the hospital for some time. He had three cracked ribs, two missing teeth, hairline fractures in his right hand and femur, a bruised spleen, a fractured eye socket, and dozens of bruises and abrasions. The doctor commented that if he didn't know better, he would have assumed Gunnar had been hit by a truck.

Karl was in the intensive care unit of the same hospital. The firefighters had found him in the president's office, sitting in the president's chair, behind the president's desk. That was how he had wanted to die, like a captain determined to go down with his ship. He was unconscious by the time they found him, and the office was filled with smoke and toxic fumes. They had managed to drag him out and carry him down a fire escape moments before the building collapsed. He had been in a coma ever since.

Over the next few days, Gunnar occasionally envied his unconscious brother. An unremitting tide of bad news threatened to overwhelm him. First, he learned that the company complex was nothing but a field of scorched rubble. Then came the fire inspector's initial report finding clear signs of arson and noting that traces

339

of diesel fuel, apparently from the building's backup generator, had been found both around the building and on Karl's clothes. Bjornsen Pharmaceuticals' insurance company struck next, denying coverage on the basis of the fire inspector's report. Then the FDA announced that they were placing a hold on all Neurostim clinical trials until Bjornsen Pharmaceuticals could prove that the drug had not contributed to David Lee's death—a task that became practically impossible the next day, when blood tests showed significant levels of Neurostim in Karl's blood as well.

A week after the fire, the last straw broke the company: A major wholesaler announced that it was going to switch suppliers because of uncertainty over when—and if—Bjornsen Pharmaceuticals was going to resume production. Gunnar had a long conference call with Henrik Haugeland and Tim Hawkins, the company CFO. Both agreed that the company's financial situation was untenable and was only likely to grow worse.

After the call ended, Gunnar lay back in his bed, physically and mentally exhausted. His body was a mass of aches, and the after-effects of the concussion made focused thinking difficult. Still, it didn't take much concentration to see the obvious next step. He called Ben Corbin and asked him to begin preparing a bankruptcy petition for Bjornsen Pharmaceuticals.

‡ ‡ ‡

Detective Frank McCormick sat at his desk with his morning coffee, a Starbucks venti caramel macchiato. His wife, a dietician, regularly tried to convince him to give up his macchiatos, objecting that they "aren't even really coffee—they're just hot candy bars in a cup." But then, she was in Burbank, and Starbucks was right on his way from the parking garage to the police station.

He worked through his in-box as he sipped from his cup. Near the bottom, he found a report from the fingerprint lab in the David Lee investigation. The lab had been able to compile several usable prints from the dozens of small partial prints on the Neurostim gelcaps. The prints belonged to two individuals, both of whom the lab had positively identified. One was David Lee, but the other—much to Detective McCormick's surprise—was not Kim Young. It was someone named Dr. Daruka Reddy. The big detective raised his eyebrows and put down his coffee. "And who is Dr. Daruka Reddy?"

He reached into an overstuffed Redweld folder and fished out his Who's Who list for the investigation. There was no Dr. Reddy on it. Puzzled, he pulled out the fingerprint request form he had sent to the lab. Stapled to the back of it was a long list of people for whom they had prints. Most of these were Bjornsen Pharmaceuticals employees who had access to controlled drugs and were therefore fingerprinted and given criminal background checks before they were hired. Dr. Reddy was there, listed as a "senior research scientist, development."

Detective McCormick didn't see anything linking Dr. Reddy to David Lee, but that could change with more digging. He made a note on his calendar to get Dr. Reddy's personnel file, phone records, and e-mail archive.

He sat back and smiled as he finished his coffee. He had liked Kim Young when he interviewed her, and he had wanted to believe her when she professed her innocence. That had just gotten easier.

‡ ‡ ‡

Anne and Markus walked into Gunnar's room as he was picking at an admirably healthy, but barely edible, hospital breakfast. Ten days had passed and Gunnar was well enough to go home. "Good morning," said Anne. "We've got the SUV downstairs. Are you ready to go?"

"I've done all the paperwork," Gunnar replied, "but I still need to pack." He glanced around his room, which had become something of a satellite office. A laptop computer and portable printer sat on two chairs, a BlackBerry lay on the bedside table, and at least one document adorned every flat surface.

"I've got it covered," replied Markus, lifting up a large wheeled bag, "I brought the big suitcase. I'll start loading it up."

"And I'll help you get dressed," said Anne. "I went shopping yesterday and found some sweats that should fit over your casts."

"Good thinking," said Gunnar. "Thanks." He levered himself up using his one good arm and leg, and with the assistance of a crutch was able to hobble over to the bathroom. Anne followed him in and helped him change out of his hospital gown and into a set of roomy blue and gray workout clothes that fit comfortably over both his leg cast and his wrist cast. He didn't much like having someone help him dress, but it was an indignity he would have to learn to live with for the next several weeks.

When Anne opened the bathroom door again, Gunnar saw Markus standing by the half-packed suitcase, reading a document. He looked at his father. "Dad, this is a bankruptcy petition for the company."

Gunnar's mouth curled in irritation. "Just pack. Don't read."

"I—" began Markus. Then he shrugged and dropped the document into the suitcase. "Okay."

Anne and Markus packed in silence for several minutes while Gunnar sat on the bed tapping out an e-mail on his BlackBerry. "I don't think we're going to make it," he said suddenly.

The other two stopped packing and looked at him. "What do you mean?" asked Anne.

"We haven't filed that bankruptcy petition yet, but we probably will in a few days. We'll try to reorganize and get back on our feet, but . . ." he gave a small shrug, "this is probably the end of the road."

"I'm sorry, Dad," said Markus.

"It's hard to believe," continued Gunnar. "A week and a half ago, wealth beyond the dreams of avarice hung right in front of us." He reached out as if to grab something invisible, then dropped his hand into his lap. "And now, it's all gone. Not just the multibillion-dollar new drug—everything. Everything I've worked for over the past thirty years."

Anne sat down next to him on the bed and took his hand. "I'm still rich beyond the dreams of avarice."

Gunnar squeezed her hand. "I wish I could make that true."

"Dad, do you know where that quote comes from?" asked Markus.

Gunnar looked at him uncomprehendingly. "What quote?"

"'Rich beyond the dreams of avarice.'"

"Oh. I didn't realize it was a quote from someone."

Markus looked slightly annoyed, and Anne said, "It's from *The Gamester*, a play Markus was in recently. Why don't you explain it, Markus?"

"The play is about a gambler who loses everything," said Markus. The irritation left his face as he spoke, and his voice took on some of the resonance that theater critics now noted in their reviews. "He goes to his wife and apologizes for ruining her, and she says—it wasn't one of my lines, so I don't remember exactly how it goes—but she says something like, 'You have not ruined me. I have no wants when you are here, nor wishes in your absence, but to be blessed with your return. I am rich beyond the dreams of avarice.'"

"I suppose I should . . ." Gunnar began. He meant to say, "I suppose I should get to the theater more," but he was surprised to discover that he was crying too hard to finish the sentence.

‡ ‡ ‡

Chicagoland had been blessed with warm, dry weather through most of October and into early November. The fall colors lingered on the trees for weeks longer than was typical, and restaurants kept their outdoor seating sections open past Election Day. And Bears fans—even sober ones—were going shirtless at Soldier Field.

But all that changed on the day after Gunnar came home from the hospital. A cold mass of air pushed down out of Canada, bringing with it a sharp wind and thick bands of clouds that alternately dropped sleet and cold, stinging rain. The storms stripped the autumn finery from the trees, leaving skeletal branches and clogging storm sewers with wads of dead leaves.

Markus had visited his parents earlier in the day and had built a fire before going back into Chicago to attend rehearsals for a new play. Anne made a pot of coffee and she and Gunnar sat around the fire drinking Bailey's and coffee as the wind rattled the windows and made them glad they were inside for the evening. Henrik was up in the guest bedroom, rescheduling his flight back to Norway, which he had delayed twice to help Gunnar deal with the crisis at Bjornsen Pharmaceuticals.

"It was good of Markus to come out today," remarked Gunnar. "It's too bad he couldn't stay for dinner."

"He came out most days while you were in the hospital," said Anne. "He was the one who took care of getting the gutters cleaned and the furnace checked this year."

"Did you lock the liquor cabinet while he was here?" asked Gunnar. Before Anne could answer, he said, "Forget I said that. This isn't the time to talk about his faults." He raised his mug. "To Markus."

"To Markus," replied Anne as she leaned forward and clinked her mug against his. "Actually, I haven't seen him drink anything for at least a week. He and Tom and I went out to dinner one night, and he had nothing except water and coffee."

Gunnar's shaggy eyebrows went up in surprise. "Do you think he's in Alcoholics Anonymous?"

"I wondered the same thing, but I didn't ask him. If he wants to tell us, he will."

Gunnar watched the fire and took a slow sip from his drink. "I wonder if he's finally growing up."

"I think he finally feels . . . significant," Anne said thoughtfully. "He's started to make a name for himself in the theater world. Since you went into the hospital, he's also felt that we need him out here, too. That reminds me, by the way—I've asked him to take care of the yard work while you're recovering."

"Why? We can hire someone to handle it. I only do it because it gives me an excuse to be outside for an hour or two."

Anne reached over and patted her husband's knee. "Let him help," she said. "It's good for him, and it might not be bad for you."

They heard steps on the stairs and turned to see Henrik walk in. "Any luck?" asked Gunnar.

"Yes," the accountant said as he sat down in an armchair and stretched his feet toward the fire. "SAS will let me use my original ticket to fly standby on the ten o'clock flight to Copenhagen tomorrow night. The flight is only half full, so I should be able to find a seat."

"That's great!" said Anne. "Can I get you a Bailey's and coffee or something else to drink?"

"Bailey's and coffee would be delightful," replied Henrik. "The weather outside makes me nostalgic for the summers I spent as a boy at my family's cabin in the Lofot Islands."

Gunnar laughed. "Yes, the Norwegian weather isn't always as beautiful as the scenery, is it? Every now and then, I used to think about semi-retiring and taking some low-responsibility role at Bjornsen Norge, so I could spend most of my time fishing someplace along the western coast. But then I'd remember that it's rainy and overcast about three hundred and fifty days a year."

"I suppose all positions at Bjornsen Norge will become low-responsibility soon," replied Henrik, his face growing serious. "I will be fine, however."

"Good," said Gunnar. "How about the rest of the employees?"

"I think they will be fine too. Most of them have good credentials and the Norwegian economy is strong."

Gunnar nodded. "I'm relieved. Taking care of our American staff is one of my bigger worries."

"What about you?" asked Henrik.

"Oh, we're all right. Our son Tom is a stockbroker, and he made sure our money wasn't all tied up in Bjornsen Pharmaceuticals, though we're worth a lot less today than we were two weeks ago. Still, we'll be comfortable."

"I'm not just talking about money," said Henrik. "I also meant, How do you feel now that the company is gone?"

"How do I feel?" repeated Gunnar, gazing into the fire. The light played on the strong features of his face, hiding his bruises and giving him a ruddy glow. He looked younger than his sixty years. "Free. I suppose that's the best word for it. I . . . the company was my world for over thirty years, and now it's in ruins. I don't feel depressed or angry, though, just . . . free or . . . or relieved. Like I've been carrying around a boulder for a long time and I finally put it down."

"I've always wondered whether you and Karl owned the company or it owned you," said Anne.

Gunnar chuckled softly. "When we were boys in Norway, our mother always took us to church, and I remember the minister preaching about how hard it was for rich people to get into heaven because their money was like an anchor dragging them down. That struck me as one of the stupidest things I'd ever heard."

Henrik laughed. "I can understand why that might not ring true to a young man with big plans."

"Especially when the minister always seemed to bring those passages up when he was trying to raise money for some church project." Gunnar shook his head and smiled at the memory. "But that image of the anchor . . . you know, it really did feel like I was chained to the company. I just didn't know it until the chain broke."

"Wherever your treasure is, that's where your heart is," commented Henrik. "Better to store it where the thief can't steal and the moth and rust can't eat away."

"And the idiot brother can't burn," added Gunnar with a sigh.

‡ ‡ ‡

Elena switched off her computer, grabbed her purse, and walked out through the heavy, locked doors that guarded the bullpen. She was about to push the down button on the elevator when a familiar voice said, "Hi, Elena."

She froze for a second and then turned slowly. "Hello, Sergei."

"I thought I'd stop by, since your phone seems to be broken," he said with an amused look in his eyes. "It just rings and rings and then goes straight into your voice mail. I've got my car a block away, and I'd like to take you someplace."

She turned back and pressed the down button. "I don't think that's a good idea."

"What are you afraid of? You can take your gun."

She smiled, but shook her head. "Thanks, but no."

"Come on. If you don't like the look of the place, I'll take you straight home. We don't even have to go inside. I promise."

The elevator came and she stepped inside, but she turned and held the door open. "Only if we can go Dutch."

He laughed. "Sure, if you insist."

To Elena's surprise, Sergei did not drive toward any of their favorite restaurants. Instead, he got onto the Kennedy Expressway and headed out of the city. After they had been driving for about twenty minutes, she asked, "Is this place in the burbs?"

He nodded. "It's kind of a drive, but it's a special place. We'll be there in ten minutes."

A few minutes later, he turned off into a dilapidated light-industrial district directly under the western approaches to O'Hare. "Maybe I should have brought my gun," she commented as they drove along the dark, empty streets.

"Okay, here we are," said Sergei as he parked his car in front of a rundown building with a faded sign that read, Advanced Gear. He turned to her. "Do you know where we are?"

She knew. "What . . . why did you bring me here?" she asked, her voice shaking slightly.

"Well, our conversations in restaurants haven't turned out that well recently, so I decided to try a change of scenery." He took a deep breath and pointed toward the darkened shape of the building. "A year ago, I almost died in there. If you hadn't broken a half-dozen Bureau rules and risked your own life, I would have been dead on the concrete floor of that basement. On that day, I fell in love with the bravest, most selfless woman I've ever met. And it doesn't hurt that she's a knockout in an evening gown."

Elena sat perfectly still as he went on. "The last time we talked, I said I wanted to 'get back together,' but the more I thought about it, the more I knew that wasn't true. It's too late to date. It's too late to come over to each other's apartments for dinner and a movie. It's all or nothing now.

"So that's the choice I'm offering you: all or nothing." He fished a small black box out of his coat pocket. He opened it and a diamond he probably couldn't really afford sparkled in the dim light. "Will you marry me, Elena? Say *yes*, and I'm yours forever. Say *no*, and I'll never call you or ambush you by the elevators again."

She leaned across the seat and hugged him tightly, laughing and crying at the same time.

He hugged her back and kissed her. "So, is that a yes?"

‡ ‡ ‡

Karl came out of his coma gradually. He opened his eyes on the third day after the fire and appeared to recognize faces. By the seventh day, he could sit up and eat with assistance. After two weeks had passed, he could take a few steps with a walker and respond to questions by nodding and shaking his head.

But three weeks after he was admitted, the hospital staff had done all they could for him. His lead neurologist's nurse called Gunnar and Gwen to arrange a time to discuss Karl's discharge and the care he would need after he left the hospital. Two days later, the meeting convened in a hospital conference room decorated with posters depicting the human nervous system and various maladies of the gastrointestinal tract. A long window gave a view of a parking lot and the street and strip mall beyond it. Several folding tables with imitation wood tops had been pushed together to form a makeshift conference table ringed by about twenty utilitarian chairs.

The neurologist sat at one end of the table, with therapists and long-term care specialists on either side of him. Gunnar and Anne sat together at the other end, with Gunnar's crutch leaning against an empty chair. Gwen picked a chair in a corner by the door, looking resolutely at a bottle of spring water on the table in front of her.

"Thank you all for coming in for this meeting," said the neurologist. "Before we make any decisions, we will, of course, involve Karl, but I generally try to meet with the families of brain-injured patients first, because of the significant commitment they may be asked to make to the patient's care.

"I'd like to start by giving a quick description of Karl's current condition so that we can use that as a baseline for our talk today." He opened a manila folder and flipped back several sheets of medical notes. "He has minor lung damage from smoke inhalation, and he has fractured bones in both hands, with significantly worse damage to the right hand. All of these injuries should heal fully, though he may experience arthritis in the joints of his right hand.

"He has also suffered significant neurological damage. The precise cause is unclear, but it appears to be a combination of oxygen deprivation during the fire and the presence in his body of certain compounds related to the experimental drug known as Neurostim. The presentation of this brain injury is unique, but can be best analogized to simultaneous strokes in different regions of the brain. The frontal and temporal lobes appear to have been particularly affected.

"Karl has substantial deficits in fine motor control and cannot speak. He has some short-term memory loss, but does not appear to be measurably cognitively impaired. He does not hallucinate and has not exhibited any abnormal behavior since he was admitted.

He reportedly engaged in suicidal and violently sociopathic conduct shortly before admission, but this episode appears to have been related to Neurostim use."

The neurologist turned a page and continued, "Karl's prognosis is unclear, but it appears probable that he has suffered substantial permanent damage. However, the extent of recovery from brain injuries varies from individual to individual. Further, the operation of the Neurostim compounds in the neurological system is largely unknown, which adds additional uncertainty." He closed his notes and turned to a gray-haired, white-coated woman seated to his right. "That's all I've got for now. Barbara, would you like to outline care options for Karl?"

"Sure," she said with a nod to the neurologist. "I've evaluated Karl and concluded that he is a good candidate for either an assisted living facility or in-home care. My preference is generally for in-home care in cases like Karl's, but I know that it isn't always feasible for families." She looked inquiringly at Gwen.

"I don't think in-home care will be feasible," said Gwen. She then returned her attention to the water bottle.

"If you work, I could recommend having a nursing service on-call, in case Karl needs something during the day," offered the long-term care specialist. "They could also help him with meals."

"Thank you, but in-home care isn't an option," replied Gwen with a gracious but firm smile. "You had mentioned there were some nursing home possibilities?"

The doctor looked surprised, but she didn't press the point further. "Well, yes. There are a range of options in terms of both care levels and, ah, expense."

"Karl's going to need something that fits within his income from disability insurance, Social Security, and so on," said Gwen. "I'm not sure how much that will be."

"I've seen his financial responsibility forms," replied the doctor. "There are some competent, no-frills facilities that might work. For instance—"

"Gwen, what are you talking about?" interrupted Gunnar. "If you go back to work, your health insurance will cover Karl. If you don't, you can stay home with him."

Gwen put on a smile and looked at the long-term care specialist. "Please go on."

"No," said Gunnar firmly. "Answer my question first."

Several seconds of awkward silence passed. The neurologist cleared his throat. "I think this would be a good time for a short break." He got up, as did everyone in the room except Gunnar. As the medical professionals filed out, Anne walked over to Gwen and laid a hand on her arm. "Could we talk for a few minutes?"

"Of course."

Anne walked back to Gunnar, and after a moment's hesitation Gwen followed. "What's going on?" demanded Gunnar.

"I'm leaving him," said Gwen flatly. "I'm surprised you hadn't figured that out."

"You're going to just stick him in some nursing home warehouse and go?" he asked incredulously.

She bristled. "He's lucky I'm even here today. I should be in New York or Paris looking for a job right now. Do you know there's no money left? The government seized everything two days ago. Did you know that?"

"I didn't," admitted Gunnar. "If it's . . . if it's a question of money, we might be able to help."

She stared at him for several seconds. "You'd do that? After what he did to you, you'd pay his bills?"

Gunnar nodded. "If you can't."

She shook her head incredulously. "Well, I can't—and I wouldn't if I could. And another thing: This isn't just about money. He lied to me. And then he ruined me. I'm not going to spend the rest of my life dressing him and pushing him around in a wheelchair."

Gunnar looked at her angrily. "He's your husband."

"Not for long!" she shot back. "After what he's done to me, nobody can expect me to turn my life upside down for him."

"You're right, Gwen," Anne said coolly. "Nobody would expect that from you."

Gwen opened her mouth, then shut it and pressed her lips into a hard red line. She turned and walked out without saying another word.

A moment later, the door opened and the neurologist poked his head in. "Should we reschedule?" he asked tentatively.

"Give us a couple more minutes," said Gunnar.

When they were alone again, Anne asked, "What do you want to do?"

"Maybe she can leave him in one of those places and sleep at night, but I can't." Lines of anger and frustration furrowed his granite face. "Maybe he deserves it, but I'm not going to do it. No matter what he's done, he's still my brother and . . ." His voice trailed off and he looked up at his wife. "Have you seen him?"

She shook her head.

"I did. The day before I was discharged, I was taking a walk around the hospital and I went past his room. The door was open. I didn't go in, but I could see him. He was sitting in his bed and a nurse was feeding him something—applesauce I think."

He paused and looked out the window with unseeing eyes. "We can't afford to hire a full-time nurse for him and keep him in that Gold Coast apartment, not after he burned up ninety percent of our net worth. That doesn't leave us a lot of options." He paused and looked up at her again. "What do you think about putting him in the downstairs guest bedroom, at least until we can find a decent place for him?"

"He can stay as long as he needs to," replied Anne. She bent down and kissed him. "And I want you to know how proud of you I am right now."

He shrugged. "He's my brother."

She kissed him again. "I'll tell the doctors we're ready for them."

Epilogue

Fall passed into winter and winter into spring. At UCLA, these distinctions marked changes in the academic and athletic calendars, not the weather. After the disruptions and stress following David's death, Kim's life fell into the rhythms of student life she knew so well. It was her senior year, and she was a seasoned veteran at picking classes and professors to ensure the grades expected by the top medical schools. A new wave of freshmen in her sorority needed mentors, and she and a friend adopted a few who showed interest in a pre-med track. She sent in her med school applications and in due course was accepted into two of her top three choices, including UCLA.

She occasionally searched Google News for reports on developments at Bjornsen Pharmaceuticals, but she didn't talk to anyone from the company, until one day in April, when she received a call from Dr. Tina Corrigan. "Hi, Kim. I thought I'd call and touch base with you. You probably heard that there were some pretty dramatic developments after you left at the end of the summer."

"I did. I read about the fire and Mr. Bjornsen and everything. I was really shocked."

"We all were," replied Dr. Corrigan. "I'd known him for over ten years, and I never would have guessed he would do something like that. I left work one day and came back the next to find the company gone. It looked like a bomb had gone off."

"I saw a picture on the Internet," said Kim. "I couldn't believe it was the same place. So, what happened to everybody?"

"Well, Dr. Reddy disappeared on a one-way flight back to India as soon as the police asked to interview him. I heard a rumor that he's working at a plastic surgery clinic in Bollywood."

Kim rolled her eyes. "Why am I not surprised?"

"By the way, I'm very sorry about what happened with David Lee," continued Dr. Corrigan in a more serious voice. "If I'd had any idea that someone on my staff was distributing unauthorized doses of Neurostim—or any drug—I would have stopped it immediately."

"I know," replied Kim. "Don't worry about it." She fidgeted uncomfortably with her hair as she spoke and moved the conversation away from the topic of David and Neurostim. "How about the rest of the lab? Where did people land? Where did you land?"

"A lot of people scattered, but the core R&D group moved to Abbott. They bought Bjornsen Pharmaceuticals' assets out of bankruptcy, and they signed a consulting agreement with Gunnar Bjornsen. He convinced them to hire us as a team."

"That's great! How are you liking it there?"

"It's wonderful. They have more resources than we could ever afford at Bjornsen, and the people are first-rate. In fact, I have an opening for a lab tech, and I think you'd be a perfect fit. You'd be doing a lot of the same work you did so well last summer, but you'd have more responsibilities. I know you're planning on med school next year, but most schools will let you defer for a year or two, and this would look good on your résumé. I think it would be a good move for you."

Kim remembered the sticky-hot weather, bugs, and homesickness of last summer. "Thanks, I'll think about it," she said. But she knew she would say no.

A moment later, she realized that this would be the first time in her life she had ever rejected the advice of someone she respected. It made her feel grown-up in an undefined but significant way.

☩ ☩ ☩

Noelle had spent the day using her event-planning skills to help Elena and Sergei with last-minute wedding decisions, like how to configure the seating at the reception, where the table with the wedding cake should go, and so on. Elena was an admirably low-stress bride, and Sergei wisely avoided expressing any opinions on wedding-planning matters, but there had been a lot to do, and Noelle was tired by the time she pulled into the garage.

She walked in to find Ben and Eric on the family room floor, watching *SportsCenter* on ESPN with exactly the same vacant expression on their faces. "What are you doing?" she asked.

Neither of them looked at her. "We're practicing sitting," replied Ben. "It's on the skill chart."

"*His* skill chart," pointed out Noelle. "You've got the sitting skill nailed."

"Thanks. That's why I'm modeling the behavior for him."

"Why don't you turn off the TV and play with his phonics toys while you practice sitting? I think you're both advanced enough to multitask."

"Okay," said Ben, raising his eyebrows skeptically as he reached for the toy box. "But if I get overstimulated and start to fuss, you'd better be ready with a bottle."

She laughed. "I'll go get one now." She went into the kitchen and came back a few minutes later with a freshly opened bottle of Chardonnay and two glasses. *SportsCenter* was still on, but Ben was playing with Eric, so she didn't complain.

"Thank you," Ben said as she filled a glass and handed it to him. "By the way, Emily Marshall called while you were out. She said they were starting a new campaign and she thought you could really help them out if you had the time. I told her that I didn't think you did, but that I'd pass along the message."

Noelle had been expecting this. Emily had worked to rebuild their relationship over the past couple of months. She had sent Eric a cute outfit and had called several times to chat and fill Noelle in on the latest happenings at the Field. It made perfect sense: Gwen was no longer rich and had left town to take a job with a fashion magazine in New York, so why not bring Noelle back into the fold? She was a hard worker and a good organizer. Besides, Noelle sensed that Emily really did like her in a way. Noelle had forgiven Emily, but she had no interest in working with her again. She had different priorities now.

"Yeah, between Eric, the office, and volunteering at the women's shelter, I don't have much extra time for one of Emily's projects."

"You sure?" replied Ben with a wink. "She said to let you know that Jacqui Gossard would be involved."

"Well, if Jacqui's involved, I'm sure Emily can get by without me, but I'll try to let her down easy."

‡ ‡ ‡

The morning sun rested on the rim of the world, casting infinitely long shadows across the blue-gray waters of Lake Michigan. A light, cold wind raised small waves that thrummed rhythmically against the side of Gunnar's Boston Whaler as he and Karl trolled for Coho and Chinook salmon.

Gunnar sat in the back of the boat with one hand on the outboard motor and the other holding an insulated mug of steaming coffee. He watched a sonar display as he took the boat back and forth in long, slow sweeps a mile from shore. Karl sat in the middle of the boat, gripping his seat tightly with both hands to keep his balance as the boat gently rocked. Several fishing rods stuck out from the boat at different angles near each brother. Each rod was baited with a different type of lure and set to run at a different depth.

The tip of a rod near Karl twitched and then bent sharply. "Karl, you've got one!" called Gunnar. He resisted the urge to grab the rod and set the hook as Karl reached for it with agonizing slowness. He gripped the rod by its long cork handle and, after several tries, managed to get it out of the short metal tube that held it in place. He braced himself with his feet and began to reel with awkward, jerky movements. His face was a mask of concentration and strain, and the muscles of his whole body bunched and tensed. He began to sweat despite the cool dawn breeze. But he kept reeling.

Gunnar watched silently with a mixture of pity and admiration. Five months ago, Karl's doctors had been convinced that he would never walk without a wheeled walker, but now he could get by with only a cane on all but the roughest surfaces. They had thought that he would be unable to speak again, but he had learned to force the complex muscles of his mouth and throat to obey his commands and now was able to carry on a conversation, though he was occasionally hard to understand. More recently, his neurologist and physical therapist had expressed doubt that he would ever regain the degree of fine motor control necessary to fish, yet he was well on the way to achieving that goal. Gunnar was glad that his brother hadn't decided that now would be a good time to start driving again.

The most amazing recovery of all had been the slow but steady return of the spirited relationship between the two brothers. In light of his medical condition and the small chance that he would re-offend, Karl had avoided both jail time and extradition to Russia, which was belatedly investigating Cleverlad's activities and the death of Pyotr Korovin. But Karl had not been able to avoid massive fines and liabilities to Bjornsen Pharmaceuticals' bankrupcy estate. He had lost everything and was still deeply in debt. He had no place to go—but Gunnar was somewhat surprised to realize that he didn't want his brother to go anywhere. He enjoyed retelling old stories over coffee, playing chess in front of the fire, and now being out on the water in the early morning chill. Gunnar smiled. It was good to be fishing with his brother again.

After fifteen long minutes, Karl managed to bring the fish along-side the boat. Gunnar deftly scooped it up with a net and Karl sat back, exhausted and panting. Gunnar detached the lure from the fish's mouth and dropped the salmon into an ice-filled cooler, where it would stay until it was filleted and grilled for a family dinner that evening. He tossed the lure into the lake and Karl let out line until it was at the appropriate depth and distance from the boat. "Thanksh," he said.

"Don't mention it," replied Gunnar. "That's a good fish."

"Haf . . . hafta mention it," said Karl. "Thanksh . . . for everythin'."

Gunnar nodded gravely. "You're welcome."

Karl set the drag on the reel and carefully put the rod back in its holder. "Shtill one thin' . . . You never ob . . . obeyed the judgmen'."

Gunnar cocked his head to the side in confusion. "What do you mean?"

"Never tol' me how to grow the plansh."

"Oh, that's right. Well, there's no harm in telling you now. The secret is that the seeds have to travel through the digestive tract of an elephant before they will sprout," Gunnar said. "Asian elephants work best," he added matter-of-factly.

Karl blinked. "How didja . . . ?"

"How did I know that?"

"Yeah."

"I remembered a Discovery Channel program about a tree species on a remote island where dodos used to live. The trees were slowly dying off and scientists on the island had no idea why. Then one of them realized that there were no trees younger than the year dodos became extinct, so he guessed that dodos had eaten the seed pods and that the seeds needed to go through a dodo's stomach to sprout. He fed some seeds to a turkey and, lo and behold, the seeds that came out the other end of the turkey sprouted. Something about the chemicals in a turkey's gut flipped a switch in the seeds and made them grow."

"But elephansh in Norway? Don' remember 'em from hishtry clash. An' don' remember *nors'* dodos either."

Gunnar smiled slyly and held up a finger. "But you remember Norwegian mammoths, don't you?"

Karl's eyebrows went up. "Mammosh," he repeated. "You shaid the plansh live' long, long time . . . Always won'ered 'bout that."

Gunnar nodded. "There are pines still living in the desert mountains of California that go back to the time of the last mammoths. I did some research and found out that plants in extreme climates often have long life spans. The mammoth theory also explained why the plants slowly went extinct even though Norway's mountain ecosystems had been basically undisturbed since the end of the last ice age. In the right conditions, our berserker plants could live for thousands of years, but not forever. So I decided to give it a go; nothing else we tried had worked and I was starting to get desperate. We had donated a lot to Brookfield Zoo, so I was able to persuade them to put two of the seedpods in an elephant's food. One of the seeds sprouted, and we were on our way."

Karl began to shake, and for a moment Gunnar worried that he might be choking. "Sho . . . sho," he forced out, "when you tol' me you were doin' 'off-shite reshearsh,' you were at the zoo lookin' for sheedsh wi' plashic glovesh an' . . . an' . . ."

"And an old pair of hip waders," finished Gunnar.

Karl's laugh had not been affected by the trauma he had experienced, and it broke forth now in rich peals that echoed across the water. A moment later, the brothers were laughing together.

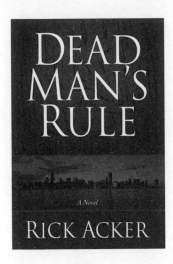

Ben Corbin's
Career Begins

Up-and-coming lawyer Ben Corbin has a bright career ahead of him, but when a seemingly simple case turns deadly, Ben finds himself fighting a sinister opponent.

Ben's client, Dr. Mikhail Ivanovsky, claims legal ownership of a safety deposit box. The case appears innocuous, but as pieces of Dr. Ivanovsky's shadowy past come to light, Ben suspects that his client is hiding something important. When the other party in the case dies suddenly, the opposing attorney invokes Dead Man's Rule. Desperate, Dr. Ivanovsky reveals the horrifying truth about the contents of the safety deposit box and Ben realizes that he *must* win this case.